KARA WAS HERE

KARA WAS HERE

a novel

| WILLIAM CONESCU |

SOFT SKULL PRESS • NEW YORK

Library of Congress Cataloging-in-Publication Data

Conescu, William.
Kara Was Here : a novel / William Conescu.
pages cm
Includes bibliographical references and index.
ISBN 978-1-59376-533-0 (alk. paper)
1. Grief—Fiction. 2. Murder—Investigation—Fiction. 3. Ghost Stories—
Fiction. 4. Mystery fiction. gsafd I. Title.

PS3603.O533K37 2013
813'.6—dc23
2013017681

ISBN 978-1-59376-533-0

Cover design by Debbie Berne
Interior design by Elyse Strongin, Neuwirth & Associates, Inc.

Soft Skull Press
New York, NY
www.softskull.com

Printed in the United States of America

With love to
Austin and Nathan

KARA
WAS
HERE

CHAPTER ONE

LATELY, BRAD MITCHELL'S WORLD SEEMED TO BE SPLITTING IN TWO. THE GREEN minivan on the highway in front of him sped along atop the ghost of itself. Brad could see a hazy outline hovering on either side of it. Only if he concentrated, really focused on the minivan, was he able to fuse its overlapping images together. The traffic signs were more difficult to control—signs announcing a gas station ahead, thirty-seven miles to Wilmington, exit 380 to Rose Hill. They emerged in the distance in adjacent pairs that began to overlap as they grew closer, until each sign passed through Brad's peripheral vision with a halo surrounding it, like a memory of the sign super-imposed on the present.

He hoped it was still safe for him to drive. It probably was, he said to himself for the tenth time that morning. Highway driving wasn't difficult, plus it was light outside. *Lord knows you drove in worse condition when we were together,* he could hear Kara saying.

A dozen years ago, sure. But the questionable vision made more sense back then.

If it makes you feel any better, I think you drove better stoned than I did, she might have told him.

The words were like a shameful soundtrack to years he never discussed anymore.

"But today—" he started to say aloud. Then he stopped himself. Today he was just seeing the world the way it had started to appear. And today he was en route to Kara Tinsley's funeral.

Brad had driven this stretch of I-40 on many spring mornings like this one. Since he and Val had gotten married five years ago, they'd been heading to the beach every year as soon as she'd turned in grades, and back when he was at UNC, he and Kara would often escape from Chapel Hill to the North Carolina coast—for spring break, or to do laundry at her mother's house, or to avoid a midterm. As far as Brad could recall, this was his first time driving this route without anyone beside him singing or fussing with the radio or insisting on a stop at a convenience store. He'd probably stopped at half of the gas stations he was now passing, so he and Val could buy sodas and the most complicated scratch-off lottery tickets they could find, or so he and Kara could stock up on cigarettes and Boone's Farm. *Strawberry Hill: seven and a half percent alcohol. Wild Island: only five percent. Choose wisely,* she would say.

He had. When she turned twenty-four and moved to New York to pursue celebrity on the stage, he stayed behind in their apartment in Chapel Hill. For a year, he got more acting work in North Carolina than she did in New York, though it wasn't as if he rubbed her nose in it. Eventually, he ended up with a realtor's license and a beautiful wife who appreciated his attempts at making brunch. Kara ended up dead on a couch in Brooklyn. The call came the night before last.

Maybe he should have anticipated getting a call like this one day: news of an overdose, a car crash, alcohol poisoning. But why brace yourself for all the things you hope will never happen? Was that supposed to make the news go down easier? It didn't seem likely.

An eighteen-wheeler sped past, edging into Brad's lane—it was not an optical illusion—and as Brad shifted his Civic from the center to the right lane, he allowed himself to wonder once again if he shouldn't have driven. It could be unsafe. But then again, the doctor had said it was probably nothing. And besides, Brad had been driving all week. He'd driven the week before. He was fine. It was daytime, this wasn't dangerous. It was nothing, he told himself. Just focus on the road.

A mileage sign announced that Brad was only twenty-two miles away from Greenwood Park, maybe twenty-four from her body. And it was only the white border of the sign that seemed to sit, transparent, beside its double.

Brad's yoga instructor had once said that mindfulness was the best way to combat anxiety, but these days, when Brad followed her advice, when he stayed in the moment and paid attention to the world around him, more often than not he saw two worlds. His moments had extra stoplights and two refrigerator handles superimposed on one another. Distant trees split like amoebas when Brad tried to be mindful of any one of them. At the gym, the lines of the machines wavered in and out of double as he crossed the room. Thresholds were becoming wider than they used to be, and making eye contact at the dinner table required choosing one of his wife's four eyes to hold in focus. Only when Brad was least mindful, when he retreated into his head and existed with little concern for what was in front of him, only then did the doppelgangers go away. Or he didn't notice them. If there was a difference. If a tree falls in the forest . . . or two trees.

"Let me ask Dr. Ziferra to look," the first ophthalmologist had said. This was on Tuesday. Brad had made himself go, though he still hadn't said anything to Val.

"Hmm," said the second ophthalmologist.

"You see?"

"*Yes*, I do."

Brad stared at a popsicle stick as they moved a small paddle back and forth over one eye and then the other. The doctors studied him; they breathed into his face. Dr. Ziferra had recently eaten something with ketchup on it. "His eyes are moving," the first ophthalmologist whispered. Then they paced across the room and had a hushed conversation, the second ophthalmologist saying "Yes," and then "Yes" and "Yes."

"When did you say this started?" Dr. Ziferra asked.

Brad wasn't certain. A month ago, maybe two.

The doctors exchanged a look.

"We want to send you to a *neuro*-ophthalmologist," Dr. Ziferra said at length. "And we're scheduling you to have an MRI—just to be safe."

"Okay," Brad said. "After I see the other doctor?"

"Sooner, actually," the first doctor replied. "What are you doing on Friday?"

Driving to a funeral, as it turned out. The MRI was postponed, and on this morning when Brad should have been sitting in the hospital waiting room, when he would have told his colleagues he had a dentist's appointment and probably would have let his wife believe he had an early showing, Brad was instead en route to Greenwood Park, North Carolina, a town just outside of Wilmington.

A Volkswagen in front of Brad forced him to slow down to sixty-five, then sixty. The car was filled with young girls in swimsuits and sunglasses, and he could hear them singing even with his windows rolled up. He checked the rearview mirror, glanced over his shoulder, then passed them with a quick look to his right. It was hard to tell who was in high school and who was in college these days. One of the girls winked at him as he drove past.

It was with a guilty sense of relief that he had left Val behind. She was eleven weeks into a difficult pregnancy, and her fear of another miscarriage was making every stomach cramp that much more painful. So Brad discouraged Val from even trying to get a substitute for her class. She'd never even met Kara; he was fine going by himself, he told her. And in truth, he preferred having this chance to say good-bye alone. *Oh, it'll be fabulous,* he could hear Kara saying. *You can light candles and prop up my corpse. We'll have a grand old time.* In death, she was probably still chain-smoking.

Brad and Kara had been one of those college couples that seemed destined to stay together forever. When she moved to New York, there were resolutions to make it work, to visit each other every month or two, to talk daily or almost daily or soon. After there weren't any more resolutions, there were still phone calls for a little while. Then a few quiet years of birthday text messages and holiday cards, until those two unsettling phone messages that Brad left unanswered. Then there was silence.

The silence made this drive a little worse. The silence and the twin exit signs announcing his arrival in Greenwood Park.

He'd made a reservation at the Greenwood Inn, because—well, he didn't need to be on the road at night. Not that it was dangerous, but it was a two-and-a-half-hour drive. After a stressful day. He might be tired.

"Supposed to be a lot of sun this weekend," said the girl working at the front desk. She wore her hair in a ponytail and had freckles and braces. "You're going to the beach, right?" she asked as she pulled up his reservation.

Headed to my ex's funeral, Kara would have said. *Looking forward to it, too.*

"Just a visit," Brad told her, and in spite of himself, he flashed the girl one of his reassuring smiles. She smiled back, and Brad dropped his gaze to the counter.

It was ridiculous how often he smiled these days. Big, toothy, dimpled smiles that Kara never would have recognized. They popped out like this, involuntarily, all the time—out of habit, not elation. When he was showing a house or at a neighborhood barbecue, at dinners and lunches and meetings, everyone could count on Brad for a smile. Maybe even a wink. He'd become a winker. He never saw it coming. It just happened once, the half-selective we're-in-this-together wink, and it seemed to appeal, so he found himself doing it again and again, and that was how he became a winker. Over the years, his lazy waves hello and good-bye were so frequently mistaken for two-fingered peace signs that he finally gave in and let them be construed as such. He'd become a regular flirt, though a benign one. Women seemed to enjoy it, men seemed to admire it, and he had no trouble signing clients.

Funny, because no one would have pegged Brad as a guy anyone would have particularly respected or admired. But aging out of his teens and early twenties, buying white oxford shirts and bright neckties, jogging and joining a fitness club, these things slowly transformed Brad until he started to look like the kind of man who played golf—and played it well. And then at some point—when was it?—he did learn to play golf. Not well, but he had the shoes. He could never have told Kara that he had the shoes. They'd had sex on a golf course once. Dropped acid and tooled around in one of the golf carts, peed in the holes. She referred to number sixteen as "the ladies' room" all night.

"I'm visiting my dead girlfriend," he said to the girl behind the desk.

The ponytailed girl held up a finger and kept typing with the other hand. Then she turned to look him in the eye. "Okay," she said, "what was that?"

"I said," Brad began—he cleared his throat—"I just said . . . um . . . thanks for the tip about the weather."

"Oh, sure," she said with a shrug. "Have fun."

<hr />

Margot Cominsky stood around the corner from the funeral parlor. She'd tried standing right outside the door, hoping for a breath of air that didn't reek of carnations, but she was immediately taken for the welcoming committee, and strangers kept hugging her and cheek-kissing her and grabbing her hand. "We're so sorry." "So young." "Too soon." What was she supposed to do, thank them for their profound and original words? We're all fucking sad, people. Look at where we are.

Inside the lobby, it had turned into a regular college reunion, but of course, no one recognized Margot. Not one person. Not the girl who lived next to her and Kara freshman year, not what's-his-name who did the lighting for *The Women*, not even that mediocre soprano they'd only cast in *Oliver!* because Margot thought they needed some fresh blood. And who wasn't tall and thin and blond? That little twig who'd understudied for Kara in *Cabaret* looked exactly like the girl she was fifteen years ago. Whereas Margot looked like she had eaten the girl she was fifteen years ago—and followed that up with a hearty dessert.

There was a time she felt certain she'd keep up with this crowd. They'd be her friends forever, she thought. But as soon as Margot moved back to New York, she lost touch with pretty much everyone. Except Kara.

Had Kara really kept up with all these people? Well, Kara could say hello to a person she hadn't seen in five years and make the girl feel like a long lost friend. Even if Kara hated the girl—and she totally hated Francis, who was now passing in front of Margot attached to a short man who looked way too young for her. Kara would have had something to say about that. Francis looked good. Unfortunately.

Margot pulled out her phone. No little envelopes. No message lights blinking. She clicked through her photos to find the image of Mike, and in her head she kissed him. Then she typed: "At K's funeral. Feel fat and angry. Wish you were here."

Seconds later, from Japan, came his reply: "But looking BEAUTIFUL no doubt. What R U wearing?"

Margot looked down at her innocuous navy dress and replied, "Hot pink tutu. You?"

The phone vibrated again: "Loin cloth + cardbord Burger King crown. XX00."

Margot smiled. "You'd fit right in," she typed.

The parade of black and grey and navy from the parking lot across the street was starting to pick up. Only a few minutes before the big show. Margot didn't recognize most of these people. The older ones might have been friends of the family or people who went to their church; the younger ones probably went to high school with Kara. And junior high. And elementary school. Everyone in Greenwood Park knew everyone else. Or was related, Kara used to say. They probably reserved the third weekend of each month for a real good town funeral, something everyone could enjoy.

Margot hadn't seen Kara in two months, which seemed kind of silly, considering they only lived an hour apart. But it was a long hour between Brooklyn and Long Island, and everyone was so busy these days. There was work, and—well, they talked more often, of course. Kara had heard all about Mike, all about the horrors of dating a man in the military. "When you meet him . . ." Margot had said so many times. It was hard to believe that would never happen now, that Kara would never meet Mike or their children. The children Margot hoped they'd have, eventually.

Margot had met Mike two years ago. She'd helped cater his brother's wedding, and there Mike was, this big hunk of a guy, biceps thick as cantaloupes, face like an oversized cherub, sneaking into the kitchen for an extra helping of potatoes or to check on the groom's cake. Margot fell for him instantly—women always did, apparently—and for whatever reason, he fell for her too. Then, five months after they met, he was stationed overseas. In Japan, thank God, and not Iraq or Afghanistan, but still. By now, she'd had more email exchanges with the man than live conversations.

But they were in the home stretch—just seven more months and he'd be back. "And it does feel real," she'd told Kara. "Sometimes it's funny how life works out."

Or doesn't. "Kara girl, what did you go and do?" she mumbled.

Kara's stepfather had called with the news. As soon as he'd identified himself, Margot knew why he must've been calling. It was just a question of how and where. An overdose. At least she'd died in her sleep.

Margot excuse-me'd her way back through the front doors and kept her eyes down as she crossed the lobby with its heavy drapes, burgundy carpet, and fake antique chairs. She passed through the wreaths and floral arrangements, passed clusters of mourners saying mournful things or laughing awkwardly. People were starting to take seats in the next room, and in there was the box. It was open. She'd heard people saying it was open.

When she crossed the threshold, the first thing Margot saw across the room was Kara's hair. It fell in familiar dark brown waves below her shoulders. Margot took a few steps forward. Kara's eyes were closed, and in a way she did look like she might be asleep, though her arms weren't sprawled all over the place. They were folded tight to her body, her hands gripping a strangely inappropriate bouquet of spring flowers in what looked like a fucking doily. Margot dropped her eyes and tried to suppress a laugh. Kara wouldn't have bothered trying. Daisies and baby's breath. A little snort of amusement escaped.

"Cougar Cominsky?"

Margot turned. "Oh, for Christ's sake," she muttered.

"It *is* you," he said.

Standing beside her was Brad Mitchell looking not a damned thing like Brad Mitchell. The face was the same, but everything else had turned all country club. The hair was parted to the side, a shiny black instead of blue or green or magenta. The face was clean shaven. He was wearing a black suit, and everything looked crisp and tailored and not stolen from the drama department's costume shop. He didn't look like he was carrying a joint anywhere on his person.

Brad drew her into a tight hug. He even smelled good. Eucalyptus and mint something. "I see you bathed for the occasion," she said.

"I did."

"Very thoughtful of you."

"I've been trained."

"Well . . . you look good," she said.

"So do you."

He stood there for a minute, smiling like the goon she remembered, as if he was all dressed up to play a romantic lead, complete with shoulder pads in his suit and mousse in his hair. He could've been a politician. For all she knew, he was one. It was crazy how easily you could lose track of people you used to see every day. Margot hadn't heard anything about Brad in years, not since Kara said he was getting married. Margot checked his hand. Yes, wedding band in place.

"Wow," he said at last. "I'm really glad to see you. I mean, I can imagine events I'd prefer."

Margot scanned the room. "I can imagine funerals I'd prefer."

⁂

Brad hadn't given much consideration to who else might be attending the funeral. If pressed, he might have acknowledged that he'd imagined a roomful of sixty-something-year-old relatives and locals, none of whom really understood Kara. When he walked into the Greenwood Park Funeral Home, he was surprised to see so many dimly familiar faces painted to varying degrees with signs of age: the hair, the figure, the makeup a little different, more sophisticated or at least less unsophisticated.

They were mostly people from the UNC theater crowd, surrounded by husbands and wives and others Brad didn't know or recall.

For a moment, he thought he recognized the poor girl from Kara's Philosophy of Ethics class to whom Kara had "confessed" that she and Brad were not only a couple but also half-siblings. *So . . . is it, like, half-ethical?* Kara had asked. After that, she and Brad somehow ran into the girl at least once a week, walking to class or at the cafeteria or in a coffee shop. Kara would stick her tongue in Brad's ear or grab his ass for show. He wouldn't have minded seeing that girl today. He'd have kept up the part, if he could.

Brad smiled a few greetings, then passed through the lobby to the back room where the casket was. He needed to see Kara before the room filled up. The casket was a lacquered white, which struck Brad as an odd choice, and as he approached, he saw that Kara was dressed in a white long-sleeve shirt with some sort of ruffles happening on the front and a dark skirt with black stockings. They'd put flowers in her hands too, as if she were an aging flower girl for the dead. She was the picture of someone who had once made a marvelous quilt, not someone who had gone for two years without owning a fork. (*What can a fork do that a spoon can't? Honestly?*) Brad stopped within a few feet of the casket. This wasn't the way he'd imagined her, even dead—her lips folded into a nothing sort of expression, a false complacency in her relaxed cheeks and brow. As he stood staring at her, Kara's tiny nose divided in two. Or maybe he made his eyes do that, as a test.

He had only been seated for two minutes when he spotted Margot. She walked into the room by herself and was laughing through her nose, amused by some private joke. So typical. She looked all grown up, a little plump, but undeniably herself. They only had time to exchange a few words before the organ started to play, so Brad invited her to sit beside him, and he was glad to have a friend from the past close by.

A mass of people moved in from the lobby, and Brad checked his watch. It was just a minute before four o'clock. Kara had never done anything on time in her life, but apparently it wasn't too late for a first. A minute later, the pastor entered the room. Then everyone stood for the family: a few older relatives, followed by Kara's mother, Lucy Ann, who refused to stop looking like a woman in her forties. Her hair was dyed in the honey brown/blond family, and she kept it short now, in a bob. Beside her was stepdad Randy, who was greyer and stockier, followed by Kara's ten-year-old half-brothers, the twins, born just as Kara was moving to New York. They were blond with bowl-cut hair, and wore matching navy suits. Then, after a gap, came Kara's sister, Gwen, wearing small oval glasses, her hair tied behind her in a dark knot. And God, somehow it hadn't occurred to Brad that the little girl who was seven or eight the last time he saw her would be so much older now. Or that she might resemble Kara.

Once everyone was seated, the pastor began with generic words of faith and sorrow, then went on to remark on the recklessness of youth, the unexpected paths people's lives take, and "the dangers our children can welcome all too readily." What followed was an invitation for anyone in the room—Kara's family and friends, her neighbors and loved ones, anyone—to step forward and accept Christ and his teachings. Right then and there.

Brad turned to Margot, who shrugged. "Eh, I'm not in the mood," she said.

Margot was the only other person Brad knew in college whose parents sent a box of Matzo every year for Passover. She never ate it, of course; neither did he. Junior year he gift-wrapped his and gave it to Margot. The next year she added a bow and gave it back. "It comes 'pre-stale,' so it's just as good as the day it was made," she said. Kara got a kick out of the fact that she knew two of the only

Jews in North Carolina. *Why does your Sabbath have to start on Friday night? It seems like such poor planning. We schedule ours for Sunday morning—that way we can sleep right through it.*

No one chose this particular moment in the funeral service to embrace the teachings of Jesus Christ, so the pastor continued, inviting up the first speaker. It was a high school musical theater teacher and friend of the family. From Brad's seat near the back, he had a tough time keeping the teacher's head from doubling. He had to look straight ahead and really concentrate, and even then, if the teacher turned his head or shifted his body, he'd split.

The teacher said things that made Brad laugh and tear up a little, as did Kara's stepfather. The pastor had said her stepfather was representing the family, so it seemed like he would be the final speaker, but then after he returned to his seat, the pastor announced that one more person had asked to say a few words. "Would Steve Donegan please come up to the lectern?"

The name was new to Brad, and he watched as Steve rose from the line of seats across the aisle and strolled up to the front of the room. He was tall and broad-shouldered, with rust-colored hair that was slicked back behind his ears and continued down his neck in what looked like a mullet. He wore a mustache and goatee, and his skin had a red, leathery tint to match. He was clearly older than Brad and Kara, somewhere in his late forties. His brown twill sport coat had what looked like a grease stain on the elbow. "Who's that?" Brad whispered.

"Roommate," Margot replied.

"Ah." Brad nodded. Kara tended to go through roommates quickly, given her habit of eating other people's food and letting months go by without paying or procuring rent. Before she lived with Brad, and later when she first moved to New York, her housing situations would emerge during crisis: She was being evicted, and another actor or waiter or singer or chain-smoker who was Kara's dearest, sweetest friend of the moment gave her a place to crash. It was only a matter of time before she'd taken over the bathroom with scented shampoos and candles and handmade soaps. Shortly thereafter, another crisis arose, and someone new had to be charmed into letting her move in.

At the lectern, Steve paused to extract a wrinkled sheet of note-book paper from inside his jacket. Then he clicked on a microphone that the others hadn't used, dropped his notes, mumbled, "Shit," which was amplified, then, "Oh, shit, sorry." Then he shook his head, took a breath, and began to speak.

"I didn't know Kara for that long," Steve announced in a New York accent that pressed against the walls of the room. "I can't tell stories from when she was a teenager," he continued, pausing for some sort of effect. "I'm not from the South. This is my first time to North Carolina. But we have one thing in common: Kara."

Brad lowered his eyes to his hand, and with a little effort, saw only five fingers. He could discern their outlines clearly, follow the lines on each knuckle.

"Kara and I lived together almost a year," Steve continued into the microphone. "I feel real lucky I got to know her. She could be funny, she could be bossy, she could be a real pain in the you know what. But she was a great person, as all you know, or you wouldn't be here. And I know she didn't have a chance to tell you all this, but she and I were going to get married."

Brad's right hand had ten fingers now. He looked up at Steve's heads.

"I gave her a ring"—he paused and swallowed—"just a week ago. I can't believe she was only able to show it to you like this." Steve gestured toward the casket, and Brad turned to Margot. He hadn't noticed a ring. Margot shook her head, her lips apart and eyes half-squinting.

"It happened real fast between us," Steve continued. "I know she was looking forward to introducing me to Lucy Ann and

Randy, who seem like great parents, and to all of you guys. I just wish we'd have been able to meet at, you know, a funner event."

A "funner event"? Brad wished he could see Lucy Ann and Randy's faces.

"I know this is a sad time for everybody, and I know a lot of you knew Kara a lot longer than me. But I want to thank you for being so welcoming to me. I know Kara would've appreciated it."

The silence after Steve spoke was pungent with surprise. Nose-blowing and whispering were kept to a minimum. Brad watched Steve walk back to his seat. The man didn't make eye contact with anyone. He fumbled with his notes, shoved them back into his jacket. He wasn't wearing a tie, and orange chest hairs protruded from the top of his shirt. He didn't look like an actor, or sound like one. He looked like someone who might've delivered pizza for too many years, or worked at an old video store renting out porn. He could've been Kara's trashy uncle, an uncle she would have made fun of behind his back. Or in front of his face. How on earth had she ended up with *him*?

He was lying. He had to be lying. Margot didn't know why, or what to do about it, but she knew it.

Didn't she?

Kara couldn't have been engaged—and to him—and not have said anything. And besides . . .

Margot took a quick mental survey of her conversations with Kara over the past year. Kara hadn't talked much about this latest roommate. There was the physical description: *Imagine a big red dinosaur transformed into a forty-seven-year-old loser—with a mullet. He's your basic mullet-saurus.* And then there were the passing refer-ences: *Mullet's got his panties in a wad . . . Not that it's any of Mullet's business . . . Mullet will get over it . . . I can handle Mullet . . .*

No, "Mullet" did not sound like a pet name or a term of en-dearment. There was not love in Kara's voice when she'd uttered the word. Contempt, frustration—that was what Margot had heard.

"Did you know him?" Brad whispered. Margot had felt his eyes on her when Mullet was speaking. She shook her head. She couldn't bring herself to speak.

Row by row, people walked past the open casket and out the door. Jews didn't do this sort of thing. Shove 'em in a pinewood box and send 'em on their way—that was the Jewish funeral. That was how Margot's mother had gone. But not Kara. Now Margot was being given yet another opportunity to gaze on her dead friend. When it was her turn to pass the casket, Margot dropped her eyes from Kara's face to the bouquet in her hands, and tucked beneath the flowers, Margot spotted it: a cheap-looking little dia-mond ring on Kara's finger.

How can you say it was cheap-looking if you barely saw it? Margot asked herself as she walked to the door. But that was how it struck her; she didn't feel like arguing with herself. Cheap, fake, impossible.

"How did that happen?" Brad asked once they were standing outside.

"I don't know," Margot said. How many times had Kara turned down Brad?

As they waited outside, groups of familiar faces passed. Some were whispering—about Kara, about the fiancé. "Oh look, there's *Brad*," someone whispered. A couple of people from college nodded past Margot to him. No one offered her any sign of recog-nition. Finally, the casket was carried outside by Kara's stepfather, Mullet, and a few men Margot didn't recognize. Then everyone headed to their cars.

"Do you need a ride?" Brad asked.

"No, thanks," she told him.

The procession to the cemetery took twenty minutes, though it was only a few miles away. There were a lot of cars to be moved, a lot of people inching along. Margot was glad to be alone in her own rental car as she sat wedged between cars of strangers who also believed they knew Kara.

Kara had been the last of her single friends, the last one without children. Margot's childhood friends from Long Island now had one, two, and three kids; their photos decorated her refrigerator doors. When she got together with them, they talked about the price of day care and finding good schools, and soccer practice and dance classes, and husbands who worked too hard or traveled too much or didn't help around the house. When Margot and Kara got together, they talked about theater and auditions and Margot's business and Kara's latest adventures. They laughed about the old days, about their lives, about nothing. There was a time they talked about Brad a lot, then intermittently, then not at all. More recently, they'd talked about Mike.

Had Margot misunderstood anything Kara said about Mullet? He really hadn't come up much in conversation.

At the cemetery, Margot pulled into the gravel parking lot and walked up the hill toward the awning. Brad had arrived already, and Margot took a spot beside him a few feet behind the awning. From where they stood, Margot could see the parking lot and could watch the line of skinny women wearing black stockings in the eighty-something-degree heat as they marched up the hill. The ground was soft from recent rain. Margot was glad she hadn't worn heels, and a little bit glad some of the other women had.

Having seen the casket open, Margot felt odd seeing it closed now and knowing that Kara was inside and that no one would open the box or look at Kara's face again. The part of Margot that always liked to double-check—car doors, grocery lists, unplugged irons, credit scores—had an impulse to look inside. She imagined herself slowly opening the lid a crack, the way she'd open the oven, careful not to upset a soufflé. She'd look close at Kara's waxed face, whisper her name, poke her with a toothpick perhaps—to be sure she was dead. Margot tried to recreate the image of Kara she'd seen at the funeral home. It really was a crumby-looking ring.

The ceremony was mercifully brief, and as soon as it ended, Kara's little sister, Gwen, pulled away from the family and lit a cigarette, just as Kara would have done. Mullet pushed out from under the awning and did the same, muttering "Oh, man" in what sounded like a stage whisper.

WHEN she arrived at Kara's mother's house, Margot wandered to the dining room, where the table was covered with moist finger sandwiches, competing bowls of potato salad, and a surprising number of cans of dry-roasted peanuts. Perhaps there'd been a sale. She tried to resist the instinct to criticize, to put on her caterer's hat and judge the menu and presentation. The carafe of chardonnay on the sideboard made her smile. *You could fill a carafe with piss, and my stepdad would call it fancy,* Kara once said. *My family really knows how to put the k in klassy.* Margot poured herself a glass and braced herself for the sharp taste and strained conversation.

She gave her condolences to Kara's mother, Lucy Ann, who seemed glad to see Margot but said very little, and to Kara's stepfather, Randy, whose thickly Southern "So-good-of-you-to-come" poured out in one word. Margot said a few words to Kara's half-brothers, who hovered in a corner, somberly passing a handheld video game back and forth, and she reintroduced herself to Gwen, who was moving about the house in a mask of officiousness. Margot even sucked it up and said hello to a few of the girls from the drama department. One of them said, "Oh my God, I didn't see you before"—which was a lie. Another said, "It's wild how different everyone looks"—but "everyone" meant Margot and "different" meant fat.

If she hadn't quit smoking last year, this would have been a good time for about thirty consecutive cigarettes, so Margot topped off her wine and went out to the carport where she and Kara used to smoke in their college days. It still smelled like ashtrays, which was a comfort, though now it had more bicycles and toys than before. The ice chest where she and Kara used to sit had been replaced by a box of sporting equipment. Margot was marveling at all the basketballs and soccer balls and baseball paraphernalia when the side door opened and Mullet walked out.

The revulsion felt like a bubble inflating inside her stomach.

"Am I interrupting?" he asked.

"No," she said, reluctantly.

He lit his cigarette, cupping the flame in his thick hand. Margot thought about going inside.

"You want a smoke?" he asked.

"I quit," she told him.

He nodded.

They exchanged silences.

"Pretty crazy shit," he said after a minute. "I'm the fiancé, Steve Donegan."

He said the words with an ownership that made Margot uncomfortable, and she wished he'd trip over a stray baseball, but she took his extended hand. "Margot Cominsky," she said. "I'm a friend of Kara's from college."

"Cool," he said. "Yeah, I remember her talking about you." He sucked on his cigarette and blew the smoke out the side of his mouth. Margot could smell it. She could almost taste it.

"You from around here?" he asked.

"New York."

"Oh yeah, me too."

"I know," she said.

They both nodded.

Margot dropped her eyes to a row of muddy sneakers beside the door. Mullet flicked an ash into the driveway.

Then Margot said, "I didn't realize you were a couple."

"Oh yeah, I know. Kara was nervous about telling people 'cause of, you know, the age difference. But I'm sure she'd have introduced us soon."

"I would hope so. If she was engaged."

"Absolutely, no doubt. It just sort of happened, you know. One minute we're talking about maybe looking for a bigger place together, the next we're saying the M-word."

Margot's throat felt dry. She took a sip of wine from her plastic cup.

"How did you two meet?" she asked after a minute.

"At a bar," he said. "Lemon Drop—you know it? Near Prospect Park? Anyway, it's a neighborhood place we both used to hang out at. We would see each other, talk. One day she needed a place to live. We started out as roommates. One thing leads to another . . ."

Mullet is acting like a giant hemorrhoid, Kara had once growled over the phone.

The story, as Margot had heard it from Randy, was that Kara fell asleep on Saturday night and didn't wake up. She'd taken some kind of drug the night before, and Mullet didn't realize she'd gone too far until the next morning when he tried to wake her up.

"So, you found her . . . unconscious?" Margot asked.

"Yeah, it was pretty crazy." Mullet dropped his eyes, then pushed his hair behind his ear, looked up, and continued. "Saturday night she fell asleep watching TV on the couch, so I went ahead and left her there, thinking no big deal. Then Sunday morning, we're supposed to go to Pancake King for brunch, so I make coffee and I'm talking to her and stuff, trying to wake her up before I realize."

Margot tried to picture Mullet saying "Good morning" to Kara's dead body. Then she tried not to picture it.

Mullet held out his pack of Marlboros. "You sure you don't want one? I wouldn't tell."

She shook her head. "I can't."

He finished the cigarette and dropped the butt into a soda can that seemed to be in the corner for that purpose. Then he lit another and put the lighter and box of cigarettes beside the can. "I'm leaving them here in case you change your mind. Kara's sister keeps bumming smokes from me, so I said I'd leave them out."

"Thank you," Margot said.

"I couldn't quit at a time like this."

"I—" She was about to explain that she'd quit a year and a half ago, when Mike left for Japan. He said smoking was more dangerous than running communications for the Army. She was about to say this but stopped herself. It was none of Mullet's business.

"Man, this is not my scene," Mullet said, shaking his head slowly.

"It's no one's scene," Margot snapped, before she could control her tone of voice. "It's a funeral."

"Yeah, I know. I meant here," Mullet said. "Like, the town, the little bicycles and shit . . ."

Margot couldn't listen anymore. She felt like she was suffocating, breathing his smoke, his air, his sweat. Through the window she saw Brad passing in the kitchen. She would talk to him. Or she'd remind another college friend who she was. "Excuse me," she said. "I see someone I should say hello to."

﹡

Brad slipped around a corner in the kitchen and down a hall to the back of the house. His head was pounding and he rubbed his fingers against his temples. Maybe he was feeling the tumor grow, pushing against the folds of his brain. Could a developing tumor kick, like a fetus? If he put a finger in just the right place at the right time, would he feel it?

Brad found Kara's room empty and surprisingly familiar, and he closed the door behind him and took a deep breath. The walls were all white except for one. *That's my graffiti wall,* she'd explained the first time she brought Brad home. In her early teens, she'd spray-painted her name on it in giant pink letters, and over time, she'd added doodles, quotes, names, phone numbers, bumper stickers. Standing in the room now, he still had no trouble finding Kara-hearts-Brad. He also had no trouble finding Kara-hearts-Mark, his predecessor from her high school days. Nothing got erased from the graffiti wall. And the wall had remained intact for all these years.

Looking around the room, Brad saw past all the things that weren't Kara's—the treadmill and television set near the entrance, the sewing machine by the window and stack of little boy pants piled next to it. The bedspread wasn't Kara's. This one was brown with white flowers; Kara's had been leopard print. But the bed was exactly where it had been before, in the center of the room, up against the graffiti wall. Across from it, beside the desk, hung Kara's poster from the movie *Grease 2*. Still. She was probably the only person on earth who'd ever hung this poster in her bedroom, and throughout her life, when asked, she continued to insist with a deadpan face that it was one of the finest films in American history.

A bookshelf that Kara had covered in neon-colored paisley wallpaper stood in the far corner of the room, with college textbooks sitting beside Roald Dahl novels and Uta Hagen's *Respect for Acting*. Kara's flute, long abandoned, sat dusty on the bottom shelf. Behind the treadmill sat Lucy Ann's old dollhouse, which she'd given to Kara, and Kara had given to Gwen, and Gwen must have outgrown years ago.

Kara's desk had always served as a vanity and was still cluttered with jewelry and bottles of nail polish and lipstick tubes and mascara. Brad looked up from the desk to the mirror hanging above it, and he could picture her looking out at him. The face he saw belonged to the thirty-four-year-old he'd seen in the coffin, but her dark hair was alive again and fell in tangled waves, and her eyes, almost black, had that mischievous glimmer he'd once adored. Her lips were painted a deep burgundy, instead of the softer pink they'd used at the funeral home, and she was showing more cleavage than they'd let her show that morning. She didn't look too different from the Kara he remembered.

"Hi," he said to her.

He could practically hear her voice. *Hey there. How was my funeral?*

"It sucked," he said.

The preacher, I know. Not the smoothest operator, but there was entertainment value.

She was wearing some sort of patchwork plaid top he'd never seen before.

Don't be critical, she said. *I love this. I found it at a thrift shop.*

"You're dead."

Yeah, but I can still spot a cool shirt when I see one. What's up with the suit? Are you an investment banker now?

"Realtor," he said.

Difference?

Brad didn't have an answer.

Ibuprofen's in the nightstand, she told him.

She'd always kept a bottle there, and he went to the drawer, pulled out the 300-tablet container, and took two. When he turned back around, she was waiting for him in the mirror.

"So," he said, "Steve, huh?"

You're not going to be jealous, are you? she asked, and she lit a cigarette. When she exhaled, he pictured the smoke penetrating the glass and rising to the ceiling.

"That was kind of a surprise," he said.

The engagement? she asked. *Or me dropping dead? Or the whole maybe/maybe not a brain tumor thing—if you don't mind my bringing it up.*

Another puff. He watched the smoke seep out from between her lips.

Do you remember my secrets? she asked. He followed her gaze to the dollhouse. A moment later, she stepped out of the mirror and into the room.

The move startled Brad. He hadn't felt himself imagining it. And yet there she was—almost—walking past him across the room. Below her shirt, she wore blue jeans and flip-flops. *Dress flip-flops,* she said. Each had a large plastic daisy clipped to the front.

When she reached the dollhouse, Kara ashed in a tiny sink and opened the miniature toilet. *I think you could use these,* she said. Brad looked inside, knowing what he would find. Before she gave the dollhouse to Gwen, Kara had always kept a few Xanax there. *For domestic emergencies,* she used to say. *You're having one now,* she told him.

"So are you," he said.

No, I'm dead. It's all very simple now. Last Saturday was a different story.

"How could you let yourself . . ." he began, but he let the words trail off. She was ignoring them anyway.

She rested a finger on the flusher of the dollhouse toilet. *I'm going to offer them up to someone else if you don't take them, so you might as well.*

"I don't do that anymore."

At least take two for your little trip through the MRI tube. Your doctor would give them to you, if you asked. That's why God invented Xanax.

Kara drifted back across the room and into the mirror, and Brad felt his eyes start to water, his vision grow blurry.

It's okay, Brad. Did you ever imagine I'd turn forty one day? Or sixty?

"What about me?"

She ran her eyes up and down him. *I think growing old will suit you—if you can manage it.*

For a solid minute, Brad stared into the mirror where the image of Kara was and then wasn't. He could remember standing in front of this mirror with her, both of them grinning and naked. Now he felt like an imposter. Being in this room. Being older than twenty-two. Wearing a tie and shoes that he'd polished. Owning shoe polish in the first place. He turned back to the dollhouse and with his finger slid two Xanax out of the toilet bowl. It felt like there were probably four more inside. He dropped the two pills into his shirt pocket.

"Did you just take——?"

Brad turned to face the door, and for a second he thought he was seeing Kara again. But no, it was Gwen. And once again he was conscious of his vision, of a transparent outline around the girl that might have been her sister hiding behind her.

He didn't have a chance to respond before Gwen was walking past him and reaching into the dollhouse. But she wasn't going for the bathroom. She was fishing through the master bedroom. A moment later, she was holding a miniature dresser, which he now saw was just a hollow box with false drawers. Crammed inside the back was a ziplock bag of marijuana. "Sorry," she said, and she turned to face him.

Brad shook his head to say no, and don't worry.

Up close, Gwen looked like a deflated version of her sister: more angular cheekbones, a smaller chest, tiny limbs, straighter hair. Her lips were thin lines, lightly colored. She was wearing a black silk dress with ornate stitching on the front and oval glasses that emphasized the darkness of her eyes.

"I remember you," she said in a matter-of-fact tone. "Do you remember me?"

"Yes," Brad told her. "You look older now."

"So do you."

He felt her studying him, and he took a deep breath. "Sorry about Kara," he said at length.

"Yeah, I know," she mumbled.

"I hope it's okay that I came in here."

"Sure, I don't care."

Gwen returned the dresser to the dollhouse, and as she did, Brad noticed dangling from her wrist a bracelet that he'd bought for Kara a dozen years ago or more. It was made up of square tiles of onyx set in silver and held together with a black leather cord. They'd gotten it on a road trip through the mountains. He wondered if Gwen had started wearing the bracelet in the last few days, or if it had been passed on to her long ago. And if so, how long ago. And why.

"Are you still an actor?" she asked.

"No," he said. "Realtor."

She nodded.

"Are you in college now?"

"In the fall," she said. "I'm going to a pre-college thing this summer." She pushed a loose strand of hair behind her ear. "It's an art program in New York. Being there was supposed to be a whole sister-bonding thing. Mom wants me to cancel now, but I mean, what else am I going to do?"

Brad felt like her question wasn't entirely rhetorical, like he should say something consoling or constructive. His instinct was to agree with her mother. New York was a hard place for anyone to navigate, let alone an eighteen-year-old who'd just lost her sister. But that probably wasn't the advice she wanted.

"I should go help out," she said.

His window of time had passed.

"Okay," Brad said. "But if you need anything . . ." He fished into his pocket and pulled a business card from his wallet.

"Like a house?"

"No. Like, to talk."

She examined his card. "You're still in Chapel Hill," she said, her voice lightening. "I'm going to UNC."

"Oh, then you should definitely give me a call. When you're there for orientation. I can buy you a decent meal."

"Maybe so."

"I'm serious. Please let me."

"Well," she said, "I should go help. People keep bringing over macaroni, and I'm in charge of putting it somewhere."

※

Margot was done. She'd said her good-byes to the family, eaten her share of funeral food, and chatted with a half-dozen people she'd probably never see again. Now she was standing in the kitchen, wondering if Brad might have left without saying good-bye, when she saw both him and Gwen slip out of Kara's bedroom down the hall. At a glance, Gwen looked a lot like Kara, and Margot was reminded of a moment long ago when she'd been standing in this kitchen, talking to Kara's mother about God-knows-what for God-knows-how-long, and saw Kara and Brad walk out of the bedroom behind Lucy Ann's back. This was early in Kara and Brad's relationship. Margot had thought *he* was the third wheel on the trip, but his face was flush and Kara was grinning. Without knowing it, Margot had become their accomplice, their decoy. She'd been furious. She pouted the whole weekend, though no one seemed to notice.

Gwen passed through the kitchen and said good-bye to Margot again as she picked up a bowl of soupy chicken salad to bring into the living room. Brad lingered in the kitchen. "You going?" he asked.

"I am, yeah. I have a flight out of Wilmington in a couple of hours. Do you still live down here?"

"Yeah, in Chapel Hill."

"I need to make a visit back one of these days. I'm in Long Island."

"I still have a couple of cousins up in New York. We try to make it up every once in a while."

Brad walked with her outside and down to her car, and they exchanged phone numbers, both typing the digits into their cell phones as if they meant to call. ("That was an eight?" "Yes, exactly.")

And Brad, she found herself thinking, was one of a handful of people she'd seen today whose wedding she wasn't invited to but whose funeral she might have attended if he'd died and she'd been told.

And who would have told her if he'd died? Kara, of course.

"This was a little surreal," he said.

"Tell me about it."

"And Steve . . ."

"I *know.*"

"It's hard to believe," he said.

"Very hard," she agreed. "I almost feel like he's lying." Margot inserted a fake laugh to lighten the tone.

"To inherit the tens of dollars she had to her name?" Brad said.

He wasn't taking her seriously.

"Kara was something," he added. "You never quite knew what to expect."

Over his shoulder, Margot saw Mullet walk out of the house and light a cigarette under the carport. He caught her eye and took a few steps down the driveway. "You going?" he called out. "Good to meet you. Maybe we can get together back home sometime."

Margot forced a smile and waved back. "Mm-hmm," she called back.

"You never met him before?" Brad asked quietly.

"Never," she said, still smiling over his shoulder. "I thought she couldn't stand him." Margot looked at Brad now, then turned away and tossed her purse in the car. "I don't know," she said, in answer to the question in his eyes. "She should have married you when she had the chance."

Brad dropped his gaze to the ground. Now it was his turn to fake a laugh.

CHAPTER TWO

WHEN THE WOMAN ON THE PHONE TOLD BRAD HIS TEST WOULD BE IN THE mobile unit beside the hospital, he thought "mobile" referred to patients who were mobile. He didn't realize his MRI would take place in a trailer.

"You're not late. Don't worry. Come on up."

Brad had circled the hospital twice before he saw a sign propped up next to the small trailer beside the hospital's front entrance. At a glance, it looked kind of like a dumpster or storage pod. Inside was a small office and the machine in the next room.

"Is anyone here with you?" the medical technician asked. "Your wife?" The guy was younger than Brad, maybe in his mid-twenties. He wore scrubs but had a baseball cap on the desk.

"No," Brad said. "I'm here alone."

"Okay. Well, first I'm going to ask you to take anything you have that's metal and put it in this tray here: your watch, phone, belt, wedding ring."

Brad emptied his pockets, took off his ring and watch. "I have a zipper," he said. "Do I have to take off my pants?"

Oh, that would be fun.

"No, your pants are fine."

Brad pictured Kara sitting in the office's single guest chair. She wore a denim skirt, a T-shirt, and leg warmers.

Leg warmers?

Kara shrugged. *It's cold,* she said, and she ashed her cigarette on the floor.

She was right. The trailer was strangely cold. It had to be eighty-five outside.

Brad set his belt on the tray and looked back at the chair. He could let himself see her there, or make himself not see her.

She smiled. *Which do you prefer?*

"The test should take about forty minutes," the technician said, and he led Brad into the next room, where what looked like a morgue drawer awaited him. "Are you claustrophobic?"

"No," Brad said. He had taken a Xanax before getting out of the car. He hoped he'd feel it soon.

You know you will, he heard Kara say. *You've had your share of recreational Xanax.*

"I'm going to need you to lie very still. Try not to sneeze or cough. If you need to come out for any reason, just hit this call button, and the microphone will come on. I'll be right next door." Brad followed the man's gaze back to the office beyond the glass partition. He probably saw bad news on that computer screen every day—though he never had to be the one to deliver it.

"It's going to be loud," the man added, and he handed Brad a pair of foam earplugs. Brad could only recall wearing earplugs once before, at some awful concert Kara dragged him to. He wedged them into his ears and lay down on his back on the metal tray. The technician inserted an IV in Brad's left arm. "This is going to feel cold," he said.

Like the tip of an ice cube running up Brad's arm.

"Do you want a blanket?"

Brad nodded, and the man arranged Brad's arms flat against the sides of his body, then slipped the call button into Brad's right hand and put a blanket over his chest and legs. A moment later, a switch was flipped, and Brad felt himself sliding backward, slow-motion, into the center of the machine.

His eyes circled the putty-colored metal tube. He waited for the Xanax to kick in. An intercom clicked on. "This one will be for six minutes."

"Okay," Brad mumbled.

There was a snap, then another, then a loud series of pulses. The sounds came in waves. The first ones weren't too bad. Others were more insistent, like someone drilling and hammering on the outside of the machine's metal casing. Collectively, the dissonance would reveal whether or not there was "a mass," the ophthalmologist had explained. It might also detect if he'd had a stroke—"just a mini-stroke," the doctor had hastened to add, "one you didn't even notice." The word "mini" was not a comfort.

Focus on your breathing, Kara whispered.

He did. He closed his eyes and counted breaths. He tried to ignore the clacks and bumps, the pulsations rearranging themselves again and then again.

Are you starting to feel it?

He was starting to feel it. He let the noise wash over him.

"This one will last for four minutes."

Another adjustment, then a new set of sounds.

It was odd to lie there, immobile in this tube. While Kara lay in her coffin underground. He wondered how he'd look in a coffin.

Depends on how they dress you. Did you see that shirt they put me in? Where did they find that?

Probably your closet, he said. In his mind.

An abandoned Christmas gift from the eighties, maybe. My God.

Brad concentrated on his breathing. If he opened his eyes and looked toward the entrance, his feet and the technician would start to double in the distance, but inside the tube there was nothing but beige. It was refreshing, in its way, to not worry about seeing.

"This one will be about three minutes."

Brad closed his eyes. He felt the closeness of his metal cocoon. And he felt Kara's presence.

It's kind of sexy, isn't it? Being in here together.

Brad pictured her pressed on top of him, her chest against his.

He wondered if Xanax was hallucinogenic.

You know it's not. But it's cute of you to pretend to forget.

Why are you here? he asked.

She licked his ear.

"Remember not to move," said the intercom.

Brad focused on his breathing, on the thumping of the machine.

I know you haven't had sex in two months, she whispered.

The thumping stopped, adjusted itself, then started again.

It's understandable, she continued. *I know it's been a difficult pregnancy.*

It has, Brad told her.

And Val's been a trooper, a saint.

The machine made a new noise, a whistling from above.

What if I unzip your pants—

No.

We're going to be here for a while.

"Three minutes."

If I just rub the tip of your—

No.

Why not? I'm not really here.

I'm married.

Brad tried to distract himself. He counted the clicks and the bumps. He tried to categorize them, but then he lost track.

What difference does it make? You're just imagining me. Besides, I'm dead. You may be soon, too.

A mini-stroke, the doctor had said. A precaution.

Kara unzipped Brad's pants beneath the blanket. He could feel her finger run slowly down the shaft of his penis.

"Everything okay in there?"

"Uh-huh," Brad mumbled.

He could feel the weight of her hand.

"Alright, this one's going to be a little longer. Eight minutes."

Brad took a deep breath and focused on the noise. He focused on the gentle pressure of her hand inside his pants. It had stopped moving and now rested there on top of him. It didn't do anything. Just held him, comforted him. It told him not to worry, through all the clanks and thumps and bumps. It told him there were a million possibilities, that most people who get MRIs are fine, that doctors don't know what they're talking about, and that he probably just needed a pair of glasses. The hand held him and told him Val would be okay too, and the baby would be okay, and he would be a good father. The hand stayed there for a long time. The hand told him that he was a good person, a brave person, and that people loved him.

I miss you, he said, or he wanted to say.

I miss you too, she whispered.

BRAD was lying on the couch when Val returned from school. "You're home early," she said.

"A little bit," he said. "How're you feeling?"

"Fine," she said. "I picked up a couple movies for you." She set two DVD boxes on the coffee table. "Something horrible and something horrible-er." She wrinkled her freckled nose. "For after I'm asleep," she added.

"Oh, you're wonderful."

"Well, you've seemed down."

Brad rose to give her a hug, but Val waved her hand and backed away. "I smell like Listerine, bile, and Febreze. It was one of those days. Let me shower first," she said, and she went huffing up the stairs.

"Breakfast for dinner?" Brad called behind her.

"I can do that. Give me a few."

"I can make."

"Even better," she called back.

Brad glanced at the coffee table—an action movie and a thriller. He'd seen one of them in the theaters without her, but the other would pass the time. It was sweet of her. She was responding to the funeral the other day, of course. She didn't know about the MRI that morning.

In the kitchen, Brad opened the fridge and pulled out the eggs and a roll of that gooey croissant dough they liked to pretend wasn't unhealthy. He preheated the oven and unrolled the dough and carefully folded little croissants on a cookie tray. If it had been any other time in their lives, of course he'd have told her about the test—and she'd have been a great support. But now, when things were so difficult for her, he couldn't bring himself to burden her with one more worry.

Upstairs the shower clicked on. She was washing away the day, the smells, the sickness. He hadn't realized how lucky she'd been during the start of the first pregnancy. She was in high spirits every morning, never complained of discomfort. This time around, she had to invent almost daily excuses to leave the classroom. There was a book she'd forgotten in her car, a message to pick up from the principal's office. She started leaving things in the teacher's lounge to facilitate these exits: an interesting poem she'd photocopied, papers she'd finished grading, cupcakes because it was Friday.

And it wasn't just the morning sickness she was hiding. It was the whole thing. They were in week twelve. Last time she'd miscarried during week fifteen, though the doctor said she'd probably lost the baby a week or two before. Once they passed the fifteenth week this time around, he knew everything would be back to normal—better than normal. So much better. But in the meantime, they'd agreed not to tell their parents or celebrate prematurely, and she certainly wasn't saying anything at school, not after last time. The memory of it haunted every day as the pregnancy inched forward.

Val taught middle school English in Chapel Hill, and everyone there loved her—the kids and parents, the young teachers and the old regime. She created the school's summer enrichment camp when she was barely out of college, and two summers ago, she walked into the cafeteria one day to find the whole camp throwing her a surprise baby shower. One of the kids started a secret ballot competition: "Guess what Mrs. Mitchell will name her baby." There were over a hundred entries.

She was at the camp when it happened. She was standing in front of a classroom, thanking a guest speaker, and her water broke. She'd been bleeding off and on, but the doctor had said she was fine. Then in the teacher's lounge bathroom, before Brad could get there, a wet mass slipped out of her into the toilet. When he arrived, he found her sitting on the floor beside the toilet bowl. She showed him what was inside: It looked like something out of an ultrasound image—little arms and legs—but broken and drowned in a murky pool. They didn't know what else to do. Eventually, she let him flush.

After that, Val stayed away from the camp during its final weeks. And for months—maybe a year—when she and Brad were out at the mall, the same kids who used to run up to her to say hello and introduce a parent or sibling or friend or pet kept their distance but stared. And Val, who had never avoided a student in public, who loved to wave across the restaurant to a smiling kid with braces, would look down into nothingness. Brad wasn't certain she even noticed the kids noticing her.

When he and Val started trying again, they decided to time it so she wouldn't show during the school year and could take the summer off. As it turned out, she got pregnant quickly, so now she was starting to show and had to get creative with her clothes, wearing light sweaters and shawls in late May, long blazers and loose dresses. During class her forehead would bead up with sweat, and she had to reapply antiperspirant at lunch. And as often as they went to the obstetrician, they couldn't help wondering the next day, would there still be a heartbeat? Was the baby inside her still alive?

Add to this the morning sickness she had to conceal every day at school—and she made light of that part, but he knew it pained her. Every day of it pained her. But soon things would be better. School would let out, and she could stop pretending. She could let her belly hang out, and live in maternity pants, and stop working so hard for once in her life. Week fifteen would pass, and they could let themselves be excited.

Val returned downstairs wearing the terrycloth robe he'd given her for Christmas, her cherry-brown hair pulled back in a clip. He could see in her eyes that she'd be in bed by nine at the latest. "How are we doing?" she asked.

The croissants were in the oven. He'd just cracked the eggs in the pan, sunny-side up. "Good, we're close."

"I'm kinda feeling the groove," she said. "Are you?"

"I can be."

"Truth be told, I've been fantasizing about it all day," she said. "I'll go set up."

Brad smiled to himself. When she bought the PlayStation, she made a valiant effort to pretend it was for him, but she'd gotten it for Trivia Master, a game show–style quiz game they could play online. She'd been a pub trivia fanatic in college, before he knew her. She also attended a Rock-Paper-Scissors competition once— for the camp value, she insisted, though he liked to tell friends she'd put herself through college on the competitive Rock-Paper-Scissors circuit.

"Our nemesis is online," she called to the kitchen. "Can we start while we eat?"

"Fine, sure."

"Excellent . . . I now know for a fact that two of my seventh graders play this game. Sarah and Max *could be* 'Smartie Pantz 007.'"

Brad carried the plates into the living room. "Isn't 'Smartie Pantz 007' from Akron, Ohio?" Brad checked the screen.

"It's a front. I said we're from Atlanta."

"How exotic."

Val took a bite of croissant—"Mmm"—and started the game. "My deep dark secret."

"'The Twinkie Express,'" Brad said. The name she'd given their team.

Val chose the topic "Word Play," and the animated host read their first question aloud. "The word *ungulate* means: (a) to fluctuate, (b) a hoofed mammal, (c) the fleshy lobe in the back of the mouth, or (d) to regurgitate."

"It's not C," Brad said.

"It's B," Val said, and she made the selection on the screen.

The host smiled. "You, my friend, are correct."

Now it was Smartie Pantz 007's turn.

"How was your showing this morning?" Val asked.

Showing? Brad hadn't seen a client all day.

But he *had* left the house early, to go to the hospital—

"Fine," he told her. "Fine. Nothing special."

A wave of guilt passed over him. But it was only a precaution, that's what the doctor had said. In a few days, he'd know it was nothing, and nothing would have been hidden.

Still he did feel a little odd about hiding it. And about imagining Kara there.

"'Facts and Figures' or 'Mysteries of Science'?" Val asked. She was back to the game.

And it really wasn't a big deal. There was no sense thinking too hard about it. "Mysteries," Brad said.

"Excellent choice," the digital host replied.

※

Margot was still thinking about the voicemail message when she pulled her minivan into the garage. It was a call from Collin, a mess of a guy who'd been Kara's roommate before they had a falling out and Kara moved in with Mullet. Margot had barely met the guy a couple years ago, but somehow he'd gotten a hold of her number. He was having a get-together next week for Kara's New York friends to celebrate Kara and what would have been her thirty-fifth birthday.

Hadn't Margot just gone to a funeral last week? Did she really need to subject herself to this?

Margot deposited the first load of groceries on the kitchen counter, then checked her computer to see if Mike was online. She'd started keeping her laptop on the breakfast table so he could keep her company if he was available. No word yet today. It was three in the morning in Okinawa, but when he was on night shifts he'd often check in before or after, or sometimes he'd text her on a break.

She was lucky, in a way. Women who dated men in the military didn't always have so much access to them. But she and Mike talked all the time—by instant messenger, text message, even phone or Skype. And he was in Japan, thank God, specializing in communications, which Margot understood to mean he spent a whole lot of time sitting safely in a room staring at a monitor. There were worse places he could be and worse skills he could have. She knew she shouldn't complain.

But she still worried about him. And although she usually heard from him several times a week, he didn't actually reveal much about his life. Boring, he always insisted, so no great loss—but it was a loss. When she tried to ask him what he was doing, or if he knew for sure when he'd be able to talk next, or whether he was doing anything dangerous, Mike would often change the subject and start asking about Uncle Bernie. "How's Bernie doing?" "I heard from Bernie the other day." "Say, what's your Uncle Bernie think of the Yankees this year?"

If anyone really was monitoring these conversations, which Mike insisted was possible, they might think Mike had a touching affection for this uncle of Margot's. But in fact, Bernie didn't exist. He was an invention Mike used to dodge questions about his work. At first it was funny. ("What do you do all day?" "Not much. Bernie get laid lately?") She pictured Bernie as the little old man who worked the register at the kosher deli over in Plainview. But sometimes Margot didn't want to talk about Bernie, or even herself. Sometimes she wanted to know things.

There was one thing she made Mike promise he would tell her—whether he was allowed to or not. If there was ever a threat of his being deployed to Iraq or Afghanistan, he promised to let her know. It wasn't his plan, he insisted, and there was little chance the Army would send him there from Japan. But Margot worried, so before he left they agreed on a code word: "eggplant." If he ever mentioned eggplant, that would mean a reassignment was on the horizon. Now Margot couldn't eat eggplant. She could barely stand seeing it at the grocery store. It didn't occur to her until after he'd left that she should have chosen a food she already disliked.

Six months, three weeks, and five days until his return. Margot had installed a countdown program on her laptop. A few months after he went away, Mike had promised Margot he was coming back to New York and wouldn't reenlist. In not too long, "eggplant" would just mean eggplant—maybe she'd even start eating it again. Uncle Bernie would be happily put to rest. She and Mike would finally be conversing in the same time zone, even the same room. It seemed so luxurious—the idea of his being there, in touching distance.

If he were here now, Margot thought, he could help her unload all these groceries—the bricks of cream cheese and bags of brown sugar, the flour and cartons of eggs. If he were here now, while she was loading up the fridge, he might say, "Boy, that does sound like an odd funeral," or, "Nah, you don't need to go to another memorial," or, "Maybe it is time we had a baby."

Margot had started feeling the maternal tick-tock a few years ago, and moving into this neighborhood hadn't helped. "More Than Muffins" had taken off while she was temporarily staying with her father, and by the time she'd moved him to a retirement facility and sold his house, she realized she couldn't afford to move back into an apartment. She was taking in too many orders. She needed to bake cakes and muffins at the same time, have cookies and pies in the works simultaneously. So instead of moving to an apartment in Brooklyn or Queens, she bought a house on Long Island with a large, tax-deductible kitchen where she put in two double ovens, a giant refrigerator, and enough counter space for— well, you could really never have enough counter space.

All the houses in her neighborhood were too big for one person, and most had at least two children inside and parents who looked at Margot with what felt like a mixture of confusion and pity. So sad that the muffin lady is all alone, they all murmured to each other. She'd be so much happier with kids. Maybe someday, they were saying, she really would have more than muffins. Margot could hear them through the walls.

Kara had given her a hard time about the move. *You're finally free to be young again, and you're giving it up,* she'd said. But by the time Margot got her father settled in Florida and bought the house, she already owned an embroidered apron with her company's name on it. She'd become the fucking muffin lady, there was no denying it. She was a long way from her days as Cougar Cominsky.

She couldn't believe Brad had called her that.

You do something once, whatever. You do it twice in a row, maybe it's cute, it's funny. It's a coincidence, it's the craziest thing. But if you sleep with three football players in the weeks before the team hits a sudden winning streak, so help you God, it's going to haunt you for the rest of your life. Not that Margot had been ashamed at the time. She thought it was funny when Reggie or—what was his name?—turned out to be a football player too. Another freshman, no less. When she got back to the dorm the next morning, she woke up Kara and Brad and told them all about it. And it was that weekend—not that any of them normally followed sports—that the team had its first win in a month. Reggie had his picture in the school paper, and somehow, in certain circles, Margot became known as Cougar Cominsky, the football team's newest mascot and secret weapon.

Badges of pride are different when you're twenty. Today, Margot was known for her cranberry/white chocolate dessert muffins. At least in certain circles. She needed to make six dozen this afternoon, which was just as well, because she didn't need to be thinking about football players or Mike or Kara.

What was she going to do about Collin's memorial thing? The idea of making small talk with Mullet and Collin and Kara's other druggie friends held no appeal. In fact, to Margot's knowledge, Kara and Collin had been on non-speaking terms for the past year. Why was he doing this, and how had he gotten Margot's phone number anyway? Well, Kara did have a tendency to shed her possessions, so maybe she'd left an address book behind. Or maybe Mullet had provided it. Lucky for Margot.

Engaged? Was it possible? Margot still couldn't make herself believe it.

Mullet had his goddamned Space Invaders video game running half the night. I can still hear the explosions going off in my head.

That was the only thing Kara had said about the man during

their last phone conversation two weeks before she died. No reference to feelings for him, the possibility of an engagement.

Could Kara have been hiding the relationship from Margot? But why bother? Could it have come on suddenly? Very suddenly. It seemed hard to believe. And even so, could Kara have become engaged to the man—or to *anybody*—and not have told Margot?

Margot needed to clear her mind. To busy her mind. And she was familiar with the art of self-distraction. She'd become something of an expert when she was taking care of her parents, and these days it could make her insane when Mike was unexpectedly "out of touch," as he liked to put it, for a week or more. Or when he jumped. God, she wished he wouldn't do it, but he earned an extra something per month if he maintained his certification to parachute out of a plane. It was such a tiny amount, in the scheme of things. She wished she could tell him she could replace that income catering an extra bar mitzvah now and then, but she couldn't say that, and he probably liked it even though he said he didn't. He hadn't jumped since before the holidays, thank God, but the times he did, she was up all night baking. Coffee shops across town were forced to try a new walnut/olive scone— "Yes, olive. Humor me," she'd say—and butternut squash pound cake. She couldn't sit still until he messaged her that he was all right.

She would never have stayed with Mike if he had decided to enlist while they were together, she'd told Kara. Unfortunately, she happened to meet Mike after it was too late. But she was glad to have met him—who was she kidding?—and he only had six months left. Well, six months, three weeks, and five days.

Margot glanced at her computer screen again—no word from Mike. And no messages on her phone either, except the unanswered one from Collin. So she sighed, picking up the phone, and sent a text message back to him. She'd try to be there, she said. Thanks for the invite.

What else was she going to do on Kara's birthday? It was going to be a horrible day no matter where she spent it.

Then Margot plugged in the food processor and dropped in the first zucchini. Six dozen muffins. That's how she needed to spend this morning: mixing the flour and butter and eggs and sugar. And a touch of zucchini in the muffin batter—her secret ingredient. Who would think to mix zucchini with cranberries and white chocolate?

Cougar Cominsky, that's who.

※

Neither of them used the word "tumor." After Brad spent thirty minutes in the waiting room surrounded by children with thick glasses, and ten more sitting alone in the examination room, he was greeted by the neuro-ophthalmologist and informed that the MRI had revealed "no unusual mass."

"So everything's okay?"

"Let me start with a few questions," Dr. Thompson said.

"Have you been in a car accident recently?"

"Do you fatigue easily?"

"Were you cross-eyed as a child?"

"Do you find yourself slurring your speech?"

"Do your eyelids ever droop?"

The answer to each of these and at least a dozen other questions was "No" or "I don't think so."

Then the examination began: She shined a flashlight in his face and studied his pupils. She moved her finger around and asked him when it doubled. She held a patch over one of his eyes then snapped it away. She had a nurse come in to take a blood sample for some obscure disorder with a long name. She poked his eyeballs with what looked like a Q-tip attached to a tiny pistol. And she repeated all the tests he'd had at the regular doctor's office, trying one lens after another. "Is this better, or this? This, or this?"

When she concluded, as the previous doctor had, that Brad had 20/20 vision, Dr. Thompson pulled out a long leather box from a drawer. It looked like the kind of box that might contain a fancy carving knife or antique jewelry, but inside was a row of about twenty foggy glass wedges. She pulled out one of the thinnest wedges, and when she held it in front of Brad's right eye, the *E*'s on the chart in the distance came together.

"This is a prism," the doctor explained. "It bends light, so the image you're seeing with one eye is shifted horizontally to meet the image you see with the other eye." She pulled the prism away, and the *E*'s split again into overlapping images. When she held the prism back over his right eye, the two *E*'s merged.

"A person with normal vision actually sees two slightly different images from the differing perspectives of the two eyes. The brain fuses these images together into what is perceived as a single, three-dimensional image. What's happening here is you're having trouble fusing the separate images on your own."

The doctor tried a few different-sized wedges to determine how much prism he needed, then concluded that one "diopter" over each eye was sufficient. The prism over the left eye would move the image to the right; the prism over the right eye would move the image a little to the left. Brad would see what was in the middle. He couldn't suppress a smile.

"Why do you think this happened?" he asked, as she scribbled out a prescription.

"It's hard to say," she said. "People are generally born with strabismus—this misalignment of the eyes—and parents notice because a child's eyes start to cross, or the child gets in the habit of ignoring one eye so it starts to drift. It's possible you've always had a very mild case and your brain was able to compensate for it, but now as you're getting older, you need a little help."

So he was always ever-so-slightly cross-eyed but never knew it?

That certainly beat the alternative scenario that had sent him into the MRI tube.

Brad left the appointment delighted to feel healthy and unremarkable. One diopter over each eye didn't seem so bad. A lot of kids had it worse. The largest prism in the box looked like it was an inch thick. How could they even make glasses out of something like that? He dimly recalled a classmate in grade school with crossed eyes and very thick glasses.

Had he ever made fun of someone with a lazy eye? Brad tried to remember and felt penitent just in case.

FIVE days later, Brad picked up his new glasses before heading over to Annie's Coffee Shop. The shop at the mall advertised lenses in an hour, so he was surprised that they needed so much time. "But sir, these are prisms," the optician had said, as if the problem were self-evident. Brad had felt himself blush and cut the conversation short.

Now he was wearing his new glasses—wire-rimmed rectangular frames that looked like ones half the people in the world were wearing—and through the lenses, each person, chair, and mug in the coffee shop remained singular. Brad surveyed the room, with its exposed brick walls and framed mirrors, and as pleased as he was to see the world in front of him more clearly, a part of Brad was seeing beyond what was there to what had been there before.

Annie's Coffee Shop used to be Tyler's Steakhouse. Then it became a Greek restaurant, then a pool hall, then Annie's. The whole place had been paneled in dark wood back in Brad's day; the floor had been clay-colored terrazzo. Near the front window, where Annie's had a few mismatched loveseats, there'd been a bar where Brad would wait for Kara's shifts to end. The bathroom in back, he discovered as he passed through its door, looked exactly the same as it had a decade earlier. The walls were painted a bright Carolina blue, the toilets and sink were black ceramic, and the stall door and walls were black too. It was like peeing in a time machine. During the summer that he'd worked as a busboy at the steakhouse, he'd mopped that black-and-white checkered floor too many times to count. Once he'd even slept on it.

He was running a few minutes early and had settled into one of the coffee shop's wooden chairs when Kara walked in the front door.

No, not Kara. Gwen. Of course it was Gwen. She wore her hair pulled back in a barrette and hanging down below her neck, and though her hair was much straighter than Kara's, from a distance, she looked like her older sister fresh out of the shower.

Gwen spotted him at once—he gave a quick wave—and she walked toward him with something of a smile. She wore a navy knit shirt with tiny buttons up the front and carried a backpack slung over one shoulder. When she adjusted her own glasses, Brad saw she was wearing the onyx bracelet again, the one he'd given to Kara.

"It's hot," Gwen said as she dropped into the chair across from him. Her brow was shiny with perspiration.

"And humid," Brad said. Kara used to sweat a lot, too.

Gwen ordered an iced tea and was on her second refill by the time the salads arrived. She told Brad all about orientation and its "eye-opening" activities. "I can't decide if I was more stimulated by the don't-rape-girls exercise or the don't-be-a-racist presentation," she concluded. "But I know I'm a better person now."

Brad had met Kara during their summer orientation. They were both assigned to the same group during a session in July, along with a pimpled surfer from Los Angeles who had a fake ID and a large quantity of marijuana. Kara and the surfer were sitting together on a bench when Brad walked past. *This one seems artsy. I bet he'll join us.* The words were spoken to the surfer but meant to be overheard. Brad stopped and met Kara's eyes, dark and inviting. They both smiled. That evening, while the rest of their group went on a Carolina-themed scavenger hunt, the three of them sat together in a dorm room and Brad was introduced to what would soon become a fixture in his college life. He did his best to pretend to know what he was doing. Months later, he admitted to Kara he'd never smoked pot before; she said she knew. She confessed the only reason she'd invited him along was to keep the surfer from making the moves on her; Brad said he chose not to believe her.

They didn't exchange numbers at orientation, but when she said she was sure they'd see each other again soon, he had a feeling they would. It was on the second day of classes. He was sitting in his 8:30 AM film class, and as soon as the lights went out, she appeared beside him. *We really should get some breakfast.* That was her greeting. Then she tapped his knee, and he followed her out the door. With that, the pattern was set: If the professor was showing a film and both of them happened to make it to class that day, they left as soon as the lights went out. It was only a month before they were having sex.

Gwen had signed up for the first orientation session available, and apparently she hadn't made any friends in her group, none that she mentioned anyway. She said she'd stayed in her room during the scavenger hunt. That's when she'd painted her nails shamrock green.

"Did you like the tour?" Brad asked.

"It was a tour. Here's this building, here's that one. It was fine, I guess." Gwen plucked a crouton from her salad bowl, then added, "It was good to get out of Greenwood Park for a few days. Just change life's window dressing."

Brad smiled. That phrase—*change life's window dressing.* It was so Kara. Was Gwen even conscious of where she'd picked it up?

She was talking now about the art program in New York. It started in a week, right after her graduation. "Mom thinks it'll be depressing to be up there, but I don't know what could be more depressing than sitting in the house all summer listening to her and Randy and the two Bobbies."

"The two Bobbies?"

"The twins: Bobby and Tommy. Did you see them? They look the same, they act the same. I really can't tell them apart." Gwen said this with a wave of her hand, a gesture of dismissal with which Brad was familiar. Only if this had been Kara talking, she'd have had a cigarette in her hand, and she'd have ashed behind her, most likely on another person.

"You don't mean that," he said.

"I'm sure it'll be a relief to have me out of the house," Gwen continued. "Then Mom can focus all of her energy on family number two."

"What are you talking about?"

"The Randy Bunch. It's a much simpler family. No dead father, no dead Kara, no bad behavior. I'm sure they'll have a much better summer without me."

"Don't say that."

"It's true," Gwen said. "She can't wait for all this to be done. Once I'm gone and all the crap with Kara is passed, I bet she becomes a Cub Scout mother, really hurls herself into it. They went camping this spring. My mother, who gets manicures like other people go to church."

Brad wished he could offer her something useful. "People handle grief in different ways," he managed after a minute. Gwen didn't respond. She picked through her salad. It wasn't a comment worthy of a response, Brad knew. Then he asked, "Did you know Kara was engaged?"

Gwen sucked on her straw, and the bottom of the tea bubbled up with the suction. "Mom always said Kara was full of surprises."

"She never mentioned him?"

"No, she did. A little. But not that they were, like, together. Did you have on glasses at the funeral?" she asked suddenly.

"No, these are brand new," he said. "What do you think?"

Gwen studied him a moment. "They look pretty good," she said. "Very Clark Kent."

"Why thank you," he said. "I'm still getting used to them."

"I've had mine since I was three."

"I remember," he told her, and he gave her a wink.

"Oh, yeah," she said, and they held each other's stare. "Do you remember that time you and Kara took me out for ice cream in downtown Wilmington?"

Brad nodded vaguely. "Sort of," he said.

"That's one of my favorite memories of her," Gwen said, retiring her fork to the side of her plate. "It was right before Kara left for New York, sort of a good-bye visit. Do you remember how insane the house was? The Bobbies had just been born and at least one of them was always screaming, and my crazy Aunt Nadine had moved in to help out. Y'all were barely there for an hour before Kara was like, let's go, and you drove me to The Creamery.

"I'd never been there because ice cream always made me sick, but Kara gave me this medicine she said would help. I thought she was making it up, but she said not to worry—if I puked, Mom would blame her, not me. So I got blue bubble gum–flavored ice cream, and it was like the greatest thing I'd ever eaten. And then I didn't get sick. I thought she was magic. Turned out it was just a lactose supplement—she gave me a whole box of them. But I remember feeling like she'd invented ice cream."

Brad dimly recalled being exhausted by the whole visit. A noisy lunch. A trip to Walmart. This ice cream run. But he'd been a twenty-four-year-old whose girlfriend was about to move away. Hearing about it now, he was sorry he hadn't paid more attention to what the visit meant, at least for Gwen. That trip ended up being his last visit to the house, until the funeral.

"Before she left for New York," Gwen added, "I remember she told me not to think about how far away she was, that I should call anytime I wanted—even after nine o'clock, if I could get away with it."

"And did you?" Brad asked.

"Yeah, but she usually didn't answer," Gwen said with a laugh.

Brad smiled. "That was pretty much my experience, too."

VAL was in the kitchen when Brad got home. Books and colored folders littered the dining room table. "I'm planning final exams," Val called out to him. "Sorry for the mess."

Brad braced himself outside the kitchen doorway. The radio was tuned to NPR, talk of another suicide bombing outside of Baghdad. Then he walked into the kitchen. She had her back to him for a few seconds, then turned around and immediately asked, "What are you wearing?"

He'd decided to be nonchalant about the glasses. "Oh, yeah, these," he said. "I popped by the eye doctor the other day because I was having a little trouble with distance. Turned out I needed glasses. I picked them up today. What do you think?" He pulled a bottle of wine out of the pantry, then reached around Val to get a glass from a cabinet.

"I didn't know you were having trouble seeing."

"It's a very mild prescription," he said, his back to her. He uncorked the wine and poured himself a glass. A pot of soup was simmering on the stove. "Chicken noodle?" he asked.

"Vegetable barley," she replied. She studied him now, her bottom lip pulled in under her teeth.

"Smells good," he said, and he sipped his wine. "So, do they look okay?"

She was angry. He could tell. But then she relaxed her mouth. It was nice to see one of her again. "They do," she said. "You know, I could have helped you pick them out."

"Oh, you've got exams to deal with . . ."

"It's hard to pick out frames alone."

"Do they look bad?"

"No, I'm just saying. You could've asked me."

"I'm sorry. Next time."

They stood in silence for a minute. A voice on the radio speculated about Iran's interest in nuclear weapons, and Val snapped it off. "I don't have the energy to be frightened about that right now." Then she met his eyes. "They look fine. They make you look kind of like Clark Kent, actually."

He chuckled. The moment was passing. "That's what Gwen said," he told her.

"Gwen?"

"Kara's sister. I had lunch with her this afternoon."

Val turned around and began stirring the soup. The metal spoon scraped against the pot with each rotation. Then she said, "Did I even know Kara had a sister in Chapel Hill?"

"She doesn't live here yet. She was just visiting for orientation. She's going to UNC in the fall. She's done with exams already," he added.

"Lucky her," Val said, and she pushed through the kitchen door into the dining room.

Brad wondered if he should follow or leave her alone, but a second later she was back. "Are you doing alright with your—with Kara's death? I mean, you didn't say much after the funeral, and now you're having lunch with her sister."

"I'm fine, yeah. I was just trying to be nice. She doesn't have a big sister who can tell her about Chapel Hill anymore, and it was easy enough for me to buy her lunch. I thought I mentioned it this morning."

"No."

"I'm sorry."

Val opened a cabinet and pulled out two bowls and set them out on the counter. "It's okay," she said. "I get it. That was a nice thing to do. It must be hard for you."

"I'm fine, really."

Val hesitated, then met his eyes. "I would like to not be the fifth person to find out you've started wearing glasses, okay? You can ask me to go to LensCrafters with you. You really can. I can handle that."

Brad tried to wrap his arms around her, but she resisted. Behind her, the soup bubbled over the rim of the pot and sizzled on the stovetop. "Shit," she said, turning her back to him.

"Let me get that."

"I can handle it."

"I know you can, but . . ."

Val shifted the pot to a cold burner. "Just give me a couple of minutes to finish dinner."

Brad walked out to the dining room and carefully started moving Val's piles to make space for two placemats.

He didn't like being dishonest with her. It wasn't the way their relationship worked. He'd have been glad for the help picking out frames. That could have made it fun. But he didn't want to have to explain his unusual prescription because that would have required explaining the tumor he didn't have and the appointments he hadn't mentioned.

This was temporary, he reminded himself. By the middle of June, they'd be able to talk like a normal couple again. And they had a lot to discuss. Last time, by this point, they'd already stenciled the extra bedroom with circus animals. He'd built the crib and attached a mobile to it, and Val had started looking at fabric for curtains. Almost every meal seemed to revolve around names or day care, or some child development book one of them was reading, or what they'd do if their child wanted to ride a motorcycle. He wanted to have those conversations again. Soon. Only about two more weeks.

Val came out of the kitchen carrying two bowls of soup. "Careful, it's hot."

Brad leaned over his bowl to sniff, and his glasses steamed up almost instantly, so he took them off and wiped them on his shirt. Val couldn't help smiling. "Smells good," he said again.

"Thanks."

He followed her back into the kitchen and got silverware for the table, and she began assembling a salad. Maybe later, he thought, in a few weeks, when she was in a better frame of mind, they might sit down to dinner and he might tell her about his little scare.

But then what would be the point, he asked himself, as he lay out the silverware. If a car nearly runs you off the interstate, what sense is there in rushing home to tell your wife about it?

Better to focus on the future. Next time he needed a pair of frames, he'd simply invite her to help him. And if Val asked about the particularities of the prescription, noticed that he wasn't exactly nearsighted or farsighted, discovered that his doctor wasn't a typical ophthalmologist—

But why bother thinking that far into the future? By the time he needed another pair of glasses, they'd have a baby on their hands. At that point, the nuances of his glasses prescription would be the last thing on anyone's mind.

※

Gwen Tinsley stopped outside the doorway of her sister's old bedroom and looked at the writing on the graffiti wall. All of the names of Kara's friends were on the wall. And favorite bands. And favorite movie stars. "Pink Ladies" was written in large pink script above the headboard. It dated back to when Kara was in a high school production of *Grease*. She'd played Frenchie. Gwen wasn't even born yet.

No one was in the house but Gwen, so she entered the room and pulled back the nightstand. Behind it, scrawled in her own little girl handwriting on the bottom of the graffiti wall, were the words, "Gwen was here." She'd drawn a smiley face beside her secret message.

Below it was Kara's reply: "I know, and she better not be here again."

Gwen opened a drawer of the nightstand and fished out a purple pen. "Now, she's back," she wrote. Something about the statement looked lonely, so she added, "Ha. Ha. Ha."

The house felt quiet.

If she ever saw this wall again, Gwen knew it would be painted over. The whole room would be white. The posters would be gone, the Mardi Gras mask that was thumb-tacked above the closet. Her mother had chosen their trip to the mall yesterday to tell Gwen about the plan to sell the house. As Gwen was packing for New York, her mother said she might want to box up anything personal and throw away anything she'd outgrown. "You never know with these things," her mother said. "Some houses take a year to sell, and some sell in a day."

I could give you the name of a good realtor, Gwen was tempted to say.

The boys were getting older, her mother explained. Soon they'd be in junior high, and she and Randy wanted them in a better school district.

"Kara and I went to school at McKimmons. It was good enough for us."

"You know what I mean," her mother insisted. "It's different now. New Hanover County is getting all sorts of attention for its new schools. And besides, it's time for the boys to have their own rooms."

Gwen knew what was happening. A part of her wasn't surprised. "Is this because no one wants to move into Kara's room?" she asked.

"No," her mother insisted. "We've been talking about this for years. Long before . . ." Dot-dot-dot.

Her mother seldom said anything about Kara's death that didn't end with dot-dot-dot. When she told people the news, her mother would say that Kara had died in her sleep, dot-dot-dot. "She was a free spirit," she might add, dot-dot-dot. Or, "She lived a hard life . . ." Only Randy seemed willing to use the word "drugs." "You may think grown-ups lay it on thick when we talk about the dangers of drugs, but look what happened to your sister. It was your mother's worst fear."

Yes, obviously it was smoking pot that did her in, Gwen wanted to say. But she didn't.

There had been times during Kara's rebellious periods—which covered much of Gwen's life, now that she thought about it—when talking about Kara was unofficially off-limits. Her mother wouldn't mention Kara, even if she'd just gotten off the phone with her, and would hardly respond if Gwen said something about her. The Bobbies barely knew Kara, the age difference was so great, and Randy didn't matter. Even when she was alive, Kara sometimes seemed like a ghost, haunting conversations in which her name was never mentioned. Not talking about Kara now felt familiar.

These past three weeks, when Gwen's mother was on the phone, it was easy for Gwen to tell when the subject involved Kara. Her mother's answers would be short and breathless and vague. Behind them was an obvious desire to change the subject or end the conversation:

"I don't know."

"Yes, I understand."

"When will that be?"

"I'd appreciate that."

"And that'll be it?"

That's what her mother wanted, for that to be it. She was ready to stop talking about it and thinking about it and seeing it. She was ready for the paperwork and phone conversations to stop. She was ready for the sympathy cards to go away; most had been swept off the mantel the week after the funeral, the flowers too. She was ready for Kara's room to be eviscerated and for Gwen to go to

New York and then to college. She was ready for a new house and a new life with Randy and Bobby and Bobby.

Her mother would never open those boxes. Steve had sent two large cartons to the house—COD—and now they sat unopened between Kara's old bookshelf and their mom's sewing machine. With a sigh, Gwen walked over and ripped open the first.

The scent was overpowering. Filth and smoke. It was as if Steve had just dumped Kara's dirty laundry hamper into a box, sprinkled a couple of ashes on top, and sent it to North Carolina. That's probably what had happened, except Kara had probably ashed all over herself. Gwen got a couple of trash bags from the kitchen and returned to the boxes. The clothes went right into the trash: jeans and shirts and slacks and bras, a coat, a couple of scarves, a black blazer, a furry hat.

Gwen paused when she saw a sleeveless blouse she'd given Kara this past Christmas. That was the last time she'd seen her sister in person. Five months ago, and a little bit. She wasn't planning to come down for Gwen's graduation. Her mom was annoyed about that, but Kara had talked to Gwen, and it was no big deal. Gwen was about to be up there for eight weeks, and they could have their own celebration. Gwen held up the shirt. She was thinking about keeping it, but it smelled too much like everything else, so she threw it in the trash.

Below the clothes, which filled most of both cartons, were some books and scripts, which Gwen piled onto Kara's bookshelf. There was a cell phone in one box, and scattered about the bottom of the other were loose earrings and necklaces and rings. Gwen lay them out on the desk. Most she didn't recognize beyond their being the kind of thing Kara would wear—silver with something extra, something simple, a twist or a stone. The one thing she was glad to see— and startled to see as well, because it made Kara's absence from the world more real—was the silver locket that Kara had found at a thrift shop a million years ago. It held a black-and-white photograph of an attractive young stranger. Kara liked to tell people it was her namesake, the late imaginary Great Grandma Kara.

Her great grandmother, Kara would tell people, had been extremely wealthy, but she kept all of her money in cash under a stack of brassieres in her closet, and so naturally in the Great Imaginary Fire, when poor Great Grandma Kara died, all of her money burned up too. Alas, young Kara was not to be a rich girl. Kara told the story to boys when she was in high school, to anyone in town who admired the locket when they were out, to Gwen's junior prom date, whom Kara knew Gwen didn't particularly like, and to every employer who required a death in the family as justification for a missed shift.

Gwen slipped Great Grandma Kara into her pocket. It felt like stealing, even though she knew she could take anything she wanted now. *Should*, in fact. She'd already taken a few bracelets from Kara's dresser. The rest of the jewelry she didn't want to throw away, so Gwen pulled open Kara's top desk drawer to sweep it all in, but when she did, she noticed in the back a finger puppet that had belonged to her. Gwen pulled out the puppet and fished under the rim of the desk into the back of the drawer and found a kazoo that had also been hers, and a lip gloss she'd loved as a child and had forbidden Kara to use. Gwen sifted through the contents that had been tucked in back. "What a bitch," she laughed. There were at least another half-dozen stupid things that belonged to her.

Gwen went to her room and brought back a carton she'd been using to pack her own things. In it, she dumped the entire contents of Kara's desk drawer, along with the jewelry that Steve had sent back. She surveyed the room and pulled off the shelf a couple of photo albums that were spilling over with high school and college photos. A picture of Kara with Brad fell out, and Gwen studied it. They were probably nineteen in the picture. Brad had no glasses and longer, messier hair. He was skinny and unshaven and handsome. Somewhere on the graffiti wall Kara had once written the words Mrs. Bradley Mitchell. Gwen scanned the wall and found the words near the dollhouse in the corner. They'd been scratched out in pencil, though they were still perfectly legible, the capital *M, B,* and *M* fat and oversized.

For the next two hours, Gwen sorted through Kara's drawers, closet, and bookshelf, filling up boxes and labeling them "Gwen's Closet." She didn't want anyone to throw away the *Grease 2* poster, but she also didn't want to be the one to take it down, so on the white wall, beside the poster, she wrote "Save for Gwen" in pencil.

It was dark outside when she finished, and she could hear that the Bobbies and her mother were back in the house, though no one had come to find her or to make her go to dinner. She'd packed the locket, the cell phone, the photo of Kara with Brad, and the bag of pot from the dollhouse in her luggage for New York. She would be there in four days.

As she was heading for the kitchen, she took one more look into her sister's room. Beyond the giant treadmill, the graffiti wall dominated the room. There was little evidence of Gwen's packing, and Steve's cartons were now gone. Gwen wondered what would feel worse, coming back to find the house sold or standing in this doorway and seeing all signs of Kara erased.

"Happy Birthday," Gwen whispered to the room. "I'll miss you."

Margot had driven many times to the Park Slope apartment Kara had shared with Collin, and to the one she'd shared with Mullet, and to other apartments that had preceded them. She had not, Margot now realized, seen the inside of Mullet's apartment, but that might have been true of one of the early apartments, too. Kara went through a lot of roommates when she first moved to New York.

But for all her moving, she'd always lived in Brooklyn. Margot had lived in Queens for a time, then moved back to Long Island.

If she and Kara met in the city, for drinks or a show or a shopping trip, they usually took trains in and trains home. But when Kara voyaged to Long Island, which had become the most common way they visited, Margot would drive her home the next morning.

"Boring Girl's Night Out," that's what they liked to call it. Margot was the boring girl—that was implied, but never said—but it was more fun being boring with Kara. They'd go to Target, rent a movie, make dinner—well, Margot would make the dinner, and Kara would keep the wine poured. Then they'd get up and have breakfast. Margot might cook, or they'd go out. Sometimes they dyed the grey strands out of their hair; sometimes they painted their nails. Then Margot would drive Kara back to Brooklyn with her haul of groceries and a box of muffins.

Kara would usually wait for the drive home to bring up anything bad that was going on. She'd been fired. She was getting back into coke. She'd been to a party and blacked out. These drives back to Brooklyn often felt like confession. Margot would say it was bad, and Kara would agree, and she'd swear she was never going to do whatever it was she needed to never do again, and— *Oh, I forgot to tell you the most hilarious story*—and then the subject was changed. Maybe Margot should have worried more about Kara during these conversations. But Kara always made it sound like she had things under control. She seemed naughty, yet indestructible—just like she'd been in college. Even her DUI a few months ago she'd managed to explain away somehow. There were the customary pangs of regret on the Belt Parkway, but those felt a bit manufactured, for Margot's benefit or perhaps more for Kara's own sense of ritual cleansing. That's how they generally felt. Maybe there was more to it, sometimes. Maybe Margot should've listened more carefully.

Today she was listening to the radio, or at least she'd flipped on the radio to fill the silence beside her. Several times she considered turning around and heading home. She didn't know Kara's other New York friends. Why did she need to meet them now?

The apartment building was red brick and five stories tall, and as she approached it, Margot saw an empty lot just beyond it and the early signs of construction. That was different. Margot remembered when there had been a taller building there, abandoned, condemned. It had been gated off, a couple of windows broken, and Margot imagined Kara imagining what took place inside. *We're right next to the empty building that's clearly a safe house for giant rodents,* Kara would tell the car service operator. *I'm one building down from the gang headquarters near the corner,* she'd tell the Chinese food deliveryman. *Okay, if I don't get killed by the arms dealers living in the bombed-out building next door, I'll meet you right outside.*

Margot rang the bell for 4C, was buzzed in without any conversation, and walked up the stairs to what was for four years Kara's home. When Margot knocked on the door, a twenty-something-year-old Asian girl with long hair and a nose ring opened the door but didn't particularly acknowledge Margot's presence. Margot walked inside and hovered around a table, which held bowls of pretzels and chips. Mullet and Collin were nowhere to be seen. An earnest, whiny rock ballad played from a pair of speakers attached to an iPhone.

There were about ten people in the small living room and at least as many bottles of wine and liquor gathered on the kitchen counter. Everyone was young and waifish, except for a thickly built man on the sofa who had a white goatee and was saying, "Girl, don't make me slap you back to Kansas," to a man wearing eyeliner. Margot had more hip and thigh and breast than the six girls here put together. Not that anyone seemed to notice her. One girl registered her presence briefly; another said "Hi" and "Excuse me" and grabbed a handful of Pringles. This didn't look like a funeral. It looked like a party.

It was strange being back in this space without Kara. The dusty floral sofa was the same, the found-on-the-curb coffee table with one leg duct-taped in place. Against one wall was a bookshelf that had once held a framed snapshot of the two of them at a wine-tasting. The poster from *Grey Gardens* was Kara's. The lamp in the corner they'd bought together.

"Are you Margot?" someone asked after what was probably a good five minutes.

"Mm-hmm."

"So great to finally meet you," the girl said. "I didn't see you come in. I'm Pepper."

The girl's tone of voice seemed to imply that Margot should know who she was, so Margot nodded. "You too," she said, and they shook hands.

"I worked at the restaurant with Kara," Pepper said. "And we went to auditions together sometimes." Pepper had spiraling red hair pulled back in a bandana. She looked like she was about twenty-five, and there was no question she'd played Annie in a high school production, talent or none. "Let me get Collin," she added, and she turned around and shouted his name.

That seemed to do the trick. He emerged from a bedroom, opened his arms, and hugged Margot as if they'd met more than once in their lives. He was wearing a spicy cologne, and his hair dipped below his eyes so he had to toss it back when he stepped away from her.

"I'm so glad you could come," he said. "I really am. I just felt like I had to do something. Did you go to North Carolina for the funeral? You did? I couldn't, and I just felt awful about the way Kara and I left things, so Pepper said *do* something, don't keep moping for God's sake, and I thought, with Kara's birthday coming up and most of us not being able to go to the funeral, that this is what Kara would've wanted, you know? A party. So anyway, thank you for coming. Make yourself at home—did you get a drink?"

Margot let Collin make her a madras, but he put barely any orange juice or cranberry in it. It tasted like colorful vodka, so she had to sip it down and add more juice herself a minute later. Cougar Cominsky would have been mortified.

She had heard about the falling out; she just hadn't heard the details. Somehow, quite suddenly, Collin was an asshole, Collin was full of himself, Collin was intolerable, and Kara was moving out. That was the end of Collin.

Before he'd disappeared from Kara's life, Collin was often the character in Kara's stories who dragged her to the next bar at three in the morning, or had a friend who could get them more Valium, or was going through a phase of bringing home Puerto Rican men, or got them into an after-party at some stranger's apartment somewhere in Brooklyn Heights. So when Margot heard that Kara was moving out, although she was predisposed to feel some sympathy for the people who lived with Kara, Margot didn't mind knowing that Collin was out of Kara's life.

"Come sit down," he said, leading Margot and Pepper to the sofa. "Everyone, this is Margot, one of Kara's friends from back in *college*."

A chorus of *Hi, Margot*s followed, reminding Margot of those AA meetings, or at least their sitcom facsimiles. "Hi, everyone," she said. She sipped her madras.

"I'm jealous that you knew Kara in college," Pepper said. "What was she like?"

"Oh, a lot like the Kara she is today—or was. Full of energy and jokes. Everybody loved her."

"Even the people she hated," said the man with the white goatee, and most of them chuckled. There was something to that, Margot thought. In college, Kara made everyone laugh; the whole drama department loved her. But in private, she wasn't always a fan of her fellow actors, and she was quite unforgiving of stage managers.

"Kara used to say the nicest things about you," Collin said. "She had pictures of you two looking young and precious. Oh, and there was some story about you doing a photo shoot at a shopping mall. Am I right?"

"Oh, yeah," Margot said. "We didn't actually do the shoot, but we did schedule it. We went to one of those photography studios for toddlers and babies, and she told the salesman that 'Mummy and Daddy' didn't have any pictures of us from our childhood, so we wanted to put together a childhood photo album now. She was very convincing—"

"Of course," Collin said.

"She told the guy we wanted to do a dozen shots dressed as children—riding hobby horses, posing as angels . . ."

We don't actually have adult-sized angel wings, the salesman had told them.

No problem. We have our own, Kara had replied. *Now can we do the bath time shot in the back? Obviously, we don't mind being naked in front of a photographer, but it could be awkward doing it in the store window.*

Margot snorted a laugh. "It got a little outrageous."

"Oh my gosh," said the man with the white goatee, clapping his hands. "Did Kara tell you about that time at Riccardo's?"

"No one but Kara could have gotten away with that," Pepper said.

"What?" Margot asked.

"She and I were walking past Riccardo's—Do you know it? Big, posh place in Soho—and I'm ogling the window, and I say I always wanted to go there but it's too expensive. So, girl hands me her purse and says, 'Wait here.' Next thing I know she's in the restaurant, standing beside this table where they just got their meals. And she says to this stuffy-looking couple she's terribly sorry but there was a problem in the kitchen and they need to remake their dinners, but they'll have replacements out in no time and it'll be on the house. One minute later, girlfriend is out the door walking beside me with two plated dinners in her hands. I mean, it couldn't have happened faster. I almost peed on myself. We ate on a stoop around the corner. She'd even grabbed two napkin rolls from the host stand—I still have the silverware. It was the best dinner I ever had."

Collin told them about an afternoon he and Kara had spent loudly shopping for matching Rolexes for everyone in the extended family. "Everyone," Kara would clarify, "except Cousin Gertrude . . . that bitch." Pepper recalled Kara's three lively days of employment at Victoria's Secret. Then Collin remembered the Great Grandma Kara routine and how Kara had used it to get free drinks at the bars and as an excuse for forgetting someone's order at the restaurant. "She was using that story in college," Margot said, "to get out of exams."

Margot was nursing her drink and keeping an eye on her watch, and at about the one-hour mark, she figured it would be reasonable to say her good-byes. But Mullet still wasn't there, and she was curious. "Has Steve been by?" she asked in a general way.

"Who?" Collin asked.

"Steve."

"Who's Steve?"

The guy with the white goatee clapped his hands together. "Is that the yummy guitar player?"

"No, that's Toby," Pepper said.

"Steve's the old guy Kara was crashing with," said the Asian girl with the nose ring. "The dude with the mullet."

"Oh . . ."

"Speaking of her guitar player," Collin said, "has anyone told him?"

There were some shaking heads. "I thought you were going to invite him to this," said the nose ring.

"I wouldn't recognize him in a lineup of one," Collin said. "I only heard about him through Pepper."

"I don't know him either," said the guy with the goatee. "But I waited on him once . . . and had inappropriate thoughts about him later."

"He hasn't been by the restaurant in a while," Pepper said. "I think Kara said he was going on tour with some band."

"Fancy," someone said.

"We should all keep an eye out for him," Pepper added, in a serious tone.

"That's going to be a fun conversation," mumbled the man with the eyeliner. "'Can I take your drink order, and by the way . . .'"

"Who is this?" Margot asked.

"Toby," Collin said.

"A guy Kara was seeing a little bit," Pepper added.

"Recently?" Margot asked.

Pepper nodded. "A couple of months, maybe. It wasn't serious, but I mean, someone should tell him, right? I wish I knew the name of his band. Did Kara ever mention him to you?"

"No," Margot said. "This is definitely the first I've heard of him."

CHAPTER THREE

BRAD WAS STILL THINKING ABOUT MARGOT'S CALL WHEN HE ARRIVED AT HIS office. Last night, while he and Val were playing Trivia Master and eating take-out Italian on their couch, Margot had been to Kara's apartment. Not the one where she'd died; the one before that.

Strange to think that a gathering like that had taken place without his even knowing, that he might have been there if circumstances had been different. He knew it was Kara's birthday. The awareness had passed in and out of his mind all day, while he was showing houses, answering email, changing for yoga class, picking up dinner. He'd wondered about Gwen, how she was handling the day over in Greenwood Park. But it hadn't occurred to him that in New York a bunch of Kara's friends would have gotten together to recognize the occasion.

Brad turned on his computer and pulled up the prior day's home sales and new listings.

If he'd lived in New York, he probably would have gone, too. Surely someone would have thought to invite him. If not that

Collin guy, then Margot. She'd have called, and Brad would have driven out for the occasion. Maybe he and Margot would have driven together.

Brad scrolled through the latest home listings. Nothing terribly exciting. One three-bedroom that might appeal to a couple he was seeing later in the day. Another house that was iffy, but he printed out the information sheet anyway.

When she called, Margot had made a big deal about the fact that Kara might have been seeing someone other than her fiancé. "Not just *might have*," Margot insisted. "*Was.* Everyone who worked with her knew about the guy. Don't you think that's a little strange?"

But it made sense to Brad, in a way. Or at least he derived some private pleasure hearing about it. Engagement ring or not, Kara and Steve couldn't have been the happy couple.

"I'm struggling to believe they were together at all," Margot said. "He wasn't at the party. No one there talked about him. The only times Kara ever mentioned him to me, she called the man 'Mullet.'"

"Classic."

"I don't recall her saying one nice thing about him."

Well, if Kara was cheating on him, what did Margot expect?

"Could you really see her with him?" Margot asked. "Did you talk to him? After I left?"

No, of course he hadn't.

"Kara and I were close," Margot insisted. "If she was engaged to someone, I can't believe I wouldn't have known it."

But the more Margot talked, the more Brad could believe it. Margot didn't seem to know any of Kara's other New York friends. She'd never heard of this Toby guy Kara was supposedly seeing. There was a time when Margot fit right in with Kara's scene, but that time was not now. Why was Margot so sure Kara would have told her all about Steve, especially if she was having problems with him?

Brad walked out of his office, winked a hello to a colleague passing in the hall, and went to the kitchen, where someone always left a box of donuts. Today there were two boxes. He went to the coffee machine. About a year ago, one of the other agents had orchestrated the purchase of a coffee machine that brewed individual cups from little vacuum-sealed packets. You could have a fresh-brewed cup of coffee in sixty seconds. Sometimes that sixty seconds felt like a long time.

If he'd moved to New York, he probably wouldn't have become a realtor. And he wouldn't have driven with Margot to Kara's memorial, because he'd have had no reason to live way out on Long Island. Because if he'd gone to New York, it would have been to pursue acting. And to be with Kara.

Brad took the cup of coffee back to his desk and closed the door. If he'd lived there for all this time, surely by now he'd have had some success as an actor. He wouldn't have put up with nearly eleven years of struggle, eleven years of failure. When he and Kara were undergrads, a grad student in UNC's drama department told them actors shouldn't move to New York unless they're invited. *That's bullshit,* Kara had said, and the advice may have sounded conservative, but there was some sense to it. There were a whole lot of actors not working in New York. Give it a finite period of time, Brad told Kara when she started talking seriously about a move. Don't torture yourself by leaving it open-ended. Give it two years or eighteen months or three years or something.

Brad gave their relationship two years after she moved. Kara wouldn't commit to a timeframe for anything. *I want to see what happens. Who knows?* she said when they talked about her expectations for New York. And that's what she said about their relationship. *Let's give it a try. Let's see what happens.* They'd visit and talk, and maybe it would work out great.

Before she left, they'd both been getting in with the graduate program, playing bit parts in its professional productions. They even talked about applying and probably would have gotten in. After she moved to New York, Brad felt inspired to show Kara that their chances were better—or at least decent—in North Carolina. He found an agent in Raleigh, someone who worked with TV and film companies on the coast in Wilmington. She got Brad a couple of commercials and two lines in a teen soap opera. Kara insisted she'd "done Wilmington" because in high school she'd worked as an extra in two movies and had a speaking part in an episode of a detective show. But the odds of getting work in North Carolina *had* to be better than in New York. To this day, he still received small checks from the soap opera when his episode was replayed on cable.

He did alright in the local theater world, too. He worked temp jobs by day, and at night always seemed to be in rehearsal for something. Kara was vague in the descriptions of her failure. She'd sent out headshots. She'd gone on another audition. She'd heard about something that was coming up. She waited tables. That's what she'd done in Chapel Hill too, he thought. Sometimes he reminded her.

Brad's phone rang, a client asking about a house she'd seen online, and Brad pulled up the listing and answered a few questions. "Why don't we check it out?" he said, and he opened the calendar on his computer. "How about tomorrow? Three? Three thirty?"

Brad was well suited for real estate. He had a knack for charming clients, and for directing buyers to the houses they wanted without wasting their time. And he could win over his sellers, too. Some of the other agents won listings by claiming they could sell at unrealistically high prices. Brad favored competitive pricing and rapid turnover. He didn't accept every house he could, because he didn't want his sign sitting on a lot for months on end.

He found himself in a real estate office as a temp when he was still acting. He was playing Patrick in *Mame* at the North Carolina

Theatre in Raleigh. NCT used a mix of local actors and imported celebrities, and Brad had what was arguably the largest role given to a local. Tuesday night through Sunday afternoon, he was dressed in expensive-looking suits, hair slicked and parted to the side. He bowed near the end. He was mentioned in a couple of reviews. Half the girls in the chorus wanted to have sex with him; that was kind of a given if you played a young leading male. And by day, he lived a less glamorous existence as a fill-in assistant at a real estate agency.

But it was fun to see how excited everyone got when one of the agents sold a property. And the commissions were a big deal. When the agency hired him as someone's permanent assistant, he got to go to houses and take pictures and help with the marketing, and sometimes, if the agent was running late for a meeting, he'd go over listings with the client to figure out which houses might appeal. So after *Mame* closed and then some awful Shakespeare production and then something else Brad could no longer re-member, he decided he was done proving his point to Kara. Hell, she was proving it herself every day. So instead of auditioning for something new, he started taking night classes to get a real estate license. It was a career that offered variety and lots of human in-teraction. And if he was going to be talking to people about buying houses anyway, he might as well start taking home his own commissions.

I don't know anyone who owns anything, Kara said when he told her about the classes. *Not a car or condo or house. You never know what's going to happen, so what's the point?* she said over the phone. *Everyone I know sleeps on a futon and moves around a lot.*

They were nearing the end of the fizzle. She'd been away for almost two years.

"Sounds like college," he said.

Yeah, you don't have to grow up very fast here.

Well, Brad was growing up. And what was wrong with that?

Growing up had its merits. Having a little money wasn't such a bad thing—a little cash so his mother could stop buying pants for him or, heaven forbid, he could open a savings account. How long was he going to want to spend every night rehearsing for some show that, odds are, he only half-liked? How many hours had he put in one week trying, unsuccessfully, to land a job advertising a mattress sale? Once he earned his license, Brad kept half an eye on audition notices, but only half an eye. He needed his nights and weekends if he was going to attract listings and make sales, and he found a new kind of satisfaction in the work he was doing, and that was okay. At a certain point, it became impractical to go out drinking four nights a week. And it wasn't hard to stop smoking pot, it just kind of happened.

Brad glanced at the clock on his computer: a little after nine thirty. He needed to head out. So he dropped a notepad and a few printouts into his shoulder bag, walked out to his car, and gave a friendly wink to one of the younger agents who passed him in the parking lot. Then he clipped the sunglass shades on top of his frames and pulled out of his parking space.

He was getting more comfortable with the glasses now, trusting them more. The night after he picked them up, he thought he was starting to see double again, but then his worries passed by morning, and now they seemed to be doing the trick. At a traffic light, Brad lifted his frames up for a moment, and a passing jogger had a light tracer behind him. When he put the glasses back on, the jogger looked fine.

The car behind Brad honked its horn, a friendly, Southern reminder that the light had turned green. Brad liked it here. He liked driving and seeing trees, and having people honk politely, and owning a nice house that was just waiting for at least one child if not two. He was glad his parents had moved from New York to North Carolina when he was in grade school. And he was right to have stayed.

But if he *had* moved back to New York after college—and there was a time not long ago when he'd slept on futons and picked apartments based on which one was fifty dollars cheaper per month—if he had moved to New York, then surely Kara's group of friends would have been his, too. He probably would look nothing like himself. He'd never have started wearing bright polo shirts instead of those thrift store T-shirts now relegated to lawn work. He might have kept his leather jacket and Converse tennis shoes, and when he had to get glasses he might have chosen thick plastic frames, ones that made him seem hip and ironic. Though if he'd been in New York for all these years, he better not have been living the way he had at twenty-four. Or Kara had at thirty-four. He better have been at least booking small parts or getting roles in second-rate national tours.

Why hadn't she connected herself with the NYU film school crowd? He would have done that. Gotten himself in short films, built up his resume, endeared himself to young directors who might have gone on to make bigger pictures or television shows, ones that needed fresh talent, and why not him? Why had she scoffed at that idea when Brad suggested it? He was trying to be helpful, supportive.

If Brad had moved up with Kara, maybe she'd have listened to a piece of advice or followed his lead. Maybe she'd have gotten herself into film, been more persistent about getting auditions. She probably wouldn't have been cheating on Brad, the way it sounded like she was cheating on Steve. And if he and Kara had stayed together for all these years, if they'd been living together or even married by now, then surely she wouldn't have wound up dead on somebody's couch.

The car felt cold and quiet all of a sudden. Brad turned down the air conditioner and flipped the vents away from him. It's not like she was his permanent responsibility.

He turned on the radio. Some awful acoustic song, but no

matter, he needed something. He had to clear his mind. He didn't need to be thinking all these things. He was approaching Wood-croft Parkway and his appointment, and he needed to be the Brad Mitchell he was, the Brad Mitchell who'd been selling real estate for eight years and picked up two new listings per month.

He wound his way into the neighborhood, onto Woodcroft and then onto Legacy Ridge. It was two minutes after ten, and a woman opened the front door the moment he pulled into the driveway.

"Hey there," Brad called out before he'd closed the door of his car. "Could we have had a prettier day for this? You must be Mindy. And Charles—okay, Charlie, you bet." They were younger than Brad, and nervous. That made things easier.

Brad shook their hands energetically and paused as they walked him into the front hallway. He needed a compliment—always a compliment in the front hall. The walls were a dull shade of beige, and the light fixture above him was brass, like the fixtures in most houses in this neighborhood. Pretty much all of them were built by the same developer in the late eighties, so there was a sameness that had to be overcome. "You have a gorgeous front yard," he said. "That's a terrific Bradford pear tree out there."

Mindy mumbled some words of gratitude and led him into the living room. Sky blue walls. Chair rails. Grey carpet—a little old, a little cheap. Too much furniture. Dog crate in the corner. "What kind of dog do you have?"

"German Shepherd."

Shit.

"That's fun," he said. "They're great dogs." Distracting as well as intimidating. Mindy said he was at the groomer's now—a good sign. Brad would have to talk with them about keeping the dog away for showings.

The dining room was small with plain hardwoods that were scratched but didn't get much sunlight from the windows, so that would help. The laminate floors in the kitchen and breakfast room were okay. Cabinets, too. Dated, but plain. Typical of the neighborhood. White walls. Bright curtains. Pig-themed kitchen paraphernalia—salt and pepper shakers, napkin holder, tchotchkes in the windowsill. Mindy seemed a little young for the cute pigs look, but Brad had walked through hundreds of houses by now. He couldn't be shocked anymore by personal taste.

Charlie led the way upstairs, where there were three bedrooms. The master was painted pink. "This was your choice, I bet," Brad said to Mindy with a wink.

"I told her we'd have to repaint it," said the husband.

"Let's not rush. It's part of the big picture. It's a soft pink, a soothing pink." Piggy pink, he thought.

The next room was painted orange. Brad had seen it out of the corner of his eye. That's where the first can of paint would have to go. He knew to pick his battles. "This is . . . fun. Definitely fun. But it may be too much," he added, as if it was an afterthought. "We'll see." The third bedroom was an innocuous shade of brown. It was set up as an office and smelled like dog.

"So what do you think?" Charlie asked.

"It's a terrific house," Brad said, following the couple down the stairs. "I bet you're sorry to leave." That's what he always said. He didn't pay much attention to Charlie's long response. They were leaving town for a job. That was the gist of it.

So, I gather you would have been a huge movie star by now?

Kara was standing in the middle of the living room. She was wearing a white oxford shirt, black pants, and a loose necktie borrowed from Brad's closet. She was dressed for a shift at Tyler's Steakhouse.

I would like to not see you right now, he said. To her, to himself.

Sorry this isn't a good time for you, she replied. *Should I make an appointment?*

"Let's take a walk around outside," Brad said to the couple.

"You got it," Charlie said.

Charlie and Mindy walked a few paces ahead of Brad, and as they circled the house, Brad searched for cracks in the foundation, corrosion in the siding, and Kara. One hedge off the back porch was dead. So was she.

You would have schmoozed with the up-and-comers at the film school, he heard her saying. *Probably would have moved to LA in a matter of weeks.*

Brad saw her on the swing set now.

"You have kids?" he asked Mindy.

"No, not yet," she said. "That was here from the previous owners."

It was a large wooden swing set with a slide attached. He approached it, approached Kara. The beams looked sturdy, and felt sturdy too. "I didn't say that," he whispered to one of the beams.

I'm so jealous of your Sullivan Toyota commercial. It's been eating me up inside.

Brad turned back to the couple. "Looks like it's in good shape," he said. "Let's sit down inside, and we'll look at some numbers. Alrighty?"

'Alrighty?' Kara muttered. *What happened to you?*

Brad followed the couple back into the house. He didn't need to allow this to happen, he told himself. Not now. This wasn't real. At the breakfast table, Brad opened his bag and pulled out a folder. He showed Charlie and Mindy a list of recent sales in the neighborhood—a list they might have already pulled off the Internet themselves or seen from another realtor. Then he gave them his shtick: the number of houses he sold per year, the way his agency made "aggressive use of online marketing strategies," the relationships he'd built with other realtors in the area. He said that some realtors might suggest setting a fairly high price, but only after the couple spent ten thousand dollars replacing the carpet and repainting the exterior, swapping out fixtures and doorknobs, etc., etc. "We can do that," he told them. "Sure. But I'd rather price you a little more competitively and ask you to spend just a little bit of your time slapping some neutral paint in the orange bedroom, maybe doing a few other inexpensive, easy cosmetic things that'll help you stand out. What do you say?"

Kara clapped her hands. She was standing in the kitchen now, smoking. *Bravo,* she said. *I'd forgotten what a gifted actor you are. This isn't boring at all.*

Why was she doing this to him? Or why was he doing this to himself? Kara shrugged, then ashed on the countertop a few inches from the sink. She always had a way of selectively missing ashtrays when she was angry.

"I think we need to talk about it," Mindy was saying. "Don't we, honey?"

Don't we honey? Kara scrunched up her face and mimed the woman's deferential glance at her husband. *I thought* I *was in hell.*

"I feel good about this," Charlie half-said and half-asked, his eyes on Mindy.

"Okay?" she said.

"Let's do it."

"Terrific," Brad said.

Terrific, Kara mumbled.

Brad made a point of looking down at the contract for the last part of the conversation, rather than looking toward the couple or past them into the kitchen. He explained the terms, the process, the timing. He scheduled a date for photos to be taken. He filled out his to-do list for them. He always liked to write this out by hand, though it was mostly the same from one client to the next: Paint such-and-such room. Put such-and-such crap in storage. Move such-and-such pet or child or aging parent out of sight. Get a front doormat. Polish the doorknobs and locks. Clear the surfaces. Remove distracting pigs from the windowsill.

While they read over the contract, Brad looked back into the kitchen. Kara was still there, staring at Brad. *Are you honestly satisfied?* she asked him.

There's nothing wrong with selling real estate, he said. I'm doing well. We're trying to have a family. This is what grown-ups do.

I suppose if I'd become a grown-up like you, I'd have an Oscar by now, and a Tony—I have had a Tony, actually.

I would've come back, if I couldn't make it work.

Yes, I know. Clearly you were a legend in the nonprofessional Raleigh regional theatre circuit. How you gave all that up, for this, is baffling.

Kara circled the counter and stood a few feet from the table. *You're so sure you'd have been better for me than Steve,* she said. *That's what you keep thinking. If only I'd been smart enough to marry you . . .*

Brad didn't respond, and Kara exhaled a cloud of smoke that covered Mindy before it disappeared.

It thrills you to think I was cheating on him. How do you know I wasn't cheating on you?

"I'm going to take another quick look up front," Brad told the couple, and he walked through the kitchen into the dining room.

Kara stood waiting for him.

How did he know? He trusted her. He had.

But you don't believe I could have loved anyone else.

I don't know. I don't know what your life was like.

No, you don't. Whose fault is that?

Brad dropped his eyes. He could remember their last conversation, the final in a series of strained how's-it-going phone calls they made to each other in the months after they gave up on the relationship. She'd interrupted a lull in their halfhearted storytelling by asking, *Are we just going through the motions out of habit?*

He said, "I don't know. Are we?" By which he meant, "Are you?"

Maybe, she said—which sounded a whole lot like *I am.*

So he stopped calling her to see what would happen, and she

didn't call him. Not until a few years later, and those were messages he couldn't return.

Brad examined the floorboards of the dining room. A little scuffed, maybe they needed some paint, too. Kara stood in the front hall waiting for an answer. Then, without raising his eyes, he saw her walk to the front door and pass through it.

A few minutes later, it was Brad's turn to pass through the same door, and he felt a fluttering sense of expectation in his stomach. Hands were shaken. Grins and winks were offered. Promises to talk soon. Thanks and enthusiasm. Then he walked outside and surveyed the street, and for a minute he thought the Bradford pear tree was splitting in two. But then he looked again, and it returned to focus. Kara was nowhere to be seen.

※

Student housing for the art institute was in an old apartment building on West 97th Street on the Upper West Side. Gwen arrived later than the other girl assigned to the apartment, so she was left with a small wardrobe instead of a closet, and her mattress made a noise when she sat on it. She was alone in the apartment now. The roommate had come to New York with two friends who were staying together down the hall. The three of them had bolted out to dinner without inviting or taking much notice of Gwen.

The bedroom had just enough space for two twin beds, the wardrobe, and a lime green metal dresser. The other room had a corduroy loveseat, a television set, two folding chairs, and a card table. There was what looked like a child's play kitchen built into an alcove of one wall. The mini refrigerator contained a two-liter of Diet Coke and a two-liter of Diet Ginger Ale. Both were labeled "Stephanie" in permanent marker.

Gwen unpacked her clothes into the wardrobe and the bottom two drawers of the dresser. She'd been on a train for ten hours, arriving at Penn Station at six, then taking the subway to the apartment. She'd never been on such a long train ride before. When she'd planned the trip, of course, Kara was supposed to have met her at the station. She'd have escorted Gwen to the apartment to check it out and drop off her stuff, and then she'd have taken Gwen back to Brooklyn to spend the night. Maybe they'd have stopped for Korean food or something exotic but still cheap, something they didn't have back in Greenwood Park. Then in Brooklyn, Gwen would have surprised Kara with the bag of pot she'd brought for the occasion. She'd been hiding it in the dollhouse for weeks. That was the real reason she'd taken the train. Not because she was nervous about flying alone.

Unpacking took all of twelve minutes. It was only seven thirty. Her first class didn't start until ten tomorrow.

Gwen had gotten an A in her art class during her senior year because she'd painted one decent watercolor—the neighbor's dog, Rollerskate, sitting in the back of a pickup truck. But that didn't make her anything special. She wasn't one of those girls who knew she was super-good at something but pretended not to think she was. People like that irritated Gwen. She was just competent at something, and her mother had latched onto it and had gone online and found this fancy pre-college art course at some institute Gwen had never heard of in New York. And it beat working at Eddie's Country Café and Pottery Shop, where she'd worked for the past two summers, so here she was.

She could call someone, Gwen thought. Margot, perhaps. She'd given Gwen her number. But not tonight. Gwen wasn't in the mood for stories about her wonderful, hilarious sister, the black sheep in the family and the life of the party. She wasn't in the mood for sympathy hugs either. She'd had plenty of those.

Graduation had been all about Kara. Gwen's mother had taken her to a salon to get her hair and makeup done, but Gwen might as well have written "Pity me" on her forehead. All her teachers kept hugging her and saying, "I'm so sorry your sister couldn't be here." She wasn't planning to come anyway, Gwen wanted to say. Get a grip. At the graduation party, most of the kids in her class stayed as far away from Gwen as possible. When they passed, they said, "Sorry to hear about your sister," and then walked on. That was pretty much the only thing anyone wrote in her yearbook during the last week of school, before she finally started leaving it in her locker instead of asking people to sign it.

Well, her arrival in New York was bound to be anticlimactic, Gwen told herself. Still, she had to eat something, and she might as well explore the neighborhood. Gwen changed into her least wrinkled shirt and skirt, then double-checked her nails, which she'd painted blue on the train. Next she set aside her glasses for a minute, applied a thick layer of eyeliner above and below each eye, and christened a new eye shadow she'd bought at the Belk make-up counter back home. In the mirror, she didn't look too different from the Gwen who hung out at Greenwood Mall, so she decided—what the hell?—to pull out the earrings that Kara had sent her for her last birthday. They were ridiculously long dangle earrings with silver feathers everywhere and little bits of garnet. The tips brushed against her shoulders when she tilted her head. There was no way she could wear these in high school, but in New York, why not? In the light of the bathroom, Gwen chose a lipstick that seemed to call out the flecks of garnet. Garnet or plastic; it didn't really matter. Last touch: a pair of black cowboy boots she'd taken from Kara's closet. She took the elevator down four flights and walked out the door.

Outside she walked toward Broadway, where there seemed to be more activity. The heat of the evening surprised her. It must have been well into the eighties. She thought it was supposed to be much cooler up North. She and her mother had visited several times, but now that Gwen thought about it, she'd only been to New York in November and December, once for the Thanksgiving parade and the other times during winter break.

At the corner, Gwen noted a storefront where she could buy coffee and a muffin in the morning, then she walked a block and saw another on the corner of West 96th Street near the steps down to the subway. She continued down Broadway for several blocks, past a crazy mix of restaurants and specialty stores, pizzerias and nail salons, busy people carrying bags and walking small dogs and talking on cell phones, cars and taxis flying past. Then, when she'd walked about ten blocks, quite suddenly, she found her legs very tired, so she slipped inside the next restaurant that caught her eye. It was called the Lizard Lounge, and it turned out to be a nicer place than she'd hoped it would be—dark wood paneling on the walls and bar, red carpet, people dressed up eating dinner. The bar had only a few people in it, and she took a seat at the first stool. The moment she sat down, her toes started throbbing. The boots were squeezing them together.

"Can I get you a drink?" the bartender asked. This looked like the kind of place where a single woman should order a glass of wine, chardonnay or something, but Gwen didn't know much about wine, except that it could be expensive. She surveyed the wine bottles behind him. "Would you like to see a wine list?" the man asked, following her gaze.

"I'll take a Stoli and Diet Coke," she said. "Stoli vanilla, if you have it."

He said he did. Then he asked for her ID.

"Your license is expired," he said after studying it for a moment.

"Well," she said to him, "I guess it's, um, a pretty good thing this is a restaurant and not a pickup truck."

It took a minute for him to respond, and she prayed the line would work. It was a Kara line, one she'd been taught but had never had cause to use. In New York, Gwen thought, she probably shouldn't say pickup truck.

"This time," he said, and he turned to get the bottle of vodka.

Audi. That would be better. *It's a good thing this is a bar and not an Audi.* Much better. Next time.

The drink tasted weak, but she was glad to be sitting down, and the bartender was handsome. He had blond hair parted to the side and a tan that was probably fake. He looked like he was in his late twenties—or he was in his thirties but wanted people to think he was in his twenties. Gwen wondered if he was an actor. Every waiter and bartender in New York made her wonder. Are you like my sister? Do you have headshots from five years ago in a box at the top of your closet? Have you gotten fired for skipping work to go to auditions? When's the last time you had a part in anything?

"Are you waiting for someone tonight," the bartender asked, "or would you like to see a menu?"

Gwen looked down at her sister's old driver's license, the hair frizzy, the mouth open, eyes glancing to the right of the camera lens, as if Kara could barely stop talking to pose for the picture.

"No," Gwen said. "Just me." The bartender strolled to the other end of the bar. Gwen slipped the driver's license back into her wallet and couldn't stop herself from mumbling, "Bitch." No one appeared to notice.

※

Margot wasn't sure what she planned to say once she got to the restaurant. She didn't know if Collin would even be working this afternoon. But, she told herself, she could always say hello and order a salad and be done with it. She was just in the neighborhood. Or sort of in the neighborhood. She'd been delivering muffins in Queens, so Brooklyn certainly wasn't on the way home, but it was closer than it would've been if she hadn't been in Queens.

There'd been no traffic at all, and now here she was, parking on 7th Avenue, only two blocks away from Three-Sixty, the restaurant where Kara had worked until a month ago. Maybe no one would recognize her.

"Margot?" someone said as soon as she'd walked in the door. It was the white goatee guy from the party last week. Devon, according to his name tag. "Good to see you again," he said. "Are you here for lunch?"

"Actually," she said, "I was hoping to talk to Collin for a minute. I was just in the neighborhood . . ."

"Well, he's probably at the coffee shop. You know he doesn't work here anymore, right?"

"I . . . didn't know that, no."

"Yeah, ever since he was in *Once Upon a Time*."

"On Broadway?"

"Girl, don't feed his ego. It was *Off*-Broadway, and he was in the chorus. Ask him to tell you what he's in now, okay? He works at Java Jones on Fifth Avenue and Baltic."

Before walking out, Margot surveyed the restaurant. *It's called Three-Sixty because you can get pad Thai, lasagna, or a really juicy burger,* Kara had explained when she started working there three years ago. *Nothing's especially good, but it's all expensive, and the plates are cool.* The presentation did look nice. The dishes were large and colorfully garnished. Among the servers, Margot saw two more familiar faces from the party. They all wore black shirts and pants and burgundy aprons. Margot could picture Kara slipping out back and pulling a cigarette and someone else's lighter out of her apron pocket. Near the kitchen door a handsome man with a shaved head was dining alone. Margot wondered if that could be the guitar player, Toby.

A few minutes later, she reparked her car right in front of Java Jones. She could see Collin through the window, and if she sat there for long, she knew he would see her. Besides, she'd already talked to Devon. There was no pretending she had nothing to say.

"Oh my God, what are you doing here, it's so great to see you," Collin said as soon as Margot stepped in the door. "How wild that you're here. It can't be a coincidence, can it? What are you up to?" Collin tossed his hair out of his eyes. It was brown but dyed, Margot now noticed, with dirty blond highlights. He smiled quickly and pushed his hair aside again.

"Cup of coffee?" she said. There were only two other customers, both plugged into laptops, so Collin told her to sit down wherever, then joined her at the table.

"I hear you're in a show," she said.

"Oh, yeah, I am. I mean, it's not high art. Have you heard of *The Nude Clown*? Yeah, no one has. It's Off-Off-Off-Off-Broadway—as far off as you can be before they call it Jersey. I thought it was going to be campy and might take off like *Naked Boys Singing* or the *Debbie Does Dallas* musical, but it really just attracts pervs. It's sort of a bad remake of *Death of a Salesman,* but with songs. And nude clowns."

"And you play . . . ?"

"A nude clown. I can't wait till this run is over so I can eat a piece of pizza. Hang on one sec."

Collin jumped up to take care of someone at the counter, and Margot formed the first question in her head. When Collin returned, she asked it. "Why did Kara move out of your apartment?"

"Ugh," Collin sighed. "I hate thinking about that." He rubbed his finger over a coffee stain on the table. "Well, it started when we auditioned for this show, *Once Upon a Time.* They had an open call, and Kara and Pepper and I went with a bunch of friends—we did that a lot—only this time, instead of all of us getting drunk afterward and trashing the show and the music director and the casting director, I got called back and ended up in the chorus. It was amazing, it was the biggest show I've ever done. They gave me a haircut every three weeks, I felt like a princess. So I quit working at Three-Sixty, and I had to take Collin-the-Party-Queen down a few notches, and Kara just couldn't deal. She got mad at me for not going out with her. She'd say snarky things about me to our friends when I was in rehearsal. Finally, I sat her down and I was like, honey, you want to know why you didn't get cast? Let me tell you.

"First of all, the girl hadn't been on a stage in years. Her resume was practically written on parchment. And second, Kara was an actress first, singer second, and dancer third. She knew she had no business trying out for a dance-heavy role like the ones in *Once Upon a Time*—especially when she'd gotten so rusty. She did that kind of thing all the time. I told her I thought she was getting way too comfortable going to open calls where she knew there was little chance she'd get a part, and then bitching about the injustice of it all later. I mean, don't get me wrong—I thought she was a great actress. That workshop she did in the Village way back when—"

"*Crooked Fields,*" Margot said.

"Exactly. She was brilliant, my God. That's the kind of thing she needed to do more of. And she could act her way through a song. I met her when we were both doing the cruise, and everyone loved her 'Little Girls' or 'There Are Worse Things I Could Do' or 'You Gotta Get a Gimmick.'"

"She was a great Sally Bowles in college," Margot said.

"Oh, I have no doubt," Collin said. "So I sat her down and I told her, all this time I've been doing summer stock and rinky-dink tours, and you refuse to travel to Queens to audition for a show. She said she might as well have stayed in North Carolina if she was going to do a show in Queens, and I said maybe she should've if this was her idea of an acting career. I told her, I said, I don't know what you did to piss off your agent, but you need to get some representation and start auditioning for character parts again. And before you do that, you need something on your resume. No matter where, no matter how small you think it is or how superior you feel, get some current work on your resume. Maybe take some classes, a little refresher. If you're serious about this, be serious. Don't just act like you are."

"Wow," Margot said. "That was good of you." She could hear the surprise in her own voice and hoped it wouldn't offend Collin. "That was a tough conversation, I'm sure," she added, "but it was good advice."

Collin waved the statement away. "I don't know," he said. "She thought I was being high and mighty and, of course, didn't listen to a word of it. After that, we argued even more, about the dumbest things. Meanwhile she was hardly paying rent. Finally when she announced she was moving out, I was like, fine. It made my life easier. Eventually Pepper moved in—she was afraid it would piss Kara off, but Kara didn't make a deal of it—and that was it. She didn't even come see me in the show."

"*Once Upon a Time?*"

Collin nodded. "I invited her. Sent her the nicest email."

"Maybe she did," Margot said. "I bet she went but didn't tell you because she didn't know what to say."

Collin shook his head. "No, honey," he said. "I'm afraid I knew her well enough to know she really didn't come."

Margot could see it, Kara dropping Collin this way. It wasn't one of her more endearing traits, but she was impossible to live with and wasn't known for warm apologies. Margot had only lived with her their freshman year, when parents paid dorm fees and everyone was too distracted by the novelty of college life to care about laundry or dirt.

"So after she moved out of your place, she moved in with Steve?" Margot said.

"Yeah."

"Do you know how they met?"

"He was just some guy she met at the Lemon Drop, this bar where we used to go. I think they bonded over coke a couple times at his place after our ugly little *tête-à-tête*."

"Did you ever talk to him?"

"No. I really only saw him across the bar. Sort of an oafish red-head, late forties, looked a little rough, kind of like he could use a shampoo and rinse. Oh, and he had this awful mullet. Pepper said that's what she called him, Mullet. That was Kara for you. Touching that she'd rather move in with *that* than be civil to me."

Margot nodded. "He was at the funeral."

"Get out!"

Margot swallowed. "He said that he and Kara were engaged."

Collin took this in for a moment. "Come again?"

"Engaged."

"As in . . ."

"To be married."

Collin's eyes widened, and he pressed a finger to his lips. "I don't know what to make of that."

"Me neither."

"Are you sure?"

"I'm sure that's what he said," Margot told him. "It didn't seem right to me either. When she mentioned him on the phone, she didn't sound like she even liked the guy, and then the other night you all were talking about that guitar player, Toby—"

"That's *right*."

"—who she was supposedly seeing. Does anyone know the name of his band? Or how to get in touch with him?"

"I don't know, I don't think so."

"I just wonder if Kara might have said anything to him about Mullet. It didn't seem like anyone at your party thought she and Mullet were together."

"God, if Pepper had heard that, she'd have told me for sure. Did he say anything else at the funeral?"

"Not much," Margot said. "He said it happened suddenly. One minute they were talking about looking for a bigger place together—"

"Wait, recently?"

"That's what it sounded like."

"I thought I heard she was looking around for sublets for the summer."

"Really?"

"I thought so," he said. "I could be wrong, I'll double-check."

"Jesus."

"But," Collin said, raising a finger, "devil's advocate here. The devil and I were like this for years"—Collin crossed his fingers—"so I feel it's my duty to be his advocate every once in a while. There *was* an Austrian guy Kara dated a couple years ago—Luke, maybe?—and I had no idea he existed until after the fact."

"You mean Lucas? He was German."

"Okay, fine."

"And I met him."

"I slept with his cousin actually—it's true, it's a long story—but my point is, Kara could keep people to herself. I mean, I only met you a few times."

Margot could only remember meeting Collin once before last week. But she heard his point.

The door opened, bringing in a swarm of customers, and Collin stood, offering a little shrug. "Espresso maker calls. I'll ask around," he said. "Maybe someone knows more about Toby—or maybe they heard about this engagement but didn't tell me. I'll talk to Pepper and we'll see what we can find out."

"Thank you," Margot said. "Please keep me posted."

"Oh, of course—here, give me a hug. I'm glad you came by."

The hug caught Margot by surprise, and as she pulled away from him, she found herself saying, "I'll have to come see you in *The Nude Clown.*"

Collin winced. "You're sweet to offer," he said, "but please don't. I wear a blue wig and a penile enhancement. It's not my finest work."

⁂

The moment Gwen saw Margot standing in her lobby she knew the night was going to be a disappointment. And she'd been looking forward to it, too. Margot had called a couple of times to welcome Gwen to New York and see how she was doing, and at first it was a little annoying, but then when she suggested a night out, that had appeal. Most of the other kids in Gwen's art program either lived in New York or had enrolled as a pretense for spending eight weeks in the city with a group of friends. Gwen's roommate fit in the second category. Stephanie couldn't even eat a bowl of cereal in the room—she had to carry it down the hall to eat with her friends. So when Gwen's first weekend in the city arrived and Margot suggested they go to a club in the West Village, Gwen was relieved to be able to tell Stephanie she was going out on Saturday night.

She spent all afternoon preparing. She made a careful modification of the expiration date on Kara's driver's license, and she bought a cheap crimping iron at the drugstore and frizzed her hair so that it would better match the picture. She picked out a low-cut dress with a loose fold at the chest, which implied the presence of larger breasts than she really had. Her new shoes were from Payless, but kind of looked like a pair she'd seen in Soho: black patent leather straps, rhinestones, thin heels. She changed rings five times, settling on two chunky, one small. And as Gwen fished through her jewelry, she remembered something one of the girls used to say in junior high: The bigger the hoops, the bigger the whore. Gwen was probably one of the few girls in her class to graduate a virgin, but the hoop earrings she had for tonight were three inches in diameter.

When Gwen's door buzzed, she hurried down to the lobby. Then the elevator doors opened, and there was Margot looking—from her flats to her silk scarf—like she was dressed for a PTA dinner. "Ready to roll?" she asked. Gwen hoped her face didn't show what she was thinking. Margot looked like she could have been Gwen's mom, chaperoning her daughter for the evening. Kara hadn't looked this old. Neither did Brad. Margot easily could have passed for forty. She had lines by her eyes and sort of a second chin. Gwen had worried she might not be able to get past the doormen at the club; now she worried Margot might have trouble.

The place was called the Red Room, a name that held such promise. Gwen had visions of a secret entrance, a line of super-models around the block, and a bouncer who'd scrutinize Gwen's stockings for pulls. She'd planned to take off her glasses while they were waiting in line. But the Red Room turned out to be a wine bar, not a nightclub. There was no line, no doorman, no trouble getting in. The bar was well decorated: dim lighting, chrome fix-tures, and red textured wallpaper with black lacing. The crowd was older—thirties, forties—mostly well dressed in suits and cock-tail dresses. Gwen tried to carry herself like a woman who came here all the time, a woman who was having a low-key night out with her fat, frumpy friend.

Margot was pretty annoying, too. She talked about her boy-friend, Mike, a lot. He was in the Army stationed somewhere in Asia, and she was constantly sending him text messages all night. At one point she asked Gwen if she wanted to say hello, and Gwen said, no, that's okay, and Margot said, no, you should, so Gwen said that Margot could say hello for her, and Margot texted hello. It was retarded. She'd probably met him online. He probably wasn't even in the Army. He was probably a teenager in Iowa messing with Margot's head.

And when Margot wasn't texting or talking about her imagi-nary boyfriend, she was asking Gwen all sorts of random ques-tions—if she'd been to any museums yet, if she was dating anyone, if she'd known Kara's fiancé well, if she'd met Kara's musician friend Toby, if she preferred painting or sculpture, if she'd ever been to a Broadway show in the Big Apple. That was annoying, too. She kept calling New York "the Big Apple," like Gwen was a child visiting Disney World. At least Margot bought her a drink.

There was one other drink, too. When Margot was particularly engaged in text-messaging her fake Army stud, Gwen wandered off and accepted a drink from a man who offered. He was older and handsome. He asked if she was new to New York. She said no, she'd been there for a couple of years. He said he was a lawyer. She told him she was a lounge singer. He was much taller than Gwen, and he looked down her dress when he talked to her.

It was all of eleven fifteen when Margot said, "My God, it's getting late." They'd been there for an hour and a half already, so it's not as if Gwen needed to stay longer, but still, a lot of people were just arriving. While they were waiting for a cab, Gwen asked if Margot smoked pot. Margot laughed and sort of snorted like a pig, and said, "Yeah, no," as if the question had been a joke.

Gwen's roommate was still out when she returned to her apartment, and she felt deeply unsatisfied by her Saturday night. She needed to complain to someone, and Kara would have been perfect. Gwen thumbed through the directory in her phone and surprised herself a little when she stopped on Brad's name. He'd left a voice-mail to check up on her. She'd been meaning to call him back at some point.

He knew Margot. He'd understand what Gwen was talking about. She hesitated, then decided, why not, and sent him a quick text message. "Awake?"

He called a minute later. "Is everything okay?" he asked.

"Yeah, sorry it's late," she said, adding half of a question mark to the end of her sentence. He sounded groggy. There was a television on in the background. Gwen could hear the laugh track. "Everything's fine," she said. "I just wanted to call you back to let you know I'm fine. Margot actually took me out tonight so we could party like rock stars."

"So where are you?"

"Home."

"Kind of like geriatric rock stars. What is it—eleven forty-five?"

"My point exactly."

"Did you have a good time?"

"No. Kind of, maybe. I don't know. It was okay. I think Margot had a blast. Going on about her pervy online boyfriend."

"Stop," he said, laughing a little.

"And what a wild and crazy girl she was."

"She *was*," Brad said. "Back in her day."

"I'm sure," Gwen said. Her left earring clanked against the phone and she took it off and set it on the dresser. "I'm sure you were, too. I actually remember thinking you were cool."

"I remember thinking I was cool, too."

Gwen smiled as she unstrapped her shoes and kicked them under the bed. She could see what Kara had liked about him.

"How are classes so far?" Brad asked.

"Good."

"And the people?"

"I went out with Margot, didn't I?"

"It's hard to meet new people."

Gwen lay down; her mattress squeaked. "Kara could make friends anywhere."

"She was amazing that way. People gravitated to her. I was afraid she'd find someone to replace me the first week she was there."

"As if. She referred to you as Mr. Tinsley."

"She did?"

"You knew that."

"No," he insisted.

"Well, she did. For a while. Why is that so interesting to you?" Gwen asked. "Didn't you break up with her and get married, like, five minutes later?"

"What?"

"I'm just saying . . ."

"Did she say I broke up with her?"

As far as Gwen could recall. But she didn't respond.

"It just ended after a while," Brad told her. "And I didn't get married for another three years."

"Okay," Gwen said. She shifted the phone to the other ear. She could hear Brad's breathing. She didn't mean to be such a bitch.

"So, how are you adjusting to the glasses?" she said, and she fumbled with her ear. She'd forgotten to take off the other earring.

"It's alright," he said. "I'm on my second pair, actually. I just had to get the lenses replaced. Turned out the prescription was too low."

"That's weird. What kind of cheapo optometrist did you go to?"

He chuckled for a second. Gwen listened to the voices in the background to try to guess what show he might be watching. Then Brad asked, "Gwen, is everything really okay?"

She didn't know the answer. She stood up and the mattress squeaked again, and in the mirror she saw her eye shadow was smudged. "Yeah, I'm fine. I was just thinking about Kara."

"It must feel funny being up there without her."

"Yeah."

"Did you visit her much?"

"Every couple years or so. She came down more."

"Did you ever get to see her in anything?"

"Um, yeah," Gwen said. She dabbed a cotton ball with make-up remover and wiped it over her eyelid. "When I was in middle school, we flew up to see her in a play they were trying out, *Crooked* Something-or-another. It had Rich Carson in it and someone else from TV I'd never heard of. Mom recognized him. It was cool."

"That's neat."

"And I saw her in the tour of *Into the Woods* when it passed through Raleigh."

"She was in that?"

"Yeah, she was in the chorus." Gwen shifted the phone to her other hand and wiped her other eye. "She understudied for Little Red Riding Hood too, and went on a few times, but not when I saw it."

"Wow . . . I almost took Val to that show."

"I'm sure that would've been awkward."

"You think?" They both laughed.

Gwen tried to remember if that was all she'd seen. Growing up, her mom had driven Gwen to Kara's shows all the time—at UNC and, during the summers, at Wilmington Playhouse. "Oh, I saw that short movie she made," Gwen remembered.

"She was in a movie?"

"Just a five-minute one. She said they showed it at film festivals and stuff. She was, like, a friend of one of the main characters."

"That's really cool."

"Yeah, it was. But it was a long time ago." Neither of them said anything for a minute, and Gwen could hear laughter again on the television. "Do you act anymore?" she asked.

"No."

"Do you miss it?"

"I haven't in a while. But lately, maybe a little."

"Seems like nobody ends up having the life they think they'll have."

Brad took a minute to reply. "That may be true," he said, "but new options present themselves. What kind of life do you want?"

Gwen wiped away her lipstick. "I don't even know."

"That's fine, you don't have to. You're eighteen. Enjoy yourself. You get to explore, have adventures. Paint—which it sounds like you're good at. Meet new people."

"I'm obviously good at that."

"Oh, give yourself a chance. It's in your genetic makeup to be quite charming."

※

Val's school was about to let out for the summer, and Brad was getting ready for the annual "June Jamboree," a display of not so much musical talent as musical enthusiasm. The drama teacher would string show tunes and Top 40 hits around an implausible plot, and every student who wanted to participate was included, at least in the chorus. Last year, there were twenty-six girls onstage singing "Hopelessly Devoted to You" in no particular key. Val had turned red holding in her silent laughter.

"Ten-minute warning," she called to him up the stairs.

"Thanks," he called back, and he pulled a navy polo shirt out of the closet and set it on the bed.

Half the fun, he thought as he stepped into the shower, was watching Val watch the kids, laughing or blushing or marveling at her favorites. "That's Emily," she'd whisper to Brad—a girl whose parents were in the middle of an obnoxious custody battle. "Oh, look at Kyle," she'd say, grabbing Brad's hand. "I'm so proud of him." Val's students always stared at Brad with unmasked curiosity. They were seeing a secret part of Mrs. Mitchell's life in him. And though he could observe the students with more subtlety, he was seeing a secret side of Val's life too. These were her kids.

Brad stepped out of the shower, toweled himself dry, then put on the navy polo shirt, khakis, and his glasses. He was tired, and though he didn't usually drink coffee at night, he thought maybe he'd make a quick stop if there was time. As he walked to his dresser, he glanced up at the clock on the wall—but it had too many hands, too many numbers. Brad dropped his eyes. Below the clock, the light switch had split in two. For a second, he thought he hadn't put on his glasses, but he reached up and there they were. This was what he saw *through* the lenses. When he lifted up the glasses and looked at the clock without assistance, the doubling was more pronounced.

How could this be happening? This was his second pair of lenses. He'd only had them for a few days. Brad looked down at his hands. He could keep his fingers in focus, but was he working to do it, he wondered, or did they just stay there? Next he turned to the window and looked outside. Each tree stood half-superimposed on its double.

Was he having any trouble during dinner? Before he took the shower? He wasn't sure, he hadn't noticed. This morning, he'd been fine, hadn't he? Though yesterday afternoon at the gym there was a slight haziness around the borders of people, little tracers behind them when they walked. He'd thought maybe he was feeling light-headed from lifting too much weight, but clearly these glasses weren't strong enough. Why couldn't the doctor get it right? How thick were the lenses going to get?

"Ready?"

Brad looked up at a blurred image of his wife standing in the doorway. He tried to hold her eyes in focus, but he couldn't.

"Do I have something on my face?"

Brad ignored his left eye, and that helped. Val's freckles dotted her nose and cheekbones. She was carrying a light jacket and wore a silk scarf draped around her neck. "No," he said. "No, you look beautiful."

Val let out a sigh. "Don't look at my ankles."

"Come on."

"Okay, quick review: Carla Henderson has decided she's a lesbian again, and likes to talk about it. A lot."

"So I should avoid her?"

"That's what most of us try to do. And Missy Blum is taking over the camp this summer. She has blondish hair—"

"I remember her."

Val rolled her eyes. "It's the legs," she said.

"It's *not* the legs."

"It's a little bit the legs."

"Okay, a little bit."

When they arrived at the school, Brad made small talk with the other teachers. They seemed to be especially nice to him, perhaps confirming Val's fear that they'd figured out that she was pregnant. But no one said anything, which was good.

He tried to make himself relax, tried not to think about his vision, but that became almost impossible once the performance began. Images split more the further away they were. He should have insisted on a seat near the front. Now, instead of enjoying the clumsy choreography or Val's hand squeezing his, Brad found himself trying to force images of people together. And that challenge only reminded him of the last time he'd been sitting in an audience doing the same thing. It was at Kara's funeral last month. In his mind, Brad saw a two-headed Steve Donegan at the podium.

"That's Steven," Val whispered.

"Steve?" Brad started.

"Steven," she said. "Remember, the *Romeo and Juliet* thing I did with my honors class? He was my Romeo."

"Right," Brad said. On the stage, a young Steven and his twin were singing a solo.

THAT night, as Brad was getting ready for bed, he decided he'd go straight to Dr. Thompson's office in the morning. She'd managed to fit him in last week to get him this second prescription; she'd just have to squeeze him in again to fix it. But when morning came and he started walking around the house, he wondered if perhaps he'd been overreacting. His vision wasn't so bad—a little off, sure, but not so awful. Maybe all he needed was a little more time to get used to the prescription.

Val left the house first but had made coffee for him, even though she could no longer drink it herself. She claimed to like the smell, but he knew better. He scribbled "XO" on a Post-it note and left it on the counter, then poured himself a cup to drink in the car. He was still trying to decide whether or not to go see Dr. Thompson, when he walked outside and saw Kara sitting on the hood of his car.

This seems to be going well, she said.

He was only half-surprised to see her.

The doctor said I'm going through an adjustment period, he said.

I can see how she inspires confidence.

She did say I might need more help with peripheral vision.

Looking straight ahead at a stage isn't peripheral.

Brad dropped his gaze to the driveway and opened the door. Now Kara was in the passenger seat.

People get older, he told her. They need glasses. It's part of life.

But not people with 20/20 vision.

This is different.

Yeah, glasses tend to eliminate vision problems. How about yours?

Brad started the car, put it in reverse, and pulled onto the road. Kara lit a cigarette and blew a cloud of smoke through the windshield.

This is bullshit, she said.

I'll go see her. She'll fix it. It'll be fine.

You sure? Because she doubled the prescription last week.

The doctor seemed to think—

The doctor seems like a moron. How much more are you going to spend on lenses? This isn't normal, no matter how much you wish it were.

Brad wound his way out of his neighborhood, and Kara sighed loudly, then propped her feet on the glove compartment. She did things like that when he was driving. She left her seatbelt off so he would tell her to put it on. He resisted the impulse to comment now.

Is it even safe for you to drive? she burst out as he turned onto Carver Road.

Of course it is.

How many cars do you see in front of you? How many lanes are there on the road?

It's not that dramatic.

It's at least twice as dramatic as it was last week.

Why are you doing this?

She pulled her feet down and turned to face him. *Look at that kid on the bicycle. Is he doubled, too?*

Brad didn't like her asking the question. He was ready for her to go now. The bicycle *did* have a double—but Brad was nowhere near the kid. It was perfectly safe for him to be driving.

Brad tried to banish Kara from his thoughts, but she wouldn't leave his mind or his car.

People don't randomly start seeing double, she said. *Something must have happened.*

What happened to *you*?

We're not talking about me.

Well, maybe we should.

Don't pretend this isn't happening.

How did you end up engaged to Steve?

Are you kidding me?

How did *that* seem like the life commitment you wanted to make?

Why can't you look at your own life, Brad?

Were you pregnant?

Can you really see me pregnant?

I can, actually.

Well, stop. Don't.

We'd talked about it. You used to say if you had a daughter—

Really, we're going to talk about my parenting now?

Brad had stopped the car at a red light, and Kara opened the door and stepped outside. *Believe whatever you want about me,* she said. *You always do. But don't delude yourself about this. You need to see a neurologist or something, because this isn't right. You know it isn't.*

The light turned green, and Brad hesitated to pull away from the corner, even though a part of him knew she wasn't there and hadn't been there in the first place. Still, the scene felt so real, and so familiar, he needed to see if she'd get back in the car instead of walking away.

A car behind Brad gave a polite honk of its horn, and Kara turned back to Brad for a moment and smiled weakly. *I torment you out of love, you know. That's always been why.*

WEEK fifteen passed without incident. Neither Brad nor Val said anything on the precise day when the pregnancy had ended last time, but they fell asleep that night holding hands. Then Val's turnover date came, beginning her sixteenth week, and she started avoiding Brad's eyes. Probably because his eyes were saying, Can't we be happy now? And hers were saying, No, not yet, I'm too scared.

So he didn't mention the fact that he was on his third pair of lenses. These were plastic, which kept them from being as thick as he feared they'd be. And he didn't feel like he could tell her about the referral he'd requested. It required too much explaining. It was simpler to handle it on his own.

The neurology department was tucked deep inside Duke Hospital. Brad had to take an elevator up, then an escalator down, then walk through twisting hallways toward the elusive Clinic 18. When he arrived, the waiting room was filled with people— mostly elderly or middle-aged, plus two younger women who Brad imagined suffered from spinal injuries or one of those disorders that had a walkathon once a year. Most people seemed to be accompanied by family members—adult children or spouses or whole families. Val would have been great in a situation like this. She'd have checked Brad in, rather than hovering in the entryway as he was doing now. She'd have researched Dr. Frick. She'd have known that Dr. Frick specialized in this and was widely respected for that. She might not have told Brad—he'd have been grateful not to know too much—but she would have known.

He didn't spend long in the waiting room before he was called to the back, where he was met by a young doctor who introduced herself as a neurology fellow. She asked a few questions, then performed a number of hasty tests—reflexes, vision. She seemed like a

pleasant woman and reminded Brad of his yoga instructor. She even
had the same calm voice as Brad's yoga instructor. "Is my finger
doubled here, or here? And now?" Maybe he'd make it to the four
o'clock yoga class, he thought. He'd kept his calendar clear for this
afternoon's appointment anyway. It might do him some good.

Dr. Frick was a small man with bifocals and a thick grey mustache, and he poked his head in after about fifteen minutes. He
studied the fellow's notes, making a few grunts, then repeated several tests without much enthusiasm. Finally, the doctor closed
Brad's chart and set it aside on the desk. "Your vision doesn't
bother you all the time?" he said.

"Well, I don't always think about it," Brad told him. "And these
new lenses are much better." They weren't perfect. He still saw
occasional doubling in the distance or at certain angles, but then
sometimes he thought it might be his nerves or imagination.

"What if I were to suggest that your double vision hasn't gotten
worse since you picked up your first pair of lenses; rather, the
degree of doubling varies throughout the day?"

The idea seemed strange.

"I'm suggesting that when you don't think about it, it's because
your vision is actually better. Does your vision seem worse at
night? Or when you're tired? Or after you've been reading for a
prolonged period of time?"

Brad tried to recall. "It's possible. I haven't really thought
about it."

"And you didn't experience any sort of head trauma recently?"
Brad shook his head. "No," he said.

Dr. Frick nodded. "Your MRI was fine. I think there's a good
possibility you might have an autoimmune disorder called myasthenia gravis. It's an unusual disorder characterized by variability,
and variable double vision is a common early sign of it.

"Myasthenia gravis is literally a grave weakening of the muscles,
which means that your muscles can fatigue easily. It often presents

itself in the eyes first—characterized by double vision or drooping of the eyelids. Some patients will only have what we call *ocular* myasthenia gravis; however, most go on to develop the generalized disorder which affects muscles throughout the body."

Brad's body felt cold. He tried to remember what an autoimmune disorder was. Something where the body attacked itself. Was multiple sclerosis an autoimmune disorder? Brad thought so. What had Dr. Frick called this?

"—very difficult to diagnose," the doctor was saying, "and the blood test often comes back with a false negative. Myasthenia gravis—"

Myasthenia gravis. *That* had been the blood test he took at the neuro-ophthalmologist's office. For a rare disorder, she'd said, one you probably don't have.

Dr. Frick was still talking. He was telling Brad how the weakness could manifest itself in other muscles, how some patients could experience problems climbing stairs, or speaking, swallowing food—even breathing.

"But let's not get ahead of ourselves." Dr. Frick said he wanted to do another test: an electromyography test, which he said would look at the activity of the muscles around Brad's eyes. The doctor went on to say something about electronic impulses and neuromuscular junctions, but a part of Brad had left his body by now and was watching the scene from on top of the cabinet across the room where he might have imagined Kara sitting. The Brad on top of the cabinet wanted to turn on a radio or make a joke or get a second opinion. Another second opinion.

The fellow led Brad into an ominous-looking room with a large examination table. Beside it sat a computer on a rolling desk. The test would take about thirty minutes, she said. How is myasthenia gravis treated? Brad asked. There are lots of ways, she said, but she'd better let Dr. Frick explain. He ran the hospital's myasthenia gravis clinic, she assured him, so Brad was in good hands.

Val would have known that. If Val had been in the waiting room, he'd have asked for a minute to talk to her, and she would have told him that Dr. Frick was one of the best there was, and she'd have hugged him, and he might have even let himself cry. But she'd have said there was no rushing to conclusions, and she would have ruffled his hair the way she did sometimes.

Even if he had it, Brad said to himself, the symptoms could come and go. That's what the doctor had said. Maybe they wouldn't come at all.

When Dr. Frick arrived, he seated himself at the computer and told Brad to lie down and take off his glasses. Brad hated that disorienting moment when the glasses first came off. This latest prescription was so strong that his eyes needed a minute to adjust to the absence of prism, and during that minute, the world didn't just split; it became something out of an amusement park—wildly uneven and out of control. He always felt like his eyes might not snap back into place.

But they did settle down, and Dr. Frick told Brad to relax and to choose a spot on the ceiling to focus on. So he chose a spot on one of the fiberglass squares above him, and he could sort of force the spot into focus, but then it would slip into two spots, which was frustrating, but it probably didn't matter. He was looking up.

He hadn't really paid attention to the doctor's description of the test, so when Dr. Frick said he was going to start, Brad didn't know what to expect. Then he glanced to his right and saw the doctor holding what looked like a silver thumbtack attached to a wire. "Look up, please," the doctor said, and Brad did. Then Dr. Frick slowly pressed the tack into the muscle above Brad's right eyebrow.

The pain was shocking.

"Keep looking up, please."

Brad stopped breathing. His whole body tensed. He felt a tear forming in his eye, sweat glands opening throughout his body.

"Relax the muscles in your face as best you can."

Brad curled his toes. He stared at his spot on the ceiling and concentrated on the tension in his leg muscles, in his feet. He started to count to ten, tried to ignore his peripheral vision, but before he got to number three, Brad saw the doctor's fingers coming, and a second pin was slowly inserted about an inch to the right of Brad's eye socket.

"Breathe," the doctor said.

He pushed the pin in deeper. The computer made a staticky sound. "You see the impulse is here," Dr. Frick said quietly to the fellow who no longer reminded Brad of his yoga instructor. "Mm-hmm," she said.

Brad could feel himself sweating heavily. His pants felt sticky. His brow was wet.

"I'm going to have to move this around," Dr. Frick said. "I'm sorry, I know it's uncomfortable." The doctor twisted the upper-most pin again, pressing it deeper into Brad's face. "Try to relax."

Try to relax, Kara told him. She lay on the ceiling, her eyes positioned on top of Brad's spot. *Look at me,* she said. *Hold my hand.*

Somehow she was six feet above him, but when he squeezed the fingers in his left hand, he was squeezing hers.

Tighter, she said. *As tight as you want.*

Dr. Frick adjusted the second pin.

Look at me.

"Just relax."

Just relax.

The air-conditioning was creating a breeze on Brad's sweaty forehead, and it was cold, and the doctor wiggled one of the pins again, and the computer said something.

Breathe, Kara told him.

I am breathing, Brad said in his mind.

In and out.

In and out, Brad thought.

I'm glad you came here, Kara said.

I'm not, he said back.

Dr. Frick repositioned the second pin, pointing it to the left and releasing slits of pain that crept through Brad's body. He pushed his head into the table.

Squeeze.

Brad crushed her fingers.

Take a breath.

He made himself do it.

All I wanted was a damn pair of glasses, he told her.

You look like Clark Kent in your glasses.

So I've heard.

You look like Superman now, she said. *Held captive and tortured by the evil Frick.*

Brad glanced to his right and tried to imagine a handlebar mustache on the doctor.

And leather chaps, Kara suggested.

Brad couldn't help smiling.

Remember when we went sailing?

That wasn't sailing. That was nearly drowning on your uncle's piece of crap boat.

Think about that. Think about lying down below the deck—

It smelled like fish.

You got to second base down there.

You were trying to distract me. I thought we were going to die.

We weren't going to die.

He did not know how to work that boat.

He was a fisherman. Of course he knew what he was doing.

"Hang on a second here." The first pin was pulled out—or twisted, Brad couldn't tell for sure—and then it—or a new pin?—was pushed into a muscle just a few millimeters higher. Brad pressed the back of his head harder into the examination table. "Try to relax," the doctor said. Then he wiggled the pin. Brad groaned, though it might have been silent.

Squeeze my fingers. Breathe. The boat.

Brad made himself breathe.

I'm on a boat. Come with me.

I'm not on a boat.

It'll be over soon, and you can go to yoga class.

I am not going to the damned yoga class.

Let's count to one hundred.

It was a stupid idea, but it was a good idea too. Brad's yoga instructor would have approved. He listened to Kara count: *Twenty-one, twenty-two, twenty-three . . .* He tried to count with her. He tried not to participate in what was happening to his face, and that was difficult, but listening to Kara helped. *Sixty-four, sixty-five . . .* When she got to eighty-seven, she stopped and said, *He's almost done.*

There was some shuffling beside Brad, some mumbling to the fellow. Then the tacks were pulled out, and Brad was told to sit up. The blood rushed from his head, and he was dizzy. His shirt clung to his chest. Someone dabbed his forehead with a cotton ball and returned his glasses to him. "Well?" Brad asked.

"I can't say for certain, but I did detect a few jitters in the electrical impulses which suggest an irregularity . . ."

Jitters. An irregularity. Some disorder Brad still couldn't remember the name of. And now Dr. Frick was telling Brad he needed to get another blood test, and had to schedule a CAT scan to check his thymus gland—what the hell was a thymus gland?—for a possible tumor.

This disorder was difficult to diagnose, the doctor said again, but for now Brad needed to behave as if he had a positive diagnosis. He'd need to avoid certain medications. The nurse handed Brad a list. It was long. Very long. Several antacids and antibiotics were included. The doctor prescribed a low dose of Mestinon, the most mild drug used to treat myasthenia gravis—that was the name. If the medication helped correct Brad's vision, that in itself would be diagnostic, but the reverse wasn't true. "Often we have to turn to stronger options."

The doctor reminded Brad that variability was the hallmark of the disorder, so he should notice whether or not his vision was changing throughout the day or week. He should also look out for other weaknesses throughout his body. "Rest if you get tired. Don't wear yourself out." They were talking to him like he was an old man. Last, Dr. Frick warned Brad that if the respiratory muscles were affected, the disorder could become life-threatening. There was a pamphlet about "myasthenic crisis" in the folder the nurse had for him, as well as an application for a MedicAlert bracelet they wanted him to start wearing as a precaution.

"There's a lot we don't yet understand about this disorder," Dr. Frick said as he was walking out the door, "but people who have it can, for the most part, live full and relatively normal lives."

Brad was going to live a full and relatively normal life. For the most part. That was a comfort.

He made his CAT scan appointment for later that week. He had his blood drawn, barely flinching when the small needle was inserted and then removed. He walked down the hall and around corners and up the escalator and down the elevator. He wound his way down the parking deck and paid the attendant. And in his car, as he headed back to his office, Brad let out a wail that sounded to him like the voice of someone else.

CHAPTER FOUR

EVERYONE IN GWEN'S CLASS WAS DRAWING SOME MAN'S BALLS. GWEN LOOKED
around the room and saw sketchpad after sketchpad of naked man.
It was embarrassing just sitting there, to say nothing of looking at
the model. Gwen wondered if her mother knew this was part of the
curriculum—showing Gwen her first pair of grown-up man balls.

She'd seen the Bobbies naked, of course, and she'd seen a few
photos of naked men on the computer at someone's house. But the
pictures were gone as quickly as they'd shown up, and those were
college-aged guys in a hot tub, and it's not as if Gwen had studied
them. This was real life, and the model wasn't especially young or
handsome. His stomach was soft—no Abercrombie six-pack—and
his penis, which hung limp over the balls, looked funny compared
to them. Smaller than she would have expected, or maybe the
balls were just bigger.

Again, Gwen's eyes scanned the room. Everyone else's drawings
were coming along more quickly. And the other kids were doing

sophisticated things with shading and curves and shadow. Gwen's drawing looked like an X-rated paper doll. But it's not as if she planned to specialize in balls. She wasn't Michelangelo.

Last week had been worse. Their teacher Lionel had asked them to think back to a picture they'd painted before and to recreate it with a different palette. So Gwen started on Rollerskate, her neighbor's golden retriever, in the pickup truck. But she painted the dog green and the truck gold, and she was trying to do something with magenta in the clouds. Meanwhile, everyone else was doing these abstract explosive kinds of paintings, surreal things, otherworldly landscapes, paintings like poetry. And Gwen had this decent-looking retriever with a yellow tongue, and it looked like a paint-by-number done by a kid with special needs. She felt like an idiot. All Lionel said when he passed behind her was, "How bright."

"Ten minutes," Lionel said to the class now. "Get down whatever details you need to finish on your own later. Feel free to walk to the front of the room if you need to."

And people did. Everyone did, in groups. Gwen knew they would. This had happened yesterday with the female model. People had studied her breasts up close. They were much bigger than Gwen's and sagged a little sideways. Gwen's chest had to be amplified with the shape of her bra. Walking back to her easel yesterday, Gwen found herself glancing down her own shirt, then realized at least one person had seen her do it.

Clusters of students took turns examining the male model now. Gwen was among the last. He politely looked off into the distance. The hair on the man's head had started to gray, but the little afro above his penis was solid black. Gwen wondered if hair grayed more slowly down there, or if it didn't gray at all, or if maybe the model had dyed that part, to get more work, perhaps? Who could she ask?

She made a mental note about the lines in the thigh, the height difference in the balls—had they moved?—the ridge around the rim of the penis.

This man's penis is older than me, she found herself thinking, and she almost laughed. Right there.

This was the kind of thing she'd have told Kara.

Tell me everything. A lot of actors do figure modeling. I wonder if I know him.

I almost laughed when I walked up.

Penises can be hilarious. I'm surprised you didn't laugh.

That would have been so rude.

Sneezing would have been rude. Laughing seems like an occupational hazard. Now tell me.

Okay, but I have questions too.

Absolutely. You know there's not a stork involved?

Kara had been the one to tell Gwen about the birds and the bees, or rather, the absence of birds and bees in that whole process. *I assume Mother has not taken you aside to tell you about vaginas and penises yet? I think she's waiting to tell me first, and I'm thirty. Now before we get started, you know there's not a stork involved, right?*

There were just certain conversations she had with Kara.

Gwen added a few quick lines to her drawing, lowered one ball, added some definition to the man's arm. Other kids in the class had the man looking off in the distance with pride or distraction, but the guy looked bored to Gwen. Creative license, she supposed. She'd do something with the eyes later.

As she put her pencils away and closed her sketchpad, Gwen imagined the call she would've made as soon as she got outside, once she was out of earshot from everyone else. I have to finish drawing this naked dude, Gwen would have whined with laughter in her voice. Stephanie and I are going to be in our tiny apartment this week drawing the same balls. Or maybe she had a different naked man. We're not in the same class.

Well, look at her picture too, and tell me what he looks like. I could know both of them. Both men, that is. Not balls.

Kara, I'm not as good as these other kids, Gwen might have said next.

Of course you are. You're probably three times as good. Now come on over.

⚉

As soon as Brad and Val walked out of their appointment with the obstetrician, a woman with big blond hair and a big round stomach jumped up from her seat in the waiting room and said, "Mrs. Mitchell, you're pregnant!"

Val looked dumbfounded. Brad gave her a moment to try to collect herself, then wrapped an arm around her and squeezed her shoulder. "Hi," he said to the woman, reaching out to shake her hand. "I'm Brad Mitchell."

"Congratulations!" the woman said. "Oh, that's wonderful. I'm pregnant, too! I'm Kimberly Barnes, Alex's mom. Alex was in Mrs. Mitchell's class."

"Last year," Val mumbled. Her face had lost its color, but she was regaining her composure.

"Great to meet you," Brad said. "Congratulations."

"Yes, congratulations," Val said.

"When are you due?" Kimberly asked.

"Early December," Brad said. "How about you?"

"Thanksgiving Day. I told everyone, I'm off duty. You bake the turkey this year."

"You bet! Listen," Brad added, lowering his voice, "we had some trouble last time we tried, so we're trying to keep the pregnancy quiet for the short run. We'd appreciate it . . ."

"Oh, of course. My lips are sealed. But that's so exciting! I'd heard you weren't running the camp this summer, and I was surprised. Now I know why!"

"Mum's the word," Brad added with a big grin.

"Absolutely."

"Thank you," Val said. "Tell Alex I said hi."

As they walked off, Val shook her head. "No," she mumbled to herself. "Don't tell Alex you saw me. Why did I say that?"

"Because you're a good teacher and a nice person, and you always say that to parents." Brad led her by the arm out of the women's hospital.

"Thank you," she said a minute later. "You were very good."

"Hey, if I can't schmooze, what kind of salesman am I?"

Neither of them spoke again until they reached the elevator of the parking deck. Then he stated the obvious. "It was bound to happen."

"I know."

"And it's bound to happen again."

Val didn't respond.

Week fifteen was now comfortably behind them. They were about to enter week seventeen, yet this afternoon she still told the obstetrician she didn't want to know the baby's sex. Brad did want to know, though he hadn't said anything.

The elevator doors opened, and Val punched the button for the third floor. "What floor are you?"

"Same," he said. "That was pretty amazing, wasn't it?" Brad pulled out his phone. He'd made a video of the ultrasound.

"We don't need to watch it again right now."

"Okay," he said, and he put the phone back in his pocket. "But let's show it off. Why don't we call Sophie and Les? Maybe go somewhere to celebrate."

"Let's don't," she said. "Not yet."

That's what she'd said last time he asked. "You can't hide out for the next five months."

"Can we not talk about it this second?" she said as they stepped out of the elevator. "That was a little unsettling . . . Of course Kimberly is going to tell people. And if anything happens—"

"It probably won't."

"But it could. It very likely could. I'm high risk, Brad."

He followed her for a few steps. "Want me to drive you home?"

"No, how will you get your car? I'm fine."

"Okay. I can pick up dinner?"

"Fine."

"Or I could come straight home?" he suggested.

"No, dinner is good. I'm going to go now. We don't need to keep standing in the parking lot."

"Sorry I was late," he called to her as she turned to walk away.

"Well, fortunately the doctor was running behind, too."

It was the CAT scan that had delayed Brad. He'd been in Durham that morning for the test at Duke Hospital. He'd planned to head back to the house to pick up Val and drive her to the North Carolina Women's Hospital. But his appointment took longer than he'd expected, so he ended up having to meet her at the obstetrician's, and still he was late.

Val pulled out ahead of him, and as Brad followed her down through the parking deck, he was thinking it's not just these appointments where they needed to worry about running into someone. He'd had a similar run-in that morning. While he was waiting to go in for his CAT scan, a realtor from another agency passed in the hall and caught Brad's eye. They exchanged polite smiles of recognition as the man walked by, and now Brad kept imagining the guy mentioning to a mutual friend that he'd seen Brad in the radiology clinic at Duke. Something like that could happen any day. Given the number of appointments he kept having—with Val and now by himself, too—his odds of bumping into familiar faces were increasing. Neighbors, colleagues, teachers who'd recognize him from school events. There was no telling when some sort of rumor would start working its way through their world.

He picked up Chinese food for dinner, and when he arrived home the table was set with white melamine plates. He wanted to transfer the ultrasound video from his phone to the computer and play it again, but he could tell she still didn't want to, so he resisted the temptation. He asked if she wanted to play Trivia Master after dinner. She said no, not tonight.

He would have liked to tell her, over dinner, that the pills didn't seem to be doing a thing—which was good, because if they fixed his vision, that would mean he had this disorder and might have a lot bigger problems. The CAT scan seemed like a long shot. It was supposed to show whether or not his thymus gland was enlarged or had a tumor in it. He'd found out where the thymus was: behind the sternum. Removing it sounded involved. It could require heart surgeons and broken ribs. Brad had started reading the pamphlet about it, then stopped himself. Because most likely he was fine and all that would be unnecessary. That's what he wanted to be able to tell Val, and he wanted her to tell him back.

Instead he told her about a "Don't Mess with Texas" themed bathroom he'd seen at a showing the day before, and he tried to make the story lively, and she smiled at the appropriate moment, but there was a falseness to the smile, and the story wasn't very funny anyway. Then instead of saying that she was ready to tell their parents about the baby, or that she'd learned something disarming about thymectomy surgery, or that he probably had some fluke eye problem, and what did doctors know anyway, she said, "The Lemon Chicken is really good tonight," and he said, "Yeah, it's becoming one of my favorite dishes they make."

The dinner had a familiar feel to it. A lot of these dinners did lately. They reminded Brad of life after the miscarriage. Not immediately after. First there'd been the open misery, the fits of sadness and anger and gloom. Then they'd gone on a trip to Las Vegas, stayed at a fancy hotel on the Strip. They ate and drank lavishly, allowed themselves $500 each to lose in the casinos, which they did. No photographs were taken for their vacation album. Then they returned home, turned the nursery back into a guest room, and had many dinners just like this one.

"Do you need more rice?"

"No, I'm fine, thanks."

After dinner, Val loaded the dishwasher then lay down on the couch with a book on Henry VIII's wives. Brad went to his computer and pulled up a week-by-week pregnancy calendar. He and Val had done this together during the last pregnancy. They had a book they'd consult each week. They still had it; it was on the bookshelf. He thought they'd be looking at it together by now.

Week 17: Your baby's hearing is starting to develop. Soon, if you talk loudly, the baby may be able to hear what you're saying.

But we're not saying anything, Brad thought. That's the problem. There's nothing to hear.

THE NEXT evening after Brad's last showing, he headed through the end of rush-hour traffic toward the interstate. His parents lived in Winston-Salem, about an hour and a half away from Chapel Hill, so it was easy for him to visit for dinner without making it an overnight event. He'd scheduled the dinner thinking this would be the night he and Val would make their big announcement, but since she still didn't want to say anything about the baby, she was staying home. He'd left a message for his mother that morning to let her know.

Brad began the inventory of topics he'd have to address or avoid during the meal. Obviously, he'd have to explain why Val wasn't there. School had let out, so he couldn't blame exams. They didn't know she wasn't working at the camp, but he didn't want to lie and say she was, or explain why she wasn't. He'd just keep it simple, say she wasn't feeling well, which was true.

Then there were the glasses. His mother would have a million questions about those. He'd have to deflect.

At a traffic light, Brad checked his reflection in the rearview mirror. The electromyography test with the thumbtacks had left tiny bruises above and beside his right eye, but those had faded now. There should be no questions about them. They probably could have passed for acne, even at their worst.

Still, Brad was a little surprised—and almost offended—that Val had never noticed the spots. Maybe it was because the glasses partially obscured them. Or maybe she didn't really look at him these days.

Did he look at her? he wondered as he turned onto the interstate. When you know someone, how often do you really look at them? He had seen her belly starting to grow. But she had a small frame, it was obvious. She complained about her ankles sometimes, and her face, but he didn't notice any weight there. Brad tried to picture what she was wearing when he left the house, but he had no idea.

He could visualize her, of course—her cute cherry-brown hair so often pulled up in a clip, the line of freckles across her nose and cheeks, the way her nose turned up a bit at the end, her lips and that raspberry-colored lipstick she liked. But it was a composed Val he had in his mind, not the Val of that day, or a year ago, or two.

If anything, it was the Val of his fourth date that lived in his mind, the Val he fell in love with. He met her almost eight years ago through his colleague, Sophie. Brad had recently gotten his real estate license, and he and Sophie were sharing an office. She and some of the other women at the agency had started referring to Kara as Brad's imaginary girlfriend, because she'd been in New York the whole time he'd been working there. But by the time Sophie announced her engagement to Les, Brad's relationship with Kara had reached its quiet end, so when Sophie insisted that he escort her friend to the wedding—"unless your imaginary girlfriend is going to be offended"—Brad surprised her by saying yes.

The first three times he saw Val, she was dressed to the nines: for the rehearsal dinner, then the wedding brunch, then the evening wedding and reception. Brad wasn't doing her any favors, he knew. He learned later, without surprise, that Val had not begged Sophie to find her a date. Sophie had done the begging.

They weren't alone until their fourth date, and when Brad picked Val up, for the first time he got to see her hair up in one of those clips. She was wearing jeans too, and a blue cotton sweater. She invited him into her apartment, and he saw a stack of papers piled on her sofa, beside Shakespeare's *Twelfth Night* and an open bag of Cheetos. "Midterms," she explained, and after she hugged him, she caught him looking at her hand, which was tinged orange. "Oh, I didn't get anything on your shirt," she said, and he must have double-checked, because she added, "I promise, it's fine. I have a system. This is my Cheeto hand. It never touches papers, or furniture, or clothes." Even when she cooked and there were no Cheetos involved, Val called the hand that was too messy to open a cabinet or touch a student paper her "Cheeto hand." He fell in love with that Cheeto hand, and eighteen months later, he slid an engagement ring on it.

Brad arrived at his parents' house in Winston-Salem a little after seven, and he knew before he was out of the car that there was a meatloaf in the oven.

"Honey, come in, I'm making your favorite," his mother said when she opened the door. Then she looked at him. "What are you wearing?"

Brad shrugged what he hoped was a your-little-boy's-getting-older shrug.

"What is that, for driving?" she asked, pushing a dyed brown curl out of her eyes.

"And life."

"What's the prescription?"

"I don't know."

"Let me see."

"Mom, leave it."

"Henry," she called out, "come look at your son. Henry, where are you?"

"I'm here. Oh my goodness, how is my boy?"

"Are you looking?"

"I'm looking."

"Do you see the glasses?"

"I see the glasses. You wear glasses. I wear glasses."

"But Bradley doesn't wear glasses."

"Now he does. How you been?"

"Fantastic," Brad lied. "You?"

"Terrific."

"Guess what your mother's making?"

"I told him."

"I know," Brad said.

Meatloaf and mashed potatoes. It had been his favorite meal as a child, and now she made it religiously every time he visited alone. She prepared it with what seemed like two parts ketchup to one part meat; it was a wonder the thing held together. Val was silently horrified the first time she experienced a giant, ketchupy chunk, so to prevent a repeat, they decided to tell his mother Val had given up all red meat. That lie had come with its own degree of shock and horror.

"She eats chicken?"

"Yes."

"But not roast?"

"No, not roast."

"But pork, yes? No? Not pork?"

"We're the kind of Jews who eat a lot of bacon," Brad had to explain to Val early in their relationship.

"But not in the house," his mother added. "If God put us in North Carolina, He must have meant for us to eat pork."

The Metropolitan Life Insurance Company had "put" the family in North Carolina, transferring Brad's father down from New York when Brad was eight. They'd lived in the same house ever since. In the attic, his mother had boxes filled with every Lego set and electric train he'd ever had. She was waiting for a grandchild so she could give the gifts again.

"Tell Val we're thinking about her," Brad's mother said as she carried the meatloaf to the table. His father grunted an assent. That was all that was said on the subject. Brad had said Val was sick; they didn't believe him, but wouldn't ask. If pressed, Brad knew his mother believed Val was either pregnant, or they were fighting. Why else would she stay at home? God willing, she was pregnant and healthy. Brad's father, if pressed, might have said, "It's because she hates your mother's cooking." But he only would have said it to tease his wife, even though he probably believed it was true.

"Your father's eating fish," Brad's mother said as she carried out the last serving plate and set it on the table.

Brad eyed the fish, which looked pleasant.

"Tell him," she added.

"You can tell him."

"You tell him."

"I had my cholesterol tested," Brad's father said.

"It's through the roof."

Brad's father shrugged. "It's low high."

"What is 'low high'?" his mother snipped. "It's two-forty-two. That's high."

"But it's still low high."

"There is no 'low high.' There's low, high, and regular. That's it. You're high. If you want to get granular, say the number. Bradley, you should get checked. It can be genetic."

"Maybe we should all be eating fish," Brad suggested. "Did you get checked?" he asked his mother.

She nodded. "Doctor said I'm perfect."

"There is no perfect," Brad's father said with a smile. "You're 'regular.' If anything, 'perfect' would be 'low.'"

"No, some cholesterol is good. 'Low' is too low. Bradley, is your piece big enough? Let me cut you another."

"What's new with you?" Brad's father asked.

And Brad must have said something in answer to the question, but as he spoke he looked down at the peas and the mashed potatoes. He wanted to tell them they were grandparents. Last time he'd told them at seven weeks, the day the doctor confirmed the pregnancy. They were so excited, he hated to deny them that now. The excitement could have taken focus away from the other news he should have been telling them now, but how could he tell his parents about this medical limbo when he hadn't even told Val? Not that he wanted to frighten them—or Val—but he was a guy who still told his parents when he had a dentist's appointment.

The rest of the meal seemed to be a maze of questions he couldn't answer and prompts he had to dodge: When does Val's camp start? How long have you had these glasses? Did you hear your cousin's pregnant? Do you ever talk to Kara's mother? Did you see any familiar faces at the funeral? Even after the meal ended, when Brad asked for Tums, his father produced Maalox, which for some reason was on the list of drugs Brad had to avoid. He pretended to take one, then threw it away.

It was after ten by the time Brad started the trip home. He felt like an undercover agent for nothing—all that fumbling and deflecting. It had left him uneasy. He was still replaying the evening's more uncomfortable moments in his mind an hour later when his phone vibrated. For a moment, his heart tripped. No one called him this late.

But it was just a text message from Gwen: "Awake?"

He found her number and dialed. "Hey, yeah, I'm up. Driving back from my parents' house."

"Oh, y'all are in the car. I'll let you go."

"No, it's okay. It's just me. Val stayed home."

"I remember Kara saying your parents are funny. Is that right?"

"Oh, to an outsider, yes, I guess they are." Brad used his shoulder to prop the phone against his ear, then fished in the door pocket for his hands-free headset. He felt confident driving, but he still wanted both hands on the wheel. "So, this is my exciting Friday night," he told her as he switched on the headset. "Let me live vicariously through the young. What's up with you?"

"Let's see, so far I've painted my nails yellow and washed my bras."

"You really haven't found anyone you like? How about your roommate? Is she any fun?"

"Is bronchitis?"

Brad smiled. Kara had used that line sometimes, though she varied the ailment.

"You need to put yourself out there. Ask someone to do something. If they say no, or if it's boring, then who cares? How long is the program?"

"Eight weeks. Five and a half more, but who's counting?"

"You'll probably never see these people again, so what's the harm? Kara had a theory about this. Did she tell you?"

"What?"

"If a perfect stranger decides not to be nice to you, you have license to think whatever you want about him. 'Judge me and I'll judge you back.' I think that was how she put it. So anyone who was rude to her was, in her mind—this isn't nice."

"I think I can handle it."

"A goat-fucker."

Gwen laughed, and Brad laughed too.

"That's lovely," she said.

"Apparently, a very freeing life philosophy. I don't know why goats in particular."

"You know, there was supposedly a guy in Greenwood Park

arrested for, um, inappropriate intimacy with goats. I don't know if it was real or, like, an urban myth. If you can call something in Greenwood Park 'urban.'"

"The mystery revealed . . ."

"Well, my roommate is a major goat-fucker then."

"Her loss . . . well, and the goat's."

"The other day she told me I was eating my cereal too loud. So after she left, I took her Diet Coke out of the fridge and replaced two inches of it with water. Does that make me a bad person?"

"That's hilarious," Brad said. He could feel her self-satisfaction through the line. "Does she mark it, like a liquor bottle, to be sure you're not stealing?"

"Probably."

Back in college, he and Kara had replaced so much of the alcohol in their parents' liquor cabinets that they'd left little more than water behind. Gwen was probably doing the same now. It was strange—Brad had to remind himself that he was almost twice her age. It didn't feel like so many years had passed, though it did feel adventurous to be having a phone conversation after eleven at night. Val was almost always asleep by 9:30; he would follow at 11:30 or later. Back in the day, this was when the night began. You made plans at ten, or eleven, or twelve.

"So, do you have anyone stealing your liquor yet?" Gwen asked. "Do you have, like, kids and stuff?"

Brad swallowed and shifted lanes to pass a minivan. "Well," he said, "we have the stuff."

"What does that mean? Your wife's pregnant?"

He felt his face open into a smile. "Yes," he said. And it was Gwen, there was no harm telling her. "Yes," he said, "congratulate me. You're the first person I've told."

"Wow, congratulations. I feel honored. So is it, like, real early?"

"Not exactly," he said, moving back into the right lane. "We're in the second trimester, but Val's worried about people finding out in case . . . it doesn't go well."

"That sounds a little morbid."

"I know. We had a miscarriage last time."

"I'm sorry."

"But to be honest, I think she's driving herself crazy. She's barely leaving the house. She's scared of running into people, and she's a teacher, so it's like she knows everyone."

"Get her out of town," Gwen said.

"What?"

"If she's worried about running into people, take her someplace she won't. After Kara died, Mom kept asking if I wanted to stay home this summer, and I was like, hell no. Get me away from these people."

Interesting. Maybe Gwen was right. He and Val had planned to stay home this summer to save money and let him work, and because Val liked being close to her doctor. But it was worth considering. "You're a smart girl," he told Gwen.

"One of my many gifts," she said. "So, you must be very happy?"

"Oh, yeah," Brad said. "Generally—yeah, of course."

※

Margot was supposed to go to Becky and Allan's house for dinner, but she canceled. She said she wasn't feeling well.

"Are you sure?" Becky asked.

"I'm sure," Margot told her.

"Are you *sure* sure?" Becky asked again, the way they had in elementary school, and junior high, and high school. "Scotty loves seeing his Aunt Margot."

Margot strolled to her refrigerator and looked at her most recent picture of the four-year-old Scott. She held favorite "aunt" status with many of her friends' kids. But tonight she couldn't face child-friendly conversation. It was raining, and the weather fit her mood. So she said she was "*sure* sure," then coughed twice and got off the phone.

Of course these kids love seeing you, Kara had said once. *You bring a tin full of cupcakes every time you visit.*

"But that's okay," Mike said later. "That's part of who you are. I fell in love with your muffins and your 'muffins' at the same time."

Ba-dum-bum.

He was such a cornball. Margot wished he were free tonight. Before he left for Japan, she'd suggested they do something together while he was away. Like read a novel. "Or learn French?" he'd offered, with fake earnestness. "We can quiz each other over the phone. That'd be hella romantic." He proposed horror movies; they settled on Hitchcock. She bought them each a boxed set. So far they'd watched *Rear Window, The Birds, Rebecca, Vertigo, The Man Who Knew Too Much,* and *North by Northwest.* The first two they'd spread out over multiple visits, but now they aligned their schedules so they could get through a whole movie in one sitting—Mike in a bunk with his laptop, Margot lying on the couch, each with a phone in hand thinking of the other. If he were around tonight, she'd have suggested they watch *Strangers on a Train.* It would have been nice to pretend he was there with her right now.

"OOO," he'd type, as he did at least a dozen times per movie.

"She should not have done that," Margot would respond.

It probably wasn't the way Hitchcock intended for his films to be watched, but it worked for them.

"This looks so fake," he'd written during the Mount Rushmore scene in *North by Northwest.*

"While the aliens in *Star Wars* were wholly convincing."

They had fun with it.

"I love her dress," she'd say.

"I'd love to see U in that dress—and out of it."

Margot smiled. She wished she could hear his voice. But it wasn't happening tonight. She didn't even know where he was. There was threat of a typhoon, which happened with bizarre frequency, so Mike had evacuated Okinawa and taken up temporary residence who knew where. That was half of what he seemed to do: pack up tons of equipment and schlep it onto a plane, then wait out the storm—usually in a nice hotel, he said—then schlep it all back afterward. Margot was monitoring the storm's progress on her computer. It didn't seem like it would hit Okinawa. She liked the fact that it was raining on Long Island, too. She imagined herself linked to Mike by one giant dark cloud.

What a cloud. She did feel it hovering over her. She'd filled Mike in on her suspicions about Mullet. It was hard to sit with the uncertainty, the fear that something wasn't right. She would try to push the thought out of her head, but then something would remind her of Kara—a song or a place. Or a conversation. She'd talked to Collin that morning. He and Pepper had asked around. No one in their world had any idea Kara was dating Mullet. And Collin was right: a few months ago Kara *had* told a friend from work to keep her posted if he ended up subletting his place for the summer. She sure didn't sound like a woman about to get engaged.

A shock of thunder shook the house, and Margot poured herself a glass of wine. Not long ago a storm like this had hit while Kara was visiting. They'd gone to the Stop & Shop to pick up a bottle of wine. *Is there a particular box you'd recommend?* Kara asked one of the stock boys. And then he *did* have a recommendation, so they bought it and made a dent in it that night. It was fun to drink wine during a thunderstorm. If Kara were around, Margot might have been with her tonight.

Really, she asked herself, do you think Kara would have come out here in this storm? Would you have driven to Brooklyn? In this? Maybe. Or maybe not. Kara probably would have been busy anyway. But the idea occurred to Margot all the same. She might have been hanging out with Kara.

Without thinking, Margot sat down at the computer, clicked past the countdown to Mike's return (five months, three weeks, four days) and the map of the typhoon, and pulled up a search engine. She typed, "New York criminal records." The computer announced twenty-eight million results. So she changed her search to "Brooklyn criminal records," and that helped. A mere four million.

Margot scrolled through a few pages. Most sites wanted to charge money: only $19.95, $24.95, $27.95. She liked the bargain-orientation. "Peace of Mind for Under $30." "Screen4Less.com." Then the sex offender registry emerged. It was free and government-sponsored. She typed Mullet's last name.

There was a wait. It felt long.

Then, no. No sex offenders named Donegan in Brooklyn.

She ran the name through all five New York boroughs. Still nothing came up. The database let you search by zip code, and she did. There were seventeen sex offenders in Kara's zip code. Margot looked at the first: He'd raped a thirteen-year-old girl. It wasn't Mullet though. She clicked to the next; this one had raped two women. Margot looked at each of the seventeen people on the list, and none of them was Mullet. Then she typed in her own zip code. Four names came up. One of them lived five minutes away. He looked like anyone you'd meet on the street, like one of the guys who worked at the deli or grocery store.

Margot didn't like to think of herself as a woman who spent her Saturday nights drinking wine alone and searching the sex offender registry. "This really isn't me," she said aloud, for the benefit of her ears only. Then she took another swallow of wine, pulled out a credit card, and did a New York criminal record check on Steve Donegan.

His name came up. Three convictions: two for drug possession, one for assault.

Assault.

This was the man Kara was living with, the man who said he was marrying her. A man no one seemed to know and no one seemed to think she even liked. A man she might've been planning to move away from. The convictions weren't recent, for what that was worth. Margot tried to get more information, but all she could find were the sentences. Just probation and community service. No prison time.

She pulled out her phone and wrote to Mike. "R U there?" No response. Then she tried the instant messenger on her laptop, just in case. Mike still didn't answer.

So she called Brad and left him a message. Then she called again to see if he would pick up. He didn't.

Collin was onstage at the moment—wearing nothing but a clown's wig and penile enhancement, or so he said. She wanted to talk to someone.

Toby. Margot typed the words "Toby" and "guitar" into a search engine. Over eight million results. Next she added "New York." Down to three million. It was so frustrating, because if someone knew his last name, they could probably find him on Facebook or somewhere. But Pepper had asked all the servers at the restaurant, and all anyone remembered was that he was touring with some band. No one knew the name of the band or Toby's last name, and one of the servers thought his name might be Moby and not Toby, but Collin felt that had to be wrong. "Because Moby's a pretty famous musician, and wouldn't it be embarrassing to be a musician named Moby but not be the *real* Moby—and who's named Moby anyway?"

Kara's own Facebook page was sparsely populated with the occasional out-for-drinks photo or random update (*Running late for dinner—who me? Ha ha ha*). None of Kara's Facebook friends were named Toby. Margot sifted through the wall posts and comments, as she'd done once before, still finding no sign of Toby's existence, no indication that Mullet and Kara were a couple. She waded through Kara's friends' friends, but the only Toby that Margot found was a teenager from Albuquerque.

Enough. Margot made herself stand up. She checked her grocery list, then her calendar of upcoming jobs, then the dried berry and nut supplies. She could go to the store. Or make a list, then go to the store when it stopped raining. She glanced back at the computer screen, then her phone, then the computer again. She closed the Facebook window to check on the typhoon, but it was Steve Donegan's criminal record that returned to the screen.

Assault, it said.

"And you could have married Brad Mitchell," she whispered.

Things could've been different for Margot, too. She'd turned down Benji Cohen and Paul Jacobs. She and Kara had encouraged each other. They were too carefree, too convinced of their youth to think about marriage. In those first years after college, when Brad was pressuring Kara and Margot's mother was trying to push her into the arms of every nice Jewish boy on Long Island, Margot and Kara had laughed the idea of marriage away.

That had worked out. Margot's mother died when Margot was twenty-five, and the next few years vanished into medical bills and her father's depression. Then Margot's father decided to move to Florida, so she had to find a good place for him and pack up the family house. And all the while friends were marrying and giving birth, and Margot was missing out.

Margot checked her flour and sugar supplies. She did get something during those difficult years: the baking, the business. More than one person had suggested Margot create a saccharine story about it. "I started baking to stay connected to my late mother and to share her wonderful recipes with the world." But in truth her mother was a pretty mediocre cook. Margot had no special memories of her mother baking and no reason to believe she'd gotten any pleasure from the act. Margot only started baking after her mother died as a way of keeping herself busy—or sane—when she visited her father.

He would just sit there and watch television, not talking much, not interested in going out, hardly eating. Margot would wander the house, not sure what to do, and one day she stumbled upon her mother's old recipe books and tried baking muffins. Maybe he ate to be polite; maybe he did it because it didn't feel like eating, it was just a snack. So Margot experimented, adding fruits and vegetables, even protein powder. And he started to look healthier, and Margot started to feel better.

During the next year, when she wasn't researching retirement communities in Florida or getting the house ready to go on the market, she was baking—first for one of the caterers in town, then for a deli run by a family friend. She quit a boring clerical job, moved in with her father, and enrolled in a course on small-business management. After she finally got him down to Florida, she stayed in the house while it sat on the market and used the kitchen to see if "More Than Muffins" would take off.

Thank God it did. Those months of taking her father to synagogue on Saturdays paid off. The women started passing Margot's name around, then sharing it with caterers and wedding planners. She brought samples to coffee shops all around Long Island, and when cupcakes became popular, she added icing and chocolate to her muffin recipes. Then they wrote her up in the *Long Island Press*, and that didn't hurt. Now she did sweet breads, muffins, cupcakes, cookies, cakes, pies, dessert squares, even wedding cakes now and then. She was a successful small business owner. "And I have perfectly natural hips for a woman who's carried three children," she'd said on more than one occasion—to Kara, to Mike. "It just so happens, I haven't carried any yet."

No one laughed.

It was raining. Margot tried Brad and Mike one more time each. On the computer, she saved Mullet's police record.

"Stop all that thinking and come to bed," she said aloud in the cartoonishly deep voice she used to mimic Mike when she was teasing him about something. She wished he really were there—to talk her down, to hold her in his big arms.

Maybe she would bake something, use up all those dried cherries.

Maybe she would dye her hair. *We're never more than twelve dollars away from our natural hair color,* Kara used to say.

Eight, if there's a coupon, Margot thought. That was always her line.

She poured herself another glass of wine and waited for someone to call her back.

※

Sophie was pulling into the parking lot as Brad and the Garcias were walking out, and Brad offered her a two-fingered wave, then hurried into his car before she'd turned off the ignition. She kept asking about Val and suggesting they all get together, and Brad couldn't believe they weren't telling her yet. He and Val had asked Sophie and Les to be godparents last time. If she ever bumped into Val in public, there'd be no question. There was no hiding it anymore.

Brad pulled up to the exit of the parking lot and waited for the Garcias' gold Camry to appear in his rearview mirror. They were going to follow him to a neighborhood off Ephesus Church Road, then jump in one car and look at a few properties together. While he waited, he glanced down at his phone and saw that he'd missed a call: Margot. Again.

He was surprised to keep hearing from her. She'd left a message last night, and another early this morning. There'd been a few hang-ups, too. She was sad, of course, but as often as he saw her in his college days, they didn't have a one-on-one relationship. They shared the Jewish thing and the New York parent thing and could laugh about gefilte fish and Sunday school, but she was really Kara's friend who was going out to brunch with them, or to the movie, or the beach. She was a fellow cast member in *Hair*. She was never a person Brad would have called on the phone.

He turned onto Weaver Dairy Road then dialed her number.

"Hey, good to hear from you," she said. "Sorry for all the calls."

"Don't worry about it," he said, and he shifted the call to his headset.

"I'm a little freaked out."

Brad checked his rearview mirror. The Garcias were behind him. "It's sad, I know," he said. "Hard to digest."

"No, it's more than that," Margot said. "I found something out."

Brad thought he'd talked her out of her worries the last time they'd talked a few weeks ago.

"Steve Donegan had a police record," she said.

"Who told you this?"

"I found out on the Internet. I did one of those criminal record checks."

"Good lord, Detective Cougar Cominsky at your service . . ." Brad wound his way down a curve in the road.

"I'm serious, Brad. He had an assault charge."

Brad hesitated for a moment, then said, "You can't believe everything you read online."

"It was a criminal records database."

"Are you sure it was him? I'm sure there are a lot of people with similar names in New York."

"They had a photo," Margot said.

Brad sighed. "What did it say?"

"That he was convicted of assault. No jail time, but still."

"He did look like a guy who could get drunk at a bar and hit someone. Can't you picture it? This could've been decades ago."

"It was seven years ago."

"Okay. Still. Does it shock you?"

"I think it's scary."

"Is that all it said? One assault charge that didn't even put him in jail?"

"And two arrests for drug possession."

"Well, I wouldn't be surprised if Kara had at least two herself. Did you look up her record?"

"Are you making fun of me?"

Brad was smiling a little. He checked the rearview mirror again.

"This is a big deal," Margot said. "I don't think Kara even liked this guy. Get this: He told me at the funeral they were talking about getting a bigger place together, but I found out she was asking around about sublets."

"What am I missing here? If she was looking for a bigger place—"

"She might've been looking for just herself."

Brad rolled his eyes. "That is true, she might've been. Sounds like things were rocky. But relationships are not always good."

"She would've talked to me about it," Margot said. "She was not quiet about relationship problems."

"She didn't necessarily tell you everything."

The pause that followed was longer than he expected. What had Kara told Margot about him? "What about that guitar player you said she was seeing?" Brad added. "She didn't tell you about him."

"They'd only been going out for a few weeks, and she told everyone she worked with. Eventually I'd have heard."

"Well, I guess eventually you'd have heard about Kara's engagement. And the reason for it. Or maybe it would've just gone away."

"But what if I'm right?" Margot said. "Think about it. Why would a man pretend to be engaged to a woman who died in his apartment? She didn't have any money. What could he gain? A man with a history of assault? I'll say it. What if he raped her—"

"I don't think—"

"I'm serious. He could have raped her and killed her and said they were engaged to cover it up."

"Come on." Brad couldn't believe it. So Kara told this guy she'd marry him—fine. The guy might have gotten drunk and punched someone seven years ago—sure. But still. "This is a lot of jumping to conclusions."

"But it's possible. Bad things happen to people." Margot paused for a moment. "You don't care."

"Of course I care," he told her. "I care," he said again. "Okay, sure, maybe we could call the Brooklyn police—just to alleviate your fears, to be sure they've done their due diligence. I can call. I'll say we bumped into these records, and we were surprised to hear about, you know, her being engaged."

"No one knew."

You didn't know, Brad wanted to say. But he didn't. "I'm sure they looked into this," he told her. "I'm sure they have some satis-factory information about how she died. I don't have much trouble believing she could have overdosed. Do you? Honestly?"

The other end of the line was silent for a moment. Then Margot said, "No. But this guy—"

"He's a trashy fellow. I'm not saying he's 'klassy with a k.'"

Brad paused to see if Margot would pick up on his Kara refer-ence. She might have, but there was no laugh. "You've gotten yourself worked up," he continued. "I'll call and check, okay?"

"Okay," she said, and she let out a sigh. "I appreciate it." Then she said, "I saw Gwen. When she first got here for that summer program. It was like a fucking time warp. She looks just like Kara, don't you think?"

Brad didn't respond. He slowed for a traffic light. The signal hanging on the wire in the distance was split in two. He hadn't had any vision problems thus far that morning, hadn't noticed, anyway, but traffic lights always seemed to double. Always or often? The two images almost converged by the time he stopped in front of them.

"Listen, I need to run," he told Margot, and he promised to let her know what he learned.

As he drove the last couple of miles, the Garcias' Camry behind him following with every turn, he began to visualize things he didn't want to visualize. But then he stopped himself. That wasn't what happened. Kara died of an overdose. She always acted like every drug she tried was harmless. Now her recklessness had caught up with her. It was unfortunate, but that's what happened. Margot was having trouble letting herself accept it, and *he* was letting his imagination run wild.

So he would call the police, pass on the information. They'd say they knew, it was nothing, and everything would be fine.

Brad stopped the car in front of the house—a split-level in need of a paint job. The Camry pulled up behind Brad, and he took a deep breath and plastered on a smile. Then he opened the door, stepped outside, and said, "Would you look at those gorgeous trees?"

※

Gwen's painting class had gone to the Museum of Modern Art, as had about nine million tourists. The lobby echoed with conversation in various languages. Visitors swarmed in and out of galleries, and guards hovered in almost every threshold. There were fifteen people in Gwen's class, and their teacher Lionel led them up to the fourth and fifth floors, where they saw Jasper Johns, Jackson Pollock, Andy Warhol, and Salvador Dali. Gwen had never been to "MoMA," as everyone kept calling it—she'd never been to "the Met" either—and it was cool to see all this famous stuff in person. But at the same time, once you've seen something like van Gogh's *Starry Night* or Matisse's five naked ladies dancing on the cover of a textbook and on postcards and T-shirts and shower curtains, it's hard to feel totally wowed. Gwen and her mom had gone to the mall once to see the soap opera star Juliette Drake and get her autograph. Gwen thought it would be more exciting to see her for real, but in person, she looked pretty much the same as she looked on TV, only closer and a little shorter. *Starry Night* was smaller than she expected it to be, too.

Now Lionel had given them an hour for "private exploration." Everyone broke up, mostly in groups of twos and threes. Gwen was a group of one. She passed her classmates periodically—in front of a giant sculpture of Jell-O, looking at the mannequin made of rubber bands. She studied couples studying the paintings, passed families speaking French and Russian and German. Gwen wondered if this was how it would feel to travel to Europe. It all seemed so different and cosmopolitan. Everyone was so well dressed. Not only the Europeans, but the New Yorkers, too. Gwen had been in New York for three weeks now, and she never saw anyone looking like she'd just rolled out of bed and thrown something on.

She walked slowly, not looking too hard at anything. Her feet were tired from standing for the past two hours. She was back on the fifth floor when she spotted Richard walking by himself. Gwen followed at a distance.

Richard was older than most of the kids in Gwen's class, probably twenty-two or twenty-three, and Gwen was pretty sure he was from New York. He wore oxford shirts that he left untucked, and he had hairy arms that were often stained with paint. She'd only spoken to him once. She'd asked if he could recommend a good place to get sushi, and he did. She'd hoped he would offer to get dinner with her; maybe he was busy that night, or maybe it didn't cross his mind.

When he spoke, he startled Gwen. "Color is a means of exerting direct influence upon the soul," he said. He didn't turn around. Gwen was standing about six feet behind him in front of a series of abstract paintings. She couldn't help staring at his neck, which was prickly, like he shaved it. She blushed.

"Color is a keyboard," Richard continued. "The soul is the piano, with its many strings."

Gwen swallowed. "That's beautiful," she said.

"Kandinsky," said a voice behind her. Gwen turned. It was Molly, one of Stephanie's friends.

Richard turned as well. "He painted these for the founder of Chevrolet," he said, looking past Gwen to Molly.

"What money can buy," Molly said, and she circled Gwen and joined Richard in front of a placard on the wall. Her breasts were huge, and her purse looked expensive. "'Color is a keyboard,'" she read. "I love it." She had one of those condescending accents, more snobby than regional. "Aren't you a Donald Keagan fan?" she asked Richard. "They have one upstairs."

"Let's go," he said.

And they went, neither one glancing at Gwen, as if she wasn't there.

She took a few steps forward and reread the Kandinsky quote on the placard. She'd thought Richard was being poetic. Now she was embarrassed. And angry. She took an elevator to the first floor and headed outside to finish her "private exploration" with a cigarette. She felt stupid. She wanted to cry. She couldn't make a single friend at a tiny little art school. What was college going to be like? Worse. She was pathetic. Gwen pulled out her phone and was about to dial Kara's number.

Then she stopped herself. "Fucking, fucking shit," she whispered.

She sucked on the cigarette, and the ash flared red. "I hope you're pleased with yourself," she said, this time a little louder.

Another puff. She couldn't smoke fast enough.

Who else could she call? Her mother would be useless. "Everyone likes you, Gwennie. You just need to put yourself out there. Give people a chance." Thanks, Mom. Very helpful. Kiss Bobby for me.

She didn't know who to call. She didn't want to talk to anyone who'd give her dead sister sympathy. A dead sister makes people not know what else to say to you. She wanted to hear what Kara would say right now: *That Molly sounds like a real cunt. I'm sure she'll be knocked up and living in a trailer within five years. She sounds the type.*

But Molly's from Connecticut. Do they even have trailers in Connecticut?

Of course they have trailers in Connecticut. Or maybe her "baby daddy" will be from rural Pennsylvania. They can put the trailer behind his parents' house.

Not Richard.

No, Richard's gay. That's obvious from what you've told me.

I don't think he's gay.

I know a lot of gay, and he sounds gay. Trust me. Now, do you have any pot left? I'm working, but I think my favorite busboy has something on him. You tell Mom you're going to the grocery, and I'll take a smoke break, and we can take a few hits together, okay? Don't get upset about some stupid art class filled with losers. It doesn't mean anything. Wait, I have to take an order. Hold on, don't hang up. God, I hate this table.

Gwen sighed a cloud of smoke. She had a bag of very good pot that had been sitting in her suitcase for three weeks now, assuming Stephanie hadn't stolen it and written her name on it. A bag she was supposed to share with Kara, then figured she'd smoke with the friends she'd make in New York.

She couldn't even smoke a joint by herself because Stephanie would probably tell on her once Gwen lit up in the apartment. Or the other kids down the hall would smell it. Somehow she'd get in trouble and they'd call home. That's all her mother needed. Gwen could imagine the histrionics. "After what happened to your sister . . ." Dot-dot-dot. The thought only made Gwen want a joint more.

She pulled out another cigarette and lit it from the butt of the first, and as she was tossing her cigarettes back into her purse, she saw Kara's phone. For a minute she just stared at it.

She hadn't tried to turn it on yet. It didn't seem right. But now Gwen pulled the phone out of her purse, flipped it open, and pressed the power button. She was just checking. The screen lit up. It had a charge. Her thumb clicked through the contact list, and there it was: Steve's number.

The thought had crossed her mind before. If Kara were alive, the three of them would have been hanging out all the time. They would have smoked through Gwen's whole bag by now. Gwen wouldn't have cared about the stupid kids at her school.

She took a puff of her cigarette.

He said to call. He said they should get together when she was in New York.

So Gwen pulled out her own phone and dialed the number. No answer. And then his voicemail picked up.

"Hi, Steve? This is, um, Gwen Tinsley—Kara's sister. You, ah, let me bum a bunch of cigarettes from you when you were in North Carolina, and now I'm in New York and wanted to return the favor."

※

Brad was upside down in a bridge pose in his yoga class. There was a time when he would have admired the woman in the purple spandex who was positioned about ten feet away, but now he kept his eyes closed for as much of each class as he could. It was simpler. He left his glasses in the locker room.

He had taken up yoga after the miscarriage, and he'd continued to go ever since. When he could give in, allow his mind to abandon all thought, it was cathartic. It helped him manage the stress of sales—busy times, slow times, uncertain times—and it kept him feeling healthy and young.

He moved through the cycle of poses, breathed in deeply, but today his mind refused to concentrate on the breathing because of the conversation he'd had right before class. He'd called the nurse in neurology to check on the test results and to report that he'd been on Mestinon for a week and hadn't noticed any improvement. He was expecting her to say that the CAT scan and blood tests were fine, then maybe change the dosage of the medication. Part of him imagined she might say that based on the tests, the doctor had ruled out the disorder and Brad was dismissed from their care. But instead, she put him on hold for several minutes then asked him to come into the office that afternoon. "Should I be nervous?" he asked. She made a sound that wasn't exactly a "no," then said, "See you soon."

"Upward Facing Dog." The instructor who looked vaguely like the neurology fellow was walking down the row. He could hear her footsteps. "Thighs off the ground," she said to someone behind him. Brad tensed his legs and held the pose. Had the CAT scan shown a tumor? Did something show up in his blood?

During the meditation at the end of class, Brad tried to succumb to the instructor's words. He tried to imagine the sounds of a running stream, to concentrate on his breathing, but instead he asked himself if he felt any weaker today than he had in weeks past. Was he having more difficulty than usual holding a pose, balancing on one leg? Yesterday, on the treadmill, had he become winded just a little too soon? It was difficult to know for sure. But maybe, possibly. "Feel the weightlessness of your body," she said, and he wanted to feel it, to feel himself rising up on a cloud, up and up into the air.

"WE haven't forgotten about you," said the receptionist in the neurology department's waiting room. "Should be just a few more minutes." Later, she said it again.

Brad had heard these same words on the phone two days ago when he'd called a police station in Brooklyn and asked to speak to a detective about the Kara Tinsley death. They kept him on hold for at least twenty minutes, checking back periodically. "We haven't forgotten about you," the operator said. "Should be just a few more minutes."

The detective who finally took Brad's call didn't have the thick nasal accent of television police. The man didn't have much of an accent at all. He had a smooth, calm voice, slightly high in pitch. Brad told his story to a chorus of *okays*, *uh-huh*s, and *I-see*s. To simplify matters, Brad said he'd been the one to check Steve's police records online. "I'm sure you've done everything you can," Brad said. "I just wanted to be sure this doesn't merit investigation or anything."

"Mm-hmm. And what was your relationship with the deceased, Mr. Mitchell?"

Brad answered.

Another *mm-hmm*. "And you hadn't talked to her in . . . ?"

"About eight years."

"Okay. Uh-huh. Eight years." There was a pause on the other end, and then the detective continued. "I feel for your loss, Mr. Mitchell. I really do." But, he explained, without eyewitness testimony or tangible evidence of a crime, the precinct would have to be contacted by Kara's next of kin or the medical examiner in order to pursue any further investigation. "You understand what I'm saying?"

Brad understood. He shouldn't have called. He was Kara's ex. He was saying he'd been searching the Internet for dirt on Kara's fiancé. Why had he imagined a call from him would carry much weight? Of course they weren't going to take him seriously.

But they wouldn't have given Margot much more credit, and if she'd been the one to make the call, she probably would have followed it with a call to Kara's poor mother. The prospect was horrifying. "You can't do that," he told Margot when he called to fill her in. "This is your suspicion, and that's all it is. You can't call Lucy Ann out of the blue, tell her Kara was living with a dirtbag, and start making these kinds of wild speculations. You can't do that to a person."

"Bradley Mitchell? The doctor can see you now."

Brad sat in the examination room for only a couple of minutes before Dr. Frick arrived and informed him that the CAT scan had been inconclusive. Brad's thymus was larger than normal for a person his age, a trait that was common among myasthenia gravis patients, but there were no tumors, which was the immediate concern. Still, surgery would always be an option, if they could confirm a positive diagnosis and his symptoms became "problematic." Removing the thymus could help alleviate symptoms. Sometimes. For some patients. Researchers weren't certain why.

The blood work had come back negative too—which was also inconclusive. Like the electromyography test with the thumbtacks, like Brad's response to the Mestinon pills. "Seems like a lot of inconclusiveness," Brad said.

"I want to try something else," the doctor told him. "I'll be right back." Then the nurse handed Brad a consent form, and he was left alone in the examination room.

This was getting a little ridiculous, actually. Brad had something wrong with his eyes. All these tests were coming back fine. What was the point of another one?

Look at the silver lining.

Kara. Brad looked up. He could hear her, but couldn't see her.

You're an ex-smoker who had a CAT scan of his chest, she said. *That can't hurt.*

She had a point. People with lung cancer usually found out after it was too late. The CAT scan might have been able to catch early warning signs, if there'd been any. Brad made a mental note to ask the neurologist if that was right.

Then he made a mental note not to ask.

Because he liked the suggestion. It felt good to think the CAT scan might have proved that by quitting in his mid-twenties, he'd undone any damage. Why go to the trouble to disprove something that was a small comfort?

You're so good to yourself, Kara said.

Then all at once, the six-by-eight examination room became crowded. The nurse and doctor returned, along with the fellow and a couple of medical students. Someone else arrived with a video camera, and instructions were given for where to set up a tripod and where to put a chair. Kara was somewhere. Brad saw the smoke from her cigarette rising to the ceiling, but he still couldn't see her.

Someone removed Brad's glasses, and they gave his eyes a moment to adjust. He'd signed the consent form, but had barely read it and didn't know what was going to happen. Then they turned on the camera, and the penlight was brought out and moved into various positions. Did he see double here? And here? Yes. And yes. Then Brad was told to roll up his sleeves, the nurse wrapped a blood pressure cuff around his left arm, and in the other arm the doctor inserted a needle.

Brad felt hot. Very hot. His heart started pounding.

"Quickly now. Do you see double here? Look carefully." The fellow was holding the penlight now.

"Yes," Brad said.

"What about here?"

"Yes."

"I'm injecting another three milligrams," the doctor announced to the room. "It's normal for you to feel a little warm," he added.

Sweating. Brad was sweating through his undershirt. He heard his stomach rumble.

"Do you see double here?"

He could see the cigarette smoke. But Kara?

"Brad? We need you to answer quickly. Do you see double now?"

"Maybe."

"Yes or no?"

"I don't know. Yes, I think."

"I'm injecting another two milligrams."

Hot. So hot. He felt his forehead dripping, his clothes clinging to his body. And the smoke, and all the people.

"And now?"

The dot of light in front of him appeared to be singular, but he was boiling.

Kara?

"I don't think so," Brad said.

"Look carefully."

It wasn't splitting.

"Yes or no?"

"No," Brad told her.

The fellow moved the light. "Do you see double now?"

"No," he said again.

The fellow moved the light to the far left. No again.

Someone covered one of Brad's eyes, then uncovered it. The doctor studied his pupils.

"Look," the fellow said.

The doctor said, "Uh-huh."

Burning, and the smoke. Was Kara behind the—?

"Look straight at me, please. You're doing great. Almost done."

Cover, uncover. Cover, uncover.

Then the doctor stood in front of the video camera. "Patient was injected with an initial two milligrams of Tensilon," he said loudly. "No change in diplopia noted. With an additional three milligrams, double vision was appearing to resolve. By eight, it had resolved completely. Thank you, everyone."

The camera was switched off. The tripod was removed. Brad's heartbeat was slowing down, and the room cleared out, leaving just the doctor, the nurse, the fellow, and Brad. The smoke was gone, too. Brad knew what the doctor was going to say.

"I'm afraid this does give us a positive diagnosis for myasthenia gravis. For now, let's double the dosage of Mestinon . . ."

Brad's mind was in the currents of a running stream. The water rippled through the folds of his brain.

The doctor was saying something.

". . . spontaneous remission . . ."

It could go away.

"We'll monitor you for slight variations in muscle strength and to see if your symptoms move beyond the eyes. It could end up being ocular myasthenia gravis," he said, "but within the first year or two most patients do go on to experience temporary weakness throughout the body—in the limbs and facial muscles, sometimes in the throat and respiratory muscles." It was crucial that Brad get enough rest and be prepared.

The doctor said more, and the nurse said more. Brad was reminded of papers he'd been given and medications to avoid. They talked about MedicAlert bracelets and support groups and sleep schedules and follow-up visits. Brad half-listened. He wasn't entirely there. He was in the clouds, floating, weightless. His undershirt was soaked, and he was cold.

After the doctor was finished, the nurse said she was going to leave Brad alone for a few minutes while the Tensilon wore off. Did he have anyone waiting for him outside? She could get his wife to sit with him, if he'd like. If only, Brad thought. No, he said. Okay, the nurse said, and she closed the door behind her.

Kara was there now. He could see her leaning against the closed door. She asked him if he remembered the time she'd driven him to the hospital their junior year. He'd stepped on a nail. She made him laugh the whole drive. *Don't be such a prima donna,* she'd shouted, playfully. *'Look at me, I have a nail in my foot. I can't look at it, I can't wrap it up, I'm in too much pain to stop for Mexican food on the way to the hospital.'*

He didn't feel like laughing today. Nothing she could say would be funny.

I could fart, she said. *A farting ghost would be a little bit funny, don't you think?*

A little bit, he thought. But only a little bit.

It could remain a vision problem.

It could.

And it could go into remission.

Right.

Or the weakness could spread. At any moment. It might not be safe for me to carry my own child.

That probably won't happen.

But we don't know that. Do *you* know that?

He wanted her to know that.

You're going to be fine, she said. *You exercise. You do yoga, for God's sake. You can become the poster child for this disease, do inspirational films for the Internet. It's perfect for you. Then you can do the talk show cir-cuit—the housewives will love you. You'll get discovered, start doing real acting again, become a movie star. This is a blessing in disguise.*

Brad exhaled deeply. I don't know why I didn't realize it earlier, he said.

Because you're a prima donna.

Brad nodded.

People are diagnosed with horrible things all the time, he thought. Bad things happen to people. I guess I shouldn't be com-plaining. Not in front of you.

That's right, she said, and she exhaled a cloud of smoke. *At least you weren't raped and murdered.*

What?

She didn't say that.

I didn't say that.

Kara's cigarette was gone. *Don't make me say those things. This isn't about me. I'm here for* you, *Brad.*

CHAPTER FIVE

MARGOT WAS DRIVING TO A CATERING JOB WHEN HER PHONE BEEPED. IT WAS A message from Mike. "U free?"

Well, shit, Margot thought. She'd missed his message a few days before when she was on the phone with Brad, and since then Mike had been tied up again with some training exercise. She felt like it had been ages since they'd talked.

At a red light, she typed, "Working tonight, but keep me company? XXOO"

His response came quickly. "U BET!"

Then the car behind Margot pounded on its horn and she saw the traffic light had turned green, so she flipped off the driver behind her and proceeded on toward Rockville Center.

So many of her conversations with Mike took place this way. She'd be at an event, or baking, or making deliveries, and he'd be coming off a shift, or on a break, or en route somewhere. And they'd talk by text message. Her thumb had gotten nimble, though her fat fingers still bumped the wrong keys sometimes.

"What's cooking?" he asked.

She typed "Made choc cake" with her left hand while her right hand steered. But then she realized she'd missed her street, so she dropped the phone on her lap and cut into a parking lot to make a U-turn. "Shit," she said to herself and the phone.

"MMM," the phone replied.

The house was lit up, and through the front window she could see that the cocktail hour had started. It was a rehearsal dinner for forty. A friend of Margot's was doing the dinner, and Margot was providing dessert. She had this kind of arrangement with a number of caterers in the area. It was a good deal. They booked the job and hired the staff. All she did was show up with the sweets.

There was a spot in the driveway set off with orange cones, and while one of the servers walked down to move them for her, she typed, "Sorry I couldn't talk the other day. You doing okay?"

"Indeed," came the quick reply. "Becoming quite a Poker Champ here."

"Oh yeah?" she typed. Then she waved her thanks to the server, pulled into the spot, and turned off the ignition.

"Three wins in a row," Mike had written.

Margot smiled. "Watch out, New York," she typed, before slipping the phone into her apron.

The server who'd moved the cones was waiting to help her unload the van. He was new, handsome. Looked all of nineteen. He said his name was Chad. Margot introduced herself and smiled.

The garage had been set up as a staging area for the dinner. Two servers were plating risotto and carrots on two long tables, and a third table had been set up for her. Chad and Margot carried the cakes to the table, and she continued to the kitchen with her pot. Her friend Zoe, the chef and manager, had an empty burner waiting. "Tasty," Margot said, eyeing the salmon and then young Chad who passed behind them.

Margot sent a quick note as she walked back to the garage: "Everything good beyond the poker tables?"

She'd made mini chocolate bundt cakes, and now started to set them out on baking sheets. They'd need to be warmed up for a few minutes, then drizzled with peppermint glaze. Two cakes had gotten crushed in the car, and she set them aside. U-turns can be dangerous, she reminded herself.

When she pulled out her phone again, she saw Mike's response. Typical. "YUP. How's Bernie? Hows the Viagra working out 4 him?"

"Smashingly," she replied.

Zoe was still using the oven, so Margot had a few minutes and she used the time to tell Mike, in shorthand, about the police records she'd found online and about Brad's call to the police and to her afterward. Brad had given her a speech about how awful it would be for them to contact Kara's mother, how terrible she was to even consider it. And fine, he had a point. If she'd died, Margot couldn't imagine someone calling her father a month and a half later and making these kinds of allegations. "But if I died and you thought there was something odd," she typed, "you'd pursue it, right?"

While she waited for Mike to say something passionate and caring, she carried the first two trays to the kitchen and put them in the oven. She checked on the glaze, gave it a stir. Still no reply. Then she returned to the garage to lay out two more trays of cakes. This kind of communication required a lot of waiting. A lot of giving the benefit of the doubt if a pause felt long, or if the tone or subtext was unclear, or if a conversation ended abruptly.

Her apron vibrated as she was about to walk back to the kitchen. "Of course!" he'd written.

Of course that's what he'd say. She fed him the line.

Margot rotated the first two trays of cakes with the second two, and carried the glaze back with her to the garage and set it on a hot plate. She was waiting for his next line now. She had decided what this one should be. She was just hoping he would think of it, too.

Zoe had left Margot a stack of dessert plates, and she spread out a dozen and plated the first tray of bundt cakes. Next, she poured a small scoop of the peppermint glaze into the center of each cake, drizzling a bit on the sides. Finally, she added a thin peppermint twig to the side of each plate. It was kind of a Christmasy dessert, but delicious. And the bride had liked the idea that everyone would end the meal with fresh minty breath. A fine consideration, since dinner was salmon.

Nothing further from Mike, so Margot pulled out her phone. "Can I ask a favor?"

Mike buzzed right back. "Ask away."

Margot hesitated. She plated the next six desserts. Then she typed: "Will you ask your father to check? To see what he finds on Mullet?"

There, she'd asked. It was done. Margot hurried back to the kitchen to retrieve the second two trays. Mike's father was a retired police officer from Port Washington. It seemed like a lot to ask, but maybe it was okay. Maybe he'd be glad to help, to do something that felt like police work again. If she was overstepping her bounds, Mike would be honest anyway.

Margot plated twelve more cakes, not even stopping to check the phone after she felt it vibrate again in her apron. Only when she'd finished did she read his message. "I do want my parents to meet U, but I wondr if this is the best way?"

She typed back quickly. "I've met them." What was he talking about? She'd catered the desserts at Mike's brother's wedding; that's where she and Mike had met. Of course, she'd met his parents. "Remember?" she added.

"Oh yeah," he said.

Margot began carrying the first round of desserts to a shelf across the garage where the plated dinners had been lined up before they were served. Chad appeared halfway through and helped her carry the rest, and Margot blushed, ashamed of the thoughts she was having. Zoe's whole staff looked young and attractive—probably aspiring actors, at least half of them. Margot wondered if any of them were sleeping with each other. *That's what catering waiters do,* she could hear Kara saying. *They sleep with each other. That's the point of being a catering waiter. To sleep with other catering waiters.* Margot smiled, and Chad caught her eye. She was too old for him. He wouldn't even guess what she was thinking.

Her apron buzzed again while she was drizzling peppermint glaze onto the last of the cakes. "Guess I can ask if he still has pull."

"Thank you, thank you," she typed.

"And feels comfortable," he added. "Can't promise."

"I know. I really appreciate it."

"OK. Will do. I hate for U to worry." Mike had a deep voice, a comforting voice. She heard it when he typed. Suddenly, strongly, she wanted to kiss him, to feel his scratchy cheeks.

"Want me to carry these over too?" Chad asked. He was standing across from her. He had dimples. Mike could break him in half with one hand.

"That'd be great," Margot said.

"LUV U," Mike wrote.

"Love you more," she typed back.

*

When Gwen emerged from the subway station on 4th Avenue, she took a moment to survey the streets and get her bearings. The one time she'd taken a subway out to Brooklyn by herself, Kara had given her specific instructions. *When you get out, you'll see a dumpy gas station in one direction and a taqueria in the other. Head away from the dumpy gas station, toward the taqueria. Then in two blocks, turn left at a shitty-looking apartment tower with the parking billboard on the side, pass the condemned building that looks like a terrorist outpost . . .* But that had been a different apartment and a different subway stop. Steve's instructions had been much less colorful.

Gwen pulled out her notes: Straight ahead to 7th Street, then right. Only she wasn't sure which direction to walk. Even when she squinted through her glasses, she couldn't read the cross street sign in the distance. So she picked a direction and started walking—it was better than standing there—and when 9th turned to 10th, she stopped, lit a cigarette, and turned around. And she walked back toward 7th Street with intention, like a girl who always took this subway home, who always fit in a quick smoke between the train and her apartment.

Gwen's apartment and art school were on the Upper West Side, which looked nicer than it did here, busier too. It was almost seven o'clock and would still be light for a couple hours, but she wondered if she'd be frightened to walk this route at night, then wait by herself in that small subway station. She could always call a cab. Of course, that would be expensive.

Steve had said there'd be a bodega on his corner, and Gwen saw it up ahead: small, door open, a couple of men lingering outside. They eyed Gwen as she walked the final block toward them. She dropped her gaze to her shoes, then looked up again and away from the shop entrance as she turned right. Behind the bodega were two doors: one at street level, and another five steps down. Gwen tossed her cigarette into the street, walked down the half-flight of steps, and pressed the doorbell. A minute later, Steve opened the door.

He was bigger than Gwen remembered—more than a head taller than Gwen, with thick arms covered in orange hair and freckles, a reddened face, and a rust-colored goatee. He was wearing a black T-shirt, and he reminded Gwen of a less country version of her high school's football coach. "Come on in," Steve told her.

"Thanks," she said.

The apartment was small and cluttered, and Gwen's eyes fell to the leather couch. It had a blanket draping off the edge, and in front of it was a wooden coffee table cluttered with dishes and newspapers.

She opened her purse and pulled out the plastic bag of weed. "Do you have a pipe or papers or something?" she asked.

"Of course, sure," he said. "You want something to drink?" He strolled toward the back of the room, which had a line of cabinets and a fridge. "Soda and coffee," he said, his back to her. "Jack, gin, vodka . . ."

"I'll take a vodka and Diet Coke."

"I only have Coke," he told her.

"That's fine."

She remained standing near the door while he opened the freezer and pulled out an ice tray and a bottle. "Looks like it's vanilla-flavored. That okay?"

It was Kara's then. "Sure," Gwen said with a shrug. "That's okay." The ashtray on the coffee table was filled with cigarette butts. One of the coffee mugs beside it has been turned into an ashtray, too.

"It's kind of a mess, I know," Steve mumbled.

Gwen looked up and shook her head. "That's fine," she said. She walked to the back of the room and took the drink from him. It tasted strong. Which was good.

Between the back of the couch and the kitchen was a wooden table with three chairs, and Steve cleared a pile of clothes off one and offered it to Gwen. Next he cleared a stack of mail and a pizza box off the table, then returned with an empty ashtray, a bag of papers, and a pink glass bong with a face drawn on the bowl. *Miss B,* Kara had called it. The lips were drawn in red marker, and the big eyes and long lashes were black. "Let's go with the papers," Gwen said.

He let her roll. She was feeling nervous. The pot was dry and she worked slowly, but she did an okay job. The resulting joint was on the thin side, but acceptable. "Want to do the honors?" she asked.

He lit the end and took the first hit.

"I've had it for a while," she told him.

"That's okay. It's pretty good."

Gwen took a drag now too, and held it. After a long pause, she exhaled. "Yeah."

"You brought this from home?"

"Uh-huh."

"On a plane?" He relit the end and took another drag.

"No," she said, "I came up by train. I brought it to surprise Kara."

Her eyes drifted away from him, and she noticed a yellow mug on the counter that belonged to a set her mother had. Kara must have taken it, and he forgot to send it back. So now it was his.

"I guess you would have been here too," Gwen said, turning back to him. Steve nodded without meeting her eyes. The joint had gone out, so she lit it again, then gave it back to Steve. "Here, real quick."

He inhaled then let it out. "Thanks," he said.

They sat in silence. Gwen sipped her drink, which was sweet and didn't seem so strong anymore. "So," she said, "that's the couch."

"Yeah. I'm real sorry—" he began.

"That must have been freaky. Finding her."

"Yeah," he said. "I'm sure it's hard, losing your sister."

Gwen lit the joint again and took a hit. "That's what they tell me," she said, and she surprised herself by laughing. "That's, like, the only thing people tell me. 'Hi, Gwen. It must be hard losing a sister.'"

"Your friends, you mean?"

"Friends, strangers, everyone. You finish," she said, giving him the roach. "I need a break." She pulled a cigarette from her purse and lit it.

"They're just trying to be nice is all."

"It doesn't help."

"No, of course not."

Gwen smiled and exhaled through her nose. "I guess people are saying the same things to you."

"Pretty much, yeah. So you're a painter, right?"

"Barely. I got an A in art class, so Mom's convinced that I'm the Mary Cassatt of Greenwood Park."

"But you got into art school in New York, right?" he said. "That's big stuff."

"It's only a summer program. I'm sure they accept anyone who applies."

"Oh come on, I bet you're great."

"I'm really not."

"I don't believe it. They got tough standards in this city. You having fun at least?"

Gwen shrugged. "Not particularly."

"Lot of homework?"

"No. I don't know. It's the people, I guess. They're all stuck-up. Here, roll another."

Steve took the bag from her and pulled out another rolling paper, and Gwen finished her drink. Her head was starting to feel light and slippery. During the second joint and the second drink, she told Steve about the last time she'd been to Brooklyn. She was sixteen, and it was right before Christmas, and she'd come to New York with Randy and her mom, but she got to take the subway to Brooklyn by herself and spend the night at Kara's apartment. That was when she lived with the gay guy, Collin. Before he turned into a conceited prick, Gwen explained. Yeah, he'd heard about that, Steve said. A shame, he said, and Gwen agreed.

Gwen told him about Richard from the museum, and how he kind of reminded her of a guy from her high school. One day at a football game, she managed to get a seat right behind him in the bleachers, and she said, "I have some pot, if anyone wants to smoke it with me," in a sort of haphazard way. In her head, he was supposed to turn around and introduce himself, and they'd go back to his car, and they'd live happily ever after. But instead, some kids beside her said sure, and she ended up in someone's basement with a bunch of people she didn't like that much. But it was okay.

That was kind of the story of her social life, actually. Kara had taken Gwen with her to buy pot a couple of times from this guy named Dean-o who worked at a gas station, and when Gwen was sixteen she went by herself, and she was nervous, but the whole thing was no big deal. And once she said something at that football game, she started getting invited to more places—to parties, or to hang out at someone's house while their parents were out of town. And it was mostly about the pot, she knew, but it was something to do. It passed the time.

Gwen sucked on an ice cube from her empty glass. "You think I'm pathetic, don't you?"

"No, of course not."

They were long finished with the second joint by now. The room rippled a bit, and Gwen's head felt heavy. But also light. Like it weighed a lot but was filled with helium.

"What do you do?" she asked. "Like, for a living?"

"I'm a super. I fix things."

"For this building?"

"And a few others."

"Were you the super for Kara's building? Is that how you met?"

"No. We met at this bar we both used to hang out at."

"And then you started dating and she moved in?"

"Kinda, yeah I guess. She was getting kicked out of her place, and I said she could crash here, and that started to last a while, and you know, one thing leads to another."

Gwen nodded, which made her a little dizzy. "Kara never said she was engaged."

"She would've. It just happened a little before."

"You'd think she would bother to tell her own sister."

"Of course she would've. She was gonna tell you first. You were gonna be one of the first people."

"Really?"

"That's what she said, yeah. She wanted to tell you in person, when you were here. Then she was going to tell everyone else after."

Gwen smiled and wrinkled her nose. "For real?"

"Of course, yeah. I mean, you were her sister. You went through a lot together."

"Not that much. She moved out when I was little."

"But you were the same blood. That meant something."

Gwen slouched down in her chair. She'd barely known their father before he vanished with a heart attack. "Kara was a lot older than me," she said.

"Age isn't everything."

"It's a lot."

"Look who you're talking to." Steve shrugged his big shoulders. "She was looking forward to your visit," he said. "She talked about it a lot."

"She probably thought of me the way I think of the Bobbies."

"The Bobbies?"

"The twins?"

"Oh, come on. No, she didn't. 'Cause you crossed over. At a certain point, everyone grows into a person. Someone you can talk to like an adult. The whole time I knew her—which I know wasn't all that long, but still—the whole time I knew her, she thought your brothers were cute, but she said Gwen, Gwen is like a person, I can talk to her."

"She said that?"

"Yeah, sure she did. She wanted me to meet you. I'm glad I did. I'm glad you came over."

"I'm glad too." Gwen was sliding down the hard back of the

chair, and she rested her head on the top of it. "I'm not sure I can go home," she said.

"That's alright. I can sleep on the couch, and you take the bed. And in the morning, we'll get pancakes."

"Pancakes?"

"Yeah, good ones. I know a place."

"Okay. That sounds good."

"You falling asleep now?"

"What?"

"You falling asleep?"

"I'm resting my eyes. I think—what? Yeah, I think so."

"Hang on then, okay. Let me get you into bed."

It was a couple of minutes after seven thirty, and Margot was in Port Washington. She was on their street, in fact, and she'd already circled the block three times, wondering if Mike planned to phone before she went in. But she didn't want to be late, and she hated to call him and have him think she didn't know how to handle herself. And besides, it was eight thirty in the morning in Okinawa.

The request to Mike's father had gotten out of hand. Mike mentioned that Margot had a police-related question, and Mike's dad suggested she come to dinner since they all lived on Long Island anyway, and then Mike's mother decided they ought to have Margot over for July 4, since they would be barbecuing. Then Mike said he would call in for the dinner so he could be there with all of them on speakerphone. So here Margot was, walking up to the Cavertons' front door, pie in one hand and phone in the other. Kids were lighting sparklers down the block, and Margot was wondering if the telephone would have its own place setting.

"Hello again, Margot," Lissy Caverton said when she opened

the door. Margot remembered that big smile from Mike's brother's wedding.

"Happy Fourth," Margot replied, and she held the pie out with one arm and used the other to accept Lissy's embrace. Lissy wore a red and white floral top with a blue skirt. Margot was wearing a blue dress with a red scarf. She'd started out with a yellow scarf, but then thought better of it.

"Is that dessert?" Lissy asked, taking the box from Margot.

"It is. Apple and cherry pie."

"Oh, mercy. That sounds delicious. It doesn't get more American than that, does it? Russell!" she called. "Russell's out back. Russell? Margot's here."

Margot followed Lissy to the kitchen with its avocado appliances and peach-colored cabinets. On the wall were photo collages of the Caverton boys: as toddlers, Cub Scouts, teenagers. Mike had two brothers close in age, and she couldn't distinguish Mike in the younger pictures, but as he got older, he started to stand out. Mike in a Little League baseball uniform, in a prom tuxedo, in a green spandex wrestling singlet. He must have been seventeen or eighteen. He looked like something out of a bachelorette party. Margot felt herself blushing. She didn't even know he'd been on the wrestling team.

"Did you say Margot's here?"

She turned to face Mike's father. He was wearing an apron with red, white, and blue fireworks on it and holding a pair of tongs. He had Mike's brown eyes and strong cheekbones. "Welcome," he said.

"Thank you."

"Did you see the picture of Mike dressed up as a butterfly?"

"Oh, stop it," Lissy said. "She just got here."

Russell shrugged and offered a look of innocence. "I want to be sure she doesn't miss the opportunity." Russell walked beside Margot and pointed to a picture of the boys as toddlers. Mike was wearing orange vinyl wings, a black shirt, and antenna. "Mitch was a fireman, little Max was a policeman, and Mikey picked out the butterfly costume."

Lissy put a hand on Margot's shoulder. "He'd just learned about caterpillars and butterflies in school."

"And he looked beautiful!" Russell said.

"Oh, stop it."

Just then the phone rang across the room.

"He's calling to defend himself," Lissy added.

And it was Mike, calling on the house line. "Mikey, let me put you on speakerphone," Lissy said. She was beaming. "Happy Fourth of July."

"It's the fifth for him," Russell said.

The conversation moved outside, where the phone was placed beside the grill while Russell flipped burgers and Margot and Lissy set the table. They could hear firecrackers going off in the neighborhood, and it did feel like a festive occasion. Margot could imagine Mike being there, the four of them sharing a more normal barbecue. Or his brothers there too, Max and his new wife, Mitch and his wife and baby. They'd all celebrate Christmas in the living room on the other side of the glass door, and Margot would bring a menorah and explain Hanukah to the kids, but deep down she'd be excited to finally have a Christmas tree. She and Mike would put presents under the tree for their kids, too. And maybe one year, they'd try to surprise the kids with a dog for Christmas, but of course the dog would bark too much, and they'd have to let him out early, and the kids would be so excited. She liked envisioning that scene on the other side of the glass. It seemed more natural than this one.

They ate on bright white dishes with blue stars, and Russell did set the phone on a plate, knife and fork carefully placed on either side. It was nearly time for the fireworks to start over the harbor when Mike reminded his father that Margot had a favor to ask.

Hopeful and nervous as she was, a part of her was sorry to see the evening's mood shift and its ulterior motive exposed.

"Is this about a speeding ticket?" Russell asked. "Or a murder rap?" He grinned like a man who'd said this line many times before.

"It is on the serious side," she said, and she swallowed. She'd rehearsed this several times during the drive over. "A close friend of mine died recently and—" Margot felt her heart start to beat more quickly. "It was a college friend. She was a little wild, I guess, and might have died of a drug overdose, but," Margot hurried on, "there's a part of me that worries that maybe . . . something bad happened."

Russell picked a roll out of the basket and began to butter it.

"There was a man who spoke at the funeral," Margot continued, "and he said he was her fiancé, but everyone I've talked to thought he was just a roommate. And I did one of those online criminal background checks, and his name came up with an assault conviction."

"Did someone tell this to the police?"

"One of our friends tried, but the detective who spoke with him said he'd have to hear from the family in order to pursue this and . . . well, this is our suspicion, not the family's, and my friend Brad thinks—and I guess I agree—that it would be wrong to call her mother out of the blue and tell her there's a chance something terrible happened. I don't know. What do you think?"

Lissy stood up and collected a couple of plates to carry to the kitchen. "That's horrible," she murmured on the way inside. "I'm so sorry."

Russell studied the butter knife.

Mike, from his position on the plate, said, "Maybe you can ask someone to run a background check, Dad? If Margot gives you the name."

"I'm sorry to hear about your friend," Russell said to Margot.

"If this is too much to ask, or if you can't—" she began.

"I can," he told her, and he took a bite of the roll as Lissy picked up another round of dishes.

Margot glanced down at the phone and hoped Mike was still there.

"Write down his name and address, if you have it, and I'll see what I can find out."

"Thank you," Margot said. "I really appreciate it. I hope I'm wrong."

Russell turned to the phone. "Mike, I hope this isn't the only reason you wanted us to visit with your friend here."

"Absolutely not. You were supposed to teach her how to grill a burger, too."

"Okay, good. That may take practice."

A moment later Lissy returned with the pie, and she was cutting slices for each of them. Before Margot's heart had had a chance to slow down, Mike said he was going to have to run before the fireworks started.

"You're going to miss quite a show," Russell said. "I was going to describe each individual burst for you."

"Tempting as that sounds . . ."

"Alright, tell your mother if she should worry."

"No, she should not."

"No more jumping out of planes for a while?" Lissy asked.

"He's good now for another three months, right?" Russell said.

"Right," Mike said.

Another three months? What were they talking about? Mike hadn't jumped in at least six months.

Unless . . . maybe he had.

Lissy was leaning in closer to the phone now. "Mikey, have they said anything more about your transfer?"

"Nope," Mike said. "Listen, I gotta run. I'll talk to you soon. Margot, you too. Happy Fourth, everyone. Thanks, Dad."

And that was it. The whole exchange was so quick, it took a minute for Margot to process.

"Lissy has to worry sometimes," Russell said, as if reading Margot's mind.

"With a husband on the police force for forty years, a son who raced cars for three horrible years, and another headed to Afghanistan . . ."

Margot was a step behind. Who raced cars? And Afghanistan? Not Mike. He hadn't said anything about—

"But she can't worry all the time," Russell continued. "So we agreed to tell her when she should legitimately worry."

"Although the night you were shot in the leg I wasn't supposed to worry."

"I wasn't supposed to get shot."

Then the first explosion burst over the harbor, and it felt to Margot as if it was taking place inside of her. Ripping at the part of her that she thought was safe. "Have they said anything more about the transfer?" Lissy had asked. Another son headed to Afghanistan . . .

He'd promised to tell her. They had a code word.

He was supposed to come back.

Another arrow of flame shot up in the distant sky, followed by another, and another. Each explosion louder than the last, each circle of lights taller, more powerful—then falling like a parachute and dissolving into the sky. From further away came another blast, the start of a competing show in the darkness behind her. Every few seconds a whiz, a painful burst, and bright-colored fire rained down.

"That's a good one," Russell said.

"Mercy," Lissy agreed.

How could this be happening? How could they sit watching this?

Margot glanced down at her phone and saw it had lit up now as well.

"Sorry," it said. "We'll talk soon."

※

For over an hour Stephanie had been talking on the phone and eating soy chips from a bag labeled "Stephanie." Gwen ate her sandwich as quickly as she could, then paced into the other room and dropped onto the bed. "Awake?" she typed into her phone, not really expecting Brad to reply. It was after ten, and he'd said he was trying to get to bed earlier. Some health kick, apparently— he did frigging yoga. It didn't matter. All she wanted to do was tell him how annoying Stephanie was. "Sleep tight," she added, then tossed the phone into her purse.

Once again Gwen found herself examining the painting that dominated one of the bedroom walls. It had come with the apartment, a three-foot-wide canvas covered in thick clumps of white paint and primary-colored half-moons that struggled to keep their shape over the bumpy surface beneath them. It was pretty rough. It didn't even look finished. Gwen wasn't sure what to make of the piece, or of its presence. She kept feeling like it was something abandoned by a former student, some poor kid who never imagined the canvas would end up filling wall space, on display and subject to criticism in this incomplete state. Pretty shitty of the institute to hang it up. Unless they were setting the bar low for future students. In any event, it was a reminder to Gwen to take or destroy anything she produced this summer.

"Oh my God," Stephanie shouted into the phone in the next room.

Gwen rolled her eyes. When Stephanie was around, she was always on the phone—talking loudly, often pausing to ask Gwen to turn down her music or the TV, or to please not leave dishes in the sink or stockings in the bathroom. This summer program would be good preparation for dorm life and college, Gwen's mother had said. Yeah, Gwen was looking forward to that.

"So what did he say?"

From what Gwen could gather from Stephanie's side of the conversation, Molly had gone out with Richard from the institute. He had paid for dinner, and she had put out. So much for Kara's theory he was gay.

"You totally should," Stephanie said, crunching on a soy chip. Gwen scooted halfway down the bed, stretched her leg out, and pushed the door closed with her foot.

She had been in New York for a month now, and she'd had a few meals with kids from her program. There'd been a few everyone's-going-somewhere situations, but that was kind of it. Her mom kept asking, Are the people nice? Is your roommate nice? Did you do anything nice this weekend? According to Mom, all of New York was supposed to be nice.

Weirdly, the only real fun she'd had was last weekend when she'd hung out with Steve. He was old—older than Margot—but he didn't feel as old as her. Just like Kara didn't feel all that old. Gwen's mom loved to say how irresponsible Kara was, but maybe that just meant Kara was youthful. She was lighthearted. Steve seemed sad about Kara, of course, but he was still fun to be around. Gwen could understand why Kara would've spent more time with him than with Margot.

He'd left a message inviting Gwen to do something again on Saturday. Sure, why not, she said to herself. She would text him, she decided, and she reached down into her purse for her phone—

But her hand pulled out Kara's.

For a minute, instead of swapping it for her own, Gwen held Kara's phone in her hand. It felt funny, foreign. It was lighter than her own, and cheaper too. She'd only turned it on once, to find Steve's number. Now she flipped it open and pressed the power button again, not sure what she was going to do.

When the menu screen lit up, Gwen's thumb tabbed over to the text message screen. There were twenty-three messages in the inbox. Three were marked unread.

Gwen dropped her arm to the bed and told herself no, it's morbid, it's none of your business. This wasn't like taking a bracelet that Kara probably would've wanted her to have anyway, under the circumstances. This was intrusive, wrong.

But there was the phone in her hand. And hadn't Gwen known she would do this, at some point? She held the phone in front of her eyes again and scrolled through the new text messages: a "what's up" from a 212 number dated right before Kara died, a message from the phone company telling her how she could pre-pay for more minutes, and one message dated last week from someone named Toby M: "Hey chick. Long time no hear."

Toby M. The name sounded familiar.

Gwen scrolled through the twenty older messages. Many were from him: saying he'd be late for dinner, inviting Kara to a show, saying he wasn't on until eleven, saying he had fun. "You did too," said one of his messages. Gwen switched to the sent-messages screen, which showed Kara's last seventeen texts. Right before Toby wrote, "You did too," Kara had written, "You looked sexy last nite."

Kara was totally flirting with this guy. Or having an affair. And at least as of last week, he didn't know she was dead.

Gwen turned off the phone and listened to Stephanie laugh in the next room. She felt invasive, sneaky. Naughty, but in an exciting way.

"Hey chick. Long time no hear."

Margot—that's who'd asked about Toby. That's where Gwen had heard the name. Had Gwen ever met him? Margot had asked. No, who was he? Oh, just some musician friend Kara had been spending time with recently. She'd never met him, Margot said, but she was curious. He sounded interesting.

Gwen smiled as she turned on the phone again and looked back at Kara's note: "You looked sexy last nite."

Gwen pressed the voicemail button. It worked. Kara had the password programmed in. The electric operator announced five new messages. Gwen felt her pulse racing. The first was from a credit card company, and Gwen didn't know how to skip past it, and the message was long and she felt impatient: a bill, past due, trying to confirm her address. The next message was from someone at Kara's restaurant, wondering why she wasn't there. Then another call about a bill. Then the fourth message: "Hey, chick. It's me again. What are you doing?" His voice sounded deep and raspy, like he'd just woken up. "We're playing some crap club in St. Paul tonight. We have a bigger gig tomorrow in Minneapolis. It's all good, but I'll be happy to be home soon . . . Just thinking about you. Give me a call if you feel like it."

The last message was from him, too. Brief: "Hey chick. Thinking about you." And then there was one saved message, from Gwen, giving the dates for her visit and the information about her train.

Gwen swallowed back a wave of sadness and looked back at Toby's text from last week: "Hey chick. Long time no hear."

He didn't know.

And who was he? Gwen wondered. Without thinking, she clicked over to Kara's contact list to find Toby's number. Then she pulled out her own phone and dialed. It was curiosity more than sympathy that motivated her. She knew that as she listened to the phone ring. What time was it? Ten forty-five, but he was a musician.

His voicemail picked up, that now familiar voice: "Not here. Blah blah blah. Leave a message."

Gwen sat up on her bed. "Hey. This is—my name is Gwen. I'm Kara Tinsley's sister. Can you please give me a call?"

※

The drive east reminded Brad of his last trip down the same stretch of highway, his solitary ride to Kara's funeral. He remembered paying close attention to the traffic signs on the sides of the road, trying to notice how badly they were doubling. He remembered himself remembering past beach trips with Val, and before those, with Kara. He remembered driving to the beach once barefoot, and staying that way for two days. That was a long time ago.

Ever since the diagnosis, Brad felt like a spectator in his own life. The pillbox he carried around with him was thin, but he could feel it creating a small lump in his pants or jacket pocket. Four times a day he took the Mestinon at the new, higher dosage, and he allowed himself to start hoping the medication would work. It was supposed to take effect quickly, and though he still wasn't sure it did anything, he'd watch himself closely after each dose. He might be showing a house or sitting at a stoplight or walking through a store, and he'd ask himself, Are you seeing double now? Is this *any* better than it was half an hour ago? The answer was usually maybe, or probably, or he'd forget to pay attention, and perhaps that meant things were better.

At the gym, he was monitoring his strength. You're bench-pressing more than him, he'd say to himself. And him. Though not him. But look, you're setting the squat machine at the same weight you've been using for months. Then he would worry: Maybe that was bad. Maybe he was stagnating, losing strength when he should have been gaining it. Was this a warning sign? He usually went to the gym in the early afternoons or mornings. Should he try going late at night?

Even his interactions with people seemed to take place outside of himself. He observed himself sell a house, and he observed himself simulate excitement over it for his clients and for his colleagues and for Val, who baked a cake to celebrate. That night, when he and Val made love for the first time in three months, he was thinking, You are making love to Val, and it's a distraction and a relief to her, and it's a distraction and a relief to you. And that's okay.

He surprised himself afterward when he suggested they go to the beach that weekend. "We need to change life's window dressing," he told her. She surprised him more when she said yes without much convincing.

Now he was driving to the beach, Val beside him with a quarter and a scratch-off blackjack lottery ticket. "Okay," she said, "we still have a chance to win one dollar, five dollars, one hundred smack-eroos, one dollar, and twenty-five dollars. Choose carefully."

"I'll take one dollar."

"Conservative move. The first or the second?"

"Second."

"Dealer has twenty. You draw a king . . . and . . . oh, sorry, it's a four."

"That is rough."

"We're still in this. My turn. Let's see . . ."

He and Val could easily drag this out for another five minutes, feigning strategy and building suspense. They could do a cross-word puzzle together, perhaps, or listen to the radio, try to muffle the clamor of their own thoughts. Or, maybe, hopefully, he could bring himself to tell her.

It was too late to tell her about the disorder with any semblance of nonchalance. She would be angry, with cause, and frightened too. Since they left the house, he'd been trying to build up the courage to talk about it. But now, as they neared the $100 prize and the end of their second and final ticket, it occurred to Brad that he probably shouldn't tell her until they arrived. In the car, she might question his ability to drive, and he didn't need her to worry about that. He'd become comfortable with the doubling. In fact, given the range of larger problems he could face if the disorder moved beyond his eyes, he was starting to think of his vision problems as a mild inconvenience—an indicator, a fact of life. He'd never had trouble driving. He never reached for a doorknob in the wrong place. His brain had somehow learned to compensate.

Val had insisted on a hotel far off the beaten path to avoid bumping into vacationing families from her school, but once they arrived, she happily disguised herself as a pregnant lady in a floppy hat and sunglasses, and Brad disguised himself as a healthy father-to-be in swim trunks and a baseball cap. He almost told her that afternoon on the beach, but they were both having such a nice time, and when they went out to dinner at a small restaurant, Brad didn't want to spoil the novelty of getting Val out into the world again. The next morning on the beach as he tried to formulate a way to explain what was happening—and what had, what might—he kept coming back to the fact that it really would be much better to be able to tell her that he had the ocular version of the disorder. The ocular version sounded less intimidating; it wouldn't impact their lives so much. Then he could explain why he'd kept it from her, how he'd protected her from the news because of the chance it might have been much worse.

Of course, she was a researcher. She'd go online and know in five seconds that almost all patients show eye-related symptoms first. But even if she knew that, and he knew she knew that, in a few months the doctor might be willing to say that it *seemed* like it wasn't going to be the generalized disorder. Then Brad could believe it was true, and Val would agree with him and say upbeat, disarming things, and that would be a relief. It would feel good. She'd read about people with myasthenia gravis who went into spontaneous remission. Some people went into remission forever; she'd learn the statistics. She would help him figure out the best way to tell his parents. She could distract him with talk of the baby. Maybe.

For now it was better to let the vacation be a vacation. If ever they'd deserved a vacation, wasn't now the time? People take vacations to get away from their worries. What was gained by dumping new ones on Val now?

All day Sunday they lay out by the ocean, reading and watching clouds and waves and time float by. In the afternoon, he brought out the Scrabble, which Val thought was funny, because they were bound to lose tiles in the sand, and they probably did. They played a long game, defending their board from the wind, and laughing over triple word scores, and useless *X*'s, and whether or not "quaff" was a word. For dinner, they went to another restaurant, like a normal couple on vacation. Val scanned the room for familiar faces, but there were none. She felt safe.

That night they made love again, and as they were falling asleep, Val spooned in his arms, Brad heard his phone beep.

"Is everything okay?" Val said.

"I'm sure it is."

"Check," she insisted.

So he unwrapped himself and looked at his phone, knowing who it would be. Gwen. She was bored, her text said. "It's fine," he said.

"Who was it?"

"It's nothing. It was Gwen."

Val turned around to face him. "Gwen? Kara's little sister?"

"Yeah."

"Calling you at eleven at night?"

"No, just texting."

"Texting you at eleven at night?" Val propped herself up.

"She just needs someone to talk to."

"And that person is *you*? Did you even *know* her when you and Kara were dating?"

"Yeah, sure. I mean, she was young."

"She still is." Val threw the covers to the side and stood up.

"Val, come on. There is nothing happening here."

"Oh, I have no doubt."

"She's lonely. She's grieving."

"I get it," Val said, pulling her hair back into a clip. "I'm going for a walk."

"What? Come on, no, let's talk about this."

"I'm awake, I need some air."

"I'll come with."

"Please don't."

"Val . . . ? What?"

Val pulled off her nightgown and slid into her beach dress from earlier in the day. Then she turned to face Brad. "Did we come to the coast for me and you, or for Kara?"

"What?"

"She grew up here, right? Is this all some elaborate mourning ritual?"

"Of course not. Kara doesn't *own* the beach. You and I have always come here. Val, don't do this. We were having a good time."

"Were we? Because it hasn't looked like you've been having a good time."

"What? What are you talking about?"

Val stepped into her sandals and grabbed her cardigan off the back of a chair. "Look," she said, "I respect what you must be going through, I do. I just thought . . . at this point, we were going through the same thing."

"Val . . ."

"I'm going to get some air."

"Please—"

"It's fine," she said. "It's just a walk."

VAL returned half an hour later, and they agreed it was best to just go to sleep and let the moment pass. Then they both lay in bed and pretended to fall asleep much more easily than they could. At breakfast the next morning, neither of them brought up the unpleasantness of the night before. As they made conversation about the eggs, Brad saw Kara sipping a mimosa a few tables away. She didn't say anything. She only met his eye once before she disappeared.

Brad napped a little on the beach that morning to make up for lost sleep, but when he opened his eyes he saw Kara walking along the edge of the water. He could choose not to see her there, he knew. If he tried, he could look toward the ocean and make her go away. But it was like ignoring one eye when his vision doubled. He'd know the ghosted image was really there.

For lunch Brad bought sandwiches from a shop near the beach, and he didn't see Kara on the water after he returned. But when he and Val played Scrabble, pointed words kept forming on his board: "actress," "perform," even "spirit." Then Val played the word "dead"—she couldn't have played "read" or "lead"?—and Brad said he had a headache and conceded the game.

On the drive home that evening, they stopped at a grocery store off the highway. They were still almost an hour outside of Chapel Hill, so Val wasn't going to run into any parents and could continue to be an anonymous pregnant lady. It occurred to Brad, as he wandered down the aisles by himself, that she probably hadn't been to a grocery store in almost a month. He was always picking meals up, or she'd leave him lists. He was trying to remember exactly the last time they'd gone shopping together when he almost walked through Kara.

She was in the cereal aisle studying a box of Apple Jacks. Kara always had to visualize herself enjoying a particular food item before she would commit to it. Abruptly she put it back on the shelf and grabbed a box of Frosted Flakes. *Don't mind me,* she said. *Just doing a little shopping.*

Hello, he said.

No, I'm serious. Keep pretending I'm not around.

Brad had argued with this tone of voice many times before. He waited. She picked up the Froot Loops.

Then he said, flatly, Is this you haunting me? Is your spirit not at rest?

Please, what movies have you been watching to fill the time? Don't be melodramatic.

I was trying to have a vacation here. What do you want?

Cereal. Isn't it obvious? She put the box down then stood in front of the Apple Jacks.

Is this about . . . what Margot thinks? I called the police.

I know, she said. *Good for you.*

Did something actually happen?

Didn't you decide I was knocked up with Mullet's baby? Maybe I do want Frosted Flakes. Pregnancy cravings. Kara examined the box.

Look, I don't want the police knocking down your mother's door if—

No, I appreciate it. That's very respectful of you. You are one respectful fellow. Ask Val.

Leave her out of this.

Just like you.

Val appeared at the end of the aisle, and Kara waved to her.

"Do we have cold cuts?" Val asked.

"I don't know."

"They have beautiful cold cuts here. Have you seen?"

They are stunning, Kara said.

"Get whatever," Brad said.

"Are you picking out cereal?"

"Yeah. I'll meet you."

"Okay," Val said, and she rounded the corner.

Kisses! Kara called after her. Then she whispered, *You might want to sneak a pill now. It's a little early, but you have a long drive ahead of you, and wouldn't want wife-y to find out.*

Brad turned to the cereal boxes, which were doubling slightly. Discreetly, he swallowed a pill with his spit.

You know, there were times I thought it was a shame you gave up acting, but look at you, you haven't given it up at all. You're fantastic. You make all this seem totally normal—buying perishable goods so far from home they'll spoil by the time you get back.

They won't spoil.

I wouldn't put them in the trunk.

She had a point. It had been over ninety degrees that afternoon.

And, Val, she's quite an actress too. If it weren't for the uterus full of baby she's hauling around, I'd never guess she was pregnant.

This is temporary, he said.

Your marriage? Your life?

The pregnancy. This thing we're going through.

Oh, I'm sorry. Right. This is your healthy, mature relationship. Totally different from ours. With you and Val, everything's going to be swell again after week fifteen, right? She's running a little late. With us, everything was going to be dandy just as soon as I bombed in New York, like you figured I would—

Oh come on, that's not fair—

Then we could begin the boring life you'd already started for us with your cute little job and your dapper haircut. I'd have fit into it just perfectly.

Val appeared at the end of the aisle again. "Brad?"

"Cereal," he said aloud. "Do you see the Raisin Bran?"

Domestic bliss, scene two . . .

Val rolled her cart down the aisle, past Kara who waved hello to Val's protruding belly. She picked up a box.

"Thanks," Brad said.

"I'm almost done," she told him.

"I'll get some . . . coffee."

"Don't we have?"

"I'm not sure," he said.

Brad walked to the end of the aisle and turned right in search of coffee. When he found it, Kara was waiting for him. *Regular or decaf?* she asked.

What do you want?

I'm simply buying groceries in Garner, like you. How do you know dead people haven't been shopping in Garner, North Carolina, for centuries?

Is this about my marriage? Is that why you keep visiting? To get between me and Val?

I would never.

Really?

Not in a million years.

You called one week before my wedding and left a message saying you wanted to move back to North Carolina and marry me.

Kara stared back at him for a moment in silence. Another customer, an older man, rolled past and through Kara with his cart. She didn't flinch. *It was two weeks,* she said.

You called twice.

Okay, fine.

Were you trying to ruin my life?

No. I meant what I said at the time.

I don't believe you.

You half-believe me.

No, I don't.

You half-believed me then.

That was a horrible thing to do.

Yet you wonder what would have happened if you'd called me back.

No, he said. I do not.

Then why are we having this conversation?

Val was back with the cart. "Are you ready?" she asked.

Kara was gone. Brad was holding coffee in his hand. French vanilla flavored, which Kara had liked and Brad couldn't stand.

"You know, I think you're right," he said. "We may have coffee at home." And he put the coffee back and followed Val to the checkout.

※

They were seated in the front row of the audience, so Gwen's feet actually rested on the stage. It was a small black box theater with five rows of seating on three sides of the stage, and the audience only looked about half-full. When the show began, the lights came up on a figure not ten feet in front of Gwen, a woman entirely encased in bright yellow gauze with a giant red bow over her head. A spotlight focused on the figure for a long minute, then from offstage came the sound of a young girl's laughter. The spotlight moved to follow the girl's entrance. She was wearing a leotard, and she picked up the loose end of the gauze from the floor and began running in circles around the yellow figure, unwrapping it from the bottom up. Light flooded the stage now, and the sound of the girl's laughter continued over the sound system.

The woman's legs were bare, and when the gauze reached the woman's upper thighs, Gwen found herself breathless until she saw a hand frozen in place over the woman's privates. The girl on stage flagged a bit as she unwrapped the torso, then picked up speed again, running in circles to unwrap the woman's chest, which was also covered by a carefully placed arm and hand. Gwen was watching the woman in profile, so she could see that the actress was wearing flesh-colored panties and a bra, but they were subtle. The woman's body was fully revealed before the girl pulled off the bow, which had been held over the woman's face with a red stocking mask.

The woman had long blond hair and bright red lips, and exposed, she still did not change her position. From around her came a cast of men whom Gwen hadn't noticed creeping onstage and through the audience doors: one man in a suit, one in a cowboy hat, one in a police uniform, one in a bathing suit. A teenage boy about Gwen's age walked past the little girl, giving her a glance, before leering at the blond woman.

The giggling continued over the sound system, and men passed within a couple of feet of Gwen. They circled the figure. They circled more closely. The woman blinked occasionally but otherwise stared straight ahead. At first, none of the swarming men touched the woman; then the cowboy removed his hat, bent his knees, and ran his tongue up the woman's stomach. Cymbals crashed offstage, the lights went out, and Gwen felt a breeze as the actors rushed past her to set the next scene.

Kara hadn't been in this show, Steve had said. But she'd been in shows at this theater. Steve had seen one a few months ago. "Not the kind of thing you'd tell your mom about, and hardly Broadway, but you can't say she wasn't acting."

The next scene had words. The blonde was clothed now, hair in a bun. She wore a green and white polka dot dress, and she was talking on the phone while spanking the teenage boy in the rear with a flyswatter. The boy was bent over a table, and the woman was leaning on the table's edge. Gwen wondered if Kara had ever worn that dress or sat at that table. "No, I'm sorry, I'm terribly busy tonight," the woman said into the phone receiver. SWACK went the flyswatter. "I understand. It sounds lovely. I only wish I could." SWACK against the boy's behind.

"Was Kara's show anything like this?" Gwen whispered.

"Yeah, same general idea," Steve whispered back. "It was over my head too."

Over his head or just plain awful, Gwen thought. Seemed like the latter. But then she hesitated. Looking at slides with her class or walking through the museum, she was often tempted to write something off as terrible, but then she had to ask why it was in the museum or worth a fortune. Sometimes she could see merits in the work if she thought about it or if Lionel or one of the other teachers started talking about it, giving it context. But then sometimes Gwen still thought it was a piece of crap, even if it did cost half a million dollars. One of her teachers said it was important to consider art that tested boundaries. But she also said each viewer was entitled to an opinion; there was no point in studying or producing art if you had none.

"Do you take my woman-sex?" the actress asked loudly.

Gwen hoped Kara had never uttered a line like that. But the fact that Kara had never mentioned she was doing a show had to mean something.

Of course, actors worked in all kinds of places. Kara once said she envied Gwen for painting because you could just do it. No one had to give you permission. It didn't require a million people—a writer, director, stage manager, actors, an audience. You paint on your own. And a year later, the painting is still there. You can even fix it if you want to.

Gwen had thought Kara was just patronizing her, patting her on the back, but maybe she meant it. Everyone in this show probably wanted to be on Broadway. And somebody might get discovered. It was New York. You never knew who could be in the audience. Gwen looked around. It was hard to tell if anyone there was important; nobody looked special. But somebody in the show might go on to be in a movie one day or on Broadway.

Somebody maybe, but not most of them.

Earlier in the week, Gwen's class had toured a few Soho galleries, and Lionel asked how many of the students expected to have a show there one day. Three-quarters of the students raised their hands—Stephanie, Molly, and Richard, among them. But not Gwen. Obviously, it won't happen for so many of you, Lionel had said. It's talent, luck, dedication, perseverance. It's a lot of things. But it's important for you to believe in yourself. That's a big part of it, too.

It was going to take a whole lot more than believing for Molly or Stephanie to ever have a show in Soho, Gwen thought.

Lionel's speech had reminded Gwen of cheerleader tryouts. She'd only tried out at her mother's insistence. Each of the girls had to scream, "Who thinks the Greenwood Park Mudcats are going to crush the Silar Mill Warriors?" and then the other girls would sit in the bleachers and clap and yell, like people did at real football games. Even though the Greenwood Park Mudcats *never* crushed the Silar Mill Warriors. It was a stupid rivalry. Gwen could hear the hollowness in her voice when it was her turn to shout the line, and she was glad to be part of the first round of cuts. Her mother had tried to coach Gwen at home, but it was hopeless. They were talking about two different teams anyway. In her mother's day, the Mudcats often did crush the Warriors—they were regional champions—plus her mother had one particular player she was cheering for: her soon-to-be husband. Very soon-to-be. She was pregnant with Kara at sixteen. So much for Mom's cheerleading fantasies.

Gwen was glad she didn't have any preconceptions about where she'd be when she was older. She didn't expect to be a successful actress or a professional cheerleader or a famous artist. She was one of a million people who could paint a decent picture. That didn't mean anything.

"Who is the answer is the answer is who," called out an actor on the stage.

And the other actors responded, "Who is the answer is the answer is who."

Gwen tried to imagine Kara as a member of the cast, perhaps playing the part of that woman in the back who was wearing a black evening dress and dishwashing gloves. Had Kara tried out for this play? Would she have been in it now if she were still alive?

"What is the answer is the answer is what," the cast chanted.

Funny to think that, had Kara made different decisions, instead of being here—or dead—she might be back in Chapel Hill, pregnant with Brad's baby. Probably not his first either. She'd met him when she was Gwen's age. When their mother was eighteen, she already had a child and was married to a man she'd known since kindergarten.

Did Gwen already know the love of her life? Would she meet him soon? In days? Weeks? Was there any chance she'd end up with him when all was said and done? The Tinsley women didn't have a great success rate. She was probably doomed to move on to Plan B. Randy. Steve.

Toby?

He'd left a voicemail on Kara's phone: "Hey chick, did you call me the other day? I got a message from a 910 area code saying it was your *sister* . . ." Gwen hadn't decided what to do.

Though she had done one thing. She had asked Steve about Toby at dinner before the show. "Toby? Yeah, I heard of him. He was a guy she worked with, another waiter. A drag queen," he added. "She used to go to his shows." Gwen had blushed when Steve said this, and for a moment she wondered if she'd misinterpreted Toby's exchanges with Kara, but then she covered a smile with her hand. No, she felt certain there was something going on. It was as if Kara had shared a wicked secret with Gwen, one they were keeping from Steve.

For the final scene of the show, the blond woman was back on-stage again, naked, or so it seemed, covering herself while the little girl laughed and circled her, wrapping her up again in yellow gauze. It was this scene that Gwen chose to recreate in her art class on Monday: the girl running with a trail of loose yellow gauze behind her, the giant ribbon waiting nearby in a menacing red. Back home, Gwen hated painting people because her classmates and her teacher knew everyone she knew. "That doesn't look like your mother," they'd say. Even if it wasn't supposed to be her mother. Or, "I bet that's Trudy. Is it? Is it Trudy? Or is it your sister? What's her name, Karen?"

Here, no one knew the people in her world or cared who she was painting. So Gwen made the woman's blond hair brown and turned the eyes and cheekbones into Kara's.

"Who do we have here?" Lionel asked near the end of class.

"An actress," Gwen said.

"This is wonderful," he told her. "You don't know if the

woman's being mummified or if she's going into a cocoon." He stared at the painting over Gwen's shoulder, and she looked at her own work now too. She liked the way he articulated it. She felt right to have chosen this exact moment for her image, and she was pleased with the way she'd included the edge of the audience in the shadows. She'd painted her own sandals sticking out onto the stage, and Steve's sneakers beside her.

"I like what you've done with the face," Lionel added. "The way she's holding her lips. It's like she has a secret."

Gwen could no longer suppress a proud grin.

She does, Gwen thought. And when he stepped away, Gwen pulled Kara's phone out of her purse and, using it, typed out a message to Toby: "I'm dead. Call my sister back."

CHAPTER SIX

IT WAS FOUR IN THE MORNING, AND WHILE MARGOT WAS PREHEATING THE OVENS and brewing coffee, she tabbed through photos on her phone. Mike in his uniform waving hello, Mike on a boat blowing a kiss, Mike lying in his bunk, Mike's lips on the camera screen. When he first left, she and Mike exchanged corny photos like these a lot. Then one day she decided to be a little racy and surprise him with a picture of her cleavage, but she was holding the phone upside down and ended up sending a photo of the overhead light fixture in her bathroom. That changed the tone of things; it was hard to send a serious photo after that. It became Mike sticking out his tongue, Mike crossing his eyes. For a couple of weeks, he sent nothing but pictures of light fixtures.

She only had four photos of him in New York, all taken the week before he left: two of him standing by himself in her living room, and two of them together, their faces squished close, smiling, the camera held an arm's length away. Margot stared at the one that wasn't blurry. This was it. Why hadn't she taken any more in the five months they'd been physically together? Why hadn't she thought about it? She had albums filled with photos of Kara. Physical albums. They were fifteen years younger in most of the pictures, but still there was something to look at. Proof of their time together, documentation of their friendship.

The coffeemaker stopped spitting out water, and Margot poured her first mug and a bowl of cereal. She's stopped eating muffins for breakfast long ago. Her phone sat beside her bowl on the kitchen table. No blinking light. No envelope.

On the drive home from Russell and Lissy's house last week, Margot had phoned Mike, but she got his voicemail. Then when she got home, she found an email from him waiting for her. Yes, he was going to Afghanistan, he said. He'd been planning to tell her. He just hadn't found the right moment. And now the timing was crummy because he was going to be out of touch for a few days, and he knew she'd want to talk. Sorry. Hang in there. Blah blah blah. Some other apologetic bullshit.

How did this not drive people crazy? They couldn't even have a decent fucking argument without some vague and indefinite interruption.

She wrote back asking when he would be free.

Two days passed before the slow-motion dialogue continued, Mike writing, "Still away—but glad dinner went well. BTW don't believe ANYTHING my Dad said about me :)"

Ba-dum-bum? Was she supposed to reply, "Ha ha"? She couldn't do it. She sat with the message for a day, then told him not to worry about waking her, to call as soon as he could.

Meanwhile, the television, radio, and Internet spared no opportunity to inform Margot about violence in the Middle East, deaths in Afghanistan, another kidnapping. Or to report on someone in New York or elsewhere whose rape, murder, or abduction was especially newsworthy. The anchor would lower his voice according to the formula, report the latest bit of horribleness, play quotes from a family member, someone saying she was so surprised; then on to the next topic. It was such a familiar sequence, it made the violence seem trite.

Her laptop continued to count down unknowingly. This morning it said five months, one week, and one day. But that wasn't true anymore. And all those faces of people's kids on her refrigerator were becoming less of a comfort. Would those ever be pictures of her kids? Pictures of her husband? What if—

Her mind conjured a coffin, but the one she pictured was the one she'd seen so recently: Kara's. Mike's would have to be wider. He had big shoulders, and his would be a military funeral. A flag appeared draped over it.

No, she needed to stop. Losing him would be too much.

Which would be worse—losing Mike or losing Kara?

Who *thinks* these things?

Margot dropped her spoon into the half-finished cereal bowl and gave up. Kara was gone. There was no going backward. That part of her past was over. But Mike, to lose him now—he'd become so much a part of her everyday life, part of who she was and who she wanted to be. She'd pictured their future together, family vacations, Halloweens with children dressed up in butterfly costumes.

He'd told her it was almost inconceivable he'd end up in Afghanistan, and he'd promised, *promised* to say something if it was a possibility. Was it mandatory? Did he volunteer?

He'd lied to her, too. She'd checked on the Internet and saw that people in the military needed to jump every three months in order to keep their "jump pay." He had to have done it more recently than December, even though he'd said his jumping had slowed down. Margot didn't know if she was more frightened or angry or hurt. It was too hard to know at four in the morning. She'd been taking hours to fall asleep.

She needed to bake. That was all she knew. Muffins and quick breads and cookies. There was a double chocolate cake she'd made the night before, and she took it out of the fridge so it could return to room temperature. A kid from the neighborhood was stopping by at six to help her with deliveries. It beat mowing lawns. She pulled out the food processor.

Then she saw him out of the corner of her eye on the breakfast table. He'd arrived quietly, as he so often did. His *hello* sat above the blinking cursor on her computer screen.

She was too drained to beat around the bush. "When do you go?" she asked.

There was a pause. Then, "I was going to tell you," he wrote back.

"So tell me," she typed.

"Why don't we Skype? Hang on."

A beeping startled Margot. It was one of the ovens preheating. She ignored it. Instead she found her purse, pulled out a brush, and ran it through her hair halfheartedly. When the computer began to chime, she sat down again at the breakfast table and a moment later was looking at Mike's face on the screen.

"Hi," he said, and he gave her a little smile.

"Hi," she said, and she couldn't help smiling back.

It was always a relief to see his face, handsome and intact. The dimple on his left cheek above the square jawline. His blue-grey eyes so often on the verge of laughter. Though not today.

"I'm sorry," he said, clearing his throat. "I really am."

Margot nodded. It could be a little awkward too, talking to him. Hearing each other's voices, when so many of their interactions involved type and shorthand and misspellings and endless pauses.

"I'll be heading over in the next few weeks."

"For how long?"

"Probably a year, maybe a little more."

"Another year . . . ?" she repeated. The words got stuck in her throat and came out in almost a whisper.

"But then I'm out."

"I feel like I've heard that before. Was it mandatory?"

He hesitated. "I wasn't forced to go, but I was strongly encouraged."

Margot swallowed.

"I've been wanting to tell you," he said.

"Well, you know how to reach me," she said, finding her voice. "Seems like this wasn't top-secret stuff. What was all that bullshit about 'code words'? Were you making fun of me?"

"I wasn't making fun of you. I was just . . . letting it be one of those off-limits topics."

Margot sniffled. She was starting to cry. She didn't mean to, but God, she felt like an idiot. She rubbed her eyes. She probably looked terrible. "Do you know I haven't eaten eggplant in over a year?" she found herself saying.

"I'm sorry."

"*Obviously* for no reason."

He nodded.

"And did you have a jump recently?" she asked.

He looked surprised for a moment, then said, "I did."

Margot sighed and bit her lip to keep what was inside from coming out.

"I don't want to be a constant source of worry for you," Mike told her. "You didn't sign up for this. You accidentally met me, and I happened to be in the Army."

"What are you talking about? Everyone 'accidentally' meets everyone."

"But it's not always convenient."

I'm an inconvenience to him, she thought. But she didn't say it.

"We only have so much time to talk," he continued. "It can't all be about you asking me what I'm doing that might kill me. I do what I'm trained to do. It's more dangerous than working in an office or baking muffins, but there are a lot of people stationed here. And there. It's not that bad."

"Will we even be able to talk?"

"Sure. I mean, it might be more difficult. But I don't want every conversation we have for the next year to be a check-in—me reassuring you that I'm not dead yet. That's not fair to you. It's not fair to me either."

Now Margot was really crying. She grabbed a napkin off the table to wipe her eyes. "I don't like you seeing me like this."

"I'm glad to see you any way I can," he said.

Margot snorted in reply.

"I run communications," Mike added.

"So you say," Margot mumbled.

"There are a lot more dangerous things people do around here. Have you really not been smoking?"

"Don't tempt me."

"I'll take that as a no. Just . . . think about it."

Margot balled the napkin in her hand and swallowed. "What am I thinking about?"

"If this is too much. I don't want to be this source of pain for you."

"Then don't lie to me."

"I don't want to. I just wish . . ."

"That we could always talk about Uncle Bernie?" she said.

"No. But a little Bernie is a good thing. How is the old guy, by the way?"

"Oh, shut up."

"I'm serious."

"He's dead."

"No, he's not."

"Well, he's sick. He's got the flu. And horrible diarrhea. He's been on the toilet for days."

"Margot?"

"What?"

"Think about it. I'm going to be out of touch for another little bit—"

"Of course . . ."

"See what I mean? This is what I do. Think about it."

It didn't take long for Toby to call back. Gwen was sitting at a deli on her lunch break when her phone lit up. The conversation probably lasted sixty seconds. She wanted to see him in person. "I only have a minute," she lied. "Are you free later on?"

"Yeah, sure," he said in that half-familiar voice. "Any time before nine."

"Great, let's meet for coffee at seven thirty. You pick the place."

He named a coffee shop in Hell's Kitchen, she scribbled down the address, and she arrived there five minutes late, knowing he would be early. He rose the moment she walked in the door. He recognized her. She would have recognized him.

He had deep olive skin and black hair cropped almost into a crew cut. His cheeks were unshaven, but in an intentional-looking way, the same way his fraying blazer and ripped jeans looked like they'd been carefully damaged by designers. He was tall and thin, and his clothes were fitted to his body. Around his neck he wore a thick silver chain.

"Gwen?" he said.

His eyes were dark too, sad and penetrating.

"I'm so sorry about your sister."

His voice sounded even deeper in person.

He wanted to know what had happened, so she told him about the overdose, the funeral in North Carolina.

"When was this?"

"May thirteenth."

"Damn, that was right after I left. I think I had a show that night. I've been leaving messages for her, I thought she was blowing me off."

"I know," Gwen told him. "I have her phone."

Toby bought her a cup of coffee and got a refill for himself, and when they were settled back in their seats again, she asked how long he'd known Kara.

"A few months," he said. "Well, actually—shit, if she died in May, I guess not even that. Maybe six weeks or so." They'd met at her restaurant. He was having dinner, and she was his server, and they were kind of flirting all through the meal. He had a show that night, and he had his guitar with him—Toby leaned down now and tapped something beside him against the wall: a guitar case, she hadn't noticed it before—and after dinner, when he'd paid the bill, he invited Kara to see his band perform. She showed up during the second set, after the restaurant closed. "It wasn't any-thing serious," Toby added. "But we had fun."

Gwen considered her words as she sipped her drink. "Did you know she was seeing someone else at the time?" she asked.

Toby didn't say anything for a moment. Then he said, "I did not." He dropped his eyes to the table and took his coffee mug in his hand. "But that's cool," he continued. "Like I said, we were just having fun."

"She was actually living with someone," Gwen added.

"Really?" Toby said. "Huh. Well, everyone's responsible for their own actions. I didn't mean anyone any disrespect. We just—" Then he stopped. "Wait. Mullet?"

Gwen didn't understand.

"The guy she was living with. The dude with the mullet?"

Gwen thought for a second. Actually, Steve did have a mullet. It was more specific than generically bad hair. She nodded, and Toby raised a fist to his mouth to half-cover a smile. "Wow," he said. "I didn't catch that. She always said she didn't want to go back to her place because her roommate was weird about having people in his space. She did not say Mullet was her boyfriend."

Now it was Gwen's turn to drop her gaze. "He's pretty nice, actually."

"Like I said, I don't mean anyone any disrespect. I'm just saying what she told me."

Gwen nodded. And she could believe that's what Kara would

have said. Kara's old roommate Collin had turned into "a self-absorbed nightmare." Brad had become "a chicken-shit yuppie." Their mother, when Kara was arguing with her, was "nothing but small-town and small-minded." Gwen herself had had many labels applied to her, "baby" and "immature" chief among them, which was funny, now that Gwen thought about it. Being called "immature" by your twenty-something-year-old sister while you're in elementary school. Of course you're immature.

"So what's your deal?" Toby asked. "You live in New York now?"

"Just for the summer." Gwen told him about the art program, the time she was supposed to have spent with Kara.

"Did you go to a school for the arts back home?"

"No," she said.

"I did," he told her. "For high school. It was cool. But that was a long time ago."

Gwen studied his face and wondered how long. He was much older than her, but younger than Kara. Was he twenty-seven? Thirty? She asked.

"Twenty-nine," he said. "Still hanging onto my twenties," he added with a grin.

Toby had a show that night and needed to eat, so he bought them both sandwiches. When he sat down again, he took off his jacket, and Gwen saw he had a tattoo on the inside of his left forearm: a snake, slithering toward the palm of his hand. He told her about his tour with Screaming Planet, which he said was sort of a cross between Maroon 5 and Pink with a little vintage B-52's thrown in. They're cool, he said. He was supposed to head down to New Orleans with them in a few months.

He'd been to North Carolina a couple of times, he said, not with Screaming Planet, but with a band he was in before, the Mayflower. They'd played in Asheville and Chapel Hill and Charlotte. Was Greenwood Park anywhere near there? Not really, she said. But she was going to college in Chapel Hill, she told him. That's cool, he said. That's where Kara went, right? Yep, she said.

"What are you doing after this?" he asked.

"Nothing," Gwen said. "Going home, I guess."

"Come see my show," he said

The request caught her by surprise.

"I'm filling in with Colored Sparks," he continued. "They're not brilliant, but they're alright, and they love me." He smiled. "They give me all sorts of time to ham it up. You should come. It's only a few blocks away."

She hesitated. "Can I even get in? I'm eighteen."

"You'll come in with me," he said. "It's done."

And so it was. They finished their sandwiches and walked together toward the club. Outside, Gwen felt older. Decidedly unimmature. She pictured herself as others probably pictured her, a young woman walking down the street with a guy in a band. Like she did this kind of thing all the time, was familiar with Screaming Planet and the Colored Something-or-another. She was someone who went to see concerts in the middle of the week.

Gwen pulled out a cigarette, and after she'd taken a puff, Toby said, "That's bad for you, you know?"

"So I've read," she replied.

Then he pulled the cigarette from her lips and took a puff. "Mmm," he said. "I quit. Now I only smoke other people's cigarettes, which doesn't count, right?" Gwen rolled her eyes. Then he reached over and put the cigarette back between her lips. His fingers touched her mouth for an instant, and Gwen felt herself blushing. But they were standing in a shadow. He probably couldn't see.

Two blocks later, as they approached the bar, Toby put an arm on her shoulder and walked her past the doorman. Inside, the bar was filled with the kind of furniture that was either found on the street or carefully distressed like Toby's jeans. She wondered how much money he made—a lot, or not much at all. For some reason, she felt certain it was one or the other, but nothing in between.

Time passed quickly. She was introduced to people whose names escaped her moments after she'd met them—members of the band, friends of the band, friends of theirs—and she took a seat at the end of a table occupied by some of them.

Soon the band started to play on the platform a few feet away, and there was no point in worrying about small talk. It was loud. Very loud. And Toby was a ham, as promised. He'd squeeze his brows as he hit a chord, then he'd toss his head back. His lips would form a snarl for part of an angry melody, then he'd inch his tongue out as they shifted into a raucous chorus. His body would hunch over sometimes, then pull back, making him taller than everyone else on stage. His T-shirt was snug and looked like it had been washed too many times, and when he pulled himself back, Gwen could see a small line of skin and black hair between the bottom of his shirt and the top of his jeans. Sometimes, Toby would catch her eye. Twice, he winked at her.

During a break between sets, she said she liked the show and he said it was okay, and as he stood beside her and talked to some other people from her table, Gwen could smell his sweat. It didn't smell like the twins after soccer practice, or the hallway outside the boys' locker room in high school, or Randy after mowing the lawn. It smelled different. Maybe because there was a tinge of cologne behind it. Or maybe that was just how Toby smelled.

She sat through another four songs and thought about how simple her life seemed back in Greenwood Park and how it felt complicated now in a way she couldn't describe. She was tempted to stay through the entire show, but nervous as well, and she was relieved when she checked her phone and saw it was after midnight. She had a field trip at nine in the morning. She needed to get back. So she mimed good-bye to the people at her table and walked back toward the exit. Toby saw her from the stage and gave her a comic, inquisitive look, and she pointed at her watch—then felt stupid, because she wasn't actually wearing a watch, she realized—but he got the message and rolled his eyes, and then a woman at one of the back tables turned around to see who the handsome guitar player was talking to.

Me, Gwen said with her smile.

The woman turned back to the show.

During the train ride home, a part of Gwen wanted to think about Kara, how she'd juggled two men, maybe more. But then most of Gwen—which won out—preferred not to think about Kara at all.

＊

Sophie stuck her head into Brad's office, her hair an explosion of auburn, her earrings large red flowers. "What do you think of my new assistant?" she asked. Brad was relieved the question was about work and not about Val.

"He seems fine," Brad said.

She walked a few steps into his office. "He looks at my breasts constantly."

Brad lowered his eyes to her chest. Sophie did tend to wear shirts that showcased her breasts. "They're nice," he said.

"Oh, I don't hold it against him. A woman reaches a certain age—"

"You're not 'a certain age.'"

"I'm almost 'a certain age.' I'm thirty-nine. He's twenty-two. I could be his Mrs. Robinson."

Brad smiled, or half-smiled. Or started to.

"He's not a racist," she added. "That joke John told in the kitchen." Sophie shrugged. "He was just kidding."

Racist? Brad tried to remember. There'd been a moment in the kitchen, a few people standing around, a few jokes. "I didn't think anything," he said. And then for good measure, Brad added, "He's nice, John. A funny guy."

"Okay. You didn't look like you were amused. You had that same scowl on your face."

"Scowl?"

"Lighten up, honey."

Had it come to this? Brad waved away Sophie's concern and forced a smile.

Or that's what he meant to do. But the muscles in his face didn't respond.

"Everything okay at home?" Sophie asked.

Brad swallowed, then tried again to push the corners of his cheeks outward. He envisioned himself smiling. He thought the word "smile." But he couldn't make his face do it.

"You okay?"

He couldn't smile.

"Huh?"

"At home? Everything okay at home?"

How can a person not be able to smile?

"Sure," he said. His voice cracked.

"How's my girl? God, I haven't seen Val in ages. She feeling better?"

He felt himself starting to sweat. "What?"

"Over that cold? We were supposed to get drinks after school ended, but she got that awful cold . . ."

"Oh, yeah. It's . . . lingering."

Here he might have inserted another smile, to punctuate the lie, to make light of it. But nothing. He felt his cheeks just hanging there.

"Okay, well, tell her I was thinking about her. And tell her I know she's screening my calls too, okay?"

"Sure."

"I'll tell John you don't think he's a racist."

"I don't think he's a racist."

"His sister's boyfriend is half-Korean."

"That's . . . great."

As soon as Sophie walked out, Brad rose from his desk to close the door behind her. Then he turned to his framed college diploma, which hung beside the door, and examined his reflection in the glass. His face was blank. When he tried to smile, the corners of his mouth moved almost imperceptibly, forming what was at best a grimace.

He opened his mouth and closed it. Then he did it again. That was fine. Again. Fine. Again. He massaged his cheeks—he didn't know why, maybe to work out a spasm?—and then he tried to smile, but the result was no better. He'd lost control of the muscles in his cheeks.

With his fingers, Brad pushed the corners of his mouth back, then let go, hoping the expression would hold, but it didn't. Twice. Three times. Four. Next he tried to wink, but all he saw in the glass was a tiny vibration in his cheek and a slight twitch in his eye.

What else should a person be able to do? He wiggled his chin left and right, could feel the movement in his jaw. That was okay. Then he tried to raise his upper lip into a snarl, but nothing happened. It was just an idea of a snarl, an image in his head. No response on his face. He might as well have been willing himself to fly.

Brad turned to face his office. He half-expected to see Kara—more than half-expected—but he was afraid, too. And alone. With myasthenia gravis, the generalized form. Of course that's what it was. How could he have been so naive as to hope it would limit itself to his eyes? It showed up in the eyes first for plenty of people, but then it moved on to affect muscles in the face, the throat, the chest, all over. Once it proved to be more than an eye problem, it could be a much bigger problem, and here it was: his problem. Now it was done, over. It was just a question of how bad it would get, to what extent it would dominate the rest of his life.

Brad felt something in his eyes now, water, tears, blurring the doubled images to which he was becoming so accustomed: his twin computer monitors, calendars, pencil cups, office chairs. He wished Val were there. He wished she could tell him to sit beside her. She would pet his shoulder, take his hand, and tell him they were in this together. She'd cite some statistic, a study that had been conducted, the odds of this and that and the other, and everything would sound like it made sense to someone at least.

But Val wasn't there. Not in his office, and what could he possibly say to her when he got home? What could he expect her to say back? At this point. She still wasn't herself, and he wasn't himself either. And now he was even less of himself. So much less.

"I can't . . ." he said, dropping into his chair, and he told himself to rest. Rest, that's what the doctor would say. Close your eyes. Give your muscles a few minutes to rest.

Someone knocked at the door.

Please, God, go away.

Another knock. "You on the phone?" Then silence. Then more silence.

Brad took a deep breath and closed his eyes.

"I can't . . ." he whispered. He kept his eyes closed for a long time. When he opened them, no one was there.

※

Margot was making deliveries to some of her twice-a-week customers in Queens and Brooklyn. Her delivery boy had taken care of Long Island that morning, and he'd offered to make this run too, but Margot needed to get out of the house. She was hoping a little New York traffic could get her out of her own head, and she'd cut off a couple of taxi drivers just for sport.

She hadn't heard from Mike since their Skype conversation a few days ago. Still no word from Russell either, but those silences felt connected. If Russell did learn anything from the Brooklyn police, he might tell Mike and leave it to him to pass on the news. Maybe they'd spoken already. Maybe Mike would be calling her soon. What would he say about Mullet, and about them?

What would she say? She didn't know.

So Margot was trying to keep busy. She'd found dried apricots on sale and bought ten bags, and she'd been inserting them into cookies and crushing them into cake filling. There were apricot mascarpone muffins, apricot pecan blondie dessert bars, apricot chocolate banana muffins. Lots of fiber in apricots. Margot's stomach was having some regrets.

And Margot's mind—when it wasn't inventing new things to do with apricots, or worrying about Afghanistan, or imagining what Russell might learn about Mullet—was stuck replaying bits of conversation, like a sadistic record player with its needle trapped in a groove: "I don't want to be a constant source of worry for you." "You accidentally met me." "It's not always convenient."

It wasn't convenient. It wasn't at all convenient. And he *was* a cause of worry for her; there was no getting around it. But how could he not be? And did he really imagine she'd trade the worrying for nothing?

Or was his asking a way of signaling he was ready for their relationship to end? Because having to be accountable to her, to worry about her, to lie to her or not lie—that was inconvenient, too.

Margot merged onto the Brooklyn-Queens Expressway and found herself remembering the times she and Mike had spent jumping waves at Jones Beach. It wasn't far from her house; they'd gone a few times. They would wade out into the deep water together, giggling as their feet left the ground, but it only took a moment for the current to buffet them back to the shallow waters.

It was a little like that with their relationship. They spent so much of it ankle-deep. If she asked him too many questions, Uncle Bernie came out. Any attempt at sexual innuendo inevitably turned to humor—because "What are you wearing?" left too much to the imagination. It was too tempting to say "Superman Underoos" or "A sailor's hat and feather boa." For both of them. And yet, what did she expect? How deep could they go with him on another continent, living in a different reality?

Back in her twenties, she'd had flings that lasted longer than five months. They weren't as intense, of course, but she'd dated people on and off for a few months and known it would go nowhere. With Mike she could picture Sunday mornings together and growing old, but there was no guarantee he pictured the same. Maybe that was the trouble—too much of their relationship was in her head. Maybe she was just some fat girl Mike had banged between tours of duty. It was amusing to keep in touch with her for a while, but now she was becoming a nuisance. Maybe that's all it was. All she was.

These were the thoughts that made apricots so attractive. Raspberry apricot cake filling, thumbprint cookies with apricot preserves, apricot walnut pear bread. Margot glanced down at her phone again. Nothing.

She timed her stops so she'd end at Java Jones. Collin had gotten the owner to start ordering muffins from her. It was nice of him, and she was relieved to see a friendly face. "Hey, Sugarplum!" he called to her when she walked in the door. "Your mixed berry muffins were selling like hotcakes, if hotcakes tasted like mixed berry muffins. Give me a hug."

He wasn't kidding. They'd sold out of the first batch in one day. He loaded up his cabinet with the day's delivery and asked to double his order for next week. And to put chocolate chips in the banana nut muffins—or at least in one, for him.

It was strange to talk about muffins with someone she'd recently thought of as a horrible influence on Kara. Not long ago, before Margot and Kara would buy hair dye and spend way too much time applying it and ruining Margot's towels, Kara and Collin would be out ingesting questionable substances and doing things they wouldn't remember in the morning. But here he was now, and here was Margot, and they were engaged in a thoughtful conversation about the virtues of semisweet chips over milk chocolate, the muffins that people preferred in Brooklyn versus Long Island.

"And who likes strawberry apricot poppy seed muffins?" Collin asked. "No offense, but that's a lot of words."

"It's a new recipe," Margot said. "Call it an 'apricot surprise.'"

The "surprise" postscript had been used to explain away many an all-night baking jag.

"Did you hear back from your policeman friend?"

"No," she said. "Still waiting. Anyone ever find the elusive Toby?"

"No sightings yet. I guess he must still be on the road. Honey, sit down, you look tired—are you doing alright?"

Margot told him she hadn't gotten much sleep lately. Then she told him about Mike. "I don't even know what to think anymore," she concluded.

"Do you love him?" Collin asked.

"I do. Is that ridiculous?"

"Of course not. Do you think he loves you?"

"I thought so. Now . . . I don't know. I feel like all this time he's been shutting me out and I didn't even know it."

"Well, I guess he was, in a way. But you got more sleep when he did, right?" Collin tossed his hair back and sighed. "When my dad was sick a few years ago, he said he wasn't going to tell me all the gory details. There were unpleasant things happening inside him, and they would kill him one day, but that wasn't really a surprise to either of us, so he just wanted to talk about my life instead. Actually, he said he wanted to talk about the 'non-queer' things in my life. Imagine if I'd been in this show, flailing around a prosthetic cock eight times a week. He'd have loved that. Do you know my understudy is an actual stripper? This is the caliber show I'm in."

"Is he cute?"

"No. Mildly. Yeah." Collin smiled.

"My mom had cancer a few years back," Margot told him. "I did know the gory details."

Collin reached over and squeezed Margot's hand. It was strange how something little like that could be such a comfort. Before Mike, no one had squeezed her hand in ages. Since he'd left, she could only imagine his touch. Sometimes it was difficult to remember.

"I actually didn't know all the gory details with Kara," Margot added after a minute. "I didn't see that side of her . . . the drug part. I always saw her later, the next day, when she was feeling hungover and guilty."

"And hungry," Collin added. "Tired, stupid. Smelly. I know that feeling well. I didn't see her as the overdose type—but I guess we were both probably too trusting, and sloppy. Who knows whose drugs we were taking or what was in them? Lord knows we didn't spend much money on them."

"I used to wonder how she could afford . . ."

"Oh honey, she couldn't. She didn't pay for much besides pot, the occasional tab of ecstasy. The one time she and I spent any real money, we bought a good size bag of coke and lost it in the bathroom of a bar within two hours. It was classic. 'I thought you had it.' We were like two idiots in a sitcom. No, we used to call ourselves 'opportunistic users'—which means 'poor.' Or 'cheap' or 'lazy.' But people had a tendency to share—coke or pills or whatever. It was fun for a while, and it's not like we did it all the time. Mostly, we just drank too much vodka and laughed at people."

"We did our share of that in college."

"She was good at that."

For a moment they sat together with their memories, then the door opened, bringing them back to the present.

"I should let you get back to work," she said.

"Okay," he said, giving her hand another squeeze. "It was good to see you. Good luck with your military man. I hope things work out."

"Thank you. Me too. Have a good show tonight." She was almost outside when she called back across the coffee shop, "Good luck with the stripper." Two customers looked up from their reading to see Collin blush.

※

When Brad returned home from his last showing on Sunday evening, the table was set with bright blue and yellow floral dishes that he hadn't seen in some time. There were fresh flowers in a ceramic vase that Val's mother had given them for one of their early anniversaries, and Brad smelled something cooking that he knew he hadn't brought home from the grocery store. He walked into the kitchen and peeked into the oven: steak and red potatoes. On the counter sat a casserole dish filled with brown sugar-glazed carrots, beside a wine glass. There were lipstick marks on the glass, and Val caught him staring at it when she walked in behind him.

"Half a glass for me," she said. "That way I can feel naughty."

She pulled another glass out of a top cabinet and poured Pinot Noir for him. He didn't ask. He followed her lead, clicking his glass to hers. Minutes later they were sitting at the table.

If Val had gone out in public, there was no hiding that belly. Were they celebrating her public unveiling? The end of this awkward hiatus in their lives? They'd just entered week twenty, the halfway point. Maybe this was the milestone Val needed to reach. The pregnancy calendar said she'd start to feel the baby kick any time now. Had she felt it? Would she start having regular reminders directly from the baby that he—or she—was alive and well in there?

Brad was curious, but he didn't want to push her. It had taken her a while to get to this point. He wanted to let her enjoy the moment and tell him in her own way.

So as they began their salads, he told her about the offers he'd made—two in one day. The couple moving down from Roanoke was offering too little; the seller probably would counter. But the other couple—had he mentioned them, a sweet couple about to have their third child?—they'd offered something just shy of the asking price. The odds were high he'd get a yes tonight. Brad pulled out his phone and set it on the table beside him. Sophie had sold a house that morning, too. This was going to be a good week for the agency.

They moved on to the main course. She'd just gotten a craving, Val said, for red meat. So she'd driven back to Garner—"To *Garner*?" he repeated—to the grocery store where they'd shopped together the other night. "It was laid out so nicely," she said, "and the bakery smelled so good. It was less than an hour's drive, and the weather was nice. I had fun," she said. "Be happy for me. It was your idea."

Brad wasn't thrilled, but he said, "Well, okay, good," and he started to give her a smile, but it wasn't turning into a smile. He could feel himself not smiling. He glanced down at the clock on his phone: 8:24. He was an hour overdue for his next pill. Time had a way of disappearing when a sale was imminent. He hoped his face hadn't done anything embarrassing in front of the Roanoke couple.

This was how it had gone for the past few days. When the next dose was due, he could feel it. His vision would sometimes get worse in spite of the glasses, his limbs would begin to feel heavy, and then there was his face. He'd lose control of it.

"Do you like the steak?" she asked.

"I do."

"It's not too tough?"

"No," he told her.

But at the mention of its toughness, his jaws began to tire. He and Val didn't eat steak often; the chewing felt like an unfamiliar chore.

"I left it in the oven a little longer than I meant to. But I think it turned out okay. My mother used to serve it well-done, so it kind of brings back memories."

Brad was still chewing. He'd taken an especially big bite, and it seemed as if it wouldn't go away. He took a sip of water, the meat still in his mouth. Then he chewed again.

"Speaking of my parents," Val said, "I guess this is why they were on my mind . . . I think I'd like to go visit them. For a little while."

Brad looked up.

"I've been thinking about it, and I can't stay home all the time," she continued. "You've said it, and you're right. But I can't go through what we went through last time either."

"But you're healthy," he said.

"What?"

Brad's mouth was still full, so he held a napkin to his face and pretended to wipe while he spit out the meat. "You're healthy," he repeated. "The baby is healthy. It's not the same."

"I know it's not. And I know you think I'm crazy about this, but please let's not argue. It'll be good to see my parents."

"Of course, it'll be good."

"And it'll only be for a few weeks."

"A few weeks?"

"I don't know. I don't want to set up some arbitrary timeline."

It was so rare that Val echoed Kara. She'd said the same thing when she left for New York.

"You can visit," Val added weakly.

"Is this about the beach trip?" Brad asked. "The text from Gwen?"

"No. Well, maybe—a little."

"I told you it was nothing."

"I know, but . . . I felt good today, being far away and out and about. And you're obviously having some difficulty with this . . . this loss of yours. So it got me thinking."

I haven't seen Kara in years, he was about to say—but that wasn't quite true anymore. Brad took a sip of wine to wash down the thought, then discovered that he couldn't swallow.

This hadn't happened before, but he'd read about it. He knew it was a possibility. He was surprised by the chilly calm that came over him, and he tried to think of how a person makes his throat work, what parts of the mouth have to move where.

"Are you okay?" she asked.

He nodded.

"My parents live two doors down from an obstetrician, and my doctor recommended someone . . ."

She paused. It was his turn to say something, to be angry, and he tried to swallow. He insisted that his throat open up, but it would not. So he lifted his wine glass to his mouth as if he were taking another sip, and let the liquid slide back into the glass.

"I thought you were just thinking about this," he said finally. "You've already talked about this with the obstetrician?"

"Well, of course I wanted to run it by her."

"Before talking to me?"

Val missed a beat, then said, "I'm talking to you now."

Brad reached into his pocket for the pillbox, but it was in his jacket, he knew, which was on the chair in his office. He stood up.

"Where are you going?"

"I'll be right back," he said.

"What?"

"I'll be right back."

"I can't understand you. Are you angry? What would you do if you were me?"

His legs didn't feel like legs. They were like long, iron tubes that had to be lifted and dragged. But they had to look like legs. He had to look like a man who was just walking across the room.

"Brad, I'm trying to have a conversation with you. You're not even going to answer me?"

Just a man walking away, out of the dining room, into the living room, all the way across to his office, where he closed the door. He had to close the door. The jacket was on his chair. The pillbox was in his jacket.

He put one pill in his mouth and lifted up a coffee mug from hours earlier and tried to down the pill with a swig of old coffee. But he couldn't swallow. Of course he couldn't swallow. So he let it all spill out into the mug—coffee, pill—and put a new pill in his mouth and held it under his tongue. Then he lay down. Had to lie down. This was good, he thought. It would dissolve. It had to dissolve. He could already taste the bitterness.

"Brad?"

She was outside the door. He was lying on the floor a few feet away from her.

"Can we talk about this?" she asked through the closed door. "I think we should talk about this."

"I need a minute," he called out.

"What?"

"I need a minute."

His words were coming out wrong. It was hard to form the words with his mouth. But she couldn't walk in. He couldn't have her walk in to find her husband lying on the floor incapable of movement or speech. She would panic. She would be terrified. He didn't want to think what that might mean. With all his strength, he formed the words that meant privacy for any real estate agent with a sale imminent: "On the phone," he called out.

"Seriously?" she said. "Brad? *Jesus* . . ."

He could hear her footsteps as she walked away.

Brad lay there beside his desk, the pill under his tongue, and waited. And breathed. Slowly. That was what he needed to do, concentrate on the breathing.

The pill tasted bad, but it wasn't dissolving, not quickly anyway, but it was probably a matter of time. He just needed to relax, let go of the fear, and the anger. He needed to transport himself to a calm place, he imagined his yoga instructor saying, but then the yoga instructor turned into the neurology fellow, who turned into Val's mother, and that wasn't helping, and the pill wasn't dissolving. So he lifted his right arm all the way up, off the ground, then around and down, toward his mouth. He put his index finger into his mouth and pushed on the pill, hoping that would help it dissolve. His finger pressed, wrestled against the pill and his tongue, and she was kissing him the way she always did after a fight, her tongue firm and determined. She was breathing oxygen into him. She circled his tongue with hers. She pulled out for a minute, and he felt a pressure on his chest. Kara's hand. Pressing down on him, shifting her weight, unbuttoning his shirt.

Which was good. The shirt was tight. It was restricting him or—what was the word?—comprecting him, compress . . . She unbuttoned his shirt and tugged his undershirt loose from his pants, and her mouth was on his mouth, and she was opening his belt. He felt her weight on his body, which made it difficult to get a deep breath, but that was okay, because it felt good. It felt heavy but good. I can't . . . *Shh,* she whispered, *just let it all go,* and she unzipped his pants and grabbed hold of him with her cold hand. Brad smiled, and Kara smiled, and she motioned upward with her eyes. They were eighteen years old. No one had touched him before. Margot was asleep on the bunk above them.

Brad lay there in her dorm room while she did the rest, taking off his pants and socks and shoes. She mounted him, and he felt himself convulse. *Easy there, partner,* she said. *At least give me a few minutes.* And as he felt himself squeezed between her legs, as she rocked up and down, her eyes closed, as all of his blood rushed down to be inside her, he forced his mind to think about other things: about the film class they were cutting, the theater history exam that was coming up, the dirty floors of the dorm bathroom, about the shower stall where he wanted to fuck her, the top bunk in his room where he'd fuck her soon too, the costume shop they'd soon discover, its old sofa surely a friend to other couples as well, then the backseat where they'd fuck during a concert, the fire escape of the math building, the golf course they'd find in a few years' time, their apartments together—the shitty one and then the less shitty one. Then the futon in her first New York apartment, which made their shittiest place in Chapel Hill look a lot less shitty.

Easy there, partner, she said. *At least give me a few minutes.* They were twenty-six. It was the last time he'd see her. He let his gaze wander to the nightstand she said she'd found in front of a brownstone three doors down, to the coatrack she'd inherited from the former tenant, to her discarded nightshirt, which said St. Louis Cardinals, although she wasn't a fan, and he wasn't a fan, and he was afraid to ask where she'd gotten it. She squeezed him between her legs—it had been months since they'd touched—and he wondered if this would be the last time it would happen, wondered if and also knew.

Stay with me, she whispered, as she pressed herself more completely around him.

"I can't."

Of course you can, she whispered. She raised herself up and then let herself down, and Brad felt himself disappearing into her. The blood was rushing out of him.

He lay there for a moment, watching her face, her eyes closed but still twittering. She finished. She sighed. She curled around him and pressed against his chest and whispered, *Stay*. He wanted to shake his head no, but he couldn't, or didn't. He fingered the carpet beneath his fingers. *Stay,* she said. He took a careful breath.

Look, she said. She was holding a Playbill now, flipping the pages. *You know how we used to joke about doing shows together? A lot of couples really do. See, they've done four shows together. On Broadway. And another couple—*

She put down the Playbill and draped her arm across his body.

Another couple I met, she continued, *they've been working together for sixteen years.*

She fondled him, teased him. Spent, he writhed from her touch. But her weight against his chest was good—heavy, but good. He could stay here. He could stay with her. If only he believed . . . If only the phone . . .

Stay, she whispered.

"I'm sorry," he said.

The phone.

I'm sorry too, she said. *But I have to be here, and you could be here with me too.*

The phone. He'd said he was on the phone, but he'd left it on the table. She was going to find out he'd lied.

No, she won't, Kara told him.

It'll ring.

No, it won't.

She'll see it when she clears the table.

It doesn't matter. You can stay.

Brad felt under his tongue. His mouth tasted tinny and bitter, but the pill was gone, mostly gone now. Just the remnant of powder lingered. He swallowed. Successfully. The powder went down.

He swallowed again. This time was a test. Slowly, he opened his eyes.

The room was dark. His clothes had been tugged open. The sun was setting through the window.

He stood, tucked in his undershirt, buttoned up his shirt, refastened his belt. He ran his fingers through his hair. He blinked. His vision was imperfect, but not horrible. There was a time when that imperfection had been maddening. That felt like a long time ago.

"Hello," he said to the air. And he heard himself: "Hello," he'd said.

This could happen again, he thought. That's what "hello" meant.

Outside his office, the house was quiet. The living room lights were off, and the kitchen and dining room too. Brad walked into the dining room. Everything had been cleared and put away, except for his phone, which sat in front of his chair, blinking a message, perhaps a sale. He glanced down at the empty chair, and hoped she hadn't discovered what was inside his napkin. Hopefully she'd just thrown it away without seeing he couldn't swallow her overcooked steak.

He found Val upstairs in bed, reading or pretending to, her eyes red. He sat down on the bed beside her. "I'm sorry," he said.

Val sighed and let the book fall to her side. "Is this even us? Are you even here?"

"Yes, I'm here," he said, and he reached for her hand. "I'm here," he told her again. "I wish you'd *stay* here."

Val set her book on the nightstand and took a deep breath. "I'm sorry I didn't talk to you first," she said. "But I think this is the right thing for me right now."

Brad nodded. This was really happening. She was going.

"It's an easy drive," she said. "You can visit."

"Of course," he said, and he pulled her close to him, and she let him. Then he pictured himself driving, losing the ability to hold his arms on the steering wheel. He thought of their recent trip to the beach, imagined rushing her to the hospital and having an episode in the car. He was taking too much for granted. No more interstates, he decided.

"Are you angry?" she asked.

"No," he said. "No, I was just surprised. But I understand. This is a good idea."

CHAPTER SEVEN

THE COUPLE ON PEARSON CIRCLE DID NOT SIGN WITH BRAD. HE WALKED through their house and complimented their fruit-themed wall-paper. He spoke of the charm of old appliances, which people who had old and valueless appliances usually found comforting. He gave his speech about how other realtors might set a high price but make the clients spend a lot first. But in the end, when the couple said they were going to think about it, he could tell that meant they weren't going to think about him.

A month ago, he could sign nearly any seller who let him visit the property. Occasionally they passed; occasionally he didn't think he'd be the best agent for a property, but he had no trouble picking up new listings. This afternoon, two sellers in a row had passed him up, and each time, when he got in the car afterward and looked at his reflection in the mirror, he could see what was missing: all sense of charm, charisma, confidence. His face wouldn't do the right things, not consistently anyway.

At the office, Sophie continued to ask why he was in a bad mood. And he often *was* in a bad mood, so he hoped that was responsible for much of what people were seeing on his face. Hoped, but knew that it wasn't. Another of his colleagues had taken to asking, "You doing okay?" instead of "Good morning" or "How are you?" Because he didn't look okay. He looked unhappy, cold, blank. Would any medicine undo this? What about that surgery, Brad wondered, the one that heart surgeons have to do?

"We never know how a patient will respond to one treatment versus another," the neurologist told him at the end of the day when he handed Brad a new prescription. He was starting Brad on CellCept, a medication primarily for patients who'd had organ transplants but one that could sometimes help myasthenia gravis patients too—yet another thing about the disorder that "doctors didn't fully understand." Dr. Frick wanted Brad to continue with the Mestinon four times a day. If this combination worked, even for a time, they could avoid medications with more significant side effects. Fantastic, Brad thought. For now, he was going to need to get weekly blood tests to make sure the CellCept didn't cause problems with his white blood cell count. Well, Brad thought, with Val leaving town, at least he wouldn't have to worry about her noticing the marks on his arms after each test.

He was walking out of the hospital after his appointment when his phone rang. It was almost five in the evening. He'd thought it might be Val calling to see if he could pick up dinner, but it wasn't. It was Margot.

"Brad, I'm glad I caught you. I've got some news."

"And hello to you, too."

"So I asked a retired policeman, who's sort of a friend of a friend, to look into Mullet's record, and there was more. It's not good."

"Okay."

"He had a record in New Jersey, too. A woman he dated had him arrested for assault and battery. She had a restraining order against him. She eventually dropped the charges, but we know what that means."

Brad crossed the street and headed for the parking garage. "When was this?"

"Four years ago. He also beat the crap out of some guy in Hoboken. Knocked the guy's teeth out."

"Also four years ago?"

"About six, but still, it isn't much of a character reference."

"No," Brad said.

"Well?"

"I . . . I don't know. What do you want me to say?"

"That maybe I'm right."

"And she was beaten to death?" Brad's words echoed through the garage. He lowered his voice. "Surely they would have noticed that."

"He could have suffocated her."

"Or she could have overdosed," he whispered. "That's what they said happened. Couldn't that be it?"

He reached his car, unlocked the door, and hurried inside.

"Are you really comfortable with this?" Margot asked. "Believing they were engaged, that it just so happens no one knew, it just so happens he has this history? You think she was going to marry that man?"

No, he didn't believe it. He didn't think she would. But, "Sometimes Kara did what she needed to do to get what she wanted," he said. "She didn't always have brilliant judgment."

"It's easier for you to believe Kara was whoring herself out—"

"I didn't say that. But compromising. Or misleading him—we don't know."

"The police said they'd pursue it if they heard from Kara's family."

Brad pictured Gwen at the coffee shop, Lucy Ann at the funeral. "Do you really need to do this to them?"

"How can we ignore this?"

"What are the police going to do? *Exhume* her?" The word tasted gritty.

"I don't know . . ."

"Why is this so important to you?" Brad heard his voice getting louder and he forced the volume down. "You want to dump this horrible question on her family to relieve your own curiosity—"

"Hardly—"

"—even though it's almost inconceivable anything could be proved? At best, you'll force everyone to look more closely at Kara's choices during her last year on earth, and that isn't going to make anyone happy."

"What if this guy is out there, and he killed her, and he got away with it? Doesn't that upset you?"

Brad closed his eyes.

"What if he decides to do it again?" Margot said. "He told some pretty lame lies and got away with it this time. Imagine if he tried a little harder."

Brad didn't want to imagine. "Don't do anything yet," he told her.

"I thought you'd support me in this. I'm going to call."

"Wait, let me check something first."

"Check what?"

"It doesn't matter. I just . . . I need to think, okay? I may be able to find out something. Just give me a week."

"I said I'd call back," Margot said.

"Jesus, it's been two months already. Kara's not going to be any more dead in a week. Give me a little space here."

After a pause, Margot sighed. "Fine. Have your week. Then I'm calling, and I hope you'll help me with this."

"Thank you."

Neither of them said anything else for a minute. Brad wanted to throw the phone through the windshield, to smash it into the concrete wall of the garage.

"It's not like I feel vindicated here, Brad. I loved her too."

When they hung up, the car felt quiet and empty, and again Brad closed his eyes. He could imagine Kara sitting in the seat beside him, flicking a burning ash onto the floor and saying, *You have a very high opinion of me.* But he knew she wouldn't be in the car with him when he opened his eyes, because he couldn't begin to imagine how the conversation would end.

"Rise and shine," he called to Gwen from the other room.

Gwen blinked at the beige sheets. Her mouth was dry—she'd smoked too much pot—and her head felt like it had a rock inside that might bruise the lining of her skull if she turned. It was morning. Or afternoon, she wasn't sure. It was sunny, anyway. Sun pressing through a vinyl window shade across the room.

"Come on," Steve called again. Something in the other room sizzled on a pan, and carefully Gwen shifted. Opposite the bed was a dark dresser with a television set and video game console and two empty beer bottles on top. Beside the dresser was a laundry hamper erupting with discarded clothes. The closet door was open, and over the edge hung a blue bath towel discolored in a few places. That was probably Kara's doing, a face cleanser or makeup remover. Gwen had towels like that.

She'd crashed again at Steve's place. He'd given her the bed and a giant T-shirt to sleep in. It supposedly belonged to Kara. It had a sports team on the front, the Cardinals, and a red bird, but part of the bird's head had peeled off from overwashing. Gwen picked up her glasses from the nightstand beside her and looked around the room for other signs of Kara. The walls were bare. In the bottom of the laundry hamper, through the crisscross of plastic weave, she could make out a spot of pink that might have belonged to her sister.

Gwen turned back to the nightstand and tried to see the wall behind it. But she couldn't, so with an effort, because her arms felt leaden, she pushed the table forward. Electrical cords draped from the lamp and alarm clock to the wall, and the floorboard was lined with clouds of dust. The wall was cracked in one place, but otherwise blank.

The first time Gwen spent the night in one of Kara's apartments in New York, she'd pulled back her sister's nightstand and repeated her childhood act of vandalism. "Gwen was here," she wrote above the electrical outlet, just like she'd written on the graffiti wall back home. Kara never mentioned it, but a few years later, when Gwen spent the night again, she pulled back the nightstand while her sister was in the shower. *Kara was here first,* Kara had written in green ink. Gwen was delighted. She grabbed a pencil off the nightstand and wrote, "Gwen is just visiting."

This morning, there wasn't a pen or pencil in sight. She pushed the nightstand back against the wall.

The apartment smelled like bacon and dirty laundry, and Gwen dragged her body out of bed and followed the bacon smell into the next room. "Lazy girl," Steve said. "Have a seat. You missing class?"

Gwen nodded. "At least the first one."

At the table, bacon sat in a little puddle of oil on each plate, and Steve approached with a bottle of champagne, which he sat in front of Gwen so she could read the note on top: "Do not drink." It was Kara's handwriting.

"I found this in the fridge. She got it for when you were here."

"For breakfast?"

"Brunch. Mimosas. Hair of the dog."

Gwen ate a piece of bacon while Steve opened the champagne and mixed it with orange juice. "I was thinking we'd go to our little place," he said, "but then it got late."

"What's 'our little place'?"

"The pancake place we've been going to on Sundays. The one on Fifth."

"Oh, yeah. That was good. Not the coffee, but the food."

"You want coffee?"

Gwen nodded, and Steve headed back to the kitchen to pour her a cup and to fry eggs.

If Kara were alive, they might have had a morning just like this one. Maybe it would have been this morning. An evening of smoking way too much pot, Gwen crashing there for the night, as she seemed to every time she visited, sleeping in a borrowed nightshirt. Maybe Steve would have woken them both up. "Lazy girls," he might have said. And he'd have made bacon like this, and Kara would have made a face to Gwen about the puddle of grease on the plate, but she'd have eaten the bacon anyway, and liked it. *Oh we must have mimosas,* she'd have said, and she'd have pulled out the bottle of champagne. *I rescued this from work. It's good.*

"Where did Kara get the champagne?" Gwen asked.

"I don't know."

"Her restaurant?"

"Probably."

Gwen nodded.

If Kara were alive, she would have introduced Gwen to Toby by now, too. Maybe they'd have gone out one night, without Steve, to a concert. Kara probably wouldn't have offered any preface. Toby would have just walked up and kissed Kara or grabbed her hand, not aware that there was anything to hide. Gwen would have been a little shocked, and Kara would have laughed it off and said, at the end of the night, not to mention him to Steve, that it was complicated.

But what would she have wanted? To explain it, eventually. Not that night, or the next, but another time, maybe a week later while they were shopping or having dinner alone. Out of nowhere she'd have wanted to explain the whole thing—how it wasn't really working out with Steve, or maybe how Toby was just for fun, or how she was experimenting with adultery, to try it out, to see what it felt like, even though she knew it was wrong and bad and whatever, or she was testing, to see if she needed someone else or if Steve would be good for her by himself. There would have been some sort of explanation that didn't entirely make sense, and Gwen would have acted like she understood and approved, or that's the reaction Kara would have solicited anyway. Both of them would have known Toby made more sense for Kara, but neither of them would have said it in quite that way.

Still, if all that had happened, would Toby have looked at Gwen the way he had? While Kara was in the bathroom, perhaps, or turned away. Would Toby have looked at Gwen like she was not just the little sister but someone in her own right, someone to look at? And would he have called her the next day, and would Gwen have replayed the message three times, to listen to the sound of his voice, before calling him back?

Maybe. It seemed stupid, but a part of Gwen felt an inevitability to it.

"Wanted to make sure you got home safely," he'd said in his message, "and that everyone was nice to you last night, and that you didn't hate my guitar-playing. Can I meet you for lunch some-time?" His voice went up at the end of the question, like he was excited and hopeful. "Can I meet you for lunch sometime?"

And she said yes. And walking out of class, out of the building, to see him leaning against a light post waiting for her, she felt like the most grown-up girl in her school. She wanted to kiss him, and she knew, she could tell, that he wanted to kiss her. Maybe it should have felt more wrong, but Kara was engaged to Steve, and Kara was dead, and anyway, the feeling didn't feel optional. Gwen's smile when she walked up to Toby probably gave everything away.

But his did too. "Hey, you," he said. This was two days ago. "Hey, you," she'd said back to him.

Steve doled out the eggs. "The coffee okay?"

Gwen looked at her mug, then took a sip. "Yeah, sure, thanks."

Steve was wearing a wrinkled T-shirt, his freckled, hairy arms exposed. And Toby was right. Steve did have a mullet. Last night, when they were getting stoned, Gwen found herself mesmerized by it. Did she comment on it? She might have. It was getting harder to picture Kara with him.

Gwen was looking at his hair as he stood at the sink, his back to her, when she remembered—

"Hey, were you playing video games in the bedroom this morning?"

"Last night," he said. "Did I bother you? I had the volume off."

It was a hazy memory, the foot of the bed weighed down, the brightness of the screen mostly obscured by Steve's wide back. "No," she mumbled.

"I don't sleep well," he added, and he joined her at the table.

Gwen sipped her mimosa. "Is it weird hanging out with Kara's little sister?"

Steve shrugged. "I don't know. You remind me of her, yeah."

"Is it weird how much younger than you I am?"

"Not really. It's just weird that she's . . . you know. But I don't really think about it. You seem like an adult." Steve ate a forkful of egg, then added, "I tell you what's weird—that you're leaving in two weeks. You should stay. You should move here. It suits you."

Gwen imagined herself deciding to stay, imagined telling Toby—him squeezing her hand and telling her how awesome that would be. She felt herself blush. Steve grinned too. Then he jingled a set of keys clipped to his belt. "I got to head out soon," he said. "Got a bunch of calls already. Are we on for Saturday again?"

Gwen took a few seconds to answer. "I might have plans."

He was starting to clear the plates, and he stopped to look at her. "You become Miss Popular during breakfast?"

"No," she said, avoiding his eyes. Toby was going to call soon to let her know if he was free. "I just might be busy," she said. "And we used up the pot."

"Oh, I can get better shit than that in five minutes." He shrugged. "Sorry, it's true. So I'll do that, and you call me later and tell me if Saturday's good or another day is better."

***

Margot had driven Gwen to the Galleria Mall in White Plains, and they were walking around—along with about seven million other New Yorkers. Gwen seemed amused by the novel familiarity of a characterless indoor mall, complete with every store in every other mall in the country. But this wasn't Greenwood Park, North Carolina. The mall was overcrowded with people who weren't meandering, as Margot and Gwen were. These people had things to accomplish. They shopped with intention.

The crowds and the noise and the stores were a good distraction, though, and gave Margot an excuse not to have to talk. She could just follow Gwen around—"Sure, we can go there, wherever you want."—without having to make conversation or act upbeat.

Mike remained "out of touch," and with every day that passed, it felt less and less likely that the Army was responsible for his extended silence. He'd let his father deliver the news about Mullet's police record, and in over a week had sent nothing but a quick email saying he was tied up longer than expected.

They couldn't go back to what they'd been before—when Mike lied to her and she believed him, when she counted on his coming home soon and he felt free to do whatever he wanted, or when she saw a serious future for them and he . . . may or may not have. Maybe he didn't think that far ahead. Maybe he couldn't. Or maybe he saw her as nothing—a buddy, someone to laugh with.

Well, someone to laugh with is important. That's not nothing. But it wasn't what she was looking for. Not all she needed.

They couldn't go back. Maybe Mike realized this too, and so he stayed comfortably "out of touch." Was he just waiting for her to end it?

"Do you like these?" Gwen asked.

They were standing at a jewelry kiosk, and Gwen was holding up a pair of silver earrings with a Celtic knot of some sort.

"Yeah," Margot said. They were nice. Kara had gone through a Celtic jewelry phase.

"I think I'm going to get them."

"You should."

Margot followed Gwen into a discount shoe store next, one Kara had always liked, and Margot did feel a little disingenuous talking about earrings and shoes when there was something so much bigger going on. "Why is this so important to you?" Brad had asked when they spoke a couple of days ago—as if Margot had invented Mullet's past, as if it were her goal to torture Kara's family. This was who the man was. Margot had just been the one to ask questions. Because she cared. She wasn't going to blindly accept this man's bullshit story about an engagement. She could believe Kara might've withheld bad things from her, for a time, but not good things. That wasn't the kind of friendship they had.

Even Mike's father thought it looked suspicious, Margot told Brad. He'd offered to call Kara's mother for them, but Margot said no, she would do it. Or Brad would—Lucy Ann might take it better from him. In any event, one of them would call her. Soon.

"What do you think of these?" Gwen asked, holding up a pair of black cowboy boots.

Cowboy boots. Margot was about ten years behind on her *Vogues*. "Very cool," she said.

Gwen tried them on and walked down the aisle of the store, testing the fit. She'd only called for the ride. Margot knew that.

After being "too busy" for dinner twice in a row, Gwen had called to ask if there were any malls nearby. "Maybe, if you're up for it, we could get lunch sometime and go to one," she'd said. It wasn't subtle. It had felt familiar. Like a call from Kara.

In college, there'd been an older Mormon girl who couldn't drink or sleep with guys, but she liked to go out and act slutty, so she was the perfect designated driver. Margot and Kara referred to her as their "car friend." That's what Margot was to Gwen. But Margot refused to believe she'd become that for Kara.

They'd aged differently, that was certain. They'd drifted in ways. But Kara seemed to have a good time when she was with Margot, and Margot certainly looked forward to their visits. It was easy to laugh with Kara. To relax completely, to be herself. They knew each other so well—or it felt like they did. They knew a part of each other, anyway. It was like being with family, that's what it was, even if they weren't the same people they once were. Or even if Margot wasn't and Kara was. Or had been, anyway.

Gwen bought the boots, then led the way into a clothing store that featured miniskirts Margot would have worn in her twenties and couldn't fit around one thigh now. And she felt like family too, in a way. Margot had watched Gwen grow up—mostly through photos, but back in college there'd been visits with Kara to Greenwood Park, and Gwen had driven out with her mom for many of their shows. Gwen clearly didn't feel any special connection to Margot. There was no substance to their conversation. Whenever Margot asked about Gwen's life, she gave one-word answers: Apparently the art program was "fine," the students were "boring," and the whole New York experience was proving to be "okay." Of course, Margot wasn't volunteering any of what was on her mind either.

"Margot?"

She looked up. She and Gwen had taken three steps out of the miniskirt store, and there was Lissy Caverton, Mike's mother, standing by herself with a shopping bag at her side.

Margot's heart began pounding.

Lissy couldn't mention Mullet. Gwen couldn't find out like this—not by accident, not from a stranger.

"My goodness, this is such a coincidence," Lissy said, with a quick glance at Gwen. "I was just thinking about you."

"Small world," Margot said. "This is Gwen," she added, with an exaggerated nod to her left, "my friend Kara's sister. You remember I mentioned Kara, a dear friend of mine who passed away recently." Margot was emphasizing virtually every syllable of every word, trying to send cues. Her eyes widened, tried to say, please, please don't.

"Oh. *Oh,* yes," Lissy said, hopefully getting it. "I'm so sorry to hear about your sister. I'm Lissy Caverton."

"Mike's mother," Margot added.

Gwen nodded. "Hi," she said.

Lissy turned back to Margot. "Russell and I were just talking—"

Not about Kara, please.

"—about you. I thought you and I might get lunch together one day. This is so funny. Just this morning, I asked Russell to leave your phone number for me on the refrigerator. But look, here you are! What a lark!"

"Look at that," Margot said. How awkward. A sympathy lunch with Mike's mother, who surely wasn't "out of touch" with her son. But Margot smiled and said, "Sure. Lunch would be great," as they exchanged numbers.

"Marvelous. I'll call you when you have your calendar in front of you. Let's do something soon."

"Soon, absolutely."

A moment later, Margot and Gwen were walking away, and

Margot felt as if she'd narrowly avoided a horrible collision. Her heart was still racing when they came upon a bath products store with a giant sale sign out front. "Want to go in?" Gwen said.

"You go ahead," Margot said. "I'll wait outside."

Margot took a deep breath as she sat down on a bench. It was too much. She felt like an old woman having an attack. She wished she could pick up the phone and call someone who would talk her down, but there was no one to call. Everyone in her life kept disappearing. Kara, now Mike. Who was going to be left in her rocket ship?

Margot sighed and rubbed her forehead. She'd played this game with herself her whole life. If the world were going to explode and she was filling up a rocket ship to the moon, who would she take with her? As a little girl, she'd made careful decisions about her toys—which bear would join her and her family, which doll would be left behind. In college, she shifted her focus to friends and brought Kara instead, Brad—because he came with her, a few theater friends, maybe the odd football player. Three months ago, she'd have had Mike and Kara in the front seats. But now . . . ?

Margot thought about her high school friends, but she saw each less and less often. And could she really invite Becky without her husband and kids and that horrible dog? Margot's ship would fill up with people her friends needed more than her. She would be everyone's "rocket friend," a nice enough person who could give them a ride to the moon, but no one they'd have chosen.

If Kara were filling a ship to the moon, would she have invited Margot? In college, sure, but more recently? Margot swallowed. Probably not. She might have taken Brad, though she hadn't talked to him in ages. But she'd have wanted to know he was somewhere safe. Maybe if it were a big rocket ship, an eight-seater . . . But maybe not even then.

Gwen walked out of the bath products store, looking like a reflection of her sister from their college days. She was studying a little bottle of something she'd purchased, not paying attention to the crowds around her, so like Kara.

"What'd you get?" Margot asked, and she took the bottle and read the label so she could say, "Wow, that looks nice."

"Want to smell?"

Margot unscrewed the top and sniffed. Oranges. She could do something with oranges. She sniffed again. And vanilla. Orange vanilla pound cake muffins? With cherries? "Nice," she said, handing the bottle back.

She should be baking; that's what she would do tonight. She could try something new, maybe get a head start on next week's orders. It would pass the time. It brought pleasure to people. And in a way, she thought, it was the one thing she had.

Gwen wasn't surprised when Toby called a couple of days after their lunch to see if she could get together over the weekend. But until she walked into the restaurant on Friday night, she wasn't certain whether his dinner invitation was meant to be a follow-up visit with his dead girlfriend's lonely little sister or if this was going to be an actual date.

The restaurant looked like heaven—or New York's version of it. The room shone with a dim blue light emanating from candles and sconces tucked beneath and behind semitransparent sapphire drapery that hung from the ceiling between booths. The booths themselves were a rich blue velvet, and the tables were a crisp white. The servers wore blue cummerbunds and tuxedo shirts, and Toby was walking over from the bar carrying two glasses of wine.

"You look amazing," he said to her, and Gwen blushed. She was wearing the same dress she'd worn to go out with Margot, but with silver knotted earrings she'd bought at the mall yesterday and forest green nail polish. Tonight's effect was much more satisfying. Toby had shaved this time, and he wore a designer T-shirt under his blazer—black with a lavender pattern of some sort—and dark jeans with lots of stitching on the back pockets.

There was small talk—of the menu, of New York apartments, of the rain the afternoon before. He was sitting catty-corner to her, and after they'd ordered, he rubbed her knee under the table. Gwen lost track of what she was saying, and that seemed to amuse Toby, and Gwen didn't mind. He asked her about her classes, what she was working on, and she described the painting she'd done of Kara in an avant-garde performance. "Did you ever see her in anything like that?"

"No," Toby said, "I never saw her in anything. Though I heard she auditioned for—what's the musical with all the teenagers in it? *Second Summer*, I think it's called. I heard she went to an open call for that. I just, I don't know, I have a vision of it. Not that she was old, and she said she was hardly the oldest person there. It's like *Grease,* though. I mean, the cast is always in its forties, right? Playing high schoolers."

Gwen had a vision of it too, and that's what she wanted to paint next. Or draw, with pastels. Two rows of young girls—their faces taken from memories of high school—auditioning on the stage, and in the row behind them, Kara, taller, with bigger, darker hair, fuller breasts and hips, arms and legs moving at a slight delay. Behind her, Gwen might show another row of less recognizable figures, though some might be visibly older, women and perhaps men too, their eyes following the choreographer in the front left of the canvas. All eyes would focus on the choreographer, all eyes except Kara's. She would be looking out for a moment at the viewer. At the painter. There'd be a question in her eyes. A question, but an understanding as well.

Even as the conversation moved on, as Toby talked about a show he had coming up and Gwen complained about her pretentious classmates, she was drawing the picture in her head, refining it and redrawing it. She might be able to find a video of an audition on the Internet, something with lots of dancing so she could note how people dressed and how the actors all looked in rows behind one another. She could revisit the Toulouse-Lautrec at the museum. And the Degas. She might need a larger sketchbook, one she could devote entirely to this image. This was why people did studies. There would be the girls in the front to consider: their movement, their faces—three of them. Or four. The choreographer in the foreground, with perhaps an arm or a leg off the canvas. The less distinct figures in back, older and younger, and then of course, Kara.

"You're not listening to a thing I'm saying."

Gwen felt herself blush, and in the bluish white light, she studied Toby's dark face. He wore a slight smirk. He was amused, not angry. He had long black lashes and the darkest eyes.

"What?" he said.

"Nothing."

She felt his hand on her knee again. It made her heart dance.

After dinner, they walked a few blocks to a basement bar with low ceilings and a live band in the front room. Toby led Gwen through a maze of smaller rooms to one with a vacant pool table and a few people sitting at a table in a corner. There was a couch on the other side, and Toby led Gwen to it. There was enough distance between them and the band for them to listen to the music or not listen to it. After a few minutes, Toby whispered, "I like you."

"I like you too," she told him.

"There's something so delicate about you. I like that."

Gwen didn't know what to say, so she looked down at the cocktail in her hands and didn't say anything.

"You look like you're afraid I'm going to slip my tongue in your mouth at any moment," Toby whispered. "I'd like to," he added, "but you don't have to be afraid of me."

Now Gwen turned to face him. He was inches from her face,

and she could see the stubble on his chin and hear his breathing. And then at once he was kissing her, his tongue pushing its way inside of her in a way that felt important and necessary. She fumbled for the table to set her drink down. His hand appeared on her hip, and she wrapped her hands around his back. She'd only kissed two boys with tongue before, but it hadn't been like this at all. The first time, the boy had quickly slid his tongue in and then out, like he was doing it on a dare. The second time, the guy's tongue had lingered in her mouth for a minute, but limp, as if it wasn't sure what to do in there.

Toby's tongue had intention. It was hard, massive, and it was filling her mouth, reaching for something, pressing its way into her, tasting, consuming her. His hand on her back had reached between the buttons of her dress so that his fingers were touching the skin above her waist, and Gwen felt a desire to be out of the dress, released from the buttons. It was an aching she'd not felt before—like the need to be free of shoes after a long day of walking.

Stop it, Gwen heard her sister say, but Gwen ignored her. He was leaning over her now, his back to the room, obstructing the world, hiding the hand that cupped her breast through her dress.

You're in a bar, Gwen. Don't be a whore.

Shut up. You're jealous.

I'm not jealous. I'm serious. You're eighteen.

Old enough.

Toby kissed Gwen's neck.

"Should we go back to my place?"

Gwen couldn't speak. But she was nodding.

Outside, the air was cooler, and Gwen felt funny, as if she'd had more than a glass of wine and a few sips of her cocktail. Toby was efficient, matter-of-fact. He led them to a busier intersection. He hailed a cab. He gave directions to Brooklyn—Brooklyn, a long drive. In the cab he asked if she was okay, and she said yes. And then, because she wanted to, and because he wanted to, and because they both knew it, they were kissing again. There was a power to his movements, and as they kissed she felt herself sliding down until her back rested on the seat of the cab. Toby was leaning over her, pressed up against her body, and she felt in his pants a hardness against her leg, a hardness that she'd never felt before, that made her feel curious and dirty, but good dirty, grown-up dirty.

Gwen, that's enough. Turn around.

You're dead. You had your chance.

This is a waste.

He was sucking on her ear. No one had ever . . . His tongue was in her ear, then on the back of her neck, then inside her mouth, and she was holding his face, and he was breathing heavily. "You are so fucking sexy," he whispered, and she tried to say, "You are too," but his tongue was filling her up again.

Gwen, I'm serious. He's just having fun.

I am too.

That's not true. This is more to you.

Shut up.

You're imagining a future together, picnics in the park and a wedding and love.

Go be dead, okay.

You like him. But he was doing this with someone else last night, and there'll be some other girl tomorrow. He dates lots of girls.

You dated lots of guys.

No, I didn't.

At least two.

No. I didn't.

Toby's hand was fumbling with the buttons on the back of Gwen's dress, but now she was aware of the jerking of the taxicab, the seatbelt that was jabbing into her shoulder, the smell of rubber and mildew coming up from the floor.

"Are you okay?" Toby whispered. He nuzzled her neck with his nose, then moved up and put her earlobe between his lips.

Why would Kara have said that?

"I shouldn't do this," Gwen heard herself saying.

"We can slow down," Toby told her, pulling himself back.

Her lipstick had smeared onto his face and neck. She'd worn too much. She wanted to tell him, but didn't. "I need to go back," she said. "My roommate will be worried."

"We could just hang out," he suggested. "You can call your roommate." But it was a weak offer. "We could go back to the bar?"

"That's alright. It's late." And then, all within a hundred seconds or so, she told the driver to pull over, and Toby insisted that she take the cab home and let him out, and he gave the driver twenty dollars, and then the cab was rounding the block and heading back uptown.

I hope you're happy, Gwen thought as she fastened her seatbelt and glared at her reflection in the window.

Her heart was still racing. Alone with the cabdriver now, she felt embarrassed, and after a minute, she pulled a tissue out of her purse and wiped the lipstick from her lips. What had she done? The smart thing, perhaps, but it didn't feel like it now. She was headed back to a tiny apartment where there was no way she'd fall asleep. Toby would probably never call her again. She'd missed her chance.

And then Gwen considered it: Had Kara really been there? Gwen glanced at the empty space beside her. In her mind, she could picture Kara's face, could see the impassive expression her sister had worn to many family meals. The face stayed in her mind for the whole ride back to her apartment. That was the only answer Gwen could get.

Val's parents were driving down from Richmond to pick her up. Brad had made a show of offering to drive her up, but only a small show, and even as he was insisting, he was thinking that a fictitious imminent house sale could get him out of it later. Of course he wanted to drive her, but he didn't trust his body anymore.

He'd been avoiding the interstate since the swallowing incident the weekend before. He knew it was his own fault he'd missed a dose, and maybe the new regimen of medications would help, but still, he needed to develop safer habits. He was going to bed early to give his body more rest; Val had even commented. He'd stopped using free weights at the gym.

But today Brad was lifting things like a capable husband. Val had lined up her bags next to the staircase, and Brad was carrying them down and leaving them by the front door. Since they'd been married they'd never been apart for more than two or three nights at a time. She'd packed a lot this time. "Careful. That one's full of books. Don't hurt yourself." "Got it," he said. On his third trip down, he saw Kara standing, arms folded, at the bottom of the stairs. He needed to talk to her. He avoided bumping into her as he passed.

When Val's parents were nearing, Brad drove to a deli and picked up lunch. At home, Val had set the table, and the four of them sat down for turkey sandwiches, pasta salad, and awkward conversation. They talked about smoked turkey versus regular, about the heat in Virginia compared to North Carolina. Brad didn't know exactly when Val had told her parents about the baby. Was it when she made plans to visit, or earlier? Had she been thinking about this trip for longer than she'd said? He still hadn't told his parents about the pregnancy. There'd never been any declaration that it was time.

What else had she told her parents? he wondered. What did they think of him?

What do you think of them?

Kara was leaning against the dining room wall, a bored expression on her face. She was watching the meal progress. At one point, she took a close look at the pasta salad and wrinkled her nose. It was heavy on the mayonnaise. Kara hated mayonnaise, and Brad wasn't a huge fan. At another point, she stood behind Val's father and mimicked him chewing with his mouth open. Finally, when Val's mother said for the third time how convenient it must be to have a deli right down the street, Kara threw up her arms in exasperation. *Enough already. Let's pack her up and move her out.* Brad shot Kara a glare, and Val must have seen it, because she gave him a quizzical look, which he met with a disarming smile. He was conscious at that moment of how nice it was to be able to form that smile.

They loaded up the car, Val's father helping Brad with the luggage and her mother asking questions about medical records and vitamins. Kara seemed to be doing her best to obstruct movement, forcing Brad to maneuver around her or walk through her with each trip to the car. He was nervous about being alone in the house with her, but before he knew it, he and Val were hugging and saying good-bye. Val was tearing up a little, and he thought he would too, but the parting was so public and fast, it didn't feel like good-bye. Quick handshakes and hugs from the parents, promises to call that night and visit soon. And then at once the house was empty. Nearly.

Finally we have the place to ourselves.

Brad felt frightened, unprepared. He walked into the dining room and started collecting dishes. When he returned for the second round, he found Kara sitting in Val's seat at the head of the table.

To think, all this could have been mine. The fancy china cabinet, the chandelier, the plaid tablecloth . . .

It's just a tablecloth.

The crystal pigeon. She stood and walked to the china cabinet. *I love the crystal pigeon.*

It's a dove.

It had been sitting on a shelf of the cabinet for so long it had become invisible to Brad, but now he saw it through Kara's eyes. It stood five inches tall and rested its tiny crystal feet on a crystal twig. "It was a wedding gift," he said.

Which you proudly display.

It was from her aunt.

It's magnificent. Kara picked it up and made the bird dance through the air around the room.

Give it a rest.

The dove, a symbol of the beauty and fragility of love. Something like that, right?

Put it down.

I'm so tempted to throw it at the wall.

I know you are.

She carried it into the living room, and Brad followed. *I could throw it in the fireplace,* Kara said. *You'd like that, wouldn't you? It would be cathartic.*

Only a little. Put it down.

It wouldn't be your fault.

Whose fault would it be?

I don't know. You could say you were robbed.

And they stole *that*?

Now Kara smiled, and Brad did too. She set the dove on the coffee table, and they sat down on opposite ends of the couch.

"I know you weren't in love with Steve," he said aloud.

No, I was not.

If I'd called you back when I was about to marry Val, you would have married me.

Yes, I would have. I'd even have moved back to North Carolina. It would have been a relief, actually. For a while. To get out of the race and focus my attention on—she picked up a throw pillow—*needlepoint tulips?*

Brad stood up and carried the bird back to the dining room. "You are something," he said as he left.

What? She was waiting for him in the dining room, standing against the far wall. *Now we can play house and see what it would've been like.*

You say no to me eleven times—do you realize I asked you *eleven* times?—then once you hear I've moved on with my life, you figure a little marriage vacation in North Carolina might be fun? You'll ditch the guy you're seeing, I should ditch my fiancée, and we can forget about the past few years.

I'll admit it wasn't my finest moment.

No, it wasn't.

Maybe I missed you.

Well, maybe you were too late.

Kara gestured to the china cabinet. *Clearly I was.*

Brad returned to the living room, and Kara met him there.

Come on, Brad. Don't put this all on me. You chose not *to move to New York as much as I chose to move there.*

Sure, at first, he thought. But the sincerity of her invitations grew questionable over time. Thrown in, like a door prize, after she rejected his more serious proposals. That last time he saw her, when she begged him to stay after they finished making love, it might've been the only moment she was sober the whole time he was visiting. She kept pouring the vodka like it was impossible to be around him otherwise.

It was, she told him. *I knew how the visit would go. You'd ask again, and I'd have to say no. You'd get fed up with me.*

That was your plan? Say no until I got fed up enough to stop asking?

Gee, it seemed like your plan was to belittle everything I did until I decided to give up and move back.

I didn't—

You did. Every proposal was drenched with your conviction that I wasn't

going to make it. My God, it was hard enough dealing with casting direc-
tors and asshole agents and snotty actors and my mother. Feeling like every
audition was a lottery ticket. But having to justify my being there every
time we talked, to prove my worth to you, it was too much.

Brad stood in silence for a moment. I never questioned your
talent, he said. It was the odds I questioned.

Well, obviously you were right. Kara settled back onto the couch.
It must be very satisfying to you that I was such a failure.

You weren't a failure.

I kind of was.

Brad stepped toward her. Kara dropped her eyes to the floor.

You struggled, but that was part of the life you chose. You got to do
some amazing things. Your tour. That movie short. The workshop.

You Googled me.

I watched the short online.

Ugh, it was terrible.

Well . . . yes, but through no fault of yours.

A half-smile flickered across her face, and Brad took a seat again
on the couch beside her. I'm sorry if I made it harder for you, he
told her. I didn't mean to.

Kara met his eyes. *I know.*

They sat for a minute in an expectant silence. Then he said, I'm
scared of being here with you. I'm scared of what this means.

It doesn't have to mean anything.

But it does. Your being here does mean something.

I like your hair like this. Dark. Natural. She ran her fingers through
his hair, then dropped a hand into his.

Margot is convinced you were killed.

And you're not?

I don't like to think it.

Then don't.

She laced her fingers through his. *Your hands are dry*, she said.
Her hands were always soft.

Margot's going to call the police. They'll call your mother. They might exhume your body. If something happened, or if something didn't, now is the time to tell me.

Kara stood now and walked to a shelf in the corner. *Didn't you have this candleholder when we were in college?*

It's a candleholder. I don't know. Yes. Now answer me.

I thought so. I think we had two.

That sounds right. Kara, please . . .

She turned to face him. *We both know how this works,* she said. *You imagine me, and I say what you think I would say.* A cigarette materialized in her hands, and she took a thoughtful puff.

I thought that's what was happening, but now I'm not sure. Maybe it's more than that. Maybe you're *making* me imagine you.

Kara shrugged in reply.

Why are you here? he asked. Did Steve hurt you and you want me to do something about it? Or are you trying to break up my marriage? Or is it—I mean, are you just waiting around until I drop dead? Is that it? Are you the welcoming committee?

Kara paced across the room and ashed in the fireplace, then turned back to face him. *Have you really not figured it out by now?* she asked. *Or do you just wish you didn't know?*

※

When Margot arrived at Java Jones, Collin looked a little too excited to see her. "Girl, I am two lattes and one skinny mochaccino away from telling you some interesting news. Hang on," he said, and he turned back to a group of customers at the counter.

She stacked her boxes on the far end of the counter and waited. She was ready for someone else's news. Something new to think about, to distract her. Maybe Collin was up for a new part. She studied the display case. Still a few muffins from a few days ago, cookies that weren't hers, the last of her banana bread. She'd brought apricot carrot bread this time. And extra muffins.

"Thanks for coming, you guys, have a terrific day, okay?"

He was the most cheerful barista in all of New York.

The customers took their drinks to go, and Collin came around the counter and sat with Margot at a table.

"First of all, honey, anything new with your sexy man in uniform?"

"No," she said with a sigh. "I haven't heard a peep from him. I'm not sure if I'm more worried that he could be hurt or angry that he's probably avoiding me."

"Ew. Not fun."

"No, it's not," she said. "Is this my future?"

"Hopefully not?" Collin said, but there was an audible question mark in his reply.

"Enough about the joys of being me. What's new with you? What were you so excited to tell me?"

Collin flicked his hair back and leaned forward. "Did you know that Kara's sister knows Toby?" he asked.

Margot wondered if she'd misunderstood. "Gwen?" she said.

"Mm-hmm. Toby was playing with this band called Colored Sparks, and Pepper's ex's sister was there, and so was Gwen. She sat at their table. Isn't that wild?"

"When was this?"

"A couple of weeks ago, but Pepper just heard last night when she bumped into her ex."

"I asked Gwen about him. She told me she didn't know him."

"What?"

"She said she'd never even heard of him. I asked her about him the first time I saw her."

"Well, maybe she just met him the other day, at the concert," Collin said.

"Yet it didn't occur to her to mention this during the four hours I spent schlepping her around the mall on Thursday?"

"Oh, that was nice of you."

"The one thing I ask her . . ."

"Okay now, don't get upset," Collin told her. "Maybe she forgot you'd asked. Or she didn't catch his name, or she knew him by some nickname. There are a million answers."

"I'd just like one."

Everything Collin said made sense, but it was still infuriating. With all the small talk and gaps of silence on that trip to the mall, Gwen wouldn't have thought to mention this? When Margot was asking if Gwen had gone anywhere fun, or met anyone interesting, or done any "New York things." No, I pretty much keep to myself, she'd said. Herself, and a crowd that included Pepper's ex's sister and Toby.

On the drive back to Long Island, Margot called Gwen and left a message, trying to sound as casual as possible. "I forgot to ask you about something last week," she said. "Can you call me when you get out of class?"

Next she called Brad, but of course he didn't answer either. It had been a week; he was probably scared to talk to her. "Hello again, Brad's voicemail. I thought you might be interested to know that Gwen *knows* Toby, the guy Kara was dating. Not that she told me when I asked."

The car beside Margot was edging into her lane, and she pounded on the horn. Then she said, "Call me back," and hung up the phone.

He obviously wanted no part of it. But he *was* part of it. It's not as if Margot asked to be involved in all this. It was time for one of them to call Lucy Ann, and Margot was fine doing it herself. Although right now, more than anything, she wanted to talk to Gwen. Actually, she wanted to do more than talk to Gwen. She wanted to shake her, to scream at her. What did the girl have against Margot? "I am so fucking angry," she shouted at the car in front of her.

Angry with Gwen, or with Kara?

A valid question.

This was very Kara-like behavior—using Margot for a car ride and dinner, not retuning calls until it was convenient, leaving Margot out. Margot didn't know Kara's New York friends, her New York life. After all they'd been through together, after four years of college, after that . . .

Well, after that, time had passed. More than a decade. Kara probably knew some of these other people more intimately than she knew Margot.

But that was hardly Margot's fault.

Kara was selfish. She always was. When Margot's mother died and Margot was going through all that drama with her father, getting him to the doctors and arranging the move to Florida and packing up the house, Kara was barely there. It's not that Margot wanted Kara's advice on retirement facilities or moving companies or powers of attorney, but a few more invitations wouldn't have hurt, a little more reaching out. Where had Kara been? She was around. They had dinner now and then. And went shopping . . .

Margot was reminded again of the phone messages Gwen had ignored until she wanted Margot to take her to the mall. It was maddening. And familiar. And disappointing.

All evening, Margot's anger sat like a pound of dough in her stomach, and that night it put lumps in her pillow so she slept poorly and woke with a stiff neck. No one returned her calls the next morning. No word from Mike either. One call came mid-afternoon: a canceled wedding, which Margot took as a personal affront. All day she baked muffins. She forgot to put raisins in the carrot batter.

These calls that weren't being returned, they confirmed every-thing: that Gwen had lied on purpose, that she was keeping Toby a secret out of spite, that Margot was old, too old to relate to a teen-ager anymore, too old even to relate to old friends. Brad was done with Margot, probably thought she was crazy, probably wished he'd never bumped into her at the funeral, surely wished that. And Mike had just been stringing her along—for a goddamned year and a half—but never had any intention of marrying her.

Well, fuck Brad and his cold shoulder, Mike and his lies. Margot was done with all this tiptoeing-around bullshit. She needed to be frank with Gwen. Maybe Gwen could tell that Margot was keeping something from her. Maybe that was part of the problem—they were both pretending. Well, enough of that. It was time for complete candor. She was a big girl. They could have a real a conversation that would answer some questions for both of them.

Margot was driving into the city before she knew it. It was a little after seven o'clock when she arrived at Gwen's apartment building and pressed the buzzer for 7B. Another girl answered.

"Is Gwen there?" Margot asked.

"No."

"She's out?" Margot snapped.

"Yes."

Margot wasn't convinced. "I'm a friend of the family, and I have something important to talk to her about."

"Why don't you call her?" the girl said flatly.

"Yes. I'm having trouble getting a hold of her. Do you know where she is or when she'll be back?"

There was a pause, then the girl answered, "She probably won't be back until the morning. She went out with Kara and Steve, and she usually spends the night in Brooklyn when she sees them."

Margot wondered if she'd misheard. "Kara and Steve?" she said.

There was an even longer pause now. Then the girl's voice came back over the intercom. "Yeah, her sister and brother-in-law. Didn't you say you were a friend of the family?"

Margot didn't respond. She pulled out her phone and called Gwen again. "Please call me back as soon as you can," she said to the voicemail box. Then she called Brad, who of course didn't answer. She tried Collin, but his phone was turned off; his show started in less than an hour. Mike wasn't there and probably wouldn't respond, but she sent him a text anyway. Then she just stood at the corner of West 97th and Broadway, holding her telephone and doing nothing, while people walked around her and past her and hurried home or to appointments or dinners or dates. She stood there, not walking to her van or the subway or anywhere until someone stopped and asked her if she was lost. She said no, thanks, but the answer was yes. She had no idea where to go.

CHAPTER EIGHT

"I WAS KIND OF SURPRISED YOU BLEW ME OFF LAST WEEKEND," STEVE SAID.

The salads had just arrived, and Gwen kept her eyes to the table. "I'm sorry," she said again. "I got busy."

"But you could've called."

She'd met him at the restaurant half an hour ago. While they were waiting for a table, it was all laughs and small talk.

"If you'd said you weren't coming," he continued, "I could have done something different, instead of sitting at home."

"You didn't have to wait for me."

"I didn't want you to come all the way out to Brooklyn and not be able to get in. You asked me to get more pot, so I bought—" He lowered his voice. "I was all set for you to come."

The tables were lined up close to one another, and Gwen stole a glance to her left to see if the middle-aged couple at the next table appeared to be paying attention, but they were engrossed in a conversation of their own, about a Julia Roberts movie. For a minute, Gwen listened to them. "I was surprised," the woman said.

Gwen didn't feel like having this conversation with Steve. She didn't owe him an account of her weekend. That cab ride with Toby and Kara—so embarrassing and strange. But then Gwen had been drinking, must've been drunk, that was the only explanation. It wasn't something she wanted to think about. She'd kept to herself for the past few days. She didn't have to call Steve back the second he called her. Or Toby. Or Margot, for that matter. She'd called five times in the past twenty-four hours, twice since Gwen arrived at the restaurant this evening. She was probably in the mood to let loose and dance the night away—until nine thirty. At a Starbucks.

"This was one of Kara's favorite restaurants," Steve said. They'd been sitting silently, picking through salads to fight the tension. Gwen looked up now: white walls, white linens, overcrowded tables, dinner specials written in a pretentious script on a chalkboard with prices that seemed too high for pasta. Maybe the food was good, but Gwen couldn't picture Kara loving it here.

For the past three days, Gwen had been working on new images of Kara, drawings in a sketchbook, the starting point of a triptych. She'd pulled out the old photograph of Kara and Brad from her luggage. They were nineteen or so in the picture, and Gwen based her first Kara on this image. She drew her sister from the neck up with the nineteen-year-old's carefree smile and wild hair, but she aged Kara a little to make her plausibly thirty-four. Next Gwen drew her again, but cropped Kara's hair above the shoulders and straightened the frizz. She gave Kara some of the weight from Margot's face, some of the sharpness and confidence from Brad's. She turned her sister into a version of herself that people liked to imagine she could have become.

Last Gwen drew another version of the party girl aged to thirty-four, hair the same as the first, earrings the same, but with eyes that were more tired and a smile that wasn't as big. The difference between the first and third Karas was important, and Gwen needed to solidify the image in her mind. Her teacher Lionel saw Gwen working the sketches yesterday morning and called it her "future self-portrait." He walked away before Gwen had a chance to explain.

It was the third Kara whom Gwen imagined complimenting this restaurant. Steve had probably paid. What else was she supposed to say? "It seems really nice." That's what Gwen said.

Her phone vibrated again while Steve was in the bathroom, and when Gwen looked at the screen, she was amused to see Brad's name. It was funny to think of him existing in the present after she'd spent three days looking at the photograph of his nineteen-year-old self.

"Hey," she said. "I'm at dinner. Can I call you tomorrow?"

"Um, maybe—want to call me on the way home?"

"Tomorrow would be better."

"Are you sure? Margot said she called you a few times—"

"She has a severe phone-stalking problem."

The woman at the next table glanced over, and Gwen forced a smile. "Look, I gotta go," she told him. "I'm at dinner now. I'll talk to you tomorrow."

Steve arrived as Gwen was hanging up, and he looked more than curious. Nosy. Entitled. "One of my many admirers," Gwen couldn't resist saying.

"I'm sure," Steve replied.

The pasta was fine—not better than the place in Wilmington they went to sometimes for her mom's birthday, but Steve seemed very pleased with himself and the restaurant and the bottle of wine he'd ordered for them, so she agreed that the meal was excellent. After they left the restaurant, as she followed him down 5th Avenue in silence, Gwen thought about going home. He was kind of moody tonight, and she wasn't sure she could deal with any more weirdness. She could invent a headache and skip out. If she said something before 10th Street, she could turn left and be on the subway in a few minutes. But then again, Steve had talked up his marijuana like it was the greatest grass grown on the planet, and Gwen needed something to make her relax. And what would she do back at her apartment? Nothing. Mope.

This was one of those nights when she would have called Kara. They'd have smoked a cigarette together, or a joint, over the phone. Gwen might have poured herself a cocktail from the carefully rationed bottle of vanilla-flavored vodka Kara had bought her for Christmas. They'd hidden it in a box in Gwen's closet, underneath old Halloween costumes. Their mom was mad because she thought Kara had been stingy with Gwen for Christmas, only giving her the bottle of pink nail polish that was under the tree. "It's a really good bottle," Gwen told to her mother, pleased with her word choice, knowing she'd later quote herself to her sister.

Maybe tonight she'd pretend she was getting stoned with Kara instead of Steve. Gwen glanced behind her and imagined the first Kara from the triptych walking a few paces behind. There were probably a few ounces of vanilla vodka left in the freezer. Kara's vodka. She was sharing. She knew how Gwen felt.

When they reached the apartment, Steve walked down the concrete steps and unlocked the door. Gwen remembered the first time she'd visited, how anxious she'd been to feel comfortable, how much she'd needed to relax. That was how she felt tonight too. She'd barely spoken to anyone in days. She was civil. She worked on her sketches. She mumbled thanks when her roommate offered her the last half-ounce of coffee from the pot. But Gwen had been stewing around in such a funk since that cab ride with Toby, and tonight's dinner with Steve, which was supposed to have been relaxing, wasn't. So now this next part, which was supposed to be enjoyable, needed to be.

Gwen sat at the table, and Steve poured her a drink: vanilla vodka and Diet Coke. He'd bought the diet for her; she should have said thanks, but didn't. Then he pulled out a bag of pot and a pack of rolling papers from a kitchen drawer, but Gwen asked for "Miss B," Kara's bong, the pink one with the big lips and eyes.

Steve pulled the familiar instrument from a kitchen drawer, filled the bowl with water, and packed in the weed. Then he held the lighter and took a hit. Finally he passed Miss B to Gwen, she inhaled . . . and it was stunning. The waves of her brain relaxed instantly. It was like a mental trip back in time to last week, or to many weeks ago, or to the beach with a breeze in the air. After a minute, she could hardly remember why she'd been tense these past few days. It was like cotton candy from the State Fair, or like a kiss on the lips from someone who'd done it before.

Gwen took another hit, and as Steve took his, she studied Miss B's eyelashes and tried to understand them. She half-listened when Steve told a story about the guy who sold him the stuff. Then she told a story about Dean-o, who sold to her and Kara, and the contrast was funny, hysterically funny, though a second later, Gwen couldn't remember why. Maybe it wasn't funny after all. But it was good to laugh. Gwen could hear Kara in her own laughter.

The third Kara sought out moments like this. This was how she relaxed the tension in her cheeks. That was the thing, really, the tension. That's what Gwen needed to show in the painting, that difference, the tension that came with forcing a smile. Plus the eyes, the difference. Eyes can smile, or not smile.

Gwen went to the bathroom, pulled off her glasses, and studied her own eyes in the mirror. They didn't look happy, even though at that moment she felt distinctly happy. That was how she felt herself feeling, even if she didn't look it. She leaned in close to the mirror, wondering if there was anything to be learned from her reflection. She had the same lips as Kara. They had the same nose, almost. Gwen's was smaller. She put her glasses back on. Miss B didn't have a nose.

Steve met her outside the bathroom door. He was blocking the doorway at first, just standing there, and Gwen was like, "Dude, I can't get out if you don't scoot back." So he moved back, and she went out, and he went in. And for a minute, Gwen stood at the edge of the living room, scanning her surroundings, trying to place her sister there. Then she saw something she hadn't noticed before. In the far corner of the room, on the end table beyond the couch, behind a pile of newspapers and mail, was a picture frame that looked familiar. Gwen walked over and picked it up.

It was a violet, dried and pressed between two pieces of glass and framed in white, distressed wood. Kara had stolen it from the ladies' room of a seafood restaurant they'd gone to when she was visiting home one time. *My fish was gross,* Kara said to Gwen as they walked out. *The only thing likeable about that place was the flower in the bathroom. Did you notice?* And while the Bobbies were getting in the minivan, Kara opened her purse wide enough for Gwen to see what she'd taken. Gwen must've been twelve at the time, and she remembered thinking her sister was so wicked—and so awesome. The next day, Gwen walked past a policeman and felt, with pride, like the accomplice to a crime. She'd seen the framed violet again beside her sister's bed at Kara and Collin's apartment. And now here it was, kept by Steve as a memento or, more likely, an oversight. Gwen nudged the papers aside and set the frame back down amidst a clutter of pens, pencils, and coins. There was an ibuprofen bottle on the table as well. Gwen took two. Then she dropped onto the couch.

The couch. Where *it* had happened. She and Steve always sat at the table, not on the couch, though Steve slept here when Gwen spent the night. She turned back to the end table and saw she'd set the frame on top of a rubber band—no, it was a ponytail holder.

Steve returned from the bathroom, grabbed the bong from the table, and joined her on the couch. "What're you looking at?" he asked.

"The flower," she said.

"Oh yeah, that was hers."

Over the next hour, sitting on the couch felt less and less un-natural. It was more comfortable than the chair, though a little dirty, because when Gwen was smoking a regular cigarette she missed the ashtray a couple of times, and Steve did too. But they dusted it off, and it was fine, and at some point it occurred to Gwen that she'd worn the locket tonight, and she held it up. "Recognize this?"

"Yeah, of course."

"Know who's inside?"

"Of course," he said again. "Your great grandmother."

For a minute Gwen was surprised. She almost laughed. She'd never thought of Great Grandma Kara as her own imaginary ancestor, only as Kara's. But of course, they were sisters, so she could claim the fictitious great grandmother too. She liked that idea. "Exactly," she said, and she waited for Steve to break into a smile. "She died in a fire," Gwen prompted.

"Yeah, I know. I'm sorry."

"She was very rich."

"I heard."

"But all the money was in her closet. It burned."

"I know," Steve said. "That really sucks. She should've had a bank account."

That's when her phone rang, and Gwen looked and it was Brad again. She answered, but instead of "Hello," she said, "Do you remember Great Grandma Kara?"

"Are you drunk?" Brad asked.

Steve furrowed his brow, and Gwen shrugged and rolled her eyes.

"I've had a drink," she said. "Do you remember Kara's locket? With Great Grandma Kara?"

"From the thrift store?" he said.

"I have it," she told him. "I'm wearing it."

"That . . . makes sense. It's sad."

"It's also funny," she told him. "Some things are sad and funny at the same time."

"Are you okay?"

"I've got to go now."

"Gwen, are you okay? Maybe we can talk for a few minutes."

"I'm fine. Yeah. I've got to go."

Gwen hung up the phone and shrugged again at Steve's unasked question. For a moment they looked at each other through the cloud of their smoke, a haze that seemed like an extension of the haze in her brain. Somewhere in the fog was Kara; she was watching, listening. But it was too difficult for Gwen to see her, even in her mind. Gwen turned and lay down on the couch, her knees bent, her toes touching Steve's thigh. "I'm done," she mumbled. The pillows were soft.

"Done?"

"Done," she repeated. "Cooked. Fully baked. I've got to go to sleep."

"Want me to get you to bed?"

"No, thank you."

"You want to sleep here?"

"Mm-hmm," she said.

"You sure?"

Gwen stretched out, and for a second, she looked behind her, upside down, at the end table. Beyond the stack of papers, she saw the framed violet atop a ponytail holder, the ibuprofen bottle, an assortment of pennies and quarters, pencils and colored pens. And behind the table, on the wall, she saw a mark, a smudge, a familiar scribble. It seemed to say the words *Kara was here.*

Once Val left the house, Kara did not. She sat on the other end of the couch when Brad watched television in the living room. She perched on the bathroom counter while he shaved. At night, she lay down next to him in bed or watched him fall asleep from across the room. When his mother called and Brad told her nothing was new but that no, it wouldn't be a great weekend to visit, Kara waved hello. He told his mother Val said hi.

He and Kara were working through a quiet stalemate. They'd gone through similar periods in their relationship, when uncertainty lingered in a heavy silence. He still didn't know what to make of her presence, but it had only been a few days since Val left and Kara installed herself in the house. It seemed like it could only be a matter of time before she made her intentions clear.

In the meantime, Brad was avoiding Margot's calls. The week he'd requested had ended. Her first call came yesterday when he was at the agency, trying to close a sale. He was explaining to his seller why an offer $20,000 below the asking price was worth considering, particularly given other houses that had recently come on the market. It wasn't a pleasant conversation. He knew he'd priced the house too high. It wasn't his style, but it was a terrific house, and he'd wanted to sign the listing. Now, six days after they went on the market they had this offer: good news and bad simultaneously.

Margot's message wasn't exactly good or bad news: Gwen apparently knew that guitar player, Toby, and hadn't told Margot about it. Brad didn't know Margot had been asking Gwen about the guy, and was a little annoyed to hear that Margot was grilling the girl. But if Gwen lied, maybe it was because Margot wasn't her favorite person. Brad certainly didn't want to call Margot back to talk that through.

Now she was calling again. Brad was reading the newspaper in his living room while Kara sat in the easy chair beside him. They both watched the phone ring, lit up with Margot's name and number. With a glance at Kara, he asked if she knew what Margot would say. Kara didn't respond.

The message said that Gwen was spending the night with Steve.

Steve?—Brad played the message again. How was that possible? But that's what Margot said. She said Gwen's roommate was actually under the impression that Gwen was staying with both Mullet and Kara.

"Why—" he started to say aloud.

But why not? he asked himself. Gwen was lonely. Kara was engaged to this man. Maybe he'd called her. Or she'd called him. He was supposed to be family.

Brad shuddered.

Kara was watching him. She flickered her fingers into a wave, but didn't speak.

That's when he called Gwen. He wasn't sure of what he'd say, and then suddenly she was on the other end of the line. "Hey, I'm at dinner," she said. "Can I call you tomorrow?"

At dinner with Steve, he knew, though she didn't say it.

"Um, maybe." He cleared his throat. "Want to call me on the way home?"

But she didn't. She blew Brad off, hurried him off the phone. Not that Brad had figured out what to tell her. He didn't want to frighten or confuse her—he was confused himself—and he certainly didn't want to alarm Steve.

The idea of her at dinner with Steve.

Steve, who had a restraining order against him, who'd been charged with assaulting a woman. Steve, who actually might have murdered Kara.

Brad paced to the doorway of his office, where he wasn't surprised to find Kara. She was sitting at his desk. "Am I right to be nervous?" he asked.

Well, she said with a shrug, *you are.*

He remained on the threshold. I'll call back later, he said to her and himself.

And what will you say?

Brad tried to think.

I'll tell her there's a problem with Steve, that she maybe shouldn't hang out with him, because there's a chance . . .

Mm-hmm, this is going well. And then you'll hang up the phone and pull out a crossword puzzle?

I'll talk to her for as long as she wants.

That's sweet, yeah. Or she could talk to Steve about it.

Margot's there.

She seems wild about Margot, don't you think?

Margot was your friend.

Gwen trusts you. And she trusts Steve.

Maybe I should call her mother.

Do that. Lucy Ann will handle this well. Maybe she'll have Randy call Gwen and ground her.

What else am I supposed to do? I guess I could go up, at some point.

Yes, you could.

I could check flights.

Kara stood up from the desk and pointed to the computer. *It's New York. They run about every two hours.*

Are you saying I need to go there now?

When exactly were you thinking? In two days? Two weeks? Every other month?

She held his gaze. She was doing it again.

Every other month was a lot, he said. I couldn't fly up to New York every time you wanted to see me.

Needed. Sometimes.

I was in rehearsal. I had a job. We planned a lot of visits.

Not everything in life is planned.

Nothing with you was planned.

Not much went according to plan.

Yes, I've noticed.

But that happens with a lot of people, Brad. Not just me. Take a look in the mirror. How are all your plans working out?

Brad remained standing in the doorway, and Kara beside the desk. *Right now my little sister is having dinner with Mullet,* she said.

"Okay," Brad said, and he sat down at the computer and checked a travel website for flights. He could feel Kara standing behind his shoulder. It was only seven thirty. There were flights. They weren't even horribly expensive.

If Val knew he was even considering this . . .

She doesn't have to know. You don't have to explain yourself to anyone.

Brad turned to face Kara. "This is why you're here," he said, "isn't it? This is why Val left."

Kara held his stare. Then she said, *I'm not here.*

BY THE TIME he called Margot back, he'd already bought his plane ticket. "I'll talk to Gwen the second she gets away from him," he said. "Tonight or first thing in the morning."

"I should call again," Margot said.

"No, don't. She knows you called. I talked to her for a minute."

"Tonight?"

"She got off quickly. They were at dinner."

"Did she say where?"

"No."

"I'm going to lose my mind."

Brad looked at Kara, and she pointed to her wrist. He checked the time. "I've got to go," he told Margot. His flight left in a little over an hour.

He put on a pair of jeans and a T-shirt. He threw an extra T-shirt and pair of underwear and socks into a bag, along with his medication. He turned off the television, grabbed a toothbrush. Then he and Kara got into the car and drove to the airport in silence.

He called Gwen again as he walked into the terminal. She was drunk and talked about Kara's locket and then got off the phone quickly. He'd get to her soon. He'd bump into her accidentally on purpose in the morning, or maybe she'd stay up late and text him at midnight. As long as nothing happened to her first. Why would it? He shook his head to dislodge the image.

At the airport, Brad was marked for special security. He should've expected it with the last-minute purchase. As he was questioned and wanded, he worried he might miss the flight, but when he saw Kara cracking a smile in the distance, he figured they'd make it to the gate in time.

They boarded the plane together. He was seated in the back, beside a woman who smelled of spicy ethnic food and who gasped as the plane left the ground. Periodically during the flight he felt Kara seated in her place.

Maybe there'd be a message from Gwen when he landed, a call made from a cab ride home. He'd go straight from the airport to visit her—or, no, she was drunk. He'd see her first thing in the morning. Or maybe he'd see her now, but wait to talk to her until later.

And what would he say?

You could tell her about me.

Brad didn't respond. The point was, she was going to be fine. Of course she'd be fine.

So you say. So often. It was almost a whisper.

It's true, Brad allowed himself to admit. I'm always saying things will be fine when I can't know I'm right: Gwen, the pregnancy—last time and this time, my health.

Your marriage.

My marriage really isn't fine, is it?

If Val miscarried, that could be the end for them. And if she didn't, would she trust him again—after all this?

Brad wanted to be like that family sitting a few rows up on the plane, lost in their own noisy world, a constellation of cereal and toys collecting at their feet. Right now that future felt so remote. Instead he was sitting on a plane next to Kara, while Gwen—

Brad pictured Gwen drunk, Steve by her side. Then he forced the thought out. Think about something else, he told himself.

He imagined himself with Val and the baby strolling through the park near their house, smilingly knowingly as other families walked by. But what kind of father could he be now, with his body such a time bomb? Would Val always have to carry the baby? And drive? Would every moment have to be choreographed in anticipation of the next time he'd crumble?

The plane skipped, and the woman beside him gasped. Brad caught her eye and managed to give her a wink. "Like a boat ride, huh?" he said. We'll be fine, he wanted to tell her, but he stopped himself. He felt Kara's hand on top of his. He closed his eyes and tried to rest.

As soon as the plane touched the ground, Brad turned on his phone. No word from Gwen. Or Val. Usually, when he traveled without Val, he'd call to say he'd landed safely. Tonight he hadn't even called to say goodnight, and he couldn't call her now and lie about where he was.

You've lied to her before, Kara said.

I haven't lied. That's different.

The nuances escape me.

A minute later, as if Kara could sense his reprimand, she said, *Thank you. For doing this.*

I had to, he said.

She knew.

Before putting his phone away, Brad sent a text to Gwen: "Hey, I'm in New York for a quick visit. That's why I called. Hoping to take you to breakfast. Free?"

He was hoping for an immediate reply, but none came.

BRAD waited for Margot outside the airport terminal. It was after midnight when she pulled up in a gold minivan with fake wood paneling and a personalized license plate that said MUFFINZ. "What the hell are you driving?" he asked.

"I own a business. I make deliveries. I'm driving one big tax deduction. Now get in."

Brad got into the minivan and hugged her across the center console. "If Cougar Cominsky could see you now," he mumbled.

"I'm her worst nightmare."

Margot pulled out of the airport and onto the highway, which was busier than Brad had expected. It was late, but it was still New York, and Margot drove like a New Yorker, in spite of the license plate.

"So I went back to Gwen's apartment," Margot said, "and cried over the intercom, and convinced the roommate—kind of a bitchy girl, I might add—to come down and hear me out. I said I found out about a major family situation, and I need to hear from Gwen the second she gets home, no matter what time of night. I might have come across as a tiny bit psychotic, but we'll see."

"'A major family situation,'" Brad repeated.

"I didn't know what else to say."

"I hear you. I guess we could have coordinated our stories better. I sent Gwen a text message from the airport. I said I was in town for a quick visit and was hoping to take her to breakfast."

"Oh, that's good," Margot said, and she nodded to herself. She looked all right. Better than Brad had expected. Nervous, but still in control.

"So where are we going?" he asked. Beside the highway they were passing concrete walls and obscured neighborhoods.

"Park Slope."

"I thought you lived on Long Island."

"I do, but it's an hour's drive from my house to Brooklyn in no traffic. During the morning commute, it's not practical. We're going to Collin's."

Brad nodded and tried to place the name. He didn't think he'd met anyone named Collin when he used to visit, so why did the name sound so—

"Wait," he said, "is this the Collin that Kara dated a few years ago?"

"He didn't date Kara. Did she date a guy named Collin? I don't remember that."

"Five years ago. She was going to move in with him."

"Oh, well, that's this Collin," Margot said. "But they weren't dating."

"Are you sure?"

"Are you kidding me?" she said, and she looked over at him for a second. "He's gay."

Brad hesitated. "He's gay?"

"Extra gay."

"But . . ." Brad paused. He'd never told anyone. "Kara called right before my wedding to say she was ready to marry me. She said it was up to me, she'd either marry me or move in with Collin. I could swear she said they were a couple."

"I promise you they weren't."

Brad wondered if he could have misremembered.

"That's not exactly the story I heard," Margot added. "She said you called *her* before your wedding to make a last-minute plea. She asked what I thought about you two getting back together."

"That's not what happened. She left two messages for me. I never even called her back."

"What do you know."

Brad shook his head. "What do you know," he agreed. "Well, what did you tell her? What was your advice?"

"I said I liked you two together, but it didn't bode well that you were calling her from the wedding altar."

"No," he agreed, "it wouldn't have."

Margot turned off the highway, and Brad could see Kara

everywhere—walking down every street, coming out of each subway station, popping out of convenience stores and apartment buildings. With each successive Kara he saw, Brad tried to catch her eye, but she never looked in his direction. She was always heading somewhere, oblivious to his presence.

They parked on Carroll Street and walked two blocks to a brick apartment building beside a construction site. Kara had lived there with Collin, Margot told him. She pressed a button for 4C, and they were buzzed inside.

Brad could hear Kara's footsteps echoing above them as they walked up the stairs. He was headed for a place he'd seen only in his mind: Kara moving in with Collin, sleeping with him on those soft blue sheets Brad had bought for her. Kara carrying groceries up the stairs, or take-out sushi, or a lamp she'd found on the street in front of someone's trash. *Only one more flight,* she might have growled.

"Brad, this is Collin," Margot said when the apartment door opened, "and Pepper. And this is Brad."

Collin flipped his hair out of his eyes. "Hey, it's so good to meet you," he said. "Come on in."

Brad realized he'd always had an image of Collin in his mind, but not this Collin. The Collin that Kara was going to move in with if Brad didn't marry her. That Collin was tall and charming and sophisticated. He rode a motorcycle, and when he was on coke, he fucked Kara into ecstasy. He was successful—more successful than Kara, but still an actor, or maybe he was in a band. He was blond, blonder than this Collin, who only had highlights, and he was handsome in an undeniable way that felt intimidating to Brad.

"Nice to meet you," Brad said. This Collin was still nice looking, but different. He was warmer and less macho, a type who might have traveled in their circle in college.

"Can I get you a glass of wine?" Pepper asked.

We'll have your finest white zin spritzer. That's the kind of thing Kara said at restaurants. *Do you have anything from June? I hear it was a good month.*

"Sure, thanks. Red, if you have it. Or white. Anything."

"Red it is," Pepper said.

As he took a few steps into the apartment, Brad saw Kara again and again—flipping the pages of a magazine on the ancient floral couch, hanging the poster from *Grey Gardens*, lighting a candle by the windowsill. The candlestick on the windowsill—of course. Brad walked to the window to get a better look. It was the mate to the one he had in his living room. She had the other, and she'd left it behind, and now it belonged to them.

Pepper handed Brad a glass of wine, and they took seats on the couch, Margot and Collin settling into mismatched chairs on either side: one black leather, the other a moss green fabric. The wooden coffee table had one leg duct-taped in place. Collin caught Brad eying it. "Part of the charm," he said.

I can't believe you're getting married, she'd said to Brad's voicemail. *To someone other than me.* It was the first time he'd heard her voice in years. Up to now it had been a text message on his birthday, maybe an email around the holidays, a postcard once from a cruise ship. *So I've been thinking about it, and I've decided I will marry you . . . It's inevitable, right? I can move down there. I'm packing up anyway. I'm supposed to move in with this guy I'm seeing, Collin.*

She had said *this guy I'm seeing,* hadn't she? Yes, no question. Brad had listened to the message at least a dozen times before deleting it.

I'm supposed to move in with this guy I'm seeing, Collin. He's awesome. Don't get me wrong. He's just . . . not you.

"You guys are welcome to crash in my bedroom anytime," Collin was saying. "I can sleep with Pepper—if I can sleep at all."

"At least one of us should stay up to keep an eye on the phones," Margot said.

"Sometimes Gwen texts me pretty late," Brad told them. He checked his watch. It was half past one, so he pulled out his phone and typed one last message: "Have insomnia. Bored and watching TV at hotel. Feel free to call anytime." He read the message to the group. They agreed it was a good idea.

"It was really nice of you to come up here so fast," Collin said. "You're a good friend."

"Did you know she was spending time with Steve?" Pepper asked.

"No," Brad said. "I had no idea."

"Did you know she was hanging out with Toby?" Margot asked.

"She never mentioned it, no."

Margot snorted a half-laugh. "Well, what were you talking about anyway," she said, "after midnight?"

Brad dropped his gaze to the phones on the table, though he didn't need to. He hadn't done anything wrong. "Nothing," he said. "I don't know. Growing up . . ."

Collin lit a cigarette and murmured a sympathetic "Mm-hmm."

"Making friends," Brad continued. "She was lonely. Her whole New York adventure wasn't going the way she hoped it would."

Margot nodded.

"Her roommate sounded like a bitch," he added.

"That I can vouch for," Margot said.

"Excuse me," Brad said, and he walked into the kitchen.

Was it anger he was feeling? He didn't owe Margot an explanation. And Gwen didn't owe him anything. She was a kid. She was free to tell him or not tell him whatever she wanted.

Or was he jealous? He had felt like there was some connection between him and Gwen. He thought she needed someone to trust, he thought he was being that person. But apparently he wasn't the only person, and she wasn't completely candid with him anyway.

Why did this need to bother him? It was embarrassing. It was silly, he told himself, as he topped off his wine. And when he looked up again, on the kitchen wall, he saw the words *Yay me* scribbled in ink near the telephone. The ink was dulled from what appeared to be an unsuccessful attempt to wash the words away. Who had tried to erase them? Kara? Had she gotten an audition, an actual part? A date?

Any of the above, she said.

He saw her now, sitting on the counter, a rolled bandana like a headband in her hair.

No need to be embarrassed. Only I can see your thoughts.

Brad took a sip of wine, then looked back at her.

Collin, huh? You're full of surprises.

Like Christmas.

Glad to finally meet him.

What of it? she said. *How does that change anything?*

How did it? he wondered.

This could have been ours, you know. I found the apartment. It was kind of a shit-hole, but we made it work.

Brad dropped his eyes to the floor.

Your shoes would have been everywhere, she added. *Now you put your shoes away.*

I do.

You were a slob once. She sounded disappointed.

I know. I've changed.

You have, she said. Brad waited for more, but then she was gone.

※

Margot knew she wasn't at her best, but Brad . . . looked rough. His face was almost expressionless, a portrait of fear, and had he worn those glasses in North Carolina? Not that she recalled. He must've had contacts. She remembered him looking so handsome and youthful when she last saw him, like the leading man roles he was always playing in college. Now, there was a lifelessness about him. He looked exhausted.

"Was your wife freaked out when you came up here so suddenly?" Margot asked. "Val, right?"

"Yeah. She doesn't actually know I'm here. She's at her parents' house in Richmond."

Margot nodded.

"We're sort of . . . going through a few bumps," he added, his cheeks reddening.

Well, that explained something, Margot thought. He probably hadn't been getting a lot of sleep. Not that she'd been getting so much sleep either. "I'm going through 'a few bumps' with the guy I've been seeing, too," she said.

"I'm sorry to hear it."

"It's okay. If it's over, I guess it's for the best."

"Not necessarily," he said.

"That doesn't help," she told him, and she forced a little chuckle, but Brad didn't laugh. "He's in the military. He's in Japan now. About to be deployed to Afghanistan."

"Wow."

"Of course, he didn't bother mentioning that little tidbit to me until I found out by accident."

"He would've told you," Collin interjected. "There were a few sins of omission," he added, turning to Brad.

"It's probably hard for him," Brad said. "I'm sure he's afraid too."

"Of Margot, or Al-Qaeda?" Collin asked with a grin.

"Both," Brad said. "Scared of how you'd react. And scared of being there, of the risks."

"Do you think?" Collin asked. "He's the one who joined."

"That doesn't mean it hasn't crossed his mind to be afraid," Brad said. "Maybe he just turns it off. What good would it do him to admit it?"

Brad had a point, Margot thought. "I guess he's not going to tell me. Or his mother. Or father."

"Or the guy in the next bunk," Pepper said, returning from the kitchen with the bottle of wine.

"Maybe it's understood," Collin said.

Maybe it was. Or needed to be.

Pepper topped off their wine glasses, and Margot checked her watch. Just after two in the morning; three in the afternoon in Okinawa. She suggested they might try to get some sleep, but nobody moved. They just drifted into silence for a few minutes—Collin chain-smoking, the rest of them sipping their wine—until Collin declared he needed noise and switched on the television.

Margot's phone sat on the coffee table beside Brad's, but she didn't expect hers to ring. Gwen wouldn't call her. It was Brad she would call—tonight or, more likely, in the morning. Then they could collect her and know she was safe, and tell her what she needed to know. Mike wouldn't call either. He never called or texted this late unless he knew she was going to be up, and besides, they hadn't talked for more than two weeks.

She missed him. Or at least she missed feeling like he was around. Not the real Mike—he'd been away for so long—but the signs of him that accompanied her throughout the day: the blinking light or vibration of her phone, the beep, the cursor, the little digital envelope, the announcement of some silly comment or photo, evidence that he was thinking about her at the exact same moment she was thinking about him.

Or at almost the exact same moment, anyway. She knew that during their conversations, he might be monitoring football scores, or playing a video game, or heading to some sort of training. He might be about to start a shift, on a hike, or in the middle of a conversation with a friend. Margot's girlfriend, Becky, complained that her husband didn't pay attention when she talked. Mike never had to pay attention. He could always get back to her a few minutes later, and if he was distracted when she said something, her words in type could bring him up to speed. It was true for Margot, too; she couldn't put it all on him. She could've made more of an effort to Skype or talk by phone, but typing was so much easier.

It was the idea of him that kept her company most of the time. She understood that. A part of her did. But it felt good—the way they could invoke each other's presence when they needed one another. If he returned to New York today, she knew they'd have to get used to being together. After the welcome home, the excitement of it, the sex, they might not last more than a few months. But she hoped they would. There were signs that it would work. She'd been willing to bet on it before.

Margot eyed the phones on the coffee table. She was feeling impatient. Waiting for Gwen, for Mike. Waiting for morning. It felt like all she'd done for weeks now—waited and wondered—about Mike, about Mullet. Kara and Gwen. It was so familiar, this feeling, all this waiting around. For a call, an answer, a change, an end. She'd waited for her mother to pass, for her father to recover, for her business to take off. She'd waited for a relationship, for Mike's departure, for his return.

How much of her life had she spent waiting to move on? And if the answer was most of her life, then was the waiting just life? The sitting around, or not sitting around, while waiting. The distractions—laughing, keeping company. Adding apricots, making do, making the best of. She was thirty-four years old, almost thirty-five. What was she waiting for?

Margot picked up her phone and tabbed to Mike's picture. What the hell, she thought. "I miss your horrible spelling," she typed. "I'm in this if you are. Extra year and all. But if you don't see a future in us, or if the timing is wrong, I'll understand. But please tell me either way."

There it was. She'd pointed to the escape hatch. Now it was for him to decide—in or out of the rocket ship.

When Margot looked up, she saw that Pepper had fallen asleep in a corner of the couch. Brad and Collin sat entranced by the television. Through the mild fog of Collin's cigarette smoke, Margot began watching too, losing herself in a sitcom she'd seen five years ago and in the one that followed. Then came an info-mercial for a closet shelving system, which she found strangely fascinating. At some point, Brad closed his eyes, and Collin of-fered him his bed, but Brad said no, and she saw him shifting around a few minutes later. He wasn't going to fall asleep, and neither would she.

The beeping startled them all. Even Pepper stirred. But it was Margot's phone, not Brad's. "It's Mike," she told them. Her body almost ached with relief.

"I miss you too," he'd written. "Im sorry. I wont extend again."

"I'm glad," she typed. "Then I'm going to start eating eggplant again."

"HA! I think that's a good idea."

Ha—she'd missed the sound of his laugh.

"I leave in 3 weeks. For a year. Not what U bargained for I know."

"Or you," she typed. "But I love you. I just need you to be honest with me."

The pause felt long, but this kind of communication required a lot of giving the benefit of the doubt. He could have been doing anything: walking across a room, unpacking a bag, checking a computer screen. "I luv U too," Mike wrote at last. "I'll be as honest as I can."

"I can handle—" Margot started to type, but then she stopped and erased the last word. "I can accept that," she told him.

"What R U doing up at this hour? Baking something YUMMY?"

Baking. She smiled. It was a fair guess. She looked up and saw everyone watching her. "We're good," she told them.

"Oh honey, I'm so glad," Collin said.

"That's great," Brad said.

She could feel her eyes starting to water, and she willed them to stop. It felt wrong to feel good right now, tonight. "He asked if I'm up at this hour baking."

Collin laughed.

Margot smiled and let a tear roll down her face.

She looked back at the phone. It would take so much explaining, and this wasn't what she wanted to talk about with him. She could save it for another time. For now, "I'm just hanging out with friends," she wrote. "They say hi. Go USA. :)"

"O great. THANX!"

"Can we talk later? Maybe Skype?"

"Sure. Ive missed U."

"Me too. Uncle Bernie says hi," she added. "Viagra's working a little too well, but otherwise, he's good."

"HA! That Bernie. My love to him too."

Margot set her phone down as Collin was walking back from the kitchen with coffee mugs. They were red, from Crate and Barrel. Margot had been with Kara when she bought them. "I, for one, could use a little fuel," he said. "Coffee should be ready in a few."

Margot checked her watch. It was a little after four thirty. Pepper was awake now, too. "So I guess I still have my virtual boyfriend," Margot said to the room.

"No, honey," Collin said, "*I* have a virtual boyfriend. Men take shifts playing the part. Last weekend the role was played by a bartender named Javier."

"I'm sorry, folks," Pepper said, standing with a stretch, "but I think I'm the one with the virtual boyfriend. He lives in my top dresser drawer with an extra set of batteries."

Collin poured each of them a cup of coffee, then plopped back into his chair with a sigh. "I wish I hadn't let Kara move out," he said. "No offense," he added, turning to Pepper. "I love you here. But then she might never have met Steve and none of this would've happened."

"That's not fair," Margot told him.

"No," Brad said. "But I know what you mean. It's hard not to wonder what if."

"Well," Margot said, "I wish Kara had gotten a part in the *Best Little Whorehouse* revival when she first moved up here. I've sometimes thought that could've made all the difference. Would have helped her figure things out. Maybe she'd have taken better care of herself."

"Learned to pay rent," Collin said.

"Washed her clothes on a regular basis," Margot added.

Collin smiled. "I wish *I'd* gotten a part in *Best Little Whorehouse.*"

"Hello," Pepper said. "Me too."

"Did you audition for that?"

"Yeah."

"Oh my God, I could have met you two years earlier."

"I wish."

Margot was watching Brad, whose face was so blank. "What do you wish?" she asked him.

He took a long minute to think, and Margot imagined him taking an inventory of the past, looking for a split in the road that might have made all the difference. So many moments, so many decisions, and some of them were his. If he'd moved with Kara to New York, if he'd returned her last phone calls. Margot wondered if those messages haunted Brad, especially with his marriage in trouble now. What if he'd married Kara, or tried to? Would it have lasted? Would they have been happy? He and Kara had grown into very different people.

"I don't know what I wish anymore," Brad said at last. "I guess right now I wish Gwen would call and say she's in a cab heading home."

Margot didn't have anything to say after that, and the silence was contagious. It cloaked the room again, and five o'clock passed. They finished their coffee. Pepper brewed a second pot.

Even though they'd switched from alcohol to caffeine, the evening had something of the quality of a college night—staying up, smoking too much or sharing a joint, drinking wine or wine coolers or Boone's Farm, waiting until sunrise to fall asleep and planning to wake up in time for the second class, or the third, or else a really late lunch. That had been life for four years with Kara and Brad. So long ago. These days when she stayed up all night it was out of fear, not for amusement. Tomorrow, her hair was going to smell like Collin's cigarette smoke, but a part of her didn't mind. It was nice not being alone.

Around six the sun began to emerge, and they watched the early morning news. Brad asked how soon they thought he could start trying Gwen; they agreed he should wait until a little past seven, and he did. Then at 7:06, he dialed. The call went straight to voicemail. "Just keep hitting redial until she turns her phone on," Margot said. He did. Over and over again.

They ran out of coffee by seven thirty, and Pepper offered to pick some up before going to work. She'd changed from jeans and a ratty T-shirt into a white blouse and navy suit and looked surprisingly adult. She worked three mornings a week at a podiatrist's office in Bay Ridge, she explained.

"That's alright," Collin said. "Let's get out of here and get something to eat. We can stay in the neighborhood. Maybe go to Pancake King."

"Oh, they'll like that," Pepper said.

Margot slid on her shoes as the name of the restaurant tripped through her memory. She thought back to her conversation with

Mullet after the funeral. "You know, I think that's where Mullet said he and Kara were headed the morning she didn't wake up."

"What?" Pepper asked.

Margot collected her phone. "The morning after Kara died, Mullet said he was talking to her while he was getting dressed, trying to wake her up for brunch."

"To work brunch or eat brunch?" Pepper asked.

"Eat. At the Pancake King."

Pepper shook her head. "Kara was scheduled to work that Sunday morning."

"Oh my God," Collin said. "That's right."

"Are you sure?" Brad asked.

"Yeah, I had to cover her section. She'd been working Sunday brunch for months."

"Oh for fuck's sake," Margot said. "He is such a liar."

None of them said anything else as they headed down the stairs. Brad kept hitting redial. Pepper hugged Margot good-bye and headed for the subway, and the rest of them piled into Margot's van.

As she drove, Margot imagined the conversation that would take place when Gwen finally answered the phone. Brad would say he was passing through town. They'd collect her from Mullet's apartment. Once they pulled away from the curb, they'd tell her all about Mullet. Gwen would be grateful. She'd never see the man again. He'd rot in jail. The end.

"It's straight ahead on Fifth," Collin said. "Up on the left in a few blocks, so keep an eye out for parking."

This had been her neighborhood. Kara's. Mullet's. Brooklyn was waking up. The street was filling up with commuters. They were heading to subway stations, slipping in and out of storefronts with newspapers and coffee. Men in ties, women in large sunglasses, and—

"Oh my God," Margot said. "That's him."

He was across the street, walking by himself.

"Are you sure?" Collin asked.

"I'm very sure. The mullet."

"I think that is him," Brad agreed as the van passed him.

Through the rearview mirror, Margot saw Mullet turn into a coffee shop. "Are you calling?" she asked Brad.

"Yeah. Still no answer."

She drove past the Pancake King and turned right on 9th Street. "You need to go get Gwen," she told him.

"Go . . . ?"

"To the apartment. Now."

At 4th Avenue, she turned right at a pawnshop, then saw another two doors down. The storefronts had chain-link gates pulled down in front of them and jewelry in cases inside the windows. Neon signs offered top dollar for gold and diamonds. "Oh my God," she said, slowing to look, "this is where he bought her ring." The thought occurred to her as the words came out of her mouth, and as she heard herself, she knew she was right.

"What?"

"Kara's ring. He bought the engagement ring after the fact. After she was dead, he ran around the block and bought a ring. That's why no one knew they were engaged."

No one said anything, and Margot hated what she'd just said. But she didn't question it. It was a fact. The morning after, Mullet had bought himself proof that he hadn't raped Kara.

Margot's stomach churned. Just get to Gwen. They were so close. Margot turned right on 7th Street and stopped the van just past the corner at the back of a bodega. "It's the basement apartment," Margot said. "Right there. Hurry."

"Okay," Brad said.

"We'll circle."

"There might be a space," Collin said. "Or we could wait for you at—"

"Just walk toward Fifth Avenue, and if you don't see us, call."

Brad stepped out of the van. Behind the shop on the corner, beside a line of trash cans and a bicycle locked to what looked like a water pipe, were two doors. One was a half-flight of stairs below street level. That one was Kara's.

Margot was still idling in the van behind Brad, and when he looked back at her, she mouthed the word "Go" through the van's window. Brad waved her on; Gwen didn't need a whole rescue crew waiting outside. Margot nodded as if to say, "Okay, okay," and pulled away. Brad's gaze followed the van down the street, passing brownstones that looked more like the kinds of places he'd imagined a person in Brooklyn might live—a little rundown, but nicer. He wished he were standing in front of one of them.

When Margot turned at the corner, Brad looked back at the stairway. The stairs were steep, and he could picture Kara walking down in heels after a late night out, cursing the fact that there was no railing. He could see her slipping and tearing her stockings—no, bruising her leg beneath a pair of jeans. He could hear her muttering *Godfuckingdamnitshit*. Had Gwen fallen and said the same thing?

Brad walked down the five steps and pressed the doorbell. He took a deep breath. No response. After a minute, he pressed the button again and waited. Again nothing. Next he took out his phone and hit redial again, but Gwen's phone was still going straight to voicemail. Maybe the doorbell was broken. So he knocked. "Gwen?" he called through the door.

I'm actually staying right nearby, he imagined himself saying. He tried to picture Gwen smiling and giving him a hug. I hope I'm not disturbing you, he'd say.

His next knock was more insistent. It was intended to wake her up.

I hope I'm not disturbing you. I was only in town for a day, and I heard you were staying out here.

Brad took a deep breath. Still no answer. The third time he almost pounded. "Gwen?" he said through the door. "It's Brad. I was just in the neighborhood . . . Did you get my message?" Ten seconds. Twenty.

Brad could picture Kara, dead, on a couch. He willed his mind not to transfer Gwen into the image.

Beneath him was a damp rubber doormat, and he stepped off and checked under it for a key, but no luck. None above the doorframe either. One more try with the doorbell. He didn't expect her to answer now.

After a minute he climbed the stairs and stood at street level. He was more tired than he'd realized, and he felt a strain in his legs. He'd been keeping up on his medicine, but he should have made more of an effort to sleep. The phone in his hands was starting to double when he looked down at it. "Please answer," he mumbled as he hit redial. But Gwen's phone was still turned off.

A few paces from Steve's stairway was the entrance to an alley that separated the building from the brownstones that lined the rest of the block. The lowest windows on Steve's building were at ground level and appeared to face his apartment. For a moment Brad stood at the entrance to the alley. Then he glanced down the street in both directions, walked into the alley, crouched down on his knees, and looked inside.

Peering through the first barred window, Brad felt like he was looking into a messy prison. The lights were out, and everything looked ashen brown: walls, couch, coffee table. Colonies of cigarette butts, piles of newspapers, dishes and mugs with the remnants of brown.

Brad inched forward to the next window. Same room. Now he was looking over the table and chairs. Still no sign of Gwen. Up ahead was the kitchen area and a doorway, perhaps to the bedroom. Brad crawled forward, then heard something behind him—a footstep falling, a pebble kicked aside? For a second Brad froze, then as he started to turn his neck, he felt something hard smash down on his back.

He fell forward into the pavement. His forehead stung, and his left cheek. His glasses had slipped down his face. He started to turn, but a heavy foot pressed down on his back.

"What the hell are you doing?"

Brad shifted his glasses into place. There was a scratch across the left lens. He turned partway and got a glimpse. Steve.

"I'm sorry," Brad said. "I'm looking for Gwen Tinsley." Steve's heads were blurry, even through the glasses. "I'm a friend of Kara's. We went . . . I knew her in college."

Steve didn't lift his foot. "You were looking for Gwen through my window?"

"I was just . . ." Brad began. He swallowed. He could feel his heart racing. "I got your address from Gwen's roommate. But no one answered when I knocked. I just was in the neighborhood."

Now Steve lifted his foot and backed away. He stooped to pick up a brown paper bag he appeared to have dropped on the ground. Brad flipped over, but stayed on the ground, unsure of whether or not he should rise. Steve was taller than Brad remembered, with a thick neck and arms. "Is Gwen here?" Brad asked.

"No."

"I need to see her."

"Tough."

"But I heard she was staying here. That's what she said."

Steve shifted his weight. "Well, she's not here."

"But . . . she was here last night, wasn't she? And she's not answering her phone, and it's still kind of early . . ."

Steve took a step forward, and Brad scuttled backward, further into the alley. "I'm telling you," Steve said, "she isn't here. What do you want with her at eight in the morning anyway?"

"I'm only in town for the day. I was hoping to speak with her."

Steve turned now and headed for the street. "Well, she's not here," he said over his shoulder. "If you're a friend of hers and Kara's, I guess I could let you come in and clean up. You're kind of a mess."

Brad stood slowly and touched his forehead. It was bleeding. And the palms of his hands, he now saw. He felt a tremor run through his arms and legs. Did he want to go inside that place? Not really. But Gwen might be inside. He could check.

Brad followed Steve out of the alley and down the stairs and into the apartment with the brown leather couch he'd seen through the window. The couch where Kara had died. On it was a pillow and blanket. The room smelled like marijuana and stale cigarette smoke and dirty laundry.

"Knock yourself out," Steve said, pointing at the sink in the far corner. To its right was a wall of cabinets and then a door, half-closed. Just one, but to Brad it looked like double doors that began to converge as he approached. The bedroom must have been beyond them. Brad tried to steal a subtle glance inside as he turned toward the sink, but it was too dark to see anything.

His pulse slowed a bit as he rinsed his hands. He took a paper towel, wet it, and touched it to his forehead. It stung at first. The towel came back red. Then Brad ran water over a second paper towel and wiped again. Still red, but less so. He patted his forehead with a dry towel, then his cheek, then his hands. Brad could feel Steve watching him, but when he turned around, he couldn't keep his eyes from drifting to the half-closed door.

Steve began walking toward Brad and the back of the apartment. Brad looked back at the door. "Gwen?" he called out.

A horseshoe of cabinets surrounded the kitchen sink, and Brad stepped forward to extract himself from the enclosure. He was closer to the bedroom door, and Steve was closer to him.

"What is your problem?" Steve said.

"Nothing. I'm just—Gwen?"

Then suddenly Steve was right there, yanking Brad's body out from the kitchen and slamming it against a wall. He pressed a meaty freckled forearm against Brad's neck. "What are you after?" Steve hissed. His breath was hot and sour. His face was red.

Brad struggled for air. "I'm just passing through—"

"Don't fuck with me," Steve said. "You sleeping with Gwen? Was she with you last weekend?"

"What?" Brad managed to squeak. "No, I'm a friend of Kara's, I told you. Are *you* sleeping with Gwen?"

"That's none of your fucking business."

To Brad's right was the bedroom door; to his left, the couch where Kara had died. He saw her lying on it now, watching the two of them.

Suddenly, Steve released his hold, and Brad's knees buckled and he slid down the wall to the ground.

For a moment Brad sat frozen, braced for whatever Steve might do next. Then, when Steve took a step back, Brad tried to pull in his legs to stand up—but the muscles in his legs wouldn't respond.

"Get up," Steve said.

Brad's heart was pounding. On the floor across the room was a mess of pink shattered glass. One pink wedge had a cartoon eye that was staring back at him.

"I said get up."

Brad looked down at his legs and willed them to move. He grabbed his right knee and pulled it toward him so his foot rested flat on the ground. Why did this have to happen now? If he gave his legs a minute to rest, maybe he could push himself—

"I barely touched you."

"I know."

"So get the fuck up."

"Just give me a second."

"Get up before I make you get up."

"I can't," Brad almost shouted. "I can't get up, okay? I can't control my legs right now. I have a medical thing. I need to sit here a minute."

Brad reached into his pocket for the pillbox. Maybe an extra Mestinon would help.

"What the fuck? You were walking one minute ago."

The pillbox wasn't there. "It's complicated," Brad said. He tried his other pocket. It wasn't there either.

"Are you having a stroke or something? Because that's not happening in my apartment. There is no fucking way."

"It's not like that," Brad mumbled. He was feeling short of breath now. It was probably nerves. He sucked in air.

"Alright, it's time for you to go."

Brad swallowed. "Just hang on."

"I will pick you up and throw you out the door."

Steve took a step forward, but Brad held a hand up. "I have friends waiting for me who are convinced you hurt Gwen. If you touch me, they will have police cars lining the street."

Steve stopped.

"What? I didn't do anything to her. Call, ask her yourself."

The effort of holding up his arm was tiring, and Brad let it down.

"Wait," Steve said, "did you call the police on me a couple weeks ago? About Kara?"

Brad didn't respond, but his eyes darted to the couch.

"I got you now. Fine, call them again. Tell them to come on over. But you think they don't know what happened? There was a goddamned autopsy. She OD'd on Percocet."

Kara was standing behind Steve now, near the bedroom door.

"What do you people not get?" Steve asked. "I'm the one who should be upset. I'm the one she was fucking. We had something good, me and Kara. Then she goes and does this. You think I'm happy about it?"

Brad's eyes shifted to Kara, but she turned away. A moment later she pulled a bottle of vodka out of the freezer.

"We fucked all over the apartment the night before. I knew she took something after, to unwind. I didn't know she took half the bottle. But that's not my fault."

I'm just going to drink until I pass out so it can be tomorrow, Kara said to Brad as she poured herself a mug full of vodka. She'd said the same thing to him once after a fight with her mother. And after failing her second math class. And after a bad week of auditions.

"It could've been an accident—that's what her parents asked me to say—but I don't know what was going on in her crazy head. I told the police maybe her last night with me was her way of saying good-bye."

Brad could see it now through the bedroom door: Kara's pale body pinned to the bed, Steve pushing himself into her. Did she resign herself to it in silence? Had it happened before?

I don't want to talk about it, Kara said. She was standing in the kitchen now holding her drink. She used it to wash down a handful of pills. *This is what we have Percocet for. I'm just going to skip ahead to tomorrow.*

But she skipped ahead too far because by the next day she was gone. And it became Steve's truth to tell.

"I loved her," Steve said. And maybe he believed himself, too. Or maybe he'd come to believe it.

With his right leg, Brad pushed himself up the wall. "I'm going to leave now."

"I'll walk you," Steve said.

"No, I'm fine."

"You're not passing out on my stoop. That's not happening."

Brad ran his left hand along the wall and held his right one out in front of him, as if it was capable of keeping Steve at bay, as if under the best of circumstances Brad was someone a guy like Steve might find threatening. Brad moved slowly toward the door, with only a side-glance at Kara, who lay on the couch now. *I'm just ready for it to be tomorrow.* Her eyes were slits. She was falling asleep, falling away.

Outside, Brad took thin breaths as he climbed the stairs, cursing the absence of a railing. He hoped Margot's van was only one block away, but it would still be a long block and he wasn't looking forward to the walk.

He could hear Steve follow him up the stairs and could feel Steve's gaze on his back as he walked away, but Brad resisted the impulse to turn around to confirm it. He walked slowly, with heavy legs, like an old man who'd misplaced his cane or walker. The sidewalk in front of him was doubling, but it didn't matter; all he had to do was walk straight. In spite of himself, Brad felt some comfort knowing that Steve was behind him watching.

A tear blurred the diverging paths Brad was taking, and though he felt safe, he also felt deeply alone. He wished Kara could have followed him out the door, but there would have been a solitude in that, too. In fact, this horrible stranger behind him was now the one person in whom Brad had confided. It was this man, of all the people in the world, who knew Brad's secret. Telling him had felt like a compulsion, a necessity, but it had also been a choice. This man knew Brad's weakness, and Val didn't. This was who Brad had looking out for him if he fell.

CHAPTER NINE

MARGOT AND COLLIN WERE PARKED IN FRONT OF A FIRE HYDRANT NEAR THE corner of 5th Avenue and 7th Street. She'd spent five minutes circling, looking for a spot, before giving up. "If there's a fire, I'll move," she'd said. And then they waited.

She kept thinking about the pawnshops they'd passed, the cheap ring on Kara's finger, the grotesqueness of it all. And poor Gwen, sleeping over at that apartment. They'd waited too long, they should've said something to Lucy Ann sooner. They shouldn't have let any of this happen.

Maybe I should've seen it coming earlier, she thought. Kara clearly didn't like Mullet when she lived with him. She said only disparaging things about him. Was Kara always dismissive, Margot tried to remember, or were there any suggestions of danger that Margot had been too dense to pick up on? Should she have probed more?

Margot asked Collin.

"It doesn't sound like it. I'm sure she said some terrible things about me too, near the end," Collin said.

"No," Margot insisted.

He rolled his eyes. "Oh, girl, please. Remember who you're talking to."

She smiled. She was glad he was here.

What was taking Brad so long? Margot glanced down at her phone. It was on. She had a signal.

Suddenly there was a fist pounding on the window beside her, Collin let out a little gasp, and she looked up to see a red-goateed face outside her door. Mullet. He filled the window—those angry eyes, big shoulders. She reached instinctively to check the door locks, and then before she could try to make sense of his presence, he called out, "Your friend's about to pass out. He needs his medicine."

"What?"

"He said there's a blue pillbox that slipped out of his pocket."

What was he talking about?

Collin started fishing around on the floor, and Margot squeezed her phone for some reason. "Where is he?" she said through the window. "Where's Gwen?"

Mullet shook his head and motioned for her to roll down the window.

She hesitated for a moment, then did. "Where is he?" she asked again.

Mullet nodded back toward his apartment. "On a stoop."

"Got it," Collin called out from the backseat.

"With Gwen?" she asked.

"No."

Collin held up the pillbox. "Should I go . . . ? Are you okay?"

"Yeah," Margot told him, "I'll be fine here. I have pepper spray," she added, as she stepped out of the van.

"Fuck your pepper spray," Mullet said.

Collin took off down the block, and for a moment Margot stood facing Mullet—his ratty hair, the circle of sweat where his T-shirt rested on his chest, freckle-splotched arms that descended to thick hands, hands that might have done anything—to Kara, to Gwen. To Brad. "Where is Gwen?" she demanded.

"Probably in class. Or on the train."

"Did you hurt her? Or Brad?"

"No, get a grip. You're the muffin lady, right? Gwen told me about you. If she's not answering your calls, it's 'cause she's not a fan."

"I don't care," Margot said.

Mullet turned and started walking back toward Brad and his apartment. "Kara wasn't such a fan of yours," Margot shouted after him. "What did you do to her?" Someone walking across the street glanced over, then continued on.

Mullet stopped and turned around. She could see his face reddening as he walked back. "You don't know shit." He kept walking until she was backed up against the van, inches from his chest. "I did nothing to Kara but love her," he hissed. "Ask your friend down there what happened. Ask her own goddamned mother."

He spit on the ground beside Margot, and it was so forceful and sudden that she almost raised her pepper spray.

"Why don't you go take care of your friend who's fainting all over the fucking street, instead of trying to play hero for people who aren't even here?"

With that, Mullet backed away, this time heading in the opposite direction from his apartment. Margot hesitated. She didn't know what else to say. Then she looked down the street toward Collin and Brad.

She walked toward them. They were seated on a stoop half a block away. Was he hurt? Margot picked up her pace. She hoped he was okay. She started to run, her breasts flopping up and down, slapping her stomach. He was leaning back against the railing—now only two doors down. His forehead looked like it was bleeding, and his cheek.

"Are you alright?" she said as soon as she reached him.

Brad nodded.

"What happened to you? What's going on?"

"He was holding this," Collin said, and he held up a wrinkled card. "'In case of myasthenic crisis . . .'" he read aloud, struggling with the pronunciation. "I don't know what any of this means, but he didn't want me to call an ambulance."

Brad shook his head. "I'll be alright," he whispered.

He looked exhausted, and his eyes were closed, but he seemed to be breathing normally. "I have a . . . bit of a health issue," he said, and he opened his eyes.

"So I see. Do you need a doctor?"

"No," he said. "But I shouldn't have stayed up all night. I'm a little . . . fragile."

He did look fragile, but he was starting to speak with more strength. "Did he hurt you?"

"Not much. He did find me peering through the windows."

"And Gwen wasn't there?"

"No. Sounds like she's at school."

"Do you believe him?"

"About that? Seems likely."

"And about Kara?"

Brad straightened himself up against the railing. "No," he said, "but I think other people do."

"This is bullshit."

"He said there's already been an autopsy. If they know she over-dosed on Percocet, then it's not exactly his fault—even if he does bear some responsibility, and knows it."

"At *least* some," Margot said, and she turned to look down the street. Mullet was gone now.

"I'm not sure how much success we'd have trying to prove he drove her to it—or that we'd feel very good trying."

"You don't think she killed herself?"

"I don't think, not intentionally."

"Well, I'm not sure I can pretend nothing happened," she said.

"I hear you."

"And Gwen," she added, "needs to never see him again."

"No," Brad replied, with more conviction to his voice now, "definitely not."

Gwen shifted as consciousness returned to her. The whiteness of the skin. The shading of the cheeks. She'd dreamt the painting, her triptych of Kara. Gwen could see it now.

She opened her eyes. The room was dark. Cracked plaster ceiling above her. She was lying on—

Gwen jumped up from the couch—*the* couch—and stared at it from the center of the room. Kara had slept there. Gwen grabbed her glasses from the nightstand, or end table. It was 5:34 AM. She had to leave. Now.

She was wearing her grey nightshirt, and she knew she'd brought one this time, but she had no recollection of changing into it. Could she have been so wasted she wouldn't remember?

Steve's room remained dark, the door half-opened. Gwen took a few quiet steps toward it and picked up her bag. She'd packed a change of clothes, but she just pulled out the shorts and sandals, and shoved in her boots from the night before. Then she surveyed the room. Her dress sat in a wrinkled mound on the floor. She snatched it up and put it in her bag. Then she spotted Kara's framed violet on the end table, hesitated, and put it in her bag as well.

There was a sound, a cracking of the floor behind or above her, but the room was still empty. 5:38. Old buildings make noises. She grabbed a pen from the end table, found a receipt on the floor, and wrote a quick note on the back: "Woke up early and decided to watch the sun rise. Gwen." She set the note on the coffee table beside Miss B, then felt an impulse to take the pink bong as well, but resisted. 5:41 and Gwen was outside, walking toward the subway station.

The skin would be paler on the third Kara, the hair less vibrant.

Gwen waited on the platform. There were a few commuters standing or seated on benches nearby, but only a few. (A slight droop below the eyes, lips a fraction thinner than the others.) By 5:53 she was on the train and headed to Manhattan.

She needed to paint. She could see the third Kara now. She knew the browns she'd need to mix, the shading around the temples. The smile not too big, but not too small, forced or half-forced, and betrayed by eyes that said, through a brightness, I messed up.

Those eyes stared back at Gwen now through the blackness of the glass window beside her. I messed up. She had.

Kara was there. She'd died on that couch. And before that, Kara had slept on it. Gwen wished she'd looked behind the end table to see if she'd remembered correctly, or imagined—but no matter. She was certain. She'd been so stupid. Kara had slept there every night, not in the bedroom.

The locket. Gwen reached for her neck. She hadn't forgotten it, thank God. It would go on the third Kara, and on the first Kara as well, but it would look brighter on the first Kara. Gwen could picture it.

She fished through her bag to double-check, knowing it didn't contain her sketchbook. But she didn't need it now. The triptych existed in her head. It was just a matter of getting it out. Immediately.

It was 6:42 by the time Gwen got to the West 96th Street station, and she hurried toward her institute on Amsterdam. The coffee shop where she often stopped before class to wake herself up was open, but Gwen decided against it. She didn't want to be any more awake. She didn't want to think beyond what she understood, didn't want to feel anything but what she felt now. She walked in the door to her institute, and only as she was signing in at the security station did it occur to her that the building might have been closed. But it wasn't.

The second floor studio was unlocked, and Gwen pulled out her easel and a new canvas. She stripped out of her nightshirt and put on the clean T-shirt from her bag. Then she pulled her hair back into a ponytail and grabbed a smock from the back of the room.

She collected her paints, but began with a pencil, sketching an outline of the first Kara: the young-spirited Kara, the grown-up teenager, the Kara everyone thought they knew, no different at thirty-four than she was before. This Kara would shine—the skin, the hair, the eyes, the lips. This Kara would have an electricity behind each color, a sexiness. People would want to kiss this Kara, to taste those lips, which would glow with red. Kara the confident charmer, the actress. The locket would dangle above the line of this Kara's cleavage, above large breasts concealed by the beginning of a dress at the bottom of the canvas.

The next Kara, as Gwen outlined her, had shorter hair and thicker shoulders. Another fabrication, this Kara might have driven a minivan, might have had two babies by now, might have baked muffins, and might have turned into the wife that Brad probably needed. The Kara that wasn't. She'd wear a blue-grey dress—Gwen could see it—a little higher in cut. A different necklace, a jewel of some sort, a gift she'd received, something feminine and expensive that sparkled.

Next Gwen made space for the last Kara, whose shoulder would cut in front of the second Kara, Gwen now realized. They were crowded on the canvas, the three Karas. They needed to be. They'd fill it. This Kara, so much like the first, but with the eyes that Gwen had dreamt and the smile. Gwen moved from pencil to paints. She began with the hair of the third Kara, mixing a dark brown that lacked the depth she would use for the first. She painted the curve of the face, a little thin, perhaps, Gwen's paintbrush said. So it was. Gwen let her hand lead her—around the curve of the face, to the eyes and nose, to the lips, so important, and then down to the muted locket resting above the chest, the dress below.

It was the third Kara that held Gwen's attention, the third one that needed to be seen first. The real Kara, the Kara who wasn't nineteen, who wasn't as carefree anymore, who still wanted but had begun to doubt. This Kara, you could tell from her eyes, understood better than anyone else the difference between herself and the Karas she wasn't. Something had gone wrong—more than one something, Gwen now saw. But she was still trying to smile. She still had a measure of hope and a sense of humor about her. That was important.

Gwen was startled when the door opened behind her and she turned to see another student. Behind the girl, in the hallway, Gwen could see several other students passing by, and above the door, Gwen saw the clock. 9:52. She'd been working for three hours. The time had disappeared.

She turned back to the canvas. The three women had assumed their places, had taken their shapes. The first two Karas were incomplete—only outlines with eyes and hair, but Gwen could fill them in. She knew she could. This was why she'd come to New York.

A wave of sleepiness rushed over her, and she grabbed her bag. She hadn't slept much at all, she remembered, and she was vaguely hungover. She decided to run down and get a cup of coffee before class. It was safe to return to the reality of the world. Maybe if she had time she'd try to catch her teacher and talk to him about school. He'd been talking to her about the College of Design at NC State and offered to help her try to transfer, if she was interested. And if it was possible, well, why not?

Outside, as she walked to the coffee shop, she pulled out her phone and turned it on. There were text messages from Brad, who was in town apparently, and there were voicemails too. First a message from Brad. He was in New York, hoping to catch her for breakfast. She'd have to call him, make plans to see him after class, if he could. Then a message from Steve, who was angry at her again, this time for skipping out before breakfast. Then another message from Brad. He and Margot were worried about her. They'd stopped by Steve's and now were driving into the city. "We need to talk to you as soon as you get this message."

※

Brad lay on the backseat of the minivan and slipped in and out of sleep. He was only dimly aware of the whispered conversation in the front seat as Margot drove to drop Collin at work. "Call me, okay?" Collin said when he opened the door. "I will," Margot whispered back.

They'd gotten a quick breakfast while waiting for Gwen to call back, and when the check came and she still hadn't called, they agreed she was probably in the city and they might as well drop off Collin and head in that direction. Brad's phone finally rang as they were coming off the bridge. She was fine, Gwen said. She'd been at the studio all morning, working. Now she was waiting at a coffee shop, where they could meet her and explain everything.

Margot was uncharacteristically quiet during the drive—urging Brad to rest, not to worry. At one point she asked if he wanted to call Val, but she was polite enough not to follow up. When they reached the upper nineties and Margot jerked into a parking place, Brad leaned up and combed his fingers through his hair. His vision was imperfect but had improved, and as he stepped outside, he found that his legs were working fine. He felt tired, like a man who'd stayed up all night, but not much worse. Not for the moment.

The coffee shop was called Buona Mattina, and as they approached, Brad could see Gwen watching for them through the front window. "What happened to you?" she asked as soon as he walked in the door. Brad reached up and touched the Band-Aids on his forehead. Margot had put two there, another on his left cheek, and several on his hands. The result did leave a lot to the imagination.

"I'm fine," he told her. "This is probably overkill."

"I hope," Gwen said, her grin tinged with doubt.

Margot went to the counter for coffee, and Brad sat across from Gwen at a table. They looked at each other for a moment in silence. She was smaller than he'd remembered. Smaller than Kara had been at her age. She had dirt on her arms, Brad noticed. Or maybe it was paint. Brown.

"You wouldn't believe the traffic getting over here," Margot said when she returned with two mugs.

Gwen nodded without feigning interest. She was bracing herself for something. Brad could see it in her posture, in her eyes. Her whole face was hardened, but Brad could picture her dissolving when she heard what he and Margot were going to have to tell her. He could see the tears, the running to the bathroom, the call to Lucy Ann, the phone being passed around from one of them to the other. Kara wasn't the kind of person who would break down like this, but Gwen might be.

Brad cleared his throat. "We need to talk to you about Kara and Steve."

Gwen sighed. "You want to tell me their engagement was a bunch of crap, right?" she said.

"What?" Brad turned to Margot and saw his own surprise reflected in her eyes. "Yes," he told Gwen.

"Did Steve tell you that?" Margot asked.

"No," Gwen said. "But I kind of figured it out." She fingered the locket around her neck. "He didn't even know about this," she said. "He thought Great Grandma Kara was real. I don't know why it took me so long to realize. She couldn't have liked him that way." Gwen looked from Brad to Margot and back. "So this whole engagement was just a bunch of crazy wishful thinking, huh?"

Brad could see Margot squeezing her lips together. With dread. This was the dreadful part. He wasn't excited to discuss with Gwen the ambiguity of Kara's living arrangement, or to open Gwen's mind to the scenes he and Margot found themselves imagining.

"Yes," Margot said. "That's what it was."

Brad exhaled relief.

"He's kind of a loon," Margot continued, "and not the nicest person. So we need for you to never see him again."

Gwen dropped her eyes to the table. "I won't," she said. "I thought he was a cool guy at first, but . . . yeah, he was starting to seem kinda sketchy."

Brad and Margot locked eyes. This was enough.

Then Gwen looked up again. "Kara was actually seeing someone else."

There was a note of challenge in Gwen's voice, and Brad worried Margot would press, but she didn't. "That's what we'd heard," was all she said.

"He was okay," Gwen added. "He was nothing special."

The three of them sat in a nervous silence for a minute, and then Gwen smiled. "It's a little morbid, I know, but Kara would have loved the fact that she had a fake fiancé speaking at her funeral."

"That is very Kara," Brad agreed.

"An older man who Mom would hate." Gwen laughed. "She believed him."

"*I* believed him," Brad said.

"I did, too," Gwen said. "My stepdad didn't think Kara would have gone through with it."

"Well, he was right," Margot said.

Gwen studied Margot and then winced a little as she mumbled, "I'm sorry I didn't call you back."

"It doesn't matter—"

"I know you were just trying to look out for me, and I've been kind of a bitch."

Margot stood abruptly and gave Gwen a hug, then excused herself to go to the bathroom. She was starting to tear up.

"She's fine," Brad told Gwen. "She'd gotten worked up, but she can let that go now." They both watched as Margot walked to the back of the coffee shop and rounded a corner. Then Brad turned to face Gwen. "Your program must be over soon," he said.

"One more week. But it's been going better. I like it. I'm glad I came."

"Good," Brad said, and he smiled, with an effort.

His eyes were getting tired again. He adjusted his glasses, and through them, he saw Gwen picking at a spot of paint on her arm. "Am I the reason you came to New York?" she asked.

Gwen looked a lot like her older sister, but part of her was still a little girl. Brad had never looked at Kara and thought she needed protecting. Maybe that was a mistake.

"Yes," he told her. "We didn't realize until yesterday that you were hanging out with Steve."

Gwen's cheeks colored. She took a sip from her cup. "I'm sorry I had you worried," she said without looking up. "That must've been expensive."

"It was worth it," he said.

She gestured to Brad's face. "Did he do that to you?"

"Really, it's not bad," he said. "I fell. It's not important."

For a minute neither of them spoke, and Brad wondered what she might be thinking. Then Gwen said, "I was looking at an old picture of you the other day. One of Kara's." She cocked her head and studied him, and right then, with the tilt of Gwen's head, Brad was able to see his own reflection in her glasses: twin Brad Mitchells with Band-Aids on their foreheads and upper left cheeks and scrapes on their noses. It was startling to see, at first, even though he knew the bandages were there. And each reflection of himself had a ghost behind it, and beyond the lenses, he saw himself in Gwen's eyes. Multiples of Brads, and even these weren't what Gwen was seeing, because she was seeing a Brad Mitchell from a photograph, merged with the Brad she thought he was, and a Brad he might have become, and a man he might be when the damage healed. And he was seeing—in her lenses, in her eyes, in her mind—a crowd of Brads he was and would never be, Brads he knew and didn't know, Brads he might have been without knowing, and Brads he might need to become.

"Can I tell you a secret?" she whispered.

"Of course," he said, and to meet her eye, he had to pick one of his eyes to look with, and one of her lenses to look through, and a pair of his reflections to ignore, and that's what he did.

"This is going to sound strange, but lately I've been feeling Kara's presence."

Brad let the words penetrate him.

"It's like she's been trying to communicate with me," Gwen continued. "Sometimes I hear her voice."

Brad considered the things he might say to Gwen, and he knew that if he turned his head to the left, he might see Kara sitting at the next table. She might be smoking a cigarette, or stirring sweetener into a latte. She might wave. She might shrug. She might stand up and walk over to their table.

But he didn't turn. He continued to face Gwen and did his best to fuse her doubled image together. And he said, "I'm sure she is looking out for you. You should keep her with you."

TWENTY-FOUR hours later, Brad sat in a taxicab as it wound its way through Westover Hills in Richmond, Virginia. He'd spent the night at Margot's, at her insistence, and now his body felt normal again. His vision was fine. Margot had offered to wash his clothes overnight, like a lover out of a movie, but instead he asked her to take him to a mall, where he picked up a new pair of jeans and a button-down shirt. He carried the prior day's outfit through JFK Airport in a plastic bag, a rolled-up mess of sweat and fear with a little dirt and blood mixed in. But before he boarded the plane to Richmond, he tossed the bag in the trash, a decision that felt surprisingly freeing.

He'd been afraid to call Val yesterday, so he sent her a text message saying he was busy, but that he missed her and was coming for a visit. Now he was on her parents' street, only a few doors away—and there she was. His heart skipped. She was outside working in her mother's flowerbed, on her hands and knees, hair held back in a clip.

The taxicab came to a stop, and Val looked up with surprise. She looked so pregnant, her belly protruding undisguised from a pastel maternity shirt. Brad paid the driver and stepped out of the cab, and in silence he hugged her. She wrapped her arms around his back, but kept her hands off his shirt. They were covered in soil. "Two Cheeto hands," she said.

Brad took her dirty hands in his and kissed them both.

"You didn't drive?"

"I flew."

"We could have picked you up. And why wouldn't you have driven? It's not far."

Brad studied the little trail of freckles that crossed her nose.

"Well," he said, "for one thing, that's not a drive I want to make alone right now." He nodded toward the house. "Let me explain."

| ACKNOWLEDGMENTS |

Many thanks to my agent, Bill Clegg, for his insights, encouragement, and advocacy. Thanks to my editor, Liz Parker, for her thoughtful guidance, her support, and her enthusiasm. A big thanks, too, to Charlie Winton for welcoming me into the fold and to everyone at Soft Skull, Counterpoint, Publishers Group West, and William Morris Endeavor for their kindness, creativity, and assistance.

I owe a world of thanks to my talented and generous readers: Jodi Lynn Villers, Tommy Jenkins, Kathleen Laughlin, Kristine Seawell, and Nancy Conescu. I also want to thank the many teachers who helped me grow into the writer I am today, especially Wilton Barnhardt, Angela Davis-Gardner, John Kessel, Doris Betts, and Linda Hobson.

Many thanks to my wonderful and growing family. First to Austin for his love, patience, and support, and to Nathan for his drool and giggles. Next to my loving Mom and Dad; Allison, Christine, and Gracie; Nancy and Steven; and Granny and Aunt Betsy. Thanks also to Bill and Carlene; Scott, Suzy, John, Katie, and Mary Jane; Andrew and Rebecca; Crystal, Carlos, Kenzie, Jonah, Gavin, and Susie; and the many cousins, aunts, and uncles I'm so lucky to have.

Thanks to my friends who have been so supportive of me as a writer, especially Jean, Nerissa, Frank and Larry, Jonathan and

Rob, Rachel, Stephanie, and Tracy. Thanks also to my incredible former colleagues at Duke, to NC State's creative writing crowd, and to my UNC pals.

I'm grateful to the Weymouth Center for the Arts & Humanities for offering such a beautiful retreat to North Carolina writers. Finally, for their encouragement and help along the way, I want to thank David Ferriero, Virginia Barber, Katia Singletary, and Peter Vaughn.

Photo credit: © Chris Hildreth

| ABOUT THE AUTHOR |

WILLIAM CONESCU was born in New York and raised in New Orleans. He graduated from the University of North Carolina at Chapel Hill and earned an MFA in Creative Writing at North Carolina State University. He is the author of the novel *Being Written*, and his short stories have appeared in *The Gettysburg Review*, *New Letters*, and other publications. William lives in Durham, North Carolina.

For more information, visit www.williamconescu.com.

| DISCUSSION GUIDE |

1. Brad and Gwen both question whether or not Kara's ghost is real. How do their interactions with her differ? How does she bring them together?

2. To what extent are Margot's concerns about Kara's death justified? What do you think happened to Kara?

3. How does Gwen's relationship with Steve mirror the relationship that developed between Steve and Kara?

4. How does setting impact each of the central characters' sense of connection with Kara? To what extent are Gwen's actions in New York an attempt to connect with her sister?

5. Discuss how white lies are used throughout the novel. Which lies seem reasonable, and at what point(s) do you think the deception is taken too far?

6. Do you think Brad and Kara should have stayed together? How do you think the central characters in the novel would answer this question?

7. Compare Margot and Mike's relationship with other romantic pairings in the novel. Margot speculates about Mike's perspective. How do you think he sees their relationship?

8. Discuss the friendship that develops between Brad and Gwen. What does each of them get out of the relationship?

9. How do you think Brad would have handled his medical situation if Val had not been pregnant?

10. Kara's friends and family knew her as an actress both on and off the stage. When do think Kara was most herself?

11. Compare Kara and Gwen as artists. How does the reader get to know Kara through Gwen's experiences as a young painter?

12. What do you think the future holds for each of the central characters after the novel ends?

Printed in the United States
by Baker & Taylor Publisher Services